DAUGHTERS OF THE RED LAND

by

Yan Li

Sixter Vision
Black Women and Women of Colour Press

95 96 97 98 99 ML 5 4 3 2 1

Canadian Cataloguing in Publication Data
Li, Yan, 1955
Daughters of the Red Land
ISBN 0-920813-17-8
I. Title
PS8573.12D3 1995   C813'.54   C95-932502-6
PR9199.3.L5D3 1995

Edited By Pamela Mordecai

Production and Design: Stephanie Martin
Editor for the Press: Makeda Silvera

Sister Vision Press acknowledges the financial support of the Canada Council and the Ontario Arts Council towards its publishing program.

Represented in Canada by the Literary Press Group
Distributed in Canada by General Distribution
Represented and distributed in the U.S.A. by InBook
Represented in Britain by Turnaround Distribution

Printed in Canada by union labour

SISTER VISION
Black Women and Women of Colour Press
P.O. Box 217, Station E
Toronto, Ontario
Canada M6H 4E2
(416) 595-5033

To the women of China

~ ~ ~

I wish to express my sincere thanks to
Donald R. Gordon, Carol Gregory,
Sean Kelly, Barbara Kraler,
Mary Ann Scott, and Yanbin Wang.
Their genuine friendship encouraged me
to finish the writing of this book.

Contents

1

Hometown and Grandmother's Mystery

IT WAS ON AN EARLY SUMMER MORNING WHEN I LEARNED that Evergreen had died. Heart attack. My mother's voice on the phone sounded calm; obviously she had prepared herself well before she made this cross-ocean long distance call.

I looked out the kitchen window. The rising sun was beaming through the dense leaves of the firs lining one side of the large drained fountain. The bronze statue by the fountain was clearly visible in the sunshine. The tulips, lilies and some other unknown flowers were blooming loudly along the mosaic walk in the western garden. Further away by the pond, a couple of Canadian geese with their newborns were looking for food on the lawn. The world seemed as colourful and vital as usual. It was hard to believe that death could occur on a beautiful day like this.

I felt weak, though I hadn't done any work yet. I decided to go back to my bedroom upstairs. I passed by Mrs. Thompson's room. It was deadly quiet. She must be drunk again. Yes, she must be. I remembered that she didn't ask for coffee at supper yesterday. That was a signal that she was starting another tour with Vodka. At this moment, I didn't care if she stayed in bed longer. I did need to be alone for a while.

I fumbled in my suitcase and took out a cloth bag. Inside there were a few books and a letter. They had accompanied me from China to Canada, and from place to place, as I travelled in this country. The paper of the letter had worn through the years. Before it was unfolded, the squared words, which I had already learned by heart, emerged once again in my mind.

"...For as long as twenty-eight years, fate had prevented us from seeing each other and all I could do was try to picture you — what you looked like, what kind of person you were, and what your life had been like — in my imagination. The cruel fact was that, even before you came into this world, I had known too well that you were going to travel the roughest and bumpiest road life had to offer, yet there was no way that I could help you...

"Our meeting in Beijing in the summer of 1984 was the first time I had seen you since you were born. As I sat on the bushy hill of the Imperial Palace and listened to you recalling such a miserable life so equably, I wasn't surprised at all, though my heart was bleeding and my soul sobbing...

"...I have tried hard to keep my promise not to contact you. But it is such unbearable torture, I cannot endure it any more. Please forgive me, my dear child! Can you understand how much I want to see you again? Can you understand a father's feeling? Over the years I was always haunted by the fear that the first time we met each other would also be the last time I would see you..."

This was the only letter from Evergreen, the man whom I should call 'father' but never have. I was born a very indecisive person. I had been hesitating for years over whether to satisfy his wish by writing him or phoning him and calling him 'father'.

I sometimes puzzled over the question: Can I really regard him as my father? Perhaps I should, since he was the man who gave me life. But to link the affectionate word, 'father', with this man seemed extremely awkward and uncomfortable to me. We had never seen each other until I was twenty-eight years old and, for quite a long period before that, I didn't even know of his existence!

On the other hand, I could not regard him totally as a stranger and ignore him, for this man suddenly emerged as an ominous shadow in my life when I was thirteen years old, and had since secretly tortured my inner world.

I never replied to his letter. First of all, I was not sure about what I should call him, if I were to write. Secondly, my decisions took serious account of my mother's attitude. I didn't want to hurt her feelings, though her everlasting hatred towards this man seemed hard to understand. In all those years, I couldn't, and never wanted to, start any serious discussion with her about him. Both of us were clear that even a subtle touching upon this issue would open the wound and arouse waves of emotion in our over-sensitive nerves. Human souls are the most complicated creations.

Now that this man was gone forever to another world, the thorny question seemed finally solved and I did not have to worry my head over the issue any more. Yes, he had gone, like air, like dust, traceless — yet every-where. But the sky is still very blue and the sun shines brightly as usual. He didn't leave anything behind him, except a few books and an untouchable daughter. I gazed at the books. These were the only things he left to the world, books he had composed with blood and tears. Books remain. But people will all die eventually. As he had predicted, the first time we saw each other had become the last time, forever. I felt sad. But there were no tears in my eyes — they had dried up a long time ago. Perhaps I had become numb, or perhaps I had become more reasonable — anyway, I was surprised that for the first time in my life I was able to think about this man without being disturbed emotionally.

Why had it taken me so long to decide whether to write him or not? There would be no address to mail a letter to him now, even if I did want to write! I started to wonder: Would I have had a different soul if my life had not been created by Evergreen, but by someone else? Was his wrongdoing really responsible for my mother's unhappy life, as she always claimed? Was it fair to blame him for what had happened in the past few decades? Or should someone else be blamed? If so, who? All of a sudden, I was overwhelmed by the impulse to write something.

I rushed downstairs, my heart beating fast with the excitement of this new idea. Passing through the spacious sitting room, I entered the library. It was quiet as usual. I sat in front of the big carved table by the window and looked around. Against the walls, bookshelves stood one on top of the other from the floor to the ceiling. Hard-covered books, many of which seemed to be from a couple of centuries ago, were neatly laid on the shelves. The thick carpet, the hard wood furniture, the dark leather couch and chairs, the portrait of a man in a wig, the large terrestrial globe, the opened encyclopedia on a stand, everything in this room, even the cold remains of the logs in the fireplace, created a dignified atmosphere. The only thing modern and therefore somewhat inharmonious was the IBM computer on top of the table.

I had put the computer there six months ago when I moved into this house. The novelty of a new environment had already disappeared from my eyes. But at this moment, everything in this elegant room looked foreign and strange, whereas all the things I was familiar with were somewhere unreachable. My mind became vacant; the impulse to write vanished. "Who am I? Why am I in this big house, the residence of a rich Canadian woman?" I questioned myself. My mind was still clear, of course. "I am a journalist — oh, no, a housekeeper now, from China, an ancient land on the other side of the globe…"

*   *   *

EVERYONE HAS A HOMETOWN WHERE ONE SPENT ONE'S childhood. The earliest memories, sweet or bitter, leave a remote and blurred impression, with twinkles of clarity here and there like shining stars in the night sky.

To the Chinese, a hometown is not necessarily the place where you were born, but the place where your paternal ancestors have lived for generations. Where was my hometown, then? This question came to me one day in my eighth year, as I was filling out my school registration forms. I asked my mother. Her face turned stern. It took her quite a while before she answered: "Well, you may write down Han Zhong as your hometown."

This struck me as curious because Han Zhong was the place where Laolao (the Chinese for maternal grandma) had been living. I was just about to pursue the matter when I noticed my mother was staring at me with a rather confusing expression in her eye. Sadness? Regret? Resentment? Or determination…? Her eyes fixed on me, but somehow I felt she was looking at somebody else. I felt nervous and swallowed my question.

When I was six, I visited Laolao's home with my mother. Han Zhong left a strong impression on me, for the idyllic, picturesque small city formed a sharp contrast to the much more modernized metropolitan Beijing where I lived.

Han Zhong in Chinese means the centre of the Han State. It is true that the city is right in the centre of China and had once served as the capital city for an ancient state. In the early 1960s, there were no trains in this area. As the passenger bus moved slowly over the skyhigh Mount Qinling, you could see the remaining trails of the plank road, built more than two thousand years ago, running along the face of the cliff.

Mountain peasants squeezed onto the bus all the way. Their faces were tanned by year-round sunshine and their clothes were soaked with the strong smell of tobacco, soil and sweat. Carried on their backs were fully loaded baskets and gunnysacks of loquats — a sweet, juicy, apricot-like fruit — tobacco, and hand-made straw sandals, all to be exchanged for cooking oil and salt in town.

Out of the mountains, the swift-flowing Han River led us into a large basin. Through the thin mist of the early morning, we could see old, dark wooden houses among rice fields. Palm and banana trees appeared here and there around the houses. Their broad green leaves looked fresh and lively.

The square city wall of Han Zhong was more than ten metres high. Laolao's home was in the southern part of the city, on one side of a busy street laid with large pieces of slabstones which had worn out with the centuries gone by. It was said that when my grandfather was alive, the family was one of the few rich ones in the city. They had two residences then, one in the suburbs and one in town. The suburban one was their major residence, with nine connected courtyards. It was described as the most grandiose house in this area decades ago. I had no basis for imagining how grandiose it was, though, as during the Land Reform Movement in 1950, the suburban residence had been confiscated by the local government and reassigned to twenty-three poor families.

But I did see their residence in town. It was a squared courtyard, consisting of three wings with more than a dozen rooms and a very large garden at the back. When I saw it in 1961, it was no longer in its original condition, but merely a crowded yard. This residence was only partly confiscated in the Land Reform Movement. Five of the rooms in the major house were kept for Laolao and the rest were redistributed. The house facing the street was allotted to three families. The side wing was assigned to another, while one side of the major house was occupied by a family with seven children.

I stayed in Laolao's home for a month. Life there was simple and idyllic. I remember getting up early in the morning, breathing fresh air soaked with the aroma of the oleander flowers blooming in front of the broad corridor, and watching magpies fly around the tall roof of the old house singing happily. Pushing back the heavy wooden door at the corner of the front courtyard, I would find my favourite playground, the backyard.

The backyard used to be a garden years ago. Now it was overgrown with weeds. There were a few neglected banana bushes and palm trees by the wall. An old well stayed lonely in the corner of the garden with thick moss covering its stone edge, visited occasionally by sparrows jumping on top of the heavy, rusted hand winch. Laolao warned me not to come close to the well for fear a ghost might catch me. "It has been abandoned for years..." she told me. I crawled cautiously to the edge of the mysterious well one day and peered inside, only to find my own image in the deep dark water.

A fairly large pond with ducks and white clouds floating in the green water extended along the garden's farther edge. Mrs. Wang, Laolao's neighbour, a strongly-built middle aged woman, was fetching water from the pond with a long-handled pail and watering the vegetables she had planted beside the pond. She picked up some green leaves from a vine-like plant and passed them to me. I brought them back to the large kitchen house in the front yard where Laolao made delicious soup with them.

Early in the morning Laolao usually took me with her to a pastry store on the other side of the street where she would buy a few deep-fried, sweet, soft and sticky rice cakes for our breakfast.

The store was a family business. The wooden doors and the inside walls looked greasy and dark from years of smoke, cooking oil, and burning fuels. In one corner of the large room was a huge iron pot with boiling oil inside. A girl about ten years old was pushing and pulling hard on the bellows connected to the stove and adding logs of wood to the fire occasionally. Her delicate face was reddened by the fire and her thin hair looked rather untidy. The men, women, and children of the family, all sweaty, were each holding a wooden club with which they vigorously beat a large mound of dough on a big board. The sounds of their blows, rat-tat, rat-tat, could be heard from distances away down the street. Laolao explained that the more they beat the dough, the stickier and tastier the cakes would be.

There was a bazaar in the small city. Laolao had taken me there once. In the eastern part of the city was the Ancient Han King Palace built on a high terrace. It was first built more than two thousand years ago. The carved beams and the painted rafters of the richly ornamented tower in the centre overlooked the crowded residence houses and busy market streets surrounding its foot. The bronze mini bells hanging on the upturned eaves sent out a pleasant metallic sound in the gentle breeze. Outside of the palace wall, numerous pedlars with foods and crafts were lining up in crowds. Laolao bought a branch of crippled dates for me, a strange fruit in the shape of a twisted twig, light-brown-coloured and rather sweet. On our way home, Laolao took me to a few historical sites such as the Horse Feeding Pool, where the cavalry of the Han State were fed water before fighting, and the Authorizing Platform, where the Han emperor appointed his marshal two thousand years ago. Laolao talked with enthusiasm about legendary stories linked with these places. But I was too young then and showed little interest.

The relationship between Laolao and her neighbours seemed to be smooth and friendly. Now and then there were creaking sounds coming from the stone-laid streets. Vegetable pedlars were passing by the gate with their one-wheeled carts on their way to the market in the centre of the city. The families living at the front wing would shout loudly towards the back house where Laolao stayed: "Grandma, here comes the tofu cart! Don't you want to buy some for your guests?" or "Grandma, the bean sprout cart is passing!"

A few times during a day, I would hear a woman's loud voice from the other side of Laolao's house: "Grandma, what's the time now?"

It was the wife of Old Wang. The Wangs were one of the poorest families in the city. Their poverty seemed to be long-term, what with seven children to be raised and the husband an alcoholic. There was hardly any furniture in their room and they could not even afford to buy a clock. When the skinny, red-eyed husband returned home drunk at night, he would beat up his wife and children, creating pandemonium in the house. The din of the children's screaming and the wife's sobbing, with the man's roaring topping them both, often woke us up at midnight and sent Laolao scampering over to help them calm down.

One night, my dream was once more broken by the horrible and husky bellow of the alcoholic. "...I'll kill you... kill you all! ...You damned big eaters! ...You pigs make me penniless!"

Laolao sighed and got up. As she fumbled with her shoes in the darkness, she murmured in a low voice to herself, "Old Wang... drunk again..."

*   *   *

LAOLAO LEFT THE WORLD IN EARLY 1988, ON THE EVE OF the lunar New Year's Day, as firecrackers created a deafening sound and lit up the night sky. She passed away silently in her own room in the old house when everyone else was occupied preparing the new year's feast.

Her funeral, though, was a noisy one and attracted the attention of streets of people. Uncle Honesty, Laolao's only son, a high school teacher, came back to Han Zhong to organize a traditional funeral rite, for many years forbidden.

As Uncle Honesty held up a tile pot over his head and then crashed it hard on the ground in front of the old house, the heavy black coffin was raised up and a group of trumpets started to shrill the mournful funeral music all at once. Dozens of weeping men, women and children, all dressed in white, were standing on a big truck. Following behind it were three other trucks carrying hundreds of floral wreaths, elegiac couplets, effigies, houses, and furniture made with colourful papers.

The funeral procession moving slowly along the street immediately attracted attention and the narrow street was soon crowded with zealous on-lookers. Uncle Honesty walked at the very front, holding Laolao's portrait in his arms. He was no longer young, his once handsome face now shrivelled like the shell of a walnut. He was careful to put on a serious look and keep his back as straight as possible. He also pricked up his ears so as not to miss any comments from the on-lookers.

"What a grand scene! We haven't seen this for years!"

"My funeral, more's the pity, may never be as splendid as this one!"

The remarks from a few envious senior citizens greatly gratified Uncle Honesty. The route of the parade was carefully chosen. According to plan, Uncle Honesty led the procession to the family's suburban residence, confiscated decades ago. The noise created by the mourners reached a crescendo as they circled around the big yard, presently home for twenty-three families.

When the colour photos recording the funeral proceedings reached Beijing a month later, Uncle Honesty didn't conceal his pride. "I made the funeral rite very nice looking..." he wrote.

My mother was not pleased. "He was clearly using the event as an opportunity to show off. However nice it may be, a grand funeral is only display for the living, not for the dead!" she commented coldly. "Besides his vanity, he was daring enough to provoke the local government by parading on the confiscated property! Didn't he ever think that they may regard his action as contempt for communist rule?"

I didn't care much about my mother's comment. My sorrow for losing Laolao was loud and long. While I am writing this story and recalling all I know about her life, Laolao is sleeping forever in the bamboo covered green hills along the bank of the quiet Han River, on the other side of the globe.

No one ever told me the complete story about Laolao. And, when she was alive, she was always careful not to utter a single word about life in her youth.

But I could sense something unusual must have taken place in her past. I could not forget, during my last visit to my hometown before I came to Canada, the elusive smile from an eighty-year-old distant relative when he murmured, his toothless mouth moving slowly, "Your grandma, oh... indeed... has tasted... life... and the world..." A gleam of mysterious light in his dim old eyes aroused my curiosity. But barely had I opened my mouth to say something than a sharp glance from Uncle Honesty silenced his gossip immediately. The old man's wrinkled lips then tightly wrapped around his foot-long bamboo pipe and his small eyes never fell on me again.

Now with Laolao and most of her contemporaries gone from the world, it is even harder to know what really happened. In fact, the legend concerning Laolao and her family has long faded from the memory of the present dwellers in the small city. I managed to piece it together, however, from several relatives' reluctant and conservative accounts.

Born in the late nineteenth century to a tailor's family, Laolao was the second one of the three daughters who were all described as bright and beautiful — fruits dewdrop-fresh on the tree. Laolao was considered the loveliest of the three, with her unusual fair complexion and a pair of vivacious large black eyes.

It was hard to imagine that Laolao had been pretty when she was young, for the impression I had of Laolao was of any typical old Chinese woman, clad in an old fashioned, plain coloured garment buttoned on the right, with her sparse grey hair coiled on the back of her head and a pair of small bound feet about four inches long — foot binding having been a compulsory practice for women in the old times.

Rumour had it that, in her late teens, Laolao's name had been well known in this small city. Her fair skin and beautiful features were radiant. Her small feet, which had been tightly bound since she was six years old and had caused her numerous painful days and nights, now won her fame, as they were smaller than those of girls who had started the binding at a later age. She couldn't read or write. That was fine, since the tradition prized illiteracy as a womanly virtue.

The tailor's store was frequently visited by all the well known matchmakers in town. The tailor always smiled ambiguously at these eloquent visitors. He had made up his mind to make a great fortune from his valuable daughters. He had already married his first daughter off to a wealthy merchant the year before. Now it was his second daughter's turn. He knew her worth and he knew he had to be picky; he certainly was not afraid of irritating any of these zestful matchmakers.

The shrewd man never anticipated, however, that the civil war prevailing in China after the overthrow of the last emperor in 1911 would quickly upset the peaceful but sluggish life in the small city.

It was a hot windless summer day. The blazing sun in the middle of the sky forced all street dogs to hide in the shade of deep, old-style doorways. The clear clopping of horse hoofs passing through the slabstone laid streets caught the attention of many people who stretched their necks from behind the doors despite the hot air. A wartime officer who might have been stationed in town or been just passing through with his troops, chanced to glimpse a figure with an impressively pretty face by the wooden door of the tailor's store. It was a girl in a pale green garment, wearing her hair in bangs. She met the man's daring gaze and quickly turned inside the crimson-painted door, her waist-long black braided hair swaying down her slender back. Struck dumb for a few seconds, the strongly-built, dark faced man got off the back of his horse and went straight into the store.

The tailor was lying in a bamboo deck chair and waving a cattail-leaf fan.

His hands trembled and the fan dropped on the floor at the sight of a man coming in with a pistol in his belt. The deal was promptly made. Shining silver dollars piled up on the square table. Though the amount was far from the tailor's expectation, he was too scared to argue, what with a whole bunch of armed men waiting outside.

A few days later, Laolao was taken away from her hometown with the departing troops, leaving behind her the townspeople gloating over the tailor's unexpected loss.

Whether Laolao was happy and had ever grown to love the strong-built officer would remain a riddle forever. The officer was killed in a battle months after his troops left Han Zhong.

Laolao had hardly had a chance to collect herself to face the reality of her husband's death before she was shocked by even more horrifying news. The family of the dead officer were secretly planning to sell the young woman to a brothel. Their conspiracy was leaked, somehow, by a sympathetic relative, so that when the traders arrived, Laolao had already disappeared.

She had to travel more than a thousand miles to get back to her hometown. It is hard to imagine how difficult and terrifying it must have been for a young woman with tiny bound feet, not knowing how to read and write, to survive such a trip alone in the early twentieth century when warlords were fiercely fighting one another in most areas throughout China. Besides, transportation at that time was incredibly poor, with no railway or highways reaching that mountain area surrounded with dense primeval forests and rapid rivers.

But return she did. On a winter evening when the chilly wind made the bronze bells on the eaves of the Ancient Han King Palace tinkle, someone noticed Laolao's gaunt pallid figure soundlessly materializing at the corner of a street.

Precisely how she had survived the escape and the arduous journey remains a mystery to this day. No one knew exactly what had happened and no one was willing to talk about it. Laolao's mind remained clear until her last moment; still, she had never revealed anything to anybody. I had the impression that she would feel deeply hurt by any attempt to touch upon this topic, too.

The reason, I guess, related to her marital history, which she, as well as her relatives, regarded as shameful. According to the old tradition, a chaste woman should serve only one man in her life. If only Laolao had remained a widow after the officer's death, her first marriage might not have been a shame but instead, a source of pride to herself and her relatives as well. There was no lack of stories in old China eulogizing young girls who decided to 'stay with the tombstone' all their lives when their fiancés died before the wedding. They were honoured as 'models of chastity' in order to encourage other girls to follow suit.

However, not long after her return, Laolao was married off by the tailor to my grandfather.

My grandfather, a man with a pockmarked face and a tall slender figure, was then in his sixties. Smart and ambitious, he was one of the few very rich men in the city. His wife had just died. Three of his four daughters had already married. The only pity for the old man was that he had no son, which meant no heir. So my grandfather wanted to marry a young woman to have a son.

There were plenty of people eager to become his in-laws. Rumour had it that my grandfather favoured a certain girl who enjoyed the reputation of being both gentle and submissive, and was so described by the matchmakers. My grandfather asked the matchmakers to arrange it so that he could secretly have a look at the woman before he would finally agree to the marriage. The matchmakers became wary, for the girl was ugly-looking enough to shut the eyes of any groom-to-be, young or old, with her small eyes like two narrow slits on a rough pig-skinned face, so it was said.

"What can we do, God!" The matchmakers were in a panic. They had been paid well by the girl's parents to arrange this marriage. Then one of the matchmakers had the idea of letting Laolao, not the old maid, be seen by my grandfather. "Once the marriage contract is signed, he will not be able to break the agreement, whatever he discovers later!" said the crafty conniving creature.

The tailor was bribed to arrange for his daughter to appear at the next country fair. As scheduled, before lunch time that day, my grandfather and the matchmaker arrived at an exquisitely decorated tea house located in the shopping centre. There were only a few customers inside. A blind man sitting by a corner was playing a lonely tune on er hu, a two-string musical instrument. My grandfather seated himself at a table by the window.

Through the windowpane he saw across the street a couple of acrobatic performers executing breathtaking feats under the sun. A muscular man was contorting himself in the effort to insert a two-foot long sword down his throat. He stood straight with his chin raised up to create a suitable angle at which the sword could slide in. His mouth opened wide, his eyeballs protruded, and blue veins stood out on his temples, with each advancing inch of the sword. A group of adults and kids stood in a circle, watching and shouting comments occasionally. When half of the sword was inside his throat, the man stopped. A little boy with a straw-weaved dish in his hand started to beg for coins from the audience. A couple of observers threw a few coins into the dish, but most people scattered at once.

My grandfather felt suffocated as his eyesight fell unimpeded onto the man standing nervously still with the sword inside him. He turned his face away from the window and started to observe the leaves of the green tea floating in his cup. He chatted casually with the matchmaker. He lifted his eyes again only when he heard the rustle of the bamboo bead curtain hanging on the door. A young girl, accompanied by an old man, entered the tea house. The matchmaker pointed his sharp chin at the girl and winked at my grandfather. My grandfather tried his best to completely take in the girl who passed him silently and sat at a table further inside the tea house. He doubted his eyes for having such good luck!

The girl was dressed in a pearl white, short satin gown buttoned on the right, with fashionable round lower hems and wide cuffs three inches above the wrists, and a green-onion-coloured long skirt which covered her tiny pointed bound feet. Her oval shaped face and smooth skin reminded him of an exquisitely carved pale pink jade ornament in his bedroom. And the pair of large black eyes under her bangs, hiding a mist of grief, made her as graceful and tranquil as the female figure in the ancient scroll behind her on the wall. The sick feeling aroused by the sword-swallowing man was washed away by the refreshing sight. "She looks so young, younger even than my youngest daughter, and she looks gentle and soft as water." My grandfather nodded with satisfaction. In a couple of seconds his mind was made up.

But the matchmakers found they were caught in their own trap. The tailor regretted the role he had played in the tea house. "Why couldn't I become the in-law of the rich old man?" he asked himself angrily. The tailor warned the matchmakers that he would tell the old man the truth about the charade at the tea house before he signed the marriage contract.

Needless to say, everything then developed in the way the tailor had hoped. The matchmakers could do nothing but slap their own faces and apologize to my grandfather. Though their explanation that the pig-skinned girl was suddenly found too sick to marry sounded doubtful, my grandfather was so impressed by the girl he had seen at the tea house that he eagerly accepted the matchmakers' suggestion that he marry Laolao instead, despite all the rumours about her past.

Laolao did not want this marriage at all. How could a twenty-year-old young woman feel happy about marrying a man older than her own father! Especially after she had already seen that pockmarked face with her own eyes! But again, as a woman, she simply did not have a say in this matter, just as she had been obliged to show up at the tea house against her will.

The day came when Laolao was carried by a sedan chair to my grandfather's large house. Laolao was not a virgin, so her wedding was arranged as discreetly as possible. No musicians accompanied her on the way, only a couple of close relatives. Inside the dark chair, Laolao closed her eyes. She remembered the girl students from the missionary schools she had met in big cities. "They all have natural feet and can walk as fast as men. They can also read and write as men do. They are lucky. What can make women's fates so different!" she lamented, her heart soaked in grief.

In her new home, Laolao soon confronted the hostility of her step-daughter, my grandfather's youngest daughter. Fourth-Sister, as she was called by all servants, was twenty-five years old. 'New Mother', was how she addressed Laolao. Yet her heart was full of hatred towards the 'mother' five years younger than herself.

Laolao at first felt puzzled when she heard some servants secretly call Fourth-Sister 'Purple Lips'. One evening at the dinner table, as Fourth-Sister finished her soup and wiped her mouth with a handkerchief, Laolao noticed the purple colour of her unrouged lips under the bright candle light. It was not long before Laolao learned the story related to Fourth-Sister's nickname.

Twenty-five years before, when Fourth-Sister was born, my grandfather was extremely disappointed that the family had one more unwanted daughter. In a flare of rage, he ordered the servant to drown the newborn immediately. Thus Fourth-Sister was thrown into a large vat full of water. A moment later, my grandfather went into his wife's room and found her all in tears. He was sorry for his cruelty and changed his decision. The newborn was rescued from the edge of being choked to death, but ever after bore the mark — purple-coloured lips.

Fourth-Sister didn't marry as early as her three sisters did, because my grandfather planned to let her marry — and stay at home. But this was not easy. It was commonly regarded as a disgrace for a man to marry into the bride's family, because he would have to replace his own family name with the bride's. Therefore very few men were willing to do it unless there was no other alternative for survival. Also, all my grandfather's relatives were strongly against the idea of letting Fourth-Sister marry at home. Instead, many offered their sons to be adopted by my grandfather. My grandfather, aware that these greedy relatives coveted being the only heir to his large property, turned down all their offers. Therefore Fourth-Sister waited patiently for my grandfather to find the right man to marry into the family: then she would become the sole heir to all the wealth. The coming of the 'New Mother', however, jeopardized Fourth-Sister's security. Clearly, if Laolao gave birth to a male child, Fourth-Sister would have no reason to marry at home and she would have to leave!

Two years after Laolao was married to my grandfather, she became pregnant. She was sick at the sight of any food and soon had to seek the relief of a doctor's prescriptions.

Laolao had been lying in bed for days, while her personal maid, a young girl named Crabapple, concocted medicinal herbs twice a day for her. One evening after supper, Crabapple opened a new bag of herbs and poured them into an earthenware pot. She filled the pot with cold water and put it over a coal stove in the kitchen. She then left to go to the washroom. When she came back to the kitchen a couple of minutes later, Crabapple caught sight of Fourth-Sister's tall figure in front of the stove. Hearing the steps of Crabapple, Fourth-Sister quickly turned around and left the kitchen without a word.

Crabapple had been bought by my grandfather to serve Laolao when she married into this big house. She was fully aware of the tension between Laolao and the Fourth-Sister. Fourth-Sister's appearing in the kitchen at this time was suspicious. However, Crabapple had no evidence of what had taken place in the kitchen during her absence, and Laolao was waiting for the medicine. Crabapple stared at the pot steaming with a strong herbal smell. She had an idea.

A moment later, Crabapple came to Laolao's bed. She put the medicine pot on a table by the window and looked at Laolao hesitatingly.

"If you are not feeling any better after taking this medicine for three days, I see no point in continuing it," she suggested cautiously, while through the windowpane, she cast a meaningful glance at the house in the backyard where Fourth-Sister lived.

Laolao was keen enough to catch the signal Crabapple was trying to send her. She gazed at the medicine pot for a while and nodded her head.

"You are right. Please put it away then," she told Crabapple.

At midnight, when everybody was sound asleep and the nine-courtyard home finally became quiet, Laolao was woken up by a shrill noise. She sat up in her bed and listened attentively.

"Mew... Mew..." It was the sad cry of a cat. Laolao put on her garment and went out of her room. The moon was bright and she could see clearly without a lantern. There, at the turn of the winding corridor, right beneath her window, Laolao saw a black cat rolling on the brick-laid ground with its paws scratching desperately at the bricks and its eyes shining with a deathly look. Laolao recognized this cat as one of Fourth-Sister's pets. She was puzzled by the cat's strange behaviour, but she didn't want to cause trouble by asking Fourth-Sister anything. Gradually, the cat's movement slowed down and its shrill cries became weaker and weaker.

When it finally became motionless, Laolao bent down and looked at it closely. God! The cat's face was stained with blood which was still streaming out of its nostrils and mouth! Common sense told her this was clearly the sign of a poisonous death. The image of the medicine pot flashed across her mind and sent cold shivers down her spine! Laolao shuddered and hugged herself. She looked around and found the earthenware pot turned over at the foot of the raised flower bed near the corridor. Some herbs were spilled on the brick ground. Instinct prompted Laolao to cry out but she covered her mouth. The old man had been away for two days on a business trip and would not come back for a week. Crabapple was sleeping in her own room in the side wing house. She must have been so tired from the day's activities that she had not even been disturbed by the noises moments before. Laolao stood terrified by the flower bed. The night air was filled with a strong scent, not from the blooming roses, but the herbs. She felt a coldness rising from her footsoles into her heart.

The next morning, Fourth-Sister learned about the death of her pet from Crabapple. She went into the front yard and took away the dead animal silently. Her face was white as a piece of paper and her hands were trembling. She didn't even ask a single question about the abrupt death of her cat, though the rising sun exposed everything in the yard clearly to her eyes — the blood, the earthenware pot, and the spilt herbs on the brick laid ground. Laolao watched everything quietly from her window. She had already made up her mind not to mention anything to anyone.

A year later, my grandfather held a large banquet celebrating the first 'full month' of his son, Honesty. Hundreds of guests came to his large country residence and congratulated the old man on his finally having an heir, and in his sixties.

Fourth-Sister didn't step out of her own house the whole day. A rich merchant's wife had died recently and the vacancy was going to be filled up by her, my grandfather had just informed her. She hated the idea, but there was no reason to stay at home any more. The noise of the banquet from the front yard almost drove her crazy. She shouted at all servants trying to approach her door and stamped her feet on the floor. She chased her pets around the house with a feather duster. When she was exhausted, she threw herself into bed and buried her face in the pillows and started to weep in desperation.

To comfort the unwilling bride, my grandfather prepared an abundant dowry for Fourth-Sister. On the wedding day, people in town gaped enviously as a fifty-man team carried furniture, bedding and trunkfuls of expensive clothes to the groom's home.

Fourth-Sister's new rival was her mother-in-law. Only a few months after Fourth-Sister's wedding, her aged mother-in-law died after frequent conflicts between the two. The merchant's whole family believed Fourth-Sister's hot temper and disobedience to be the direct cause of the old woman's death and so decided to punish her. The merchant blackmailed my grandfather for a large sum of money, compensation for raising up a daughter unsuited to wifely duty. But the ransom was not enough to quell their rage. The dead woman's body was kept in an empty room for days while Fourth-Sister was ordered to kneel beside it to atone for her crime. It was in the humid summer days and maggots soon appeared in the decomposing body. Fourth-Sister was forced to pick out the maggots from the body with a pair of chopsticks. The fetid odour and the horrifying sight made Fourth-Sister faint on the floor several times, but she was repeatedly slapped awake to endure her sentence.

When the dead woman's body was finally buried and the cruel torment was over, Fourth-Sister lay down and never got up again.

Laolao went to see her as she was dying. Fourth-Sister was lying in bed. She tried hard to open her eyes and murmured, "Are you coming to laugh at me? Sure, I know... It's retribution..."

"No! Believe me, I am very sympathetic..." Laolao's eyes became moist, as she watched the purple lips moving with difficulty. She forgave the dying woman everything. Fourth-Sister, Laolao suddenly felt, was just like many ordinary women, victims of a strong but unknown power.

After Fourth-Sister was buried, the rich merchant was ready to marry for the third time. Laolao was appalled to learn that her father, the tailor, was planning to marry his youngest daughter to the merchant. It was obvious that the tailor wanted his daughter to inherit the rich dowry left by Fourth-Sister.

Laolao was disgusted by her father's plan. "He is too greedy! Hasn't he heard about the merchant family's inhuman treatment of Fourth-Sister? How can he ever think of sending another lamb into the mouth of a tiger!"

She went home and pleaded with the tailor not to marry her sister to the merchant. But the tailor simply waved his hand impatiently to shoo Laolao away. "What's the matter with you? Don't you understand that a married daughter is just like spilt water? You don't belong to this family any longer!"

"Father! Father!" Laolao shouted out angrily at the tailor's back as he was leaving. "Isn't it enough that you have destroyed my life? Must you destroy my sister's, too?"

As Laolao turned her back and walked towards the door, she told herself that she would never step into his house again. "I won't cry any more. I won't leave myself at the mercy of others again! There is no sympathy in this cold world!"

Laolao's determination and strength of will, formed over time after the sequence of unexpected events in her youth, constantly made my grandfather frown. He did not anticipate that his young and pretty wife would turn out to be such an independent-minded one, a far cry from the image of soft water.

"You want to have a say in all family matters and you take every opportunity to learn how to read! Would you simply shut up your mouth and close your eyes? Don't you know that illiteracy is the virtue of a woman and a wife is supposed to be obedient and submissive to her husband?" he often castigated her in icy tones.

Of course Laolao knew all these things. But what she wanted was a change — the chance to control her own life.

2

A Young Girl in the Whirlpool of the Times

"RUFF-RUFF! RUFF-RUFF!" IT WAS MAX BARKING FIERCELY. I went upstairs and stopped outside Mrs. Thompson's bedroom. I knocked at the door.

"Mrs. Thompson!" There was no answer.

"Mrs. Thompson!" I raised my voice.

"Ruff-ruff! Ruff-ruff!" Max was scratching the door from inside.

"I can't wait any longer," I told myself, "or Max is going to relieve himself in the bedroom again, as he has done many times before."

I turned the knob and pushed the door open. A black-skinned, short-tailed Doberman shot out and rushed downstairs. I closed the door and followed him down.

I opened the door to the back porch and we both went out. Across the twenty-metre-wide back lawn was a marble railing with stone steps leading to the river down below. There was laughter. I leaned over the railing and looked down. Through the open spaces of the densely growing trees, I saw a canoe floating downstream fifty metres below in the river. A couple of young people were talking and laughing.

I looked at my watch. It was almost two o'clock in the afternoon. The mailwoman must have come. "Max!" I walked towards the cottage. The dog liked to have his B.M. in this place.

Across the eastern garden and the oak woods was an old dark cottage, standing high above at the corner where the stream on this property joins the river. The two-piece doors were off, leaning against the outside wall. In the centre of the hall was a small tractor and some tools were lying on the floor. There was a fridge on the right hand, and a fireplace and a couch on the left. Inside the small room on the left were a few pieces of bedroom furniture. Everything here looked grey and dusty and the air smelled mouldy. A door at the corner of the hall led to a long overhanging deck suspended in the air. I stepped on it carefully, fearing the aged structure might crash at any moment, and looked through the screen. Down beneath my feet was the broad surface of the river.

"Oh!" Max appeared silently by my knee and gave me a start. "Let's go and get the mail!" I said to him.

We walked on the winding driveway towards the entrance. Mini-sized old cabins emerged here and there among the bushes beside the road. They must have been built for the animals decades ago by the owner of the property, I thought. In front of us on the lawn there were two large deer with mixed light brown and white coats. Max shot out like an arrow to chase them. The deer were startled and bounced up towards the pine woods farther down the lawn. Their bushy white tails waved up and down behind their backs.

"This place is just like a zoo," I said to myself. There seemed to be all kinds of animals living here. I remembered the startling scene last winter when I had seen a red fox lingering on the snow by the fountain in front of the house. It was hard to believe that just outside of this six-acre property was a busy shopping plaza surrounded by streets of houses.

At the turn of the driveway was a cement bridge. Standing in the middle of the bridge were George and an old woman. George had been the gardener here for more than twenty years. He and his wife lived in the stone house beside the abandoned tennis court. His wife had passed away three months before. He was almost paralyzed with grief and wanted to resign from his job.

George was talking in a low voice to the woman, who was smiling and looking down over the bridge at the gurgling water below. I felt happy to see he had recovered from his sorrow and was meeting a new lady. I waved to them as I passed by. "I like the Canadian people's attitude to life..." I thought. "In China, an old man like George would arouse malicious gossip if he dated a girlfriend at the age of seventy-two."

Back at the big house with the mail, I found Mrs. Thompson was still not up. "A heart attack?" I started to worry.

I went to her bedroom and knocked at the door again. There was no answer. Could it be that she had passed away silently? Horrified by the thought, I pushed the door open and rushed to the bed. Thank God, she was still alive!

I shook her body under the blanket. She opened her eyes. "Oh, Lilac... What's the time now?" Her voice was dreamy and weak.

"It's two-thirty." I replied. "Do you want your breakfast now? I have got your grapefruit and toast ready."

"No... later." She closed her eyes again.

"You'd better eat something," I insisted and reached to help her up. "Come on! You can't lie in bed the whole day."

"No, thank you... Lilac..." she murmured, still with her eyes closed. Her hands were cold and shaking. I sighed and gave up my effort.

On the small table in front of the TV was an ashtray filled with cigarette ends and an exquisitely carved long glass which was her favourite container for liquor. By the foot of the table on the carpet lay an empty bottle of vodka. "She must be so drunk this time," I thought, "that she forgot to hide the bottle away."

She had finished the forty-ounce bottle in a couple of days. I was conscious enough of the harmful effect alcohol could have on people and I had wanted to discuss this with her ever since I had discovered her 'hobby'. However, Mrs. Thompson was conscientiously trying to conceal this hobby from me and therefore it would embarrass her if I mentioned it. I noticed a few times that when she was running out of her stock, George would sneak into the house and leave a brown paper bag and some change in the pantry. She would then come downstairs with unsteady steps and take the bag with her back to her bedroom, cautiously avoiding my eyes. Noticing the guilty smile on her face, I had to pretend that I saw nothing.

Max emerged from somewhere and jumped onto the king-sized bed. He settled down in his usual place beside Mrs. Thompson, with his mouth touching her head. He had been here for seven years. They were like mother and son.

I stared at the scene numbly. The sparse white hair and the pale wrinkled face gradually faded into those of another old lady.

*   *   *

THOUGH MY GRANDFATHER WAS GREATLY DISAPPOINTED with his pretty but unfortunately strong-willed young wife, there was one thing he really felt grateful to her for. Laolao had given birth to his only son, Honesty, a beautiful looking boy.

Following the birth of Honesty, Laolao had two more daughters, Lin and Qin. After Qin was born, my grandfather told Laolao: "I have too many daughters. I'll give two acres of land to anyone who wants to adopt the newborn!"

"No!" declared Laolao, refusing his suggestion firmly. She knew what was in the old man's mind. He wanted to have more sons before he was too old. But Laolao insisted on breast-feeding her own children and turned down all the wet nurses he found for her. Her insistence on feeding her own baby prevented her from getting pregnant again soon, and that was why the old man wanted to give the baby girl away!

All three children had inherited Grandfather's tall, slender figure, and Laolao's fair complexion. Needless to say, Honesty was the apple of my grandfather's eye. At a very young age, Honesty was already aware of his unique position in the family.

One afternoon when the adults were busy with preparations for the annual celebration of the Mid-Autumn Festival to take place the next day, eight-year-old Honesty took his two sisters to the bazaar in town. He left them in a busy street and ran away alone. Back home, he announced proudly to his parents: "See! I have got rid of the two useless things for you!"

The adults were confused by his words and didn't understand what had happened.

"Didn't you always complain that it is useless to bring up daughters, who are good for nothing?" Honesty asked my grandfather.

"...What! How could you...?" When the adults finally understood the nature of the 'heroic'" deed performed by the boy, they were seized with panic and a search party was immediately sent out.

Meanwhile, the two little girls found themselves alone and lost in a completely strange place, surrounded by crowds of pedlars and noisy bargaining voices. Six-year-old Lin was a gentle, timid girl. Frightened by the situation, she started to cry.

"Don't cry, Sister!" said Qin. "Let's find our way home." The four-year-old girl was braver than her older sister.

The two little girls walked hand in hand along wide streets and narrow lanes. They stopped and looked around now and then to find familiar objects. They dared not ask for help. They had heard too many stories about child abductors who were on the lookout especially for lost kids.

After who knows how long, the busy streets gradually had become empty and the shades of dusk spread through the air. They kept their mouths shut and their feet busy. Though hungry and tired and nowhere near home, they knew they couldn't stop.

When the moon was rising, they suddenly found they were already out of town in the suburbs. A winding road stretched in front of them, leading where, they did not know. There were fewer residential houses around. Willow woods and bamboo bushes alongside the road formed mysterious dark shadows. The little girls kept their eyes in front and resisted the temptation to look sideways. They didn't know if they were on the right track, but they knew they must go, and keep on going.

"Ah!" As the road turned around, they came to an open space and found they were at the Han River ferry. The broad surface of the water was rippling under the bright moonlight. A small ferryboat was idling by the pier. They stopped. There was no further to go. The autumn breeze swept over their faces and they both shivered with cold.

"Listen!" Qin heard someone calling their names and looked in the direction from which the voice was coming.

Along the riverbank came two figures holding a red paper lantern in the darkness. The red light was like a cosy fire in a winter night.

"Lin! Qin! Where are you?" It was Laolao's voice!

"Mom! Mom!" Lin and Qin shouted as they ran towards the red light.

Laolao passed the red lantern to Crabapple standing beside her and hurried over in her unsteady footsteps.

"Mom!" The two girls burst out into tears and threw themselves into Laolao's arms.

"Thank God!" Laolao wanted to smile, but tears of relief came welling up first. "I was so afraid that you had drowned in the river..."

* * *

QUITE A FEW YEARS HAD GONE BY SINCE THAT EPISODE. The three children were grown up. European-style school systems had been established in China and women were encouraged to become educated, though few people could afford this and female students were limited to well-to-do families. Laolao insisted on sending her two daughters as well as her son to school, in the strong belief that educated women would survive better in society. Laolao always felt sorry that she had had no chance to go to school when she was young. She liked these educated young people very much and often entertained her children's schoolmates in her home.

Honesty was a typical pampered dandy, well dressed, good at every sport and possessing a special eye for every new fad appearing in town. Lin's gentle manner and peaceful personality were nodded at approvingly by both old and young alike.

Qin was quite a controversial girl. With long legs, a slim figure, rosy cheeks, black vivacious eyes, and pearl-like teeth in gracefully delineated lips, her beauty widened the eyes of everyone who saw her. On the other hand, her strong personality characterized by frank talking, sharp comments and eagerness to succeed in everything, earned her the reputation of 'a thorny rose'. She played a leading role in every field — in class, on stage, in sports and speech competitions. But it was only at the time of her father's death that the people in town were truly impressed by the extraordinariness of the youngest daughter of the wealthy family.

The year my grandfather was knocked down in bed by a serious stroke, Qin was only thirteen years old. One day he called his three children to his bedside and looked at them silently for quite a while. They stood there like three small white birches, young and tender and smelling fresh and vital. Tears oozed out of the old man's eyes and dropped onto his grey beard.

"If I leave a very large sum of money to you after I die," he asked slowly. "What will you do with it?"

Honesty replied without much thought: "Buy real estate, perhaps."

"I have no idea..." Lin's voice was low and weak.

The old man's eyes fell upon Qin.

"Practise usury!" She uttered the two words snappily and then, as she often did, drew her lips tightly together in a gesture of confidence and determination.

The old man was silent. Then he sighed heavily and closed his eyes: "Oh... What a pity that Qin is not a son!"

My grandfather passed away a few days later. The death of a penniless man may not create much sensation. When a wealthy man dies, however, the nerves of almost all his relatives are taxed.

It was the last day of the vast seven-day funeral rite, and the climax was approaching.

Outside of the residence gate along half a mile of the street were various neatly lined up, paper-made household items. They were gifts from relatives and friends and would be burned at the funeral to secure the buried man a worry-free life in another world. Beside the figures of both male and female servants were four life-size horses made of silver foil, pulling a sedan cart made of gold foil. Right behind the cart was a human figure pulling a two-wheeled paper rickshaw, a new transportation tool recently introduced from big cities into Han Zhong.

Inside the gate, in the front yard, the huge, heavily painted black coffin which lay in the centre of the main room was waiting to be carried out at the chosen hour. During the previous week the nine courtyard suburban residences had been filled with people: relatives and friends coming to pay their tribute, workers hired for decorations and the funeral rites, sixteen Buddhist monks praying for the dead day and night, and musicians to create the solemn atmosphere.

Laolao felt exhausted, but she tried hard to look calm and keep everything in order in the overcrowded residence. According to tradition, a funeral was a 'white ceremony', just as a wedding was a 'red ceremony'. Both were events which must be held as extravagantly as possible to display the host family's riches and distinguished social status. The local people, particularly the picky relatives, enjoyed comparing, commenting on and finding fault with these ceremonies, and Laolao had to be very careful lest anything go wrong and provide a source of gossip. The task facing her was a doubly heavy one, as she planned to finish the funeral one day, and hold the wedding for Honesty two days later.

When my grandfather was very sick, he had chosen a girl for his seven-teen-year-old son. But the old man died just nine days before the wedding was to be held. Invitations had been sent out and everything for the wedding had been arranged. Old tradition held that if the wedding was not carried out as originally scheduled, it would have to be postponed for three years to show the son's filial piety to his father. Laolao decided to keep the original plan and hold the two big ceremonies one after the other, as both were time-consuming, money-costing, and people-exhausting events.

Feasts had been held from morning till night; the stove fire had not ceased for days. Guests came and went. Sitting around ten tables, they watched hot and cold dishes being carried out one by one from the large kitchen house in the side yard. Laolao walked around giving orders. Her bound feet were sore and her back was aching. She glanced anxiously at the large clock hanging on the wall once in a while, hoping the last few minutes would pass smoothly...

Suddenly, she sensed something unsettling brewing in the atmosphere in the yard. Some guests at the tables were winking at each other. Before she could find out what was wrong, seven or eight male relatives had left their seats and taken up positions in front of the coffin like a solid wall blocking access to it.

One of the men, obviously the chief plotter, was my grandfather's younger brother. With a toothpick still in his hand, he pointed at Laolao and informed her how they thought she should divide the dead man's property.

"If you don't cooperate, well," he threw the toothpick on the floor, a ferocious light gleaming in his small narrow eyes, "We will not let the coffin be moved a single inch!"

"Right. We simply won't let it be carried out!" the rest of the men threatened, waving their arms and stamping their feet on the floor.

Cold sweat promptly covered Laolao's back. Clearly, everything had been planned. "But how could I accept these harsh terms!" she thought. "They would strip almost everything from the family." She looked at the familiar faces in front of her and thought with pain that many of them had benefitted greatly from the generosity of the old man. How could they change face so quickly once he passed away?

She pleaded with them to show mercy to the widow and children. "The dead man treated you all nicely, didn't he?" she asked, her voice full of disappointment.

The hour chosen for the burial was close at hand. It was commonly believed at that time that any delay in the ceremony would be ominous for the family. Besides, the planned wedding would also have to be postponed, and the whole schedule upset, as a result.

Laolao talked herself hoarse. The men simply sneered at her as they glanced arrogantly off in the direction of the setting sun which was sliding behind the roof of the house on the western side of the yard. There were titters in their noses, but not the slightest movement in their steady feet.

The courtyard, a moment ago noisy, was deadly quiet now. People squeezed by the door and the windows of the main room and, holding their breaths, observed with great curiosity. The air in the main room felt thick. Laolao stared at the legs which seemed to be nailed in front of the coffin. Her hands were shaking. She fumbled behind her back, subconsciously looking for something to support her body.

At this crucial moment, Qin, Lin and the seventeen-year-old groom-to-be, who had been watching this scene from a side house for quite a while, became worried at the situation Laolao was trapped in. All the visitors and servants had gone to the hot spot and there was no one else around.

"What can we do, brother?" Qin asked Honesty anxiously. They all knew that young people were not supposed to argue with the older generation.

Honesty was sitting in a chair, looking pensively into the air. His mind was occupied with something else and he paid little attention to Qin's anxiety. He had been unhappy for many days. The quiet moon-faced girl was by no means an ideal wife as far as he was concerned. She was the only daughter of a wealthy landlord who owned the largest property in the town where he lived. The girl was said to fill all the criteria tradition set for a woman. But Honesty had received a modern education and was resentful of the old fashioned practice of arranged marriages.

"There were quite a few beautiful girls in the school, so why did father select this plain looking one! And she is as quiet as a dead person!" he thought, aggrieved. "The moon-faced girl will become my wife in two days and there is simply nothing I can do to prevent it!"

"What should we do, brother?" Qin pushed at his shoulder and asked him again.

Honesty's eyes turned in the direction of the main room and he replied carelessly: "What I can do? Let them do whatever they like... Who cares!"

Lin, truly frightened, was fearfully peeping from behind the curtains of the window. She looked at Honesty and Qin, and sighed, but said nothing.

Qin cast a final glance at her sister and brother. Her elegantly shaped lips closed tightly and two large dimples appeared in her rosy cheeks. She stood up. "This is no time to think what kind of behaviour is proper for a girl," she told herself.

She rushed into the kitchen house and seized a heavy chopping knife. Clad from head to foot in her traditional funeral costume of white linen, she then ran to the main room and pushed through the crowd at the door. "Give me room! Give me room!" she screamed. Everyone was shocked to see the pretty young girl, flushed, her angry eyes wide open.

Arriving at the centre of the main room, she said loudly to Laolao: "Mother, these people are not to be reasoned with!"

She then turned to face the wall of men. Suddenly she raised the shining knife above her head, announcing clearly word by word: "I'll chop anybody who dares to make trouble!"

Before finishing her last word, she waved the sharp knife menacingly towards the wall of men blocking the coffin. As the surrounding crowd screamed in alarm, the men held their heads with their hands and jumped away from the coffin in a big panic. Everyone believed that the little girl was mad and might do what she threatened, so they scrambled in haste for the door.

Laolao grasped the chance and gestured to the workers standing by. They quickly came over and raised up the coffin.

＊　　　＊　　　＊

SHORTLY AFTER QIN'S ASTONISHING BEHAVIOUR AT THE funeral, a new story about her bravery became a major topic among the people who met daily at the tea house downtown to gossip. This time, however, the young girl's rival was not the old fashioned relatives dressed in long robes and black skullcaps, puffing at foot-long pipes. Instead it was the mayor of the small city, a man who had formal education and whose nicely cut European-style suit and shining leather shoes had once been the model for all the followers of fashion in town.

After many people boycotted the unreasonably exorbitant taxes and levies from the city government, the mayor became annoyed and decided to punish one so as to frighten a hundred. He picked out Laolao, a helpless widow.

One morning as Qin was in class, Laolao's maid Crabapple came breathlessly to tell her that Laolao had been taken away by armed men to the city hall. Qin left school with Crabapple. At the entrance of the city hall, she asked the doorman politely if she could see the mayor. The doorman felt flattered that a pretty girl student was talking to him in this way, and so he agreed to help her.

The arrogant, neatly dressed mayor came out.

"Mr. Mayor, do you know that your men have brought my mother here?" Qin asked him calmly.

"Well..." the mayor looked at the girl and replied, "You are only a little girl. You don't understand that the state has its laws and that we have to punish those who are against the law. Whoever refuses to pay the tax will be arrested, too!" His voice was loud and his stern eyes swept through the people who, in their curiosity, had gathered to watch the event.

"Mr. Mayor," Qin's calm attitude was maturer than her still childish voice. "Do you know how much tax my family should pay, according to the government's regulations, and how much we have paid? We have carefully calculated it and found the fact is that we have already overpaid! You are arresting an innocent woman without proof of guilt. This is indeed something totally against the law! There are many rich people in town failing to pay their taxes. You don't touch those people but pick on us. You must be thinking that women are more easily to be bullied!"

The surrounding crowd laughed and the mayor's face turned red. He had not expected that the little girl would be so witty and sharp tongued. He noticed embarrassedly that the audience to the scene were nodding and whispering to each other in clear appreciation of the girl. He felt it had been unwise to choose this family. He took out his handkerchief, wiped away the sweat on his forehead and said to Qin: "Well, your mother was arrested simply because your family has the largest property in this city and therefore should pay much more tax than everybody else pays... If what you said is true, I would like to reinvestigate this issue..."

"Thanks. Please make a thorough investigation, Mr Mayor!" Qin quickly seized the chance and shifted her attitude. "Now I am going to take my mother home for lunch," Qin said smilingly, heading directly into the yard of the city hall. The mayor looked distracted and didn't answer. A couple of seconds later he followed Qin into the yard.

When Qin walked out of the yard holding Laolao's hand a moment later, there was a buzz in the crowd. "To have a girl like this is better than a son!" The comment found Qin's ear.

*   *   *

HAN ZHONG HAD BEEN UNDER THE RULE OF THE Nationalist Government since the overthrow of the monarch in nineteen eleven. Qin and the people in this secluded area had almost no chance to contact outsiders until World War II broke out.

During the war, the Japanese soldiers didn't come to this area, cut off as it was by natural barriers. Han Zhong was only visited a few times by their bombings from the sky. The first foreigners the local people ever saw were American soldiers serving on the US Air Force base built in Han Zhong during the war.

On the Chinese New Year's Day, students in the local girls' school were invited to attend a party held at the US Air Force base. Qin was selected to present flowers to the Commander-in-chief. Every soldier in the force received a white silk scarf embroidered with a green-coloured "Victory", a gift made by the girl students. Qin and her friends felt nervous all through the party. None of them spoke any English. They smiled with embarrassment while these big-boned Americans tried hard to communicate with the girls by exaggerated facial expressions and gestures. The music was playing and the soldiers tried to dance with the girls. The girls were horrified and shook their heads firmly when they understood the meaning of the soldiers' gestures. A man and a woman were not supposed even to touch each other's hands openly in this small city. It would become sensational news the next day if any of the girls dared to dance in the arms of a foreign man!

Gradually, the mystery of the newcomers disappeared. People in the small city started to talk about the disgusting behaviours of those 'green-eyed, red-haired foreign devils'. They were often seen in the streets, some of them with their upper bodies naked, laughing loudly or chasing after girls. Being naked in public was totally unacceptable to the local people and they were surprised to see that those Americans had no manners at all.

One morning, as Qin was passing through the city gate, she saw a scene which deeply hurt her self-esteem as a Chinese. A middle aged man was shouldering a pole with two basketfuls of animal internal organs. Qin noticed that he had a serious skin disease on his bald head. When he passed Qin, she naturally held her breath to avoid the bad smells from the baskets and his head.

By the gate, however, the man was stopped by a group of American soldiers trying to take a snapshot with the camera in their hands. With repeated body language, the Americans ordered the man to take off his shirt and stand on top of a long narrow stool outside of a small restaurant. As Qin watched the poor man's legs shaking on the stool and his back bent low with the heavy load on his shoulder, while the Americans laughed and focused their camera on him, she felt the insult, not only to the poor man, but to all Chinese.

"They are mean! They are supposed to be friends coming to help the Chinese in our fighting with the Japanese, but they have no respect for our Chinese people at all!" Qin's large black eyes flamed with indignation. She threw a sharp glance at those provoking fun-seekers and quickly left the annoying scene.

An even more unbearable event took place one summer evening. While she was walking home, a girl student was seized by a few American soldiers and put into their jeep. "Help! Help!" The girl's scared cries were heard by many people in the streets, but no one dared to come over as the jeep sped towards their base camp outside of the city.

The next day, the girl's school was boiling. The students decided to hold a demonstration to protest the violence of the American soldiers. Qin led the students as they marched through the main streets of Han Zhong shouting slogans. They came to the spot at which the violence took place and Qin gave a speech to the public, calling all people to help the innocent girl. After the demonstration, Qin also went to the local press to seek support.

There was no reaction from anywhere, however, and the girl students' demonstration was dismissed as merely a girlish game. "It was the girl's fault for walking alone in the street after dark!" Some people's comments really shocked the students. They were more disappointed when they could not even find sympathy from their own school principal. Qin and a few of her close friends decided to lead all the students on a strike, since that was the only action they could think of which might pressure the apathetic authorities.

Three days after their boycott of classes, the city government sent a man to mediate the conflict. The officials at the U.S. Air Force base headquarters formally apologized to the students. Their explanation, that the victim was mistaken for a prostitute because she walked alone in street in the evening, sounded totally unacceptable to the students. But the mediator urged them to give up their boycott: "What else do you expect of the Americans? Don't forget they came to China to help us!"

Qin hated the government's weak and submissive attitude to the foreigners. The Nationalist Government then ruling China was corrupt and rotten in her eyes. They kowtowed to the foreigners, but they knew no limits in dealing with their own compatriots. As he was working in the fields one day, a male servant in Qin's home was kidnapped by Nationalist troops enlarging their intake of recruits. During the day, as they marched with the troop, the arms of the servant and those of other raw recruits were bound with ropes. At night, when the troop stopped for rest, the recruits' pants and shorts were taken away to prevent them from escaping. The servant had left three kids at home and his wife asked help from Laolao. Laolao's efforts to get the servant back failed and she had to support the whole family he left behind.

It was to be expected that Qin would become estranged from some of her friends when they left school and became wives or concubines of the American soldiers, government officials and high-ranking officers of the Nationalist Forces. Qin was sixteen then, a proper age for marriage at that time, and many of the girl students did marry at this age. But she sneered at them. "A woman, especially an educated woman, should live an independent life, and not rely on any man!" she told herself.

When the Japanese occupied the whole of the East China coastal area, many universities moved westward to the inner territory. A few universities moved to Han Zhong, too. Young students came from all over the country, as their homelands had been taken by the Japanese.

Qin noticed that all her friends in the girls' school seemed to be in love.

It was becoming popular in those days for educated young people to choose their own spouses. After class, the favourite subject among the girls was the university students. Those students who came from the big cities seemed very charming and mature in the eyes of the girls who had grown up in Han Zhong. In their dormitories, good friends would exchange love letters and then discuss them, giggling happily. When spring came, they would go group dating in the fields which had just turned green.

To Qin, however, none of those young men was attractive. She liked to make fun of her classmates by exaggeratedly imitating their boyfriends. When she received letters from a few university students, she curled her lips and said with contempt: "All mediocre material!"

As editor of the students' monthly publication, Qin was not easily fooled. Once, her criticism of the articles offended all the writers. "If you employed half the talent you use for writing a love letter, I bet those articles would look different!" she commented sarcastically.

The girls, shamed into anger, decided to teach her a lesson. The next day, they ganged up on her and reclaimed their articles. Qin simply sneered as she watched the girls leaving arrogantly one by one. She was too proud to beg anyone.

A few days later the school newspaper was published in time. Different from all previous issues, all fifteen articles were written by the same author, Qin.

Everyone reading this issue talked about it, some admiring Qin's versatility, and some thinking otherwise. Qin didn't pay much attention to those comments. She had become used to being the focus of public opinion. What she cared about was the boycotters' reactions. When she glimpsed the boycotters gathering by the ivy-covered school wall, talking with annoyance, she almost laughed out loud.

"See, the newspaper can still be published without you lot!" she smiled in her heart. The bell for class clanked at this moment. It was announcing her triumph, Qin felt.

Somehow, not long after that, Qin found love had unexpectedly sneaked into her tender heart. It all started when a young university graduate became their English teacher as the new school year began.

Qin found English like an interesting new game, a poem and a piece of music, especially when the twenty-six letters of the alphabet were enunciated by the baritone standing in front of the blackboard. The young teacher, tall and slim, with a pair of gentle lamb-like eyes behind his round, translucent-framed glasses, always looked graceful and confident, in class and out.

It was on a late afternoon when the string of love in Qin's heart was plucked. It was summer time and the windows in Qin's dormitory were open to let cool air come in. Qin was leaning against her blanket in bed, reading a novel, when she heard a man's voice singing. Qin put down the novel and listened attentively. It was an English song, "The Last Rose of Summer", as she learned later. The voice and the tone was beautiful, bearing a tinge of sorrow. Qin stood up and came to the window, as did a few other girls in the same dormitory. Across the narrow yard, shaded with lilac and peach trees under the setting sun, was the office-dormitory of the young teacher.

He was from Qing Dao, a coastal city in East China, and planned to go to England for graduate studies in theology. Because the seaway was blocked by the Japanese, he had to wait in Han Zhong, where he was making a living by teaching English at the local girls' school.

Qin was his favourite student. Actually, he was struck by her beauty and lively personality the first day he came to her class. He wondered how this small ancient city could have nurtured a girl like this. The young teacher spent many happy times chatting with the bright girl, in his simple but neat office, around the flower-blooming campus, and among the woods overgrown with willows and bamboos on the bank of the quiet Han River. He talked about his home, about the Japanese occupation, and about his exile inland. He talked about literature, history, music, art... "He knows everything in the world." Qin listened and looked at him admiringly.

Gradually, the twenty-five-year-old young man found himself not only attracted by the beautiful girl, but developing a love for the small city too, one which contrasted strongly with his home city — a Europeanized beach city. In the ancient town wrapped around with green mountains and murmuring rivers, historical relics tracing back two thousand years were to be seen everywhere. Everything here was imbued with simplicity and the fragrance of nature.

Of course, he was fully aware that Qin, his sixteen-year-old student, had fallen deeply in love with him. As she talked to him, he could see love in her sparkling eyes and her blushing cheeks. But the more he realized this, the more pained he became.

He had been engaged to his cousin. She was a faithful Christian, just like himself and everyone else in his family.

Now, he felt, his fiancée paled, compared to Qin. But, as the only son of a pastor, brought up with a strong sense of morality, he would feel guilty hurting the innocent. Besides, he worried that Qin was not a Christian. All he could do, therefore, was try hard to hold back the flames of love, and act like a big brother to her.

Qin's love for the charming young teacher was incurable, however. When she was handing in her homework to his office, she was immediately drawn by the handsome calligraphy on the wall. "Golden beach, green waves, my beautiful dreams..." She read it silently again and again. To Qin, the beach and the waves of the sea were just like her young teacher, mysterious and beautiful dreams.

On Christmas Day, the young teacher invited all his students to the local church, built in the city a few years before the war started. It was the first time Qin had ever entered a church, as Christianity was not widely accepted by the people. She and her friends were looking at the decorations curiously, when they found an old man with a white beard and a red robe among them. The old man presented a gift box to each of the girls. "This is a gift from Santa!" he said, smiling.

"Well, this is our teacher!" Qin shrilled excitedly, recognizing the old man's familiar voice. All the girls burst out laughing happily.

Qin quickly opened her gift. It was a notebook with an exquisitely embroidered silk cover. On the front page was inscribed in beautiful handwriting: "How I hope you will become a member of the Lord's family one day!"

The next Sunday, Qin agreed to go to church with the young teacher. She observed everything seriously and tried hard to feel what her beloved teacher believed in. She was indeed sincere, but, to her disappointment, she couldn't feel the existence of the God her teacher loved so much. She admitted this honestly to the young man.

The eight-year-long war with Japan was over in the fall of nineteen forty-five. In the following spring, the day finally came when the young teacher's painful love had to come to an end. Before leaving for Europe, he asked Qin to meet him in the garden of the Ancient Han King Palace.

They gazed at each other silently, in the shade of the quiet, moss-covered old pavilion. The young teacher's gentle eyes reflected his complicated inner world.

He gave Qin a nicely-shaped pink comb. It was a plastic comb, a new product appearing in the local store that had sold only traditional bone and wooden combs before.

"When you comb your hair everyday, you will of course remember me, I hope," the young teacher said, his eyes looking pensive.

"But, I have nothing to give you." Qin felt regret that she hadn't got him a gift before she came.

"Well…" The young teacher seemed a little bit uneasy and hesitated before he said: "If you don't mind, I'd like to have a wisp of your hair… I will carry it wherever I go."

Qin felt overcome by a sudden wave of emotion. Her eyes became moist. She nodded wordlessly. As the teacher took out a pair of small scissors from his pocket and touched her straight, shoulder-long hair carefully, large beads of tears dropped onto her bosom.

She got two dozen letters from him. The first one was written on the long-distance bus leaving Han Zhong, lines of which Qin could still recite decades later: "Adieu, adieu, the tranquil river and green hills, the cordial town and the beloved girl…"

In the early days after the young teacher had left, Qin went back to her home everyday to check for letters. From his letters, she learned what he was on — the bus, the train, the ship — and where he had reached — a small town, a big city, another big city, the coast… Fully aware that he was getting farther and farther away from her, Qin always had the strange feeling that the young teacher would appear unexpectedly in front of her one day and give her a happy surprise!

Qin went into a silk store one day. She was warmly welcomed by the store owner who was smiling from ear to ear. He always saved new products of good quality for Laolao, and he was familiar with the pretty young girl. "I got some new fine stuff in the back room." He pointed at the door behind him. "I can't put them out on the counter. Some window shoppers will simply destroy them with their dirty hands…"

Qin followed the man into the back room and scanned the materials on the table. Her eyes were caught by a piece of fine, pale blue gauze. "I want a foot of this," she said, pointing at it.

For two weeks, Qin spent all her spare time on a handkerchief which she designed herself. She made tiny holes along the four sides of the fine gauze and embroidered differently shaped, small white flowers on it.

On the eve of boarding the ship to England, the young teacher received the handkerchief. In his letter, he told Qin that he pressed his lips to these small innocent flowers as he bid farewell to his motherland tearfully.

One early morning, Qin stood inside her dormitory window and watched the drizzle fall from the grey sky. It had been months since she last heard from this young teacher. He should have arrived in England long before, but... Summer was gone and fall was at hand. The lilac and peach trees in the yard seemed to weep, the drops of rain wetting their faces. Suddenly, the strange feeling appeared once again in her heart: the young teacher was coming back today! This time she felt it was definite! She was thrilled and quickly started to dress herself up. She combed her hair neatly and put on her favourite apple green shirt and a pair of pants with very loose legs, a popular style at the time.

She went to the long distance bus station directly and waited inside the small, red-roofed house, full of hope. When a bus arrived, she would stand up from her chair and rush to the door, her heart beating like a drum. As the last passenger came out of the bus, the light in Qin's eyes would become dim. She would then return to the waiting room to expect the next bus.

The whole day passed, with Qin's enthusiasm being eaten away bit by bit. Qin didn't notice the dusk was already spreading in the air. When the man came out of the ticket office and told her there were no more buses for the day, she felt the whole universe was empty. She walked home slowly drenched by the cold, endless autumn rain.

From that day on, Qin changed. She seldom laughed and could no longer concentrate on her studies. In class, she often stared at the blackboard, her mind a blank. She saw a pair of lamb-like gentle eyes on the face of every teacher coming into the classroom.

Christmas Day came again. In the evening, Qin walked into the church, dreaming of finding her young teacher there. She stood in the first row and watched the man nailed on the cross in front of her. The Christians started to sing, led by a Chinese pastor. The mysterious music was echoing in the large church. The face of the nailed man became blurred in the dim light of the burning candles...

"What? Is that him?" Qin opened her eyes wide, for she couldn't believe what she had seen: the young teacher was looking down pensively at her from the cross! And look! The pair of lamb-like eyes were filled with tears! Qin reached out her hand and waved to him. "I am here!" She burst out a crying and wanted to spring into his arms! At this moment, an old lady who had been standing beside her all this time, held Qin firmly.

His last letter was from England, a year after his departure from Han Zhong. Qin could never forget that Sunday evening when she was having supper with the whole family in their country residence. A male servant came into the dining room and passed her a thick envelope. "It arrived at our city residence this afternoon," he told her. As soon as Qin noticed the English address on the envelope, she dropped the bowl of rice in her hand onto the floor. She left the table hurriedly and ran back to her own room in the backyard.

Under the cozy candlelight, Qin opened the envelope with shaking hands. It was a long letter, describing in detail the scenery, food, clothing, and people in an exotic land. Qin laughed out happily several times as she read the young man's interesting descriptions. But her smile disappeared all of a sudden as she came to the end of the letter. "I am writing to you with complicated feelings. After careful consideration, I have finally made up my mind to remain single all my life. I have already informed my parents of my decision and I am sure they will be happy to know that I want to dedicate my life to our Lord. If you can understand me and forgive my delay in writing to you, I hope we can continue our pure friendship..."

Qin's eyes stayed fixed on the last lines. She was totally confused. "Pure friendship... Pure friendship?" The words were turning over and over in her mind. She kept the same position in the chair for a long time. The candle went off and the room turned dark.

There was a knock on the door. Someone walked in with a new candle. It was Laolao. She sat silently on the bed beside Qin. Qin looked into Laolao's eyes. Suddenly she felt she could control herself no more.

Laolao had long noticed the changes taking place in her younger daughter, despite Qin's awkward attempt to disguise them all along. The thick envelope and the spilt rice on the floor at dinner time finally confirmed her suspicion as to the source of Qin's abnormal behaviour. It was high time to arouse her daughter from this dangerous passion, doomed to bury her youth.

"...You are so young, only seventeen," Laolao said softly after Qin told her everything. "I don't want to see you being tortured by love so early and forgetting your study... You understand how much I wanted to become a student when I was young... I hope you will treasure your school years and prepare well for your university entrance exams next year. Forget that man! He will never come back, I am sure..."

The next morning, Qin went to the post office downtown. She bought enough stamps and stuck them carefully onto the envelope. "What is he going to think when he reads this?" She held the letter heavy-heartedly. "Will he feel relieved of an emotional burden?" Qin bit her lips, suddenly threw the envelope into the mail box and ran out of the post office.

Qin didn't have time to ponder the outcome of her abruptly-ended love much longer. The civil war between the communist troops led by Mao Zedong and the Nationalist Government soon broke out and the whole country was thrown into chaos.

Her first romance was actually a small wave in the sea of her eventful life, but Qin had always cherished a trembling attachment to the long disappeared teacher of her early youth. She had been seeking 'true love' — she used these words — all her life, but was disappointed to meet none, except the very first one...

*   *   *

THE THREE YEAR CIVIL WAR WAS BROUGHT TO AN END IN late 1949, with the communists seizing power over the whole country and Chiang Kei-Shek's Nationalist Government being exiled to the small island, Tai Wan.

Though the revolution led by Dr. Sun Yat-sen had overthrown the last emperor of China in 1911 and declared the founding of the republic, the Nationalist Government had never been successful in unifying the whole country.

After the death of Sun Yat-sen in 1925, the Nationalist Government ruled by Chiang Kai-shek continued to remove separatist warlord regimes, suppress peasant uprisings, resist the communist-led armed forces, and deal with the invasion of the Japanese during World War II. Among all his enemies, Chiang regarded the communists as the elements most dangerous to his rule. Hundreds of thousands of communists were massacred under Chiang's iron hand. The country was plagued by war, killings, famine, poverty and corruption.

Intellectuals, mainly university students and professors, were dissatisfied with this situation and held numerous demonstrations appealing for freedom and democracy, and opposing dictatorship, wars and famines. These activities helped to lead to the downfall of the Nationalist Government.

As for the peasants who made up more than eighty percent of the country's population, they actually could not understand or distinguish the differences between the communist ideology of Karl Marx and the Three People's Principles (Nationalism, Democracy and the People's Livelihood) put forward by Dr. Sun Yat-sen. For them, whoever could satisfy their basic need for land and food would be their God.

The Chinese Communist Party won the peasants' favour by confiscating the properties of the rich and redistributing them to the poor, wherever they went. In the long run, they were supported by the population at large in their struggle against the Nationalist Government.

Qin had been studying at a university in Xi An, the provincial capital city, for two years, when the communists came. Though not fully aware of what communist ideology meant, she joined other students in the main streets to welcome the People's Liberation Army — the communist troops — as they entered the ancient city gate. She was surprised to see there were many female soldiers among the troops, and quite moved when she noticed that the high-ranking communist officers walked and carried their own luggage, just as common soldiers did.

She and many other students were invited to political meetings where communist officials talked with them warmly and cordially, behaving quite differently from the arrogant nationalist officials. She started to absorb new ideas about communism and socialism and soon embraced the blueprint of a new classless society, where the people were to be the masters and no exploitation and oppression would exist.

Along with many other girls, she exchanged the traditional dress with high neck and slit skirt for the more fashionable suit with two lines of buttons in the front, called 'the Lenin style' and popular among the communist cadres.

It is not surprising that a young girl from a rich family should show enthusiasm for the policies of a new régime which meant to deprive her of the privileges she had been enjoying. Many educated young people at that time were patriotic and had long been dissatisfied with the war-torn country and the corruptions of the Nationalist Government. The coming of the Communist Party, they expected, would mean equity, freedom, democracy, and the turning of a new page in Chinese history.

Qin was resentful of many practices of old China which put women at the bottom of the society. She was excited to see that the new Communist Government was advocating the emancipation of women by prohibiting bigamy and wife abuse, transforming prostitutes into industry workers, and encouraging women to study and work. She was deeply impressed by the government's severe punishment of criminals and hooligans who had gone scot-free under the old regime. Public security was soon assured. Qin felt that the Communist Government was instilling vitality into a society gone rotten.

When the Land-Reform Movement started to be carried out soon after the 'Liberation' — the term for the communist takeover of China in 1949 — Qin kept on writing letters to Laolao, trying to convince her to follow the new government's policies, and to hand over the family property to the public unconditionally.

She told Laolao that these properties were actually the result of exploitation and therefore should be returned to the people. These were new ideas she had just learned at political propaganda meetings and she was eager to accept this new ideology and abandon the privileged life she had been enjoying.

She wrote those letters in a heroic mood, feeling that personal sacrifices were worthwhile, given the importance of building up an ideal new China.

It was painful for Laolao to comply, though. Knowing nothing about Karl Marx's views of capitalism, she regarded heritage and the system of private ownership as perfectly justified. After the old man died, she had tried so hard to keep the family property. She could never forget the bullying and humiliation occasioned by greedy relatives and government officials. Had it been easy for a widow to endure all those nervous years? How could she give up everything willingly now?

But what else could she do? She knew that some rich persons in town, having heard about the coming of the communists, had quickly sold their properties and escaped overseas. Among them was her dead husband's younger brother who had made trouble many years before at the funeral. Laolao's knowledge about the communists was limited only to her indirect encounter with them back in 1935. That year, the communist-led Red Army, chased by the Nationalist Government, passed through Han Zhong as it was escaping to North China. Propaganda pictured the Red Army as murderers and bandits. Laolao's family and many rich people left their country residences and hid themselves inside the closed city gates. When the Red Army left the area a few days later, Laolao returned to her country residence and found the family's huge granary had been unlocked by the Red Army and its contents distributed to the poor. Nothing else in the residence was touched. Her aged husband was heartbroken to see their empty granary. But Laolao's feelings were complicated. She didn't have a bad impression of 'bandits' who helped the poor and the needy.

Now the former 'bandits' were back as new rulers of the country, Laolao was confused about how she should react. Her children were all studying in universities far away from Han Zhong. She sought their opinions and soon received confirmation from Honesty, and Lin as well, both urging her to hand the family property over unconditionally. "You will be much safer once you become poor!" Honesty wrote.

"They must be mad!" Laolao was completely upset. "Don't they know how their living and educational expenses have been paid all these years!"

She was in a quandary. Should she escape as other rich people had done, or yield…? After a few sleepless nights, however, she finally did what Qin told her to do.

It was fortunate that she complied willingly. Soon, horrible news came. One after another, the stubborn ones refusing to hand over their properties were either dragged to the willow woods on the river bank and shot dead there, or beaten to death by angry masses right there at public 'denouncing' meetings. Among those killed was Honesty's father-in-law, the richest landlord in his town. Honesty's mother-in-law hanged herself at home before the masses of poor people rushed into her house.

Honesty's quiet moon-faced wife had never been successful in winning her husband's heart. Life was too cruel for her. Honesty had eloped with an attractive high school girl shortly after his wedding. The lovers now stayed in a large city in South China as university students, refusing to come back home, despite Laolao's attempts at persuasion. After years of washing her face with tears and swallowing all her sorrows and grief with dogged endurance, the moon-faced wife had become insane and now acted like quite a different person. People passing through her yard often heard her singing in her room. She adopted the tune of a local opera, but created the words on her own, singing everything her mind or eyes touched upon. Her mournful humming mixed with the unexpected high pitch of her voice made everybody's flesh creep.

The moon-faced woman's shrill voice disappeared abruptly one day. She drowned herself in the well at the corner of the back garden in Laolao's town residence, upon hearing of her parents' miserable deaths.

What happened in the small city was nothing compared with the figure of one and a half million landlords executed nationwide during the campaign. Laolao was deeply shocked. After the body of Honesty's wife was dragged out of the well and hastily buried, she lived every day in horror in the big lonely house. At this time she suddenly felt she was becoming old. "It's a new dynasty now, the Communist Dynasty..." she said to herself. "The future will belong to Qin and her friends."

Hundreds of acres of land were handed over to the government for redistribution among the needy and twenty-eight poor families soon moved into Laolao's residences.

It made her heart bleed as she stood behind the curtains inside her own room watching the process of the redistribution of household belongings listed as unnecessary for her personal use.

The large courtyard was chock-full of people, some standing on top of the raised flower beds. They all looked with excitement and anxiety at the fine wood furniture, silks and satins, fine china and porcelains, piled up in the yard. A large carved square table stood in the centre. On top of it was a big plate filled with silver dollars, gold ornaments, and jewelry, dazzling under the noon sun.

A skinny man in dark blue government uniform stood on top of the marble table in the centre and waved his hand to quiet down the crowd. He loudly announced the names and the goods assigned to each, according to lists on a paper in his hand. Several government workers with red bands on their left arms maintained order in the yard and supervised the procedure of distribution. The skinny man raised his voice high in order to be heard above the loud noise. His thin face was reddened by a rush of blood and he sweated under the hot sun. He took off his cap constantly to rub his face.

Laolao silently watched these poor people happily carrying home what was given to them. Among them, she found familiar faces — men and women who used to work for her family. They chatted to each other in loud voices and with hearty laughter, acting quite differently from the way they did when they were working as her servants not long ago in the same courtyard.

She noticed the smiling young face of Lotus, her personal maid after Crabapple had got married and left her some years before. Lotus was chatting with her mother and pointing her finger to the jewelry piled up in the plate. She then raised up her hand and touched her own ear lobe. Laolao saw the expression in her eyes and thought she might want to get the green jade earrings Laolao used to wear. Lotus had admired the earrings before, Laolao remembered.

The walnut table with eight chairs was assigned to nine families. This set of furniture had been made before Honesty got married. Laolao had hired more than twenty carpenters to carve the decorative patterns.

A middle aged man, whom Laolao recognized as one of her former tenants, was dissatisfied at the pair of two-foot tall porcelain vases assigned to him. He argued with the skinny man about replacing the vases with a chair. "What's the use of these things in my home?" he pointed at the vases painted with ancient ladies and scenery. "I can only use them as rice containers!"

His request to exchange the big vases for a chair was refused. "We cannot do that. If everybody wants an exchange, what will happen?" said the skinny man.

"Could you give me a couple of silver dollars instead?" The middle aged tenant was reluctant to give up at once.

"No!" the skinny man refused him harshly. "All the money and jewelry will be confiscated by the government. They will not be distributed!"

The tenant grumbled and left the yard with the vases. Laolao watched him leaving and thought: "He is so stupid! The pair of vases are Song Dynasty antiques, around seven hundred years old now. They are the most valuable things in the yard!"

At the end of the day when everyone was gone and the courtyard was empty, Laolao stepped slowly out of her room and stared at the chrysanthemums and roses trodden to the ground by hundreds of footsteps.

A young man rushed into the courtyard and hastily looked around. "He may not be on the list for redistributed goods," Laolao thought.

As his eyes fell upon a pair of red painted wooden pails behind the door of the kitchen house, he grasped them in his hands. On his way out, he noticed Laolao standing beside the pillar on the veranda and he stopped self-consciously.

The young man hesitated for a couple of seconds and forced out a smile: "You don't need these any more, do you?"

Laolao shook her head numbly.

*   *   *

IN RETURN FOR HER COOPERATION, LAOLAO WAS assigned the title 'enlightened landlord' as her class status. She felt a little bit relieved to know this, since some stubborn rich ones were given the title of 'landlord' only.

When the Land-Reform Movement was over, everyone in China was given a class status according to the amount of property he or she had owned before the movement. Those who had the titles of 'landlord', 'capitalist', and 'rich farmer', were treated as second class citizens, under the control and supervision of the new government.

Ironically, though family properties after that ceased to be inherited, the assigned class status was required to be passed on to future generations ever after. The children and grandchildren of a landlord would inherit the title of 'landlord' as their class status although their economic situations were no better and were sometimes even worse than that of those who had the title of 'the poor peasants' or 'the lower-middle peasants'.

With regard to their political rights and social life, the descendants of the landlord class received the worst treatment, despite the fact that they themselves had never exploited anyone before the Liberation.

This kind of practice was implemented for thirty years until the government finally abolished it in 1979. There was a reason for the Communist Government to classify people this way. One of Mao Ze-dong's famous sayings was that "the philosophy for communists is the philosophy of struggle", which meant that no progress would be achieved without struggle, either with nature or with mankind.

As an opposite class was always needed in the struggle between human beings, so it was necessary to keep a group of people retaining the status of a class enemy, though this practice ironically contravened the equity slogans of communist ideology.

3

Life's Bitter-Sweet Fruits

THREE YEARS AFTER QIN HAD BEEN AT THE UNIVERSITY, near the end of 1950, the Korean War broke out. To protect the security of the newly founded regime, China decided to send armed forces to Korea to fight against the UN troops headed by the Americans.

Nationwide propaganda called for volunteers to join the Chinese forces. In large cities where young people were inspired by patriotism, enthusiasm was high and the recruitment was brisk. Loudspeakers broadcast majestic martial music in streets and parks every day, from morning till night, stirring up heroic feelings in everybody passing by. Many follow-fashion parents named their newborns 'Support-Korea' and 'Resist-America'. The people believed that they were fighting with the number one enemy in the world, the American imperialists.

At Qin's university, two hundred student volunteers were selected from one thousand applicants. They were all healthy pro-communist minded youth. Qin was one of the fifteen girls selected.

Most of Qin's classmates admired her courage and congratulated her for the honour of being selected. Some, however, secretly voiced different opinions, regarding these volunteers as silly.

"We will soon graduate and be assigned to good jobs," they said, "and no career is worse than being a soldier."

"The Americans are armed with modern weapons while our equipment is poor. It would be foolish to be killed in battle so young."

Qin sneered at those opinion holders. "What cowards they are!" she commented to her friends. "A revolutionary youth should always be ready to sacrifice everything for her country, including her life!"

She wouldn't forget the insults and the bullying which the Chinese people had suffered at the hands of the Americans and which she had witnessed in Han Zhong. She felt proud of the new Communist Government for its courage in challenging the arrogant Americans.

When alone, however, she would chew over something hiding deeper in her mind. Her decision, she hoped, would be a turning point for her future. The ongoing Land-Reform Movement had already cast an ominous shadow over her family back in Han Zhong. The government's new campaign to wipe out all dangerous elements in the country in order to secure victory in the Korean War was putting tens of thousands of people to death. Many of those killed were simply innocent victims, she knew.

As one of the few very rich landlords in the small city, Laolao would certainly become targeted by the local government. She could be dragged out and put to death at any moment, with or without an adequate excuse. As for Qin, her family status as a member of the exploiting class was dangerous at that time. With this sort of family background, she would definitely be an untrustworthy person in the eyes of the authorities, despite the fact that she genuinely hoped to be regarded as a pro-communist youth.

Of course she was aware of the danger in battle, but she was determined to take the risk. Being a brave soldier, fighting and perhaps dying while safeguarding her motherland, would surely bring honour to herself and her family.

These days, Qin always thought about a distant cousin. She was six years older than Qin and they used to play together in their childhood. At seventeen, the cousin ran away from her home in Han Zhong to escape an arranged marriage and had since disappeared. Nine years later, in 1949, the cousin returned to her hometown miraculously, in a military jeep, with body guards, and with her husband, a high-ranking communist officer. People were surprised to learn that she had run to the communist base in the North and become a Communist Party member years before. Since she had now returned as a senior communist and had a certain amount of power, the local government in Han Zhong didn't dare to touch her home and her parents, also rich landlords like Qin's family, but instead, fawned on them and treated them with honour.

Qin couldn't help but envy her cousin. How she wished she would bring honour and protection to her family, too!

"Resist America and Support Korea! Protect Our Home and Safeguard Our Motherland!" Qin recited the popular slogan silently again. She felt that her action was, first of all, a realistic means of protecting herself and her home!

A few days before their departure, the university held a farewell meeting for the recruits. The auditorium, decorated with huge red paper slogans from wall to wall, was filled with students and professors. Representatives of the teaching staff, the Students' Union, the Party's and the Youth League's organizations made speeches one by one on the stage.

The chairman received a note passed on to his hand. It was from Qin. She wished to make a speech. The chairman hesitated, since all the speech makers were prearranged and the contents of their speeches had been approved. "Who knows what this girl is going to declare!" His eyes searched downwards and caught Qin's angel-like innocent face. She was looking at him with her large black eyes full of expectation. Without a second thought, the chairman decided to give her the chance.

As Qin stepped onto the stage, she was in the full glare of publicity, looking extremely attractive in a well-fitting new army uniform. With heroic emotion, she recited a poem she had just written:

> Reach out your hands, friends!
> I am bidding farewell to you.
> I am going to dedicate all I have
> including my life
> to our great motherland.
> I am going to fight
> till the last drop of my blood
> to smash Truman's greedy dream!

Her eloquence and passion met with thunderous applause and she blushed with excitement and pride as she stepped down from the stage amid the deafening sounds of drums and gongs.

In those days, Qin's poem was aired repeatedly by the city's radio station. Her fame rose quickly throughout the campus and she was always welcomed with admiring looks and warm handshakes wherever she went.

※　　※　　※

QIN WAS READY TO JOIN THE ONE MILLION CHINESE volunteers fighting in Korea. But when the train arrived in Beijing, she and many other new recruits were asked to stay. Instead of being sent further north to the battlefields, they were assigned to different forces in Beijing. As they soon learned, at that time educated young people were regarded as more useful working for the new government than fighting at the front.

Qin was assigned to work in the headquarters of the air force. It was located in central Beijing, only a few minutes' walk from the Forbidden City, the splendid golden palace left behind by the ousted emperor a few decades before.

On her first Sunday in Beijing, when the city was welcoming its first snow of 1950, Qin came to the entrance of the Forbidden City, the Tian-an-Men Gate. Standing on top of one of the five white marble bridges over the imperial river and watching streams of people and buses passing by the spacious Tian-an-Men Square in front of the magnificent Gate, she thrilled at the brilliance of the capital city and was excited to think that her new life was going to start in the heart of the country.

"I made the right choice," she thought, "I am only twenty-one years old and I am energetic. The future in front of me must be colourful and prosperous as long as I strive to win!"

The feather-like snowflakes became thicker. They fell and disappeared into the dark green water beneath the bridge and piled up on top of the hat and shoulders of her new cotton-padded army uniform. The magnificent buildings beside the Square, far or near, were blurring. The city woven with beautifully shaped snowflakes seemed more mysterious and enchanting than a moment ago. She reached out her palms to get some dancing flakes. They melted in her warm hands quickly. She did not feel cold at all. She was caught up in her imaginings and a sweet smile appeared on her face.

Qin was chosen to be trained as one of the first female pilots in China, as she was taller than most other female soldiers. She stayed in the preliminary training class for a few weeks and underwent many tests. In the end she failed, however, as her arms turned out not to be strong enough to control a bumper bar or some such thing on the plane. She could hardly contain her jealousy of the two girls in the same dormitory with her who passed successfully.

"This is nothing," she tried to comfort herself. "There are plenty of chances to prove my ability."

When she returned to headquarters, she was assigned to the air force's newspaper as a sub-editor. Her salary as a warrant officer was one people's dollar per month. This meagre pay was good for almost nothing.

One Sunday after Qin got her first monthly salary, she went out with her best friend, a girl from the same university. They came to a shopping centre in one of Beijing's busiest streets. At a department store, Qin bought a pack of sanitary napkins, a piece of soap and a tube of toothpaste. These cost fifty-five cents.

As they passed a sweet store, Qin's eyes were attracted by a young boy walking out of the door. He was sucking at a dark-brown-coloured, three-inch-long, one-inch-wide 'ice cake' in his hand. Qin had seen ice cakes while in Xi An, but not of this colour. Somehow, she felt this brown ice cake must taste good.

"Let's go inside!" Qin invited her friend. "I'll buy that for us two!" She was sure the forty-five cents left in her pocket was enough to satisfy her thirst for the novelty. Qin had developed a craving for good food in the past few months. Everyday the air force canteen served the same food — hard boiled millet and roughly stewed cabbages and turnips. Qin found it difficult to force this sort of coarse fare down her throat and she always missed the sweet, soft white rice in Han Zhong.

Inside the store, Qin and her friend seated themselves in front of the counter. She then ordered two of the brown ice cakes. "It is delicious!" they both exclaimed after taking a bite. Qin ordered two more and they soon finished these as well.

She was shocked, however, as the store clerk asked her to pay sixty cents for the four ice cakes. "Ice cakes in Xi An are sold for five cents each. Why are they fifteen cents each in this store?" Qin questioned the clerk.

"The ice cake you had in Xi An may simply be made of white sugar, but the ones you just had are chocolate ice cakes," the clerk replied, smiling nicely at the two young women in air force uniform.

Qin's face blushed. It was the first time she had ever tasted a chocolate product. She hadn't expected that it would be so expensive. Utterly embarrassed, she took out all the money in her pocket and put it on the counter. "I am a bad host," she said to her friend. "You have to make up for the rest."

Eventually, Qin found a place where her sweet tooth was greatly satisfied, at no cost. The air force headquarters gave a ball every Saturday evening to entertain the Russian air force officers working in China. Besides the few dozen Russians, Chinese officers were also invited to the ball. But there was a difference between the sexes. Where the men were concerned, invitations were only given to officers holding the rank of lieutenant colonel and above. Where the women were concerned, however, invitations were given to the young and pretty ones, regardless of their rank. Needless to say, Qin was always invited.

In the big hall under the dim lights, musicians played waltzes while the Russian and Chinese officers swivelled their women soldier partners on the waxed floor. As the males greatly outnumbered the females, Qin felt it was hard to get rid of the men who came to her one after the other. She was not at all interested in dancing with these men. Carelessly or deliberately she stepped on their feet all the time. Her attention was focused on the large tables at the four corners of the hall. On them were glass dishes full of chocolate candies, small cups of various ice creams, bottles of soda, and packages of expensive cigarettes.

Qin often sneaked out of the ball when it was halfway through. As soon as she walked into her office, she would quickly dump the contents of the two large pockets of her uniform onto the desk. The young officers not invited to the ball, both male and female, would rush over joyfully to grab the candies and cigarettes on the desk.

"While the soldiers are fighting and being killed by the Americans on the front, these high-ranking officers are giving balls in the rear!" a young man lit up a cigarette and commented.

"If they invite only lieutenant colonels to the ball, why don't they invite those female veterans with small bound-up feet as well?" another young man said sarcastically.

"Of course it is for their selfish purposes that they only select young and pretty girls to invite to the ball. This is totally contradictory to communist ideology!"

Qin understood that those young officers were angry at not being invited to the ball and she wanted to comfort them: "I don't care what they do, I just go there to get the candies for all of us!"

One day, as Qin was filling out a form collecting personal data, she came upon the item, "Name and address of your lover." She was confused by the word 'lover' and consulted her best friend.

The girl told Qin that 'lover' was the word the communists used for 'spouse'. Qin felt the communist expression odd, while her friend warned her: "Since you don't have a lover, you'd better make up a name, or the Communist Party may assign a senior revolutionary officer to you!"

"How dare they? I'll drive them away!" Qin waved her fist jokingly. It was common in those days for most of the newly recruited female soldiers to marry the senior officers promptly, as there was a rule during that time that marriage was permitted only to male officers who had served fifteen years or more in the army. There were also cases of assigned marriages for the veterans.

"I didn't come here to become somebody's wife!" Qin told her friend confidently. "I believe in my own ability. I will become a captain within five years!"

Her friend twitched her mouth: "You are too naive! Who is going to promote you? You are not a Communist Party member, not even a Youth League member! Instead you are from a landlord's family and, you are a female!"

Qin shook her head proudly and said: "What's wrong with being a female? I'll show everyone. Just wait and see!"

Somehow, their conversation was overheard and reported to their supervisor, who gathered the new soldiers the next day.

"Many of you have joined the revolutionary force with your bourgeois ideas. Our task is to wash them out of your minds!" His face looked stern as he spoke. "These senior officers have sacrificed their youth for the people and the new China. You should be sympathetic to them and respect them, not laugh at them!" His sharp eyes rested on Qin's face for a few seconds. "I remind you all, it's a great honour to marry them!"

Qin's friend secretly made faces at her. But Qin was not looking at anyone. Her eyes stayed fixed on the portrait of Chairman Mao hanging on the wall behind their supervisor. "I won't love or marry anyone," Qin said to herself silently. The pair of lamb-like gentle eyes appeared in her mind once again. Although the young teacher had been gone for several years, she had always cherished the hope that he would emerge in front of her unexpectedly one day. Because of this hope, she had refused proposals from all sorts of men in high school and at university. It was on the evening when she bade farewell to her student life and became a soldier that she had finally decided to bid farewell to the young teacher in her heart and to forget the lamb-like gentle eyes forever!

"I won't expect any man to change my life any more. My future is going to be woven with my own hands!" she thought, her face solemn.

Shortly afterwards, a campaign for culture and education was started in the Chinese Liberation Army. Qin volunteered to go to different companies under the air force headquarters as a cultural teacher. She settled down with the soldiers and worked hard teaching them how to read and write.

There was no doubt about Qin's hard effort, her genius and her contributions in the air force. In the fall of the next year, the local government in Han Zhong was informed of her achievements. A team of government men soon sent a bulletin in crimson paper, announcing Qin's meritorious service, to Laolao's residence in town. At that time, every household of a soldier would receive a red-painted board inscribed with golden characters saying "The Honoured Family of A Soldier." As Laolao's class status was 'landlord', no such board was delivered to her home. Now that Qin was awarded a certificate for her achievement in the air force, the city government in Han Zhong decided to send the board, together with the bulletin, to Laolao.

Laolao was surprised when she saw the team arriving with deafening drums and gongs, attracting attention in the streets. The family had been ignored for quite a long time — ever since the Land-Reform Movement had ended. Laolao's hands trembled as she received the distinguished board and bulletin in front of so many people. She walked around with uncontrollable happiness, offering cigarettes and hot green tea to the government men. Everyone present praised Qin as an honour to the city as well as to the family, as she was the first woman from the city to become an award winner since the beginning of the Korean War.

Ever since that exciting moment, each fall when flocks of honking wild geese passed over the cloudless blue sky in the small ancient city, and dense leaves of the old honey locust tree over the roof turned golden-yellow, Laolao would comb her grey hair carefully and listen attentively for any noisy steps passing through the courtyard gate facing the street.

Year after year, the walls in Laolao's room were decorated with various prize posters, award winning notices and photos of Qin in army uniform standing in front of various splendid architectural structures in Beijing. The old woman's lonely heart would thrill with pride whenever her eyes fell on them.

Qin was the only source of honour and protection for the family. The Land-Reform Movement had deprived the family of all its past glory and it would actually have been discriminated against, had it not been for Qin.

Laolao's only son, Honesty, was called back to Han Zhong from his university by the local government when the Land-Reform Movement was over. He was assigned the class status of 'landlord' and was not allowed to go back to his university in the South. Reluctantly he accepted the government's arrangement to labour in the farm fields with peasants every day. His lover, the attractive high school graduate, now left him and married a high ranking communist official. It was Qin's contribution in the air force that rescued Honesty from his sorry fate. He was reassigned as a primary school teacher in a mountain area. Though the school was fifty miles away from Han Zhong and there was no transportation available besides one's feet, Honesty felt relieved that he no longer had to toil in the fields.

Five years after Qin entered the air force, on a cold early winter morning, Laolao's sharp ears discovered some familiar sounds at the entrance of the courtyard. Her heart suddenly started beating fast in her chest as she stood up. Through the withered branches of the oleander tree in front of the window, she saw a familiar figure standing in the shadow of the deep doorway.

It was Qin. The light grey plaid coat and white gauze kerchief around her neck had replaced the militant bearing of the army uniform in her photos. Closely held in her arms was a small baby with an apple-like face.

At dawn three days later, when pieces of pink clouds had just broken the dark grey eastern sky, Qin silently bade farewell to the old house. As her sight fell on the month-old baby, sleeping quietly beside Laolao's pillow, tears blurred her view. She remembered her discussion with Laolao the night before, about the girl's name.

"You'd better give her a name before you leave," Laolao suggested in a soft voice.

"...I have thought about one." Qin was lost in some memories. "It is 'Cease'. Let all disasters and bad fortune cease at once!"

"Well, 'Cease' doesn't sound auspicious." Laolao disagreed. "Why not 'Peace'? Yes, let's call her 'Peace'!"

Across the high wall around the old house, the drawling cries of early pedlars, with their vegetable and tofu carts running on the stone-laid streets, created the first noises of the day. A crow resting on the honey locust tree in the backyard was wakened and started to fly and caw around the roof of the old house.

Qin swallowed a sigh and wiped her eyes quickly. A moment later her figure disappeared from the courtyard gate.

✻   ✻   ✻

"LILAC! LILAC!" MRS. THOMPSON'S VOICE CAME FROM THE staircase.

I turned off the running water and hurried to the staircase. "Yes?" I looked up.

"Could you bring me some coffee?" She was looking down over the railings.

"OK!" I went back to the kitchen and prepared the coffee for her.

"So, she has finished the week-long cycle today and is going to be sober for two weeks," I said to myself.

When I brought the coffee into her bedroom, she was seated comfortably on a sofa watching the TV; the huge satellite dish in the tulip fields allowed her hundreds of channels. She was in her pink flowered pajama coat, the fingers on her right hand were holding a lighted cigarette, and her left hand was gently patting Max's shining back.

"Thank you," she smiled at me. The bright red lipstick looked loud on her pale face. It reminded me of the Joker played by Jack Nicholson in *Batman*.

I sat on the soft top of a piece of fancy furniture. I had never seen that sort of strangely shaped sofa and I wasn't aware of its name. There were a couple of books on it. I glanced at them. The cover photos told me they were biographies of Jacqueline Kennedy and Elizabeth Taylor.

"Mrs. Thompson, " I told her, "the writers are coming this afternoon."

"What writers?" She was surprised, clearly having forgotten the event.

"Do you remember that I told you there is an editing group for local authors? They meet once a month in a member's home. This afternoon it is my turn to be the host."

"Oh, yes, of course I remember it," she nodded.

"Would you like to meet them when they are here? Some of them are famous writers!" I said half-jokingly.

"Famous? Who are they? Is Peter Newman coming? I'll come downstairs if he comes," she said. We both laughed.

I looked at my watch. There were fifteen minutes left. I took a bowl of Red Delicious apples and some mugs into the library and put them on the coffee table. I looked around, making sure everything was in order.

My eyes fell upon the old album on the lower level of a side table. Well, that was something that must be hidden. I put it inside a cabinet.

I first saw it while I was dusting the library. I opened it and found it was a wedding album. The faded photos still kept the brilliance of a blond bride. She smiles joyfully at all the guests coming into a luxurious hotel in Manhattan, while the aged stout groom looks up proudly at his young wife, half-a-foot taller than he. She is in her early twenties then, a slim, fresh, juicy peach. Though the bride is completely different from the white-haired full figure now lying upstairs, the similar smiles could be traced without difficulty to one owner. She looks cute, with a beret on her neatly combed hair, like a movie star in the nineteen forties. But there is a hint of nervousness on her lips as she smiles.

She is the bride, the focus of the wedding, but the camera exposes her as someone from a different social circle. The protruding knuckles on her hands do not fit with the graceful dress and the elegant decorations in the room, suggesting a background full of mystery.

The groom, on the other hand, displays confidence and relaxation, as easy as a fish in familiar water.

I closed the album. A thought lingered in my mind: what brought this seemingly incompatible couple together? How did they ever get to know each other?

✳   ✳   ✳

FOR THE REST OF HER LIFE, QIN ALWAYS GRUMBLED ABOUT her unfortunate fate. The hell started with that damned short marriage which left her nothing but a plain-looking, eccentric daughter and a road full of misfortune in front of her. It seemed just like a nightmare whenever her thoughts fell upon it.

...How could a talented writer and poet who was sure to have boundless prospects suddenly become a prisoner? ...A counter-revolutionary? A spy? ...What terrible words! And how could all this happen? She had never doubted that her otherwise bright future was totally destroyed because of this man. She was never successful in pushing the memory out of her mind, though it was extremely painful to touch upon it.

The last time she saw Evergreen, she had been seven months pregnant. In the dark jail where there was only a one-foot-square window letting light in, she noticed there had been big changes in him over a short period.

They first met at a conference sponsored by the army for award winners. He was then a very promising young officer in the army, teaching officers how to read and write. He had published a few books about teaching methods and one on writing skills, which was particularly applauded. After the war was over, many revolutionary veterans put down their rifles and grasped pens in their rough hands, perhaps for the first time in their lives. They wanted to write their memoirs but writing seemed to be much more difficult than fighting.

Evergreen's books appeared at the right moment. His teaching methods were introduced widely in the army. He was promoted several ranks in a year and given a special grade prize, which was a great honour, as it was the sole prize for the whole Chinese People's Liberation Army. The method he had created for the quick mastery of writing skills was named after him. In the early 1950s, his name and photo appeared frequently in newspapers and magazines, and his fame grew quickly.

Evergreen was invited to give lectures to all cultural workers in the army. Qin attended his training course for a period of four weeks. He was by no means a prince charming in her eyes, merely a warm-hearted, energetic young man with a plain-looking dark face and a stout figure. As a matter of fact, Qin was impressed by him only once. It was at a party held on a Saturday evening. Evergreen was pushed by his comrades to sing a couple of popular revolutionary songs. Qin was surprised that his voice was much more beautiful than his appearance. She was even more surprised as she saw him performing a solo dance. His energetic jumps and flexible movements on the hardwood floor, to the accompaniment of an accordion, reminded her of a Ukrainian dancer she saw in a Russian movie.

But Qin noticed that several young girls regarded Evergreen as an ideal choice for a husband — passionate, diligent and talented, besides being a distinguished special grade prizewinner. They all believed he was assured of a bright future.

When the course was over and everybody was about to leave, one of the girls, Qin's roommate, asked Qin to pass on a message of admiration to Evergreen. This was a common practice at that time, since an individual would feel embarrassed to express his or her love directly to the beloved, and instead would ask someone else to pass on the information. Qin was eager to help her and told Evergreen about the girl's admiration for him. Quite unexpectedly, the young man looked straight at her face, bright with youth, and replied: "It is you whom I really like very much, not her."

Qin drew her mind back to reality. Her numb eyes fixed on the miserable man sitting in the dark corner of the jail. "Oh, what a difference!" she thought painfully. "Every happy incident seems to have taken place just yesterday..."

When Evergreen was applauded at a big conference where his smiling face received admiration from thousands of people...

When Qin waited happily at the corner of the Tian-an-Men Square for Evergreen who was attending a state banquet held for outstanding heroes...

When they attended poem-reciting parties and danced to the encouragement of the loud music of "Youth Waltz" in the Imperial Palace on Sundays...

When they walked along the main street, discussing their new publications and future plans excitedly, the lotus-shaped street lamps shining extremely bright and soft, as if just for their benefit...

When they watched firecrackers dyeing the sky colourful on the night of the National Day, their youthful laughter drenched with good wishes for the newly-built country...

And now, how could it be that everything was turned upside down without warning? In this small dark room where the light was dim, Qin shivered with the cold, though it was summer time and she could hear the tedious chirping of cicadas from the dense leaves of the poplar trees outside the window.

Her thoughts went back to the abrupt search of their small apartment home, a few months after they had married. As Evergreen was taken away from the messy home by the agents from the Party's organizations in the army, his lips trembled with anger and he protested in a loud voice. With a troubled heart, Qin slowly picked up the books and manuscripts rudely thrown on the floor. She repeatedly told herself to stay calm, in the hope that he would be released soon after investigations were done.

It was at the time of the nationwide campaign to "uproot hidden counter-revolutionaries," and tens of thousands of people had already been arrested and shot dead. But they must have made a mistake in arresting Evergreen, she believed, for he was not only a promising young officer in the Communist Army, but also a special prizewinner, an honour granted to him by the Party!

A few months seemed ages long, amid her anxious waiting. The announcement from the army's Party organizations, however, finally smashed her last hope. The following charge was brought against Evergreen: he was suspected of being a member of an association of writers opposing the Communist Party's ideology, namely, Party Chairman Mao Ze-dong's ideology. He was also suspected of being a spy for the Nationalists in Tai Wan. His task, they believed, was to attack the Communist Government from the cover of his post in the army.

During that movement, most people convicted of such a crime would be seriously punished, to the extent of either life imprisonment or the death penalty. Considering Evergreen's outstanding service to the army, and his status as a special grade prizewinner, the authorities had decided to reduce his punishment, so they sent him to a labour camp in a swampy area near the border of Soviet Siberia.

And now it had come to the last encounter between the couple. Evergreen could see what was in her mind from her calm attitude. There were no more sweet smiles on her pale face. Her usual twinkling black eyes had gone dull. He was afraid to listen to what she was going to say, though he had anticipated the inevitable moment ever since he had been notified of his punishment. His self-esteem forbad him to show any weakness. Still, he collected his remaining strength and pleaded in a hoarse weak voice: "Qin, please trust me. I am indeed innocent... They have wronged me... Please... believe me..."

Her heart shrank. She felt it cruel to leave him now. In the few years since they had met and finally married, his success and fame had brought so much honour and hope to her life. They had cooperated well in their careers and made new achievements together. Besides, she had enjoyed all the small advantages of being taken care of by a loving husband. Though she had always suspected that she had never loved him but married him only for his fame, she could not forget the time when she was pregnant and found it hard to fall asleep in hot weather. Every night Evergreen sat beside her bed waving a fan until she was sound asleep. She also remembered him, sweating all over, riding a bicycle to look for ice all up and down the city, under the burning summer sun, simply because she wanted to eat iced watermelon. He was undoubtedly a caring husband and it would be too cruel for him if...

Then, should she yield to fate and remain his wife? The man in front of her looked so weak and hopeless... Where had all his brilliance gone? Once the shining circles around him had faded, he looked incredibly common and plain! She was surprised to find this.

At this moment she clearly realized that it was not the man, but his past fame that she had loved. "Hero plus beauty, a perfect combination!" She remembered the compliment of a guest at their wedding. She was uneasy at the moment when she heard it, but hadn't given it a second thought. Why? She examined herself now.

Before she agreed to marry Evergreen, she had been in the air force for four years. Though praised constantly for her hard work, she didn't get promoted. When she noticed that all the other female soldiers, except herself, had married and left the air force headquarters, she was puzzled. Perhaps it was impossible for a woman to achieve a higher position in the air force which was fundamentally a man's world. As a twenty-five-year-old single woman, she was already regarded as an old maid, since the traditional marriage-age for a woman was before she became twenty.

The day came when she was also told to leave the air force. She was totally disillusioned. It was at that moment that she decided to get married, a temporary acquiescence to fate. Yes, she realized now, that was why she had felt uneasy at being regarded as a beauty only, not a hero!

"And now, what kind of future can I expect from a man who has been pronounced guilty politically? All the honour and glories have gone! And the future? Awful even to think about it! As wife of a spy and counter-revolutionary, I would lose almost all my rights as a citizen, let alone my long cherished splendid dreams! That has been the reality in China ever since the Liberation, everyone knows that..." she thought painfully. "Is this the punishment brought by fate for my indiscretion?" Overwhelmed by a deep regret, she focused her resentment on the man sitting there.

"You have destroyed not only yourself, but others as well. You want me to believe your innocence, but the Party's men told me you have pleaded guilty!" Qin said to him, trying to hold back her anger.

"No! That's not true!" Evergreen raised his voice quickly. "They told me I would be allowed to go home once I acknowledged all the charges. I was worrying every day that your delivery date was close at hand and you would need me to stay beside you. In desperation, I resolved to acknowledge their charges. But, Qin, believe me, I am innocent indeed..."

She closed her cold fingers tightly in her palms. Her lips trembled and finally released the decision she had thought over numerous times. "But how can I suspect the Party? I can only trust the judgement made by the Party..."

Looking at her pale face and mounting abdomen, Evergreen realized sadly that he could no longer handle the fate of his wife and the unborn child, who would need a peaceful and comfortable life which was now beyond his ability to provide. In this nightmare where there was no justice for right or wrong, he had lost all power to defend his innocence, and was not even trusted by his wife! He felt totally exhausted. Well, when a man could not maintain his own dignity and basic rights as a human being, how could he expect his wife, especially a proud young woman like Qin, to undertake the inhuman treatment that could very well be ahead of her? It was selfish to try to keep her now. The relationship between a wife and a husband was just like that of birds in the woods. As disasters befell, the birds would fly in separate directions. That was fate... He lowered his head and nodded weakly.

When she stood up and turned slowly towards the door, he felt his heart crumpled by a hand. Subconsciously, his arms reached out as if he wanted to keep her figure from moving away, while his throat was choked and could not utter any sound... The door closed silently. The room became darker. His hands fell, limp. Despairing tears rapidly filled up his eyes. He suddenly felt so lonely in a large but empty world. He knew too well that he would never be able to see Qin nor the unborn child again...

*   *   *

THAT FALL, THE BABY CAME TO THE WORLD DURING A rainstorm. Qin had a difficult labour which lasted thirty-six hours. But she did not cry out even at the most painful moment, fully aware that crying wouldn't help, and no one would care. The obstetrician and nurses were considerate and kind to her though, thinking she was different from the pampered young women who cried out loud in the arms of their husbands as soon as they entered the hospital.

Qin had been planning to send the baby, once born, to someone else, perhaps a childless couple. Life as a single mother would be unpredictably tough, she realized.

But the moment she saw the little thing crying, tears filled up Qin's eyes and she forgot totally about her plan. She held the small girl carefully in her arms and looked anxiously for any resemblance between herself and the baby. The healthy girl looked attractive with thick black hair, double-fold eyelids, a round pink face and a lovely large dimple on her left cheek. "What a good looking baby!" Qin smiled joyfully. But her happiness lasted only a few seconds. Her heart sank once again, as the baby started to cry and Qin clearly noticed the traces of Evergreen on the baby's face.

She moved her eyes away from the baby and gazed at the garden through the window. Yellow leaves were falling from lines of poplar trees onto the neatly trimmed lawn. It was deep in the fall. The man had been expecting to see his baby for a long time and, together, they had chosen numerous beautiful names before she was born. But he would be opening up wild lands in the snow-covered frozen north now, and, Qin suspected, would never be able to see his daughter in his life.

Qin was then working at an educational institute. She brought the baby back with her to the institute's dormitory three days later. The first month of life with a newborn passed clumsily and left Qin unbearably exhausted. The month seemed as long as a year. She had reached the point where she could no longer endure the pressure and inconvenience of being a single mother.

One Saturday evening Qin left the baby with a sitter and went out to relax. As she was eating alone in a small restaurant near her institute, she bumped into a man who shouted out excitedly as he saw her. The handsome young man used to be her university classmate and had been one of her many suitors then. They had a cordial chat and he was as enthusiastic as before, until he learned that she was already a mother. The temperature fell quickly and the man hurried through his meal and left politely. Qin gazed numbly at the empty beer glass, ablaze with lights, and, unaware, bit her lower lip. Her self-esteem was deeply hurt. As she left the restaurant an hour later, she finally made up her mind to let Laolao take care of the baby.

Being winter, it was cold on the train and bus, and Qin wrapped the baby in a thick cotton quilt. She was silent all the way through the three day trip. The baby was silent, too, until a passenger mistook her for a bundle of luggage and sat on her.

The baby's sharp crying made Qin's heart quail and she lost her self-control. She had a serious quarrel with the man, who in turn blamed her for wrapping her baby up like a piece of luggage. She wept for a fairly long time, although the man had already stopped rebuking her. Perhaps the quarrel served as a good excuse for her to release her long pent-up grief and indignation. Anyway, nobody on the trip knew her and she did not have to worry about being recognized. When Han Zhong came in sight, she finally stopped her weeping.

"Mother is getting old, and I should not add any more sorrow to her life," she thought, as her moist eyes watched the familiar scene passing outside of the bus window. "Anyway, I have removed myself from disaster and I am still young. I can work harder and demonstrate to the Party that I am really an excellent worker and pro-communist youth! And I will!"

The Making of a Rightist: the Anti-Rightist Campaign in Nineteen Fifty-Seven

ON A SUNNY SUNDAY MORNING, QIN CAME TO THE NORTH Sea Park in central Beijing. It was previously the emperor's private garden. In the summer time, the park was famous for the large pink lotus flowers on the lake, its surface reflecting colourful palaces and a huge white marble pagoda built atop a hill on a small island.

Qin walked into the big-roofed, crimson-painted Five Dragon Pavilions on the lake, which were connected by zigzag bridges. She had acquired a new zest for life after leaving the air force. She wore a white seersucker shirt tucked into a silver grey skirt. Her black leather shoes were the popular flat-heeled laced style and her recently permed short hair curled up beside her ears.

She stopped at the last pavilion, leaned over the carved wooden railings and looked down into the water beneath her feet to appreciate her new image. She was familiar with this place. A few years before, she and Evergreen had waited for each other many times here to go boating on the lake...

Her image in the water blurred. It had also been on a summer day when the lotus flowers were blooming on top of the large round green leaves covering the lake... Qin remembered a girl dressed in the greenish air force uniform, her two pigtails stretching out from under her brimmed cap. She was rather slim, in fact a little bit too skinny. But her eyes looked bright in her smiling rosy cheeks and her laughter was confident as the small boat glided onto the flowered water...

Qin stared at the water and her mood changed. Yes, she was too familiar with the place beneath her feet. That might be why the words "Five Dragon Pavilions" slipped without hesitation from her tongue when Tian-zhi asked her where she would like to go for their first date.

"I am not a girl any more, but a woman." Qin said silently to the figure in the greenish water. The skinny girl had grown fuller, more womanly, after giving birth to a daughter. "Daughter... If Tian-zhi knew I had a daughter, would he still want to see me?"

To a traditional Chinese man, a woman who had been married before had much less worth. Tian-zhi's situation could allow him to choose a perfect girl as his wife. Therefore, Qin was overjoyed when Tian-zhi asked to see her again after they were introduced by a mutual friend. But she had held back the truth about her daughter, fearing his enthusiasm might be dampened. "When should I let him know, then?" Qin pondered seriously. "Perhaps I'll have to wait till our relationship is on a firmer footing."

When she raised up her head, she found Tian-zhi coming towards her. The first thing she noticed, however, was not what he was wearing on that day, but a round bamboo basket which he had in his hand!

"Sorry, I am late." Tian-zhi said smiling in apology. He had a pair of honest eyes that gave Qin a very good impression when they first met. "I stopped on the way to buy this." He showed the round basket to Qin.

"What is this for?" Qin smiled at him. She knew very well that this sort of basket was often used as a container for waste paper in the washroom. But she asked him deliberately, for she was a little bit unhappy to see Tian-zhi bringing this thing on their first date.

"This is for the washroom at home." Tian-zhi didn't know what was in Qin's mind and answered honestly. "My mother has asked me many times to buy one but I never had the time. As I passed the household supplies store outside of the park today, I remembered her words and dropped in."

Qin said nothing. She felt it must look funny that they walked around the Park with that ugly basket in his hand. As it was Sunday, the only holiday in the week, the park was full of people boating on the lake and walking around palaces decorated with glazed tiles and crimson paintings.

When they walked to the huge 'Nine Dragon Wall', a green-and-yellow-coloured relief sculpture shaded by dense-leaved trees, Qin slowed her steps and squinted at Tian-zhi walking beside her. He was about four inches taller than she. He had a rectangular-shaped face with a high forehead, clear-cut nose and lips, and a pair of large, honest-looking eyes. His white shirt was tucked inside his light grey long pants. "He is a nice-looking man," Qin said to herself, "but the basket in his hand is extremely ugly and out of harmony with the beautiful and romantic scenery!" She wondered if people passing by were laughing at them secretly and thought Tian-zhi was too casual. She deliberately kept a few steps behind him. But Tian-zhi seemed totally ignorant of what was in her mind.

"...Maybe I should regard this as a good point," Qin comforted herself this way. "A man focussing on his career pays little attention to trivialities in daily life."

*   *   *

TIAN-ZHI WAS A MAN WORTHY OF RESPECT IN QIN'S EYES. Not only honest, gentle, kind and well educated, he was also an absolutely faithful communist. After the nightmare of her first marriage, Qin felt it was important to have a husband with a politically sound background.

Tian-zhi's childhood resembled nothing of Qin's. As a Chinese saying goes, they were like melons growing on two different vines.

Tian-zhi was born into a poor farmer's family. Before he was born, his mother had already given birth to three daughters who all died as infants. A woman who had no sons would be regarded by her husband as a worthless woman, and scorned by all relatives. The poor woman had been abused for years by her husband for not being able to produce a son. The bad-tempered man was also a constant loser at the villagers' gambling tables. Each time he lost, he would vent his anger on his wife. Piece by piece, he had lost all the land the family owned. When he no longer had anything to bring to the gambling table, he beat up his wife more fiercely and frequently.

The poor woman saw no hope in her life unless she could have a child, a male child. She decided to use the method practised for generations in that area. She would pray in the Guan Yin (Avalokitesvara, a Bodigisattva) Temple on the bank of the Yellow River and then jump off from an earth cliff tens of meters high named 'Life Sacrificing Cliff', a few steps behind the temple. If you died, that was your fate; if you survived, your prayer, whatever it was, would come true. There had been women who tried this method wishing to have a son. There were also women who did this hoping illness would leave their sick relatives. Most of them died or were seriously injured and became paralyzed. In fact, people hardly remembered any woman surviving unhurt.

Early one morning before dawn, the woman came to the temple. After kneeling and praying in front of the Statue of Guan Yin for a long time, she stood up and slowly walked out of the temple. Though her legs were shaking from having knelt so long, the dim light of the burning incense and the smiling statue behind her back gave her silent encouragement. She came to the edge of the cliff at the back of the temple. Looking down at the darkness beneath her feet, she stopped. Many women had died down there... She turned around... "No, I cannot go back. Death may not be more terrifying than my present life!" She closed her eyes and threw herself off the cliff without further hesitation.

It was a miracle. She did not die. Was not even injured. She stood up and looked at the sky full of bright stars over her head and realized she was not in a dream. Her mind was cool and clear. She started to search for a way out of the gully. When she walked close to her home-village an hour later, the day was just breaking. She met a man, the tofu maker in the village, carrying two cases of tofu on a shoulder pole.

"Hi! Why are you getting up so early? Where have you been?" The man greeted her curiously. He went out early every morning to sell tofu but had never seen any woman coming back home at dawn.

The woman simply smiled at him.

A year after her sacrificial jump, a boy was born. The birth of the baby son lit up the mud walls of the home. He was given the name Tian-zhi, meaning 'heaven-gifted', for the adults believed he was bequeathed by Heaven. Female relatives came with eggs dyed red, and golden-coloured millet, to celebrate the event. The mother held her precious son in her arms with great care, fearing that Heaven might take away her hard-won baby. The older women in the village told her that biting off the infant's toe would prevent him from being taken away. She did as they said. The infant grew up, as did her next two babies.

When the children were still small, her husband died. She didn't cry, for the memory of his inhuman abuse was still fresh. Life was extremely hard for her for she had to bring up three kids on her own. Still, she believed Tian-zhi was sent to her by Heaven and had the talent to become somebody, so she strived to send him to school despite the extreme financial difficulties at home.

In the day, she went to the rented corn fields by the river bank and laboured till her back was about to break. At night, she spun cotton into yarn with an old hand spinning wheel by the dim light of an oil lamp. Every night, her kids fell asleep to the dull buzz of the wheel.

When there was a country fair, she took the yarn there and bartered it for salt and lamp oil, and the cheapest paper and black ink for Tian-zhi. She made all the clothes and shoes for the family using coarse cloth woven on a heavy, old hand loom, and dyed into black or blue, then tailored and sewn by her two hands.

As a boy, Tian-zhi seemed no different from any other village kids. Once, lured by some adults, he took his mother's hard-earned coins which she kept in a pottery jar and joined the villagers' gambling. When he returned home after dark with all his coins lost, he was shocked to see his mother sitting in the doorway weeping sadly and murmuring to herself: "...What shall I do? What's the meaning of life? Oh, Heaven! Do you know what my child has done..."

Tian-zhi was deeply touched. He rushed over to hold his mother up. "Mom, don't cry any more! I won't do it again!" he pleaded.

"Oh, Tian-zhi, my son!" the mother said, still sobbing. "Your father indulged in gambling and he made my life miserable... Now you have started to do the same thing, I see no hope in my life any more..."

Tian-zhi became mature overnight. From that moment on, he made up his mind to abstain all his life from gambling, alcohol, smoking and prostitutes — all things taken for granted as men's privileges.

He left home when he turned thirteen and started to herd sheep for a rich family. While the sheep were nibbling green grass along river banks and on small hills, he would study high school textbooks on his own. One day, he was so engrossed in his reading that one of the sheep was lost. The rich man's wife beat him, tore up his books, and let him go hungry for a whole day as punishment.

Tian-zhi swallowed everything and studied even harder. Three years later, he finished all the high school textbooks by self-study and successfully passed the university entrance exams. He became a university student at the age of sixteen! He chose to study physics, hoping to become a scientist and to be able to provide a better life for his poor mother. As he had to borrow to pay for his education, he was careful with his money, ate the cheapest foods and wore only clothes and shoes made by his mother during his school years.

In his last year at the university, he learned about Karl Marx. A book, *Das Kapital,* was secretly passed around among the students, as the Nationalist Government forbade its circulation. After reading it, Tian-zhi suddenly understood why there was so much inequality, injustice and poverty and why it was necessary to change this ugly world. He realized, too, that his own fate would never change unless the life of all mankind were changed.

He joined the Communist Party's underground activities, studying forbidden political publications, distributing pro-communist pamphlets and giving anti-government speeches. These activities aroused the attention of the Nationalist Government and soon these activist students were on the black list. Their secret meetings were often broken up by government agents and many of them were arrested. Some of Tian-zhi's friends disappeared mysteriously one evening. A few days later, their dead bodies were found, having been buried alive in an abandoned field. To avoid 'the Terror', Tian-zhi and a group of pro-communist students secretly left the school for Yan An, at that time the communist base in Mao's charge in North China. They joined the communist forces and fought against the army of the Nationalist Government until it was driven to Tai Wan in nineteen forty-nine.

After the founding of Communist China, Tian-zhi was assigned to work in Beijing. Soon after, he was selected to study in the Soviet Union for two years. It was an honour dreamt of by many young people, as in the early 1950s the Soviet Union was regarded as the headquarters of the communist world, and the Russians, China's best friends, and big brothers.

Before he went to Moscow, Tian-zhi confessed to the Party leaders that he had a girlfriend, Rose, and asked if he was allowed to contact her while in Russia. This might sound ridiculous now, but at the time it was common practice among Communist Party members to get approval from the Party's organizations for the selection of a spouse. Tian-zhi was confident that Rose would get the Party's approval since she was a nice, kind-hearted girl working in the same institute with him.

To his great disappointment, however, the answer was "No". The reason was simple. Rose's widowed mother had been a Communist Party member in the 1920s, but she retreated from the Party at the crucial time, when the Nationalist Government had just started to kill communists. Her cowardly behaviour had been recorded as 'traitorous' in her file ever since. As the daughter of such a person, Rose was regarded as an improper choice for Tian-zhi, a pure and promising young communist. Tian-zhi was advised to discontinue his relationship with a girl from a traitor's family, or his trip to Russia would be cancelled.

The young man felt heavy-hearted. On the one hand, he loved Rose very much. On the other hand, a Communist Party member must be obedient to the Party's instructions. To him, the Party had developed into a patron, always correct and trustworthy, since its noble cause was to help and save all mankind.

Anyway, he restrained his emotions during his stay in Russia, while trying hard to ignore letters from Rose piling up on his desk day by day. He was not permitted to give his address to her, but the persevering girl traced his whereabouts with the help of the Russian Government. It was painstaking to kill the innocent love in his heart by his own hand; at the same time, he felt a tragic pride as his loyalty to the Party was attested to through his self-sacrifice.

When he returned to China two years later, he was assigned to head a department in a large research institute. He was dismayed when he learned that Rose had already gone to work in Tibet, thousands of miles away from Beijing. She left no word, perhaps out of disappointment, or perhaps, from a deeper love, she didn't want to bother Tian-zhi any more.

It was at this time that a friend mentioned Qin to him. Tian-zhi's curiosity was aroused by the friend's description.

"She is a woman you must see, or you will be sorry!" exclaimed the friend. "In one sentence, she is just excellent! But," the friend paused briefly before he went on. "it all depends on how broad-minded you are… She has married once…"

It might be that Tian-zhi's lonely heart needed warming up, or that Qin was indeed a unique woman. Anyway, Tian-zhi was at once attracted by her beauty, her intelligence, and her joyful character. "She is like a blooming rose!" He praised her silently, after they were introduced to each other in the friend's home, and they started dating.

He was even happier as she told him later that she would soon be admitted as a Party member. To most Chinese men, her first marriage lowered her value since virginity was the most important virtue when a man chose a wife. But Tian-zhi thought otherwise. He regarded her divorce from Evergreen as proving her loyalty to the Party. That was the paramount virtue.

He didn't mind about the existence of Qin's daughter, either. Qin was relived when Tian-zhi said: "I don't mind that you have a daughter..." He hesitated for a few seconds and went on, "But, to be frank, I would feel embarrassed to be called 'father' as soon as we get married. I hope we can bring your daughter to our home after our first child is born."

Qin nodded gratefully. She felt his sincerity as a responsible man and thus foresaw a secure life. They married a few months later.

✻   ✻   ✻

QIN WAS NOT BORN AT THE RIGHT TIME. HER AMBITION AND expectations were doomed to be buried, together with her youth.

After a series of political campaigns in the early 1950s, many people were horrified by the Communist Government's iron hand, and their unconditional zeal for the revolution started to diminish. People were confused. They saw the government's effort at wiping out poverty, backwardness, crime, and prostitution. But they saw the killing of innocents as well. Hundreds of thousands died simply because of their different beliefs.

In 1956, the Chinese Communist Party's Conference closed with the resolution to "Let hundreds of flowers bloom and hundreds of schools contend". Since then, people continued to hear encouraging news day after day, predicting the Communist Government's willingness to adopt a more flexible and milder policy.

In early 1957, the Party's newspaper formally called on all people to express different opinions about the Party's work and policy. People were encouraged to criticize bureaucracy, factionalism and subjectivism at various levels of government organizations.

At Qin's institute, most people were suspicious of the Party's sincerity at the beginning of the campaign and few dared to say anything. The Party leaders in the institute then went all out to persuade them to voice their opinions. "If you love the Party, you should help it find out its mistakes so as to become better!" Qin and many of her colleagues were moved by this sincerity and they started to talk.

Opinions varied greatly. Some complained that the Party leaders in the institute were unprofessional and unfair, some attacked the central government for depending too much on the Russians, and some said that the Party's radical rural policy had impoverished peasants' lives.

As an applicant to join the Communist Party, Qin naturally responded to the Party's call. At one of many public meetings, she made two comments. She first criticized the city's educational official.

"Once, when I was reporting to him," Qin recalled, "about the problems of the city's adult education, he was scanning a cartoon behind his desk and paying little attention to what I was saying. This sort of irresponsible bureaucratic behaviour should not be allowed to continue."

She noticed that the chair of the meeting was taking notes of what she said and felt encouraged to continue: "I also feel that the Communist Government has been too cruel to those accused as political criminals," she added. Undoubtedly, Evergreen crossed her mind as she mentioned this.

For a period of three months, an explosion of opinions swept through the country. At schools, universities, hospitals, government offices and the press, places where there were mostly educated people, the atmosphere was one of furious activity. Everybody believed that the Communist Party had realized its past mistakes and was willing to make changes.

But people were too naive. By the summer of 1957, the Party Chairman, Mao Ze-dong, felt it was time to mute the public voices, for some had already gone so far as to demand free speech, a free press, free elections, and even a multi-party government system!

On Mao's instructions, the Party's newspaper published an editorial on June 8 with the headline, "The Working Class Wants to Talk Now!" It attacked some outspoken intellectuals and called for a purge of the 'bourgeois Rightists' accused of being enemies of the people since they were against the leadership of the Communist Party.

The wind was blowing in the opposite direction now. In July, the focus at public meetings was no longer criticizing the government's work but instead finding out 'Rightists' who had attacked the Party. People, surprised by the Party's abrupt change-face, shut their mouths in panic. But it was too late.

In the fall, the press reported daily the names and crimes of the Rightists, ranging from high-ranking government officials and well known democratic personages, to ordinary intellectuals such as university professors, school teachers, doctors, editors and writers.

Qin observed that some of the most outspoken people in the institute were denounced as Rightists. Public criticism meetings were held day and night and the Rightists were ordered to confess their evil designs against the Party's leadership.

Qin felt puzzled: "How could these persons suddenly become the enemies of the people? All they did was criticize the Party's work... Well, I have also criticized the Party! Will they think that I am also against the Party's leadership? Oh, no, no... They won't! Everyone knows that I have always been a pro-communist youth and they should understand that I am by no means a Rightist..."

Qin became quiet and cautious. She went to her office earlier and left later. She noticed the other three people sharing the same office with her did the same. The relaxed atmosphere was gone. Other than at criticizing meetings held every afternoon and some evenings, there was a deadly silence in all the offices. Everybody feared that a careless conversation might cause unexpected trouble during this particular period.

One afternoon, the institute's "activists" were assembled by the leaders for a secret meeting. Qin was not invited but a male colleague in Qin's office was called to attend the meeting. "He is never interested in politics and has never voiced any opinion. If he is regarded as an activist, what sort of position am I in now?" Qin felt all her nerves suddenly tense up. "They are expanding the web and trying to catch more people inside. And I..." She was reluctant to think this way and convinced herself that she was being paranoid.

The next day, as she was eating her lunch in the public canteen, she noticed that there was a subtle change in some people's attitudes towards her. As usual, she bought her favourite food — a bowl of steamed rice, a dish of hairtail fish braised in soy sauce, and a bowl of spinach soup. Qin was six months pregnant then and she had a good appetite. She found an empty seat and started to enjoy her meal. At lunch time the canteen, which contained a few hundred seats, was always crowded. Qin felt a little bit odd when the people eating at the same table were unwilling to talk with her. As they finished their meals quickly and left their seats, no one else came to the table. It was clear enough that she was deliberately being avoided now. The smiles left her cheeks. She chewed her rice slowly and told herself to remain calm.

When she finished her lunch and returned to her office, Qin encountered the same cold faces from the three men sitting by their desks. "It is obvious. I have been 'caught'!" Qin said to herself. Sensing approaching misfortune, Qin spoke her thoughts aloud in a desperate attempt to avoid the unavoidable: "If anyone dares to make me into a Rightist, I swear I will take my case to the Party's Central Committee!"

Silence. No reaction from the men. Not even a raised eyelid. The atmosphere was suffocating and Qin felt stifled. Powerless.

That afternoon, Qin received a phone call from Tian-zhi, asking her to come home that evening as he had something important to talk to her about. Tian-zhi was a hard-working person. He spent almost all his leisure time reading technical books or books in foreign languages. In their almost year-long marriage, Qin seldom had a chance to have long talks with him. Their communication had become even less since the Anti-Rightist Campaign started, for Tian-zhi, as a trustworthy communist, had been appointed a member of the Anti-Rightist Committee at his institute. As a matter of fact, the couple hardly had any time together. Since she had to attend meetings frequently in the evenings, Qin often spent the night in the institute's dormitory instead of taking her increasingly heavy body on the hour-long bus ride home.

"The Party leaders from your institute came to my office today." Tian-zhi started talking hurriedly as soon as Qin entered the door that night. "They said that you have made seriously misguided remarks against the Party, and they want me to inquire about your intentions now... I was shocked to know this... Why would you say things against the Party? How could you ever do that!"

Qin stood in the doorway all the time, listening to Tian-zhi. As she caught the suspicion in his eyes, disappointment flowed through her heart. "He already believes the accusations of my institute's leaders. He has not even asked me yet what I said!" Qin thought with agony. She walked to the chair by the desk and seated herself in it, while attempting to contain the flames of rage burning inside her.

"So, you want to know what my intentions are?" Qin tried to speak slowly and sound composed, but her voice was trembling. "I'll tell you. I just don't understand what the words 'against the Party' mean!"

Tian-zhi was stunned and confused at Qin's reaction. "Don't you understand that 'against the Party' means 'against the Chinese Communist Party'?"

"A perfect bookworm!" Qin shouted silently in her heart. Her anger struggled to explode but was finally forced back. Qin understood that Tian-zhi trusted no one but the Party and it was useless to explain anything to him. The only thing she could do was hope that the campaign of terror would soon be over and that she would escape unscathed.

However, time ran out on Qin. Two days later, in the institute's assembly meeting, she was denounced as a Rightist. She felt as if a bomb had exploded under her when she heard the charges: "...Not only did she attack our Party's leadership, but she has been stubborn too, in failing to recant her wrongdoings. It was just two days ago that she claimed that she didn't understand what the words 'against the Party' mean..."

Qin opened her eyes wide! She just couldn't believe her ears! Why would Tian-zhi report her angry remark to the institute leaders? Didn't he know what this was going to cost her? Had he been completely brainwashed by the Party?

"No! This is not right!" Qin stood up from her seat and shouted out angrily. "Hasn't the Party called on people to voice different opinions? Wasn't I right to respond to its call? How can you regard me as an anti-Party Rightist when I have been applying to become a Party member for years?"

She was so beside herself that she forgot the situation she was in. Many people were stunned by her frankness and watched her in silence. The institute leaders were irritated by her strong reaction and sharp questions. They banged the table in front of them with their fists and ordered her to shut up and sit back in her seat.

When the meeting was over, Qin was called into the administrative office to sign a form acknowledging her Rightist status. When she saw the black characters, "Anti-Party and Anti-Socialist Bourgeois Rightist", printed clearly on a piece of white paper, agonized tears filled up her eyes. She rejected the title forced on her and refused to sign.

"I am not a Rightist!" she cried. "This is totally unacceptable! You are wrong! And everything is just... wrong!"

"You'd better sign it," one of the leaders replied coldly. "We have received orders from the higher authorities that those who refuse to acknowledge their crimes will receive heavier punishment!"

He paused for a second to observe Qin's reaction and then continued with a dry smile. "Of course, you need to understand that your Rightist status is already settled, whether you sign it or not, as the decision has been made by the Anti-Rightist Committee."

Oh, what a hell! Qin felt her hair standing on end. She stared at the men sitting around the desk but said nothing. Of course, she understood that if numberless people could have been executed without trial, her own power to protest or protect was insignificant in the face of the might of the huge political machine.

With numb fingers, she picked up the pen from the desk and signed her name on the form.

Perhaps it was unfair to blame the institute leaders. A five percent quota of Rightists was assigned to the institute. The leaders had to find out eleven 'Rightists', that is, five percent of the total number of employees, to fill the quota. After Qin was chosen, the leaders still had to find one more. According to the government documents, a line was drawn between intellectuals and non-intellectuals. In other words, Rightists could only be selected from educated people, including university students and white collar workers. Peasants, the blue-collars and high school students were exempt, whatever 'wrong ideas' they had expressed.

A young man, a Communist Party member at Qin's institute, was denounced as a Rightist and expelled from the Party. He worried greatly that he might lose his beautiful fiancée since he was politically out of favour now. In the hope that an equally low social status might help keep the girl from leaving him, the young man reported to the leaders that his fiancée, though she never said anything against the Party in public, had made unfavourable comments about the Party during private conversations. Although the leaders were somewhat suspicious of the young man's report, they were eager to add the woman's name to the list so that the quota could be completed.

By official accounting, about half a million people in China were classified as Rightists in nineteen fifty-seven. There were several grades of punishment for them, ranging from life imprisonment or forced labour in rural areas, to job dismissal, reduction of salary and a bad record on personal files. Since the founding of the People's Republic, this had been the first large-scale political campaign to purge intellectuals.

A few decades later, people who survived Mao looked back to find out why Chairman Mao could not trust intellectuals and why he started the Anti-Rightist Campaign. Considering the international situation at that time, Mao's worry was not groundless. When the Hungarian uprising in 1956 jeopardized communist rule in that country, it was a warning signal to leaders of all other countries of the communist world. Intellectuals were keen on terms like 'freedom of speech', 'equality', 'human rights' and 'democracy' which might breed chaos and shake communist rule.

Mao had his own way — which was actually not the Marxist way, but that of a feudalist ruler — to win a revolution and rule a country. To Mao, intellectuals were easily influenced by bourgeois fanaticism and might upset the boat at any time. On the other hand, workers and peasants, who had no chance to be influenced by any 'foreign ideology', could be relied upon.

The Anti-Rightist Campaign is now regarded as a successful ploy used by Mao to eliminate dangerous intellectuals. He let people voice their opinions so as to find out who was for him and who was against him. As an old saying goes, "to lure the snake out of its hole and then beat it to death".

After the Anti-Rightist Campaign was over, a new wave of divorce prevailed, as had happened before at the end of each huge political campaign. Many couples divorced for fear that their future might be destroyed by a Rightist spouse. Some divorced for the sake of their children's future. In that case, a parent who was not a Rightist would try to get custody. There were cases of loving couples who chose to stay together but such cases usually ended up with both the man and woman punished, although one of them was not a Rightist.

Qin's year-long marriage was endangered now. Tian-zhi was informed of Qin's Rightist status by the Party organization in his institute. He was advised to divorce her.

"It is improper for a Party member to have a Rightist wife. A divorce could prove your loyalty to the Party," he was told.

For the second time in his life, Tian-zhi was thrown into the dilemma of choosing between the Party and his personal life. He liked Qin very much and he found it hard to believe that a woman like her could turn out to be a Rightist, the enemy of the people. Hard to believe as it was, though, his logic was simple: he would never distrust the Party! If there must be someone wrong, then it had to be his wife.

Qin was eight months pregnant and would soon give birth to their first child. Since the state's marriage law forbade a man to divorce a pregnant wife, Tian-zhi suggested that they separate while waiting for the baby's coming.

"We will have to go through the divorce procedure then..." He let out the words with a heavy heart, his eyes avoiding Qin's, afraid to see her reaction — pleas, perhaps, with tears. The few seconds of silence seemed unbearably long and he had to bolster himself by repeating silently the slogans stressed in the press these days: "Against Tenderheartedness! Be Firm to the Bourgeois Rightists!"

He felt relieved as Qin nodded numbly without any argument. Tian-zhi interpreted her silence as an acknowledgement of her guilt. He started to convince himself that he had done nothing wrong.

The next day was Sunday. The sky looked heavy and thick with grey clouds. Tian-zhi called a man-ride tricycle, a convenient means of transporting luggage in the city, and helped Qin move her simple belongings out of their apartment building. The four storey grey-coloured apartment building was the dormitory of Tian-zhi's institute. When he returned from Russia, Tian-zhi brought his aged mother out of her home-village to Beijing. Since his marriage to Qin, the three of them had lived in a three bedroom apartment on the third floor. Now, as the couple separated, Qin was obliged to move out.

As Qin climbed clumsily onto the tricycle and seated her heavy body in the back seat, she encountered curious stares from people living in the same building. Some were peeping at her from behind their windows, some were watching by the building entrance. Qin felt hundreds of needles were pricking at her skin. Her face turned red with embarrassment. She drew the cotton-padded curtain hanging from the roof of her seat and asked the old man riding on the front wheel to move at once. She didn't look back, but from the corner of the curtain she caught sight of Tian-zhi's figure walking beside the tricycle as if he wanted to accompany her for a while on her trip. She realized that he must have felt guilty, and reluctant to let her go, and that there must still be some tenderness in his heart. Tears streaming from her eyes, Qin bit her lips tightly to stop herself from crying out.

Five minutes later, as the tricycle came out of the quiet residential area onto the broad busy street, Qin heard Tian-zhi calling her as if to say good-bye. She didn't look out, but she could not control herself any more. She took out her handkerchief, buried her face in it, and burst out crying. The old driver riding on the front heard the noise getting louder and louder and looked back at the curtain behind him. He couldn't guess why Qin was weeping, but he had a natural sympathy for the young woman with the pregnant belly. He shook his head silently and bent over to step harder at the foot paddles.

The serious setbacks of the past two months made Qin's heart cold. Though she had a hundred arguments for her innocence and against the unfair treatment forced upon her, they would be useless if the audience was a person like Tian-zhi. Qin was fully aware of his extreme loyalty to the Party. She had seen a photo of Rose, a pretty girl with a naive smile. Tian-zhi had told her the story about his banished first love. Crying or pleading with somebody for mercy was never Qin's philosophy, especially when she felt she had no right to do so having been labelled 'enemy of the people'. She had tried hard to look resolute in front of Tian-zhi, but she felt totally crushed now.

Once again, she had to have her child alone, in hospital. As she looked at the skinny boy beside her bed, she remembered the day two years before when she had had her daughter in the same hospital. Life had repeated the same hoax, she thought, but this time the hoax was crueler.

Tian-zhi didn't come to the hospital to see his son.

"Perhaps he has forgotten my delivery date," Qin comforted herself. "He is a hard-working man and cannot remember these little things."

She thought about the Sundays after she married Tian-zhi. She got up early in the morning, cooked hot cereal and heated steamed bread on the small coal stove for the three member family. Tian-zhi's mother would return to her own room after breakfast. Tian-zhi would take a bus to the Sino-Soviet Friendship Club on the east side of the Tian-an-Men Square, where he would watch a Russian movie to brush up his Russian. Two hours later, he would go to the Beijing Library, a part of the former imperial court, to read technical materials for hours. As for Qin, she stayed at home to clean up their apartment and prepare a rich lunch.

To be frank, Qin was not a good cook and she hated to spend time doing household chores. She had never cooked a single meal when she was in Han Zhong, where all housework was done by servants. At university, and in the air force, and after she married Evergreen, she had always relied on public canteens and restaurants. But life with Tian-zhi had to be different. There was no canteen attached to the dormitory building and Tian-zhi's mother, a thrifty woman from a poor rural area, didn't like the idea of spending money to eat in a restaurant. The old woman still held onto the traditional values of rural China, where a daughter-in-law was regarded as the mother-in-law's servant. No matter how busy or clumsy Qin was in her housework, Tian-zhi's mother never reached out to help.

Often, Qin had spent hours in washing, cutting, frying and steaming, according to instructions from a cook book, finally producing a splendid lunch. At two o'clock, Tian-zhi would come home and the family would start to eat. Qin secretly expected that her hard-prepared four-dishes-plus-a-soup would claim Tian-zhi's admiration, as it was mainly to please him that she had learned to do something she disliked. To her disappointment, Tian-zhi ate without any comment. He would quickly finish his meal and pick up the newspaper.

Qin could not accept her effort being neglected this way and would ask him, "What do you think of today's lunch?"

Tian-zhi's expression would betray impatience at being bothered with something trivial. He would pause for a couple of seconds and reply simply, "Not bad," his eyes staying on the newspaper.

Qin was not content. She would tackle him further: "Did you like the stuffing in the dumplings?"

This time Tian-zhi would raise his eyes from the newspaper. He would think for a while and not be able to remember... "Oh, Qin, what kind of stuffing did you put in the dumpling...?"

Qin would force out a smile and leave the table. There was a whole bunch of dirty clothing waiting to be washed.

Many Sundays passed in exactly the same way. Qin felt disappointed at this sort of married life. She compared it with the exciting days when she and Evergreen attended various cultural activities together, and felt at a loss. But again and again, she reminded herself that Tian-zhi was a conscientious hard-working man and that he didn't neglect her totally. There had been Sunday evenings when Tian-zhi suggested they take a stroll along the weeping willow woods by the quiet stream in a nearby park, amid the soft light of the setting sun.

The weak crying of the baby brought her thought back to the hospital she was in. Suddenly Qin had a strong impulse to call Tian-zhi and let him know that he had a son. But she didn't, fearing his coming would spell the end of their relationship, since that had been made clear before their separation. With a sigh, she closed her eyes and lay weakly against her pillow.

On her last day in the hospital, Qin finally plucked up the courage to give Tian-zhi a call. He felt happy to know he had a son and said he would come to see them the next day.

Tian-zhi came to her dormitory. He looked at the skinny baby crying in a weak voice in his cradle beside Qin's single bed. His eyes behind his thick glasses became moist with a sudden rush of fatherly love, a feeling he had never experienced before.

He didn't talk much with Qin, except for an awkward greeting when he came in. Qin responded to his careful attitude with an equal reserve, and, to protect her pride, talked briefly about the boy while Tian-zhi listened and nodded once in a while. Both of them avoided touching on the thorny issue of their future. An hour later, Tian-zhi left.

When the boy was one month old, Qin received a letter from Tian-zhi. She rushed back to her dormitory room with confused feelings. Her roommate was not in and the small baby was sound asleep in his cradle. Qin sat by her desk and opened the letter with trembling hands.

"Qin:

This is the first time ever since we have known each other that I am writing you a letter. At this moment the pen in my hand feels as heavy as my heart for I deeply regret that the letter you are going to read is not the type I should have written when we were a loving couple…"

Qin's heart became icy cold, but her hands stopped trembling. She bit her lips hard and went on reading the letter. Tian-zhi told her that he had made up his mind to go through the divorce, after fighting hard with, and finally overcoming, his 'unhealthy sentimentalism'. He was going to be totally responsible for their new-born son, he wrote, and Qin should be prepared to accept any punishment the Party meted out to her for her wrongdoing…

Qin stared at the letter in her hand, motionless. Her mind was blank and she couldn't concentrate on what to do next. Although psychologically prepared for their separation, she had secretly cherished the expectation that Tian-zhi might change his mind after he came to see his son. The letter wiped out her last hope.

On the day of their divorce, Qin went to the government registration office with her son in the afternoon. In those days there were many divorces and the small office was crowded with people. Qin met Tian-zhi at the entrance. Wordlessly, they sat on the bench against the wall and waited for their turn.

Qin looked at the small baby held closely in her arms, her tears starting to drop onto the boy's blanket. She had brought a small bundle with all the baby's clothes in it. In a while, Tian-zhi was going to take the boy and the bundle away with him. She couldn't tell if she would ever be able to see her son again, for she had not been informed of her punishment yet.

When it was their turn, Qin and Tian-zhi moved to the chairs in front of the desk. A young woman with a narrow cucumber-shaped face raised up her head from the desk and looked at them. When she saw Qin's swollen eyes, she let Tian-zhi talk first.

Tian-zhi murmured their personal information in a low voice and said they had agreed to a divorce. He was obviously nervous and took off his glasses now and then to wipe them awkwardly with a handkerchief while Cucumber-face took notes with a stern expression.

As he finished speaking, the woman asked him to hand over his copy of their marriage certificate. She then glanced at the baby in Qin's arms and said to Tian-zhi in a flat voice, "The state's marriage law protects women and children. I'll need to know your wife's opinion in regard to child custody and property distribution." She then turned to face Qin, "What is your opinion?"

"I..." Qin tried her best to swallow her sorrow and talk calmly. "I don't know what I should do..." Tears ran from her eyes again.

Cucumber-face put down the pen in her hand and looked at Tian-zhi: "It seems your wife is unwilling to divorce. What's the cause of your divorce? If your wife doesn't agree to the divorce, you will have to go to court. This office deals with agreed divorces only."

"I... We..." Tian-zhi stammered, trying to find a suitable explanation. "The cause is the Anti-Rightist Campaign... That's all... We have no property to divide, and I am willing to be totally responsible for our child..."

At this moment, Qin's silent weeping turned into a miserable sobbing. The baby in her arms woke up and started crying too. Tian-zhi took out his handkerchief from his pocket and wiped Qin's cheeks silently. His hand was trembling and he looked heavy-hearted.

Cucumber-face waited for a few more seconds and finally became impatient at Qin's sobbing. "Stop your crying!" she said sternly to Qin. As soon as she learned that Qin was a Rightist, Cucumber-face's attitude changed. "So you're feeling sad now? Then what about before? Hum! You don't want to divorce, but that's not up to you!" She pointed at Tian-zhi and continued rebuking Qin. "He is a Party member and a revolutionary official. And look at you! A Rightist! Do you think you deserve him? I tell you, he is already too generous to you, offering to take care of the baby by himself and not asking any money from you!"

Cucumber-face's reckless abuse was loud, drawing the attention of all the people sitting on the benches against the wall. Qin's agony reached its peak. She stood up, put the baby into Tian-zhi's arms, and walked quickly towards the door.

Tian-zhi was stunned at her reaction and held the crying baby clumsily. Cucumber-face leapt from her chair and shouted at Qin's back: "Come back! You haven't signed the form yet!" The door closed with a bang.

Qin wandered about the city aimlessly. The streets in Beijing were as busy as before, with streams of people riding on bicycles passing the beautiful lotus-shaped street lamps. Many big new buildings in modern

European styles had been erected during the last few years, forming a sharp contrast to the old oriental structures around the city.

As she passed through Tian-an-Men Square, grand and magnificent as always, she remembered her first Sunday in Beijing, seven years before, when she had stood on top of the marble bridge like a naive dreamer.

"Time flies so quickly. But what a nightmare I have had in those years," she sighed.

At midnight, she came to the banks of the imperial river surrounding the Forbidden City. It became a quiet place deep in the night, visited by nobody else except Qin and the crows resting in their nests on top of the willow trees and under the big roof of the wall towers. The large brick laid city wall, built five hundred years before, and tens of metres high, had been worn out by the passage of time, gaps having formed here and there. The lofty watchtower at the corner of the wall formed a shadow in the cold moonlight and looked mysterious and forbidding. Qin walked back and forth like a ghost along the bank, ignoring the dry willow branches over her head which messed up her hair, and the early winter's piercing wind which cut and numbed her cheeks.

"Did I really do something wrong?" She started to recall the road she had taken during those years: her cooperation during the Land-Reform Movement; her enthusiasm to be a volunteer soldier at the start of the Korean War; her contributions in the air force. And all to win favour from the Party.

"My efforts are not recognized! My honesty is questioned! My loyalty is rejected! Why? What has gone wrong?" She almost shouted out her agony.

Qin had never suspected the motivation for, nor the justification of, the Anti-Rightist Campaign. Like almost everyone else, she trusted the Party's policies wholeheartedly and unconditionally. Her blind worship of the Party made her believe that there were really some bourgeois Rightists who intended to overthrow the Communist Government and, unfortunately, she was denounced as one of them because the leaders at her institute mis-judged her.

"Anti-Communist and Anti-Socialist Bourgeois Rightist." The horrible words loomed once again in her mind, cutting her heart piece by piece like knives. At criticism meetings she had tried hard to explain to the public that she was innocent. But they pointed out that her criticism of the city's edu-cational official was undeniable evidence of agitation against the Party's leadership. In the month after she had delivered her boy, the leaders in her institute blamed her many times for being late for criticism meetings. She was utterly exhausted by the endless cries of the baby, the merciless shoutings at the meetings, and the annoying self-criticism reports she had to write repeatedly.

Her political life was definitely destroyed by that insulting title. As a Rightist, she was treated like those who held the title 'landlord' or 'capitalist'. Anybody could step on her at will and she had to accept any insult thrown into her face! She had swallowed enough in the past few months and she couldn't take any more.

And the second marriage, which had lasted for just a year, was finished.

"There is no understanding, no trust, no sympathy, no caring in this world... Trapped in such a situation, what point is there to life? Even death is probably better than living with humiliation for the rest of my life... Perhaps death is the only way to prove my innocence. People might realize, at my death, that I have been wrongly accused of being a Rightist. The Party leaders would realize their mistake in forcing a faithful pro-communist youth to die... Yes, that's it..."

With this desperate resolution in mind, she strode determinedly towards the river bank. She paused at the edge and lowered her numbed face to stare at the river beneath her feet. There was a thin layer of ice on the surface of the dark water, in which, she felt, lay the source of peace forever. She closed her eyes.

Just at this moment, Qin heard someone calling her from a distance. She opened her eyes and looked around. A glittering flashlight was moving closer and closer on the other side of the river bank. Was someone looking for her at this hour? Qin listened attentively. She was disappointed to find it was a woman calling out in a tired voice. Clearly, she was looking for her missing child. Qin watched as the flashlight passed by and listened as the woman's voice gradually diminished.

The moving light in darkness reminded Qin of a similar scene buried deep in her memory and she suddenly felt a gentle stream floating over her numb bosom... It was... Qin searched her mind hard... It was Laolao! Yes, it was she, holding a red lantern beside the bank of the nighttime Han River, looking for her missing daughters... "I was only four then... Today I am already the mother of two..."

"It's so chill by the river," Qin shivered with cold. She felt sober. Unaware of what she was doing, she moved away from the water's edge and leaned her back against the rough trunk of an old willow tree.

"Well, if I die, who will take care of my kids? They are too small and vulnerable to be left as motherless children! And my mother would be heartbroken to know of my death. She has cherished so many hopes... How could I let her down! I am stupid, I am selfish, I think too much about myself! Have I tried hard to overcome everything yet? No! I must live! I must try to prove my innocence with the rest of my life!"

She turned her back all of a sudden and walked quickly to escape the midnight darkness on the river bank underneath the old city wall.

In early 1958, Qin was informed of her punishment: expelled forever as a member of the Communist Youth League, a reduction of two grades in her salary, and an unlimited time of labouring on a farm. She accepted this calmly, knowing her punishment was relatively less serious than many others who were jailed, or expelled from employment forever.

Qin wrote a letter to Tian-zhi. She pleaded, for the first time in her life, that Tian-zhi give her a chance to correct her 'mistakes'. "Your report of my words to the institute leaders has helped the making of my Rightist status. But I understand your absolute loyalty to the Party and I cannot blame you for that," she let out her grievance in a mild and roundabout way. "Please believe me, I am still young and I can be remoulded."

Tian-zhi had not seen Qin for two months, ever since she ran away during the divorce procedure. Though still torn by the contradiction between the Party and his personal life, the scene of the tearful Qin holding a crying baby had strongly upset him and up to now he had not successfully overcome the 'unhealthy bourgeois sentimentalism' appearing again and again in his mind! He was deeply touched to see a proud woman like Qin crying and pleading. At night, he sat by the desk and read Qin's letter over and over under the soft lamp light. At last his sense of himself as a husband and father took the upper hand.

"I will reconsider my decision to divorce. I wish you to work hard on the farm and correct your mistake..." In his letter to Qin, he wrote this with confused feelings, not sure if his new decision was right or wrong, morally and politically.

Tian-zhi had sent their three-month-old son to a nursery in the western suburbs, built on a bushy hill. It was previously an orphanage run by the Christian missionaries. After the missionaries had been driven away in the early 1950s, the government had taken it over and it was now one of the few places in Beijing to admit infants for long-term stays. Qin was happy to know that the baby at least had someone to take care of him, for she had no idea how long she was going to labour on the farm.

One day, as the sandy seasonal spring wind from the Mongolian Plateau turned the sky over Beijing yellow and obscure, Qin packed her luggage for the labour farm.

The institute leader addressed the group of Rightists before they mounted a large truck with their simple luggage on their backs and washbasins in their hands: "The Party is giving you an opportunity to correct your mistakes. You must, while labouring on the farm, learn from the workers and peasants, sincerely remould your bourgeois ideology and strive hard to win pardons from the Party and the people... Those proved to be genuinely remoulded may have their title of 'Rightist' removed."

٭   ٭   ٭

MAX RAN INTO THE TV ROOM BESIDE THE PANTRY.

"Are you still up, Lilac?" Mrs. Thompson's silver-haired head appeared at the door.

I looked at my watch. It was 12:00 am, time for Max to take his pill. That was the reason for Mrs. Thompson's coming downstairs at this hour.

"I have just seen a movie, *Silence of the Lambs*, the Academy Award winner this year."

"I have seen that, too." Mrs. Thompson sat herself on the sofa. "To me, that movie is tasteless. I just don't understand how it became the award winner!"

"Before I came to Canada, I saw quite a few movies made in the 1940s and nineteen fifties. As you know, China opened its door to the outside world just a few years ago. But the movies we saw were excellent! I do think that the ones made in the 1940s were much, much better than today's movies!"

"Oh, Lilac! I just couldn't agree with you more!" Mrs. Thompson exclaimed. "What movies did you see in China?"

"My most favourite ones were *The Waterloo Bridge, Roman Holiday, Casablanca, Spartacus* and *Gone with the Wind*..." I named a few.

"Yes, they are all masterpieces!" She sighed and leaned her head against the back of the sofa. Her eyes reflected my own nostalgic feeling.

I watched the old woman sitting opposite to me. The question I had had for a long time came out of my mouth naturally. "What did you do in the 1940s and fifties?"

"Well," her eyes searched the ceiling and her mouth selected words cautiously, "I did a few things... different each time."

"Did you work in New York? Manhattan?"

"No... Why?" Becoming alert, she sat up straight and examined my face.

"I saw your wedding album. I noticed the wedding was held in Manhattan," I told her frankly.

"...Yes. It was." There was no smile. She seemed unwilling to talk about this.

"How did your husband pass away?" I asked, swallowing my original question, "How did you meet your husband?"

"Cancer," she replied briefly, her voice calm, her face indifferent.

"Why didn't you have children? You were young enough to bear children when you got married..." I asked curiously.

"Timing... Timing was not right... I wanted to have children. But he said he did not want to start another family at his age," she said, a coldness appearing in her eyes. "He already had grandchildren before we got married."

That was against her wish, then. But why had she still married him? Perhaps his riches and fame were an irresistible attraction.

I wanted to ask her, "Do you regret the choice made in your youth? Do you think it is worthwhile to sacrifice everything else just for money?" But I didn't. I was afraid it might hurt too much.

Undoubtedly, she got something she had dreamt about from this marriage, besides money. "I can never forget those days when we entertained Pierre Trudeau in our house," she used to tell me joyfully. "It was just marvellous..."

"Did you ever meet a man you would have liked to marry after your husband died?" I asked.

She was silent for a few seconds before she admitted, "Yes, once... That was many years ago."

"Tell me something about it!" I showed great interest.

"We met at a resort in Florida. He was a Toronto businessman, on vacation with his girlfriend. Oh, Lilac, you would be surprised to know how handsome he was! I went there with my housekeeper. He saw me in the hotel dining room and inquired from other people about me... Well, it was so funny! He left his girlfriend alone at the table and came to talk to me for a whole hour!" She indulged in some happy memory and giggled.

"What happened later on?" I urged her to go on.

"Well, he courted me for two years. And he even found my step-daughter, to ask if he could marry me..."

"I am confused here." I cut in. "Why should he ask your step-daughter if he could marry you?"

"He... She... Well, I don't know. It's all peculiar!" She waved her hand as if she wanted to get rid of something disgusting.

"Then, why didn't you marry him?" My curiosity increased.

Her eyes were rolling around the room and her hand was fumbling on the small side table for her cigarette. "Well, he stayed in Toronto all the time. I couldn't understand why he wanted the marriage if he simply didn't come here."

"But, perhaps," I guessed cautiously, "he had a nicer house than yours and he felt more comfortable staying in Toronto?"

"His house?" she exclaimed. "It's a pig shed compared with mine!" She pressed the lighter in her hand, lit up the cigarette, inhaled deeply, and let out a plume of smoke. She watched the cloud spreading in front of her eyes silently. The coldness returned to her face.

What had attracted that handsome Toronto man? Why wasn't her romance brought to a happy ending? Did money play a major role in this anecdote? Her story tonight was full of contradictions. But I had lost interest in digging any further. Poor or rich, the Canadian people's marriages and love stories all seemed much less complicated than those in China. And wasn't it a blessing to have a simple, eventless life?

5

Meeting Mother on the Labour Farm

MY EARLIEST MEMORIES GO BACK AS FAR AS WHEN I WAS two or three years old. I lived in a large garden surrounded by high grey brick walls. Trees and flowers seemed to cover every inch of land in the spacious courtyard and there were differently shaped buildings here and there in the shades of the trees. My favourite playground was a small artificial hill. On one side of the hill was a large greenhouse with numerous large pots which had goldfish and tropical fish swimming inside. A beautifully decorated four-storey high theatre with more than one thousand seats was situated in the centre of the garden.

Laolao had been with me since I had been sent back to Han Zhong as a month-old baby. It became a tough task for her to find me a wet nurse. During the first four months, I had been shifted from hand to hand among three women, none of whom qualified as a suitable wet nurse in the eyes of Laolao. On the fifth month, Laolao gave the nod to a woman whose home was on the other side across the narrow street. The woman and her husband made a living selling cold spicy noodles at home. She had just given birth to her fifth child, a girl a few months younger than I. When she learned that Laolao's daughter, Qin, was offering twenty people's dollars per month for a wet nurse, this woman found Laolao and took me home. She engaged a peasant woman to raise her newborn at the cost of five people's dollars per month and, by nursing me, earned an extra fifteen dollars herself.

Laolao understood that this mother of five would be too busy to take care of me. Taking advantage of the closeness to her residence, she dropped over to the wet nurse's home a few times a week to bath me and wash my clothing.

One day when I was close to my first birthday, Laolao found my lips were red and swollen. She suspected that my wet nurse had fed me with the leftovers of their daily sale, noodles spiced with hot red peppers. Laolao took me home at once.

Not long after that, she brought me to Xi An, the capital city of the province, where we stayed in Lin's home. Lin was then a mathematics teacher in a high school and her husband, Virtue, was an official of the provincial government.

The large beautiful garden had been previously, under the Nationalist Government, the headquarters of a warlord. Since 1949, Virtue and many of his colleagues had lived with their families in the dormitory area of the courtyard.

Lin had three sons, all under five years old. As these little brothers did, I called Lin 'Mamma', and Virtue 'Dad'. I must have been a child with unappealing looks and personality. When I grew up and looked at my childhood photos, I found all my pictures had the same expression: tightly closed lips without the slightest indication of a smile and a pair of black eyes full of suspicion. In those pictures there was no trace of happiness and innocence, only a face shadowed with melancholy.

Laolao loved me more than her other grandchildren, though the others were definitely more lovely and better-behaved. I preferred to be dressed like a boy and to fool around with my cousins in the garden until I was covered with dirt from head to toe.

Laolao took me to the studio twice a year to have my picture taken for Qin. I always refused to be dressed up like a girl and Laolao had to buy a boy's cap and coat for me. Every time Qin received these pictures, she could hardly stop herself from crying out, "Oh, look! What an ugly girl Peace has become!"

Laolao not only doted upon me herself, she could not bear other people's negligence of me. One Saturday afternoon, when all the children in the kindergarten were to go home to spend their Sunday, Virtue went to get the children. The nurses told him it was better for me to stay in the kindergarten over the weekend because I had flu. Virtue agreed and took only his three sons with him.

Back home Laolao questioned him about me and was very unhappy to learn the reason for my being left behind. She immediately set out to the kindergarten to take me home and complained to Virtue: "You only care that your sons do not get infected by the flu, but you don't care that the poor little girl has to spend the weekend in the empty kindergarten all alone by herself!"

*   *   *

AFTER BEING DENOUNCED AS A RIGHTIST, QIN HAD NO heart to tell her relatives what had happened, so for more than a year, Laolao received no letter from Qin. She became anxious and extremely worried. Her instincts told her that Qin must be in big trouble.

One day, Lin received a letter. It was mailed to her school instead of her home. She opened it hastily. After reading it, Lin felt that she was almost too weak to get up from her chair.

Qin admitted that she had been denounced as a Rightist. She asked Lin to conceal this fact from Laolao as Qin didn't want to diminish Laolao's long-standing pride in her. And, as her political status might have a nega-tive impact on the future of her daughter, Qin hoped that Lin would kindly adopt the little girl.

"...Peace has been used to calling you Mamma, hasn't she? Anyway, you have three sons and no daughter, and I hope you would be glad to take Peace as your own daughter. I am deeply in need of your help, please..." Qin pleaded in her letter.

Qin promised that she would continue to send money for the little girl's expenses, but she concealed the fact that she had actually been sent to a labour farm for about two years. She was too proud to tell her relatives about it, as this sort of punishment had connotations of criminality.

Lin found herself facing a thorny issue. She wept for her sister's unfortu-nate fate, but, being a timorous woman, she simply didn't know how to help her. During the following days, Lin and Virtue discussed the problem secretly, behind Laolao's back, and finally decided not to adopt Qin's daughter.

On the one hand, they already had three children, and there was no need to have one more. On the other, Virtue was a politically sophisticated man and could foresee the potential inconvenience of keeping the little girl in his home. In a society with a complicated and changeable political atmosphere, one could never predict what sort of bad fortune might befall. It was always a wise policy to keep a distance from any politically out-of-favour person, even a close relative.

The following day, they told Laolao that Qin must be missing her daughter, since she had not seen the child for almost four years. It might be a good idea for Laolao to take the little girl back to Qin in Beijing. Laolao, knowing nothing about Qin's situation and anxious to see if she was okay, agreed immediately.

*   *   *

MRS. THOMPSON WALKED INTO THE LIBRARY. MY FINGERS stopped on the keyboard and I turned my head. There was anxiety on her face.

"What's wrong?" I drew my thoughts back from China to Canada.

"Have you seen Max around? I can't find him anywhere!" She frowned.

"He has not been here... I'll go with you to search for him." I turned off the computer on the table, got up from the chair, and followed her out of the house.

Mrs. Thompson stood in front of the fountain and shaded her hand over her eyebrows to scan the meadow under the autumn sun. "Max! Max! Where are you?" Her old voice was shivering like a piece of thread blown away by the wind in the vastness. "Oh! It's horrible, Lilac! He usually runs right to me at my calling, no matter how far away he is... Max! Max!"

"Maybe he is just playing somewhere in the woods," I comforted her. "He will be back to the house when he is tired. You cannot keep the dog in the house all the time. He is an animal and he prefers the outdoors."

"Oh, Lilac! I've got reason to be nervous! I forgot to feed him the noon pill. I am afraid he may have already died, somewhere in the grass..."

"But I don't think the pill is that important. It's only a mixture of vitamins."

"No, Lilac! You don't know. My last dog died unexpectedly that way!" She shook her head. There were tears in her eyes.

"...If you are worrying so much, I'll have a look in the orchard, and you can go to the cottage to see if he is there..." I walked away.

As I turned around the tulip fields, I caught sight of Max's black figure under an old apple tree. He was eating something on the ground. I called him loudly, "Max!" He raised up his head, looked at me, and lowered his head to continue his eating.

What kind of food could attract him so much that he would ignore Mrs. Thompson's calling? I wondered. Oh, God! I was close enough to see he was chewing on an animal's leg. The white bone and the red meat showed it was fresh. Could it be the leg of a deer killed in a fight with some wild beast or other?

"No, Max! Come home with me!" I patted him on his back. He wouldn't leave the animal leg. I kicked the leg into the bush. Max stared at the bush, and then at me. "No! No more! Come home now!" I said firmly.

As soon as Max's figure appeared in front of the house, Mrs. Thompson screamed with joy and reached out her arms to embrace her dear pet. "Where have you been, dear? You made me worry so much!" She held Max tightly and kissed him with relief.

I watched her lips close to his and suddenly felt sick. "Be careful, Mrs. Thompson!" I warned her. "I found him chewing on some animal's leg in the orchard..."

"...What? What was he eating? Some animal's leg?" She was clearly stunned at the news and loosened her hands on Max's head. She examined Max carefully this time and noticed the bloody smirch around his mouth. "Oh! My dear! You make me sick!" she screamed with revulsion.

She immediately led Max back to her bedroom upstairs. Perhaps she wanted to clean his mouth, I thought.

An hour later, I started to prepare supper in the kitchen. Mrs. Thompson finally walked downstairs. The dog was not with her. "Where is Max?" I asked.

"He is upstairs. I have punished him! Oh, Lilac! He made me angry! I am so upset he would have done such a mean thing! He has chicken, beef, pork, liver, all kinds of meat at home. But he touched that dirty thing in the wild!" she said, deeply pained.

"You are alarming yourself too much. I don't think there is anything unusual about that. It's natural for animals to look for food in the wild. Max is no different than other animals," I commented, chopping potatoes.

"Well, Lilac! Do you think Max has been raised to search for food in the wild? He is not like the Chinese!" she looked annoyed.

"Why are you comparing a dog with the Chinese people?" I was confused.

"Of course, Chinese are known for eating just everything! Grass, barks, fungus, and mice!" Her voice was sharp.

As if someone had suddenly hit me with a club, I felt my head burning with flames, while my hands became cold and started to shake. I put down the cutting knife and turned to look at her. The old lady in the chair appeared cold and vicious at that moment. "You are insulting people!" I tried hard to repress my anger and sound calm. "Have you ever seen me eat any such things in your house? Where did you get the idea that Chinese people eat mice?"

Her eyes scanned the decorative dishes hanging on the wall, in an effort to avoid mine. There was an embarrassing silence in the kitchen.

I picked up the newspaper on the table and went into the TV room. I tried to read the news, but found I was unable to understand anything in the paper... There was no equality, no respect in this house, I thought sadly. But wasn't it my own fault? Hadn't I come looking for all these insults? I couldn't forget the sunny afternoon when I first walked into this old house and became ecstatic at the sight of the beautiful library. I pointed to the bookshelves and said to the old lady: "I suppose you have read most of these books." She shook her head and replied: "No, not at all. I have no time for that!" I didn't know what made her select me from more than a dozen applicants, as her new housekeeper. Probably the fact that my educational background, my two MA degrees, pleased the heiress of this residence of learning... I used to explain it to myself this way, but what had happened today proved I was wrong. She had never regarded me as a well educated woman. I was worth nothing compared with her pet.

"Lilac, are you mad at me?" The old lady's quivering voice woke me up. I didn't know how long she had been standing by the door. "I am sorry... Lilac! I was just too mad at Max."

I raised my eyes from the newspaper and examined her. The cold and malicious light in her eyes had gone. The pale wrinkled face once again displayed a pathetic look. The hard clot blocking my throat was melting. Anyway, she was aged, and I should forgive her for what she said, I told myself. Besides, she was my employer. If I gave up this job, where could I go? I had been looking for a job for two years and this was the only thing I had ever got.

"No, I am not mad. I am just tired and need a rest," I said to her placidly.

There was a slight sound from the staircase, a step, and each time cautious. That should be Max. I walked over and found him standing halfway down the staircase, his eyes full of fear. "Oh, Max! Come down now!" I clapped my hands.

He wouldn't move, his eyes searching for his mother. I went back to the kitchen and said to Mrs. Thompson: "Max is afraid of coming down. I don't know how you punished him a while ago..."

"Well, I'll go and talk to him," she said.

I picked up the knife on the cutting board again. As I chopped the vegetables, Mrs. Thompson's voice could be heard now and then from the hall. "...You shouldn't have disappointed me... How could you ever do such a thing... Other people will laugh at you... Don't you understand? Promise me, never do it again..." It sounded just like an angry mother castigating her naughty son.

I put down the knife again and walked to the hall. A proper thing for a friend to do at such a moment was to cut in and calm down the mother, as people did in China.

"Mrs. Thompson, don't be angry at him any more! He is already sorry for his mistake, isn't he? Look at his eyes! He's feeling guilty now. Max, tell your mother you are wrong, and you won't do it again! Tell her!" I imagined that I was really in the situation of mediating a family quarrel. I acted seriously, though I felt odd in the role I was playing.

"Mrs. Thompson," I turned to face her. "You should forgive Max this time. I am pretty sure he won't let you down again. You have made him fearful enough..."

"Yes, Lilac, I forgive him now!" She nodded to me seriously and reached out her hands to the dog. "Max, we are reconciled!"

I smiled as she rubbed her cheek against his. I should leave them alone now, I thought and turned away. Mrs. Thompson suddenly remembered something and called me to stop. "Lilac, would you please go and find that animal leg and throw it to a place where it can't be reached?"

"No problem," I replied, and left.

In the orchard I retrieved the leg from the bush. I looked around and thought hard about where to dispose of it. The valley at my feet was overgrown with pine trees. I remembered the first time I had been down to explore the stream below, Max had been too scared to follow and stopped up here. "This may be a proper place, for Max won't go down into the valley," I said to myself, throwing away the leg with effort.

The leg hit the trunk of a pine tree a few yards away. That was too close. Max could smell it and find it. I walked down carefully to pick up the leg from the bush. As my hands were holding the rough bark of the pine tree and searching in the grass, Mrs. Thompson's words once again emerged in my mind.

...Grass, bark, fungus... the Chinese ate all this things... She might not be wrong in a way. There had been times when many people in China filled their empty stomachs with things even Max would not touch.

*   *   *

IN MY MEMORY IT WAS A HOT SUMMER DAY. LAOLAO AND I went out of the grand but noisy train station in Beijing and were carried by a man-driven tricycle to a quiet street where Qin's institute was supposed to be. With the address in her hand, Laolao found the entrance with a tall iron-barred gate.

A grey-haired doorkeeper came out of the reception office and told Laolao that Qin was not here any more and that she had actually been on a labour farm for about two years. She was doing well there, the doorkeeper added in a sympathetic tone, as he noticed the shocked expression on Laolao's face.

I could feel Laolao's hand suddenly tighten. Without a word, she turned around and squinted, one hand shading her brows, at the sun falling towards the western sky. A moment later we set out on our way to the long-distance-bus station in the suburbs.

As the sky gradually became dark and twinkling stars emerged over our heads, Laolao and I walked hand in hand on a narrow winding trail stretching among endless rice paddy fields. We walked slowly, with a large bundle on Laolao's back and her tiny feet limiting her pace.

About four years old then, I could clearly remember the scene of that night. The moon was round and bright. The wooden boards laid over the irrigation ditch as a bridge looked whitish under the soft moonlight. The night air was filled with a sweet fresh aroma, a mixture of soil and blooming rice flowers. Frogs and various nameless insects sang rhythmically in the densely-planted rice fields and alongside murmuring streams.

I did not know how long we had walked on the rough and bumpy trail. I felt sleepy and tired out from the day's travelling. Now and then, Laolao shifted the big bundle from left hand to right, and right hand to left. Our paces slowed down. I squatted on the ground and refused to walk any more. Laolao put down the bundle and held me up in her arms. She pointed her finger in front and said to me: "It won't be too far away. Look, there is light! We will soon get there."

Up higher in her arms, I did see a few dim lights far away in the fields.

When we crossed a few more wooden bridges, a noisy and bright scene was suddenly exposed in the dark night, like an opera being performed on a stage.

About a dozen rows of huts lined up one after the other. Each mud hut had three or four large rooms. Through the many small windows, the light bulbs hanging from the central ceilings shed light onto the yards. Men and women came in and out from different doors with wash basins and towels in their hands. There was a water tap between every two rows of huts. Many men got water in their basins and stood in the yard washing their mud-stained bodies. Women, however, carried the water back to their rooms.

Through the nearest open door, I could see the inside of one room. There were two wide plank beds facing each other lining the walls. Each bed had about ten people's bed clothes on it. Underneath the beds were small suitcases and shoes. A thin iron wire stretching from wall to wall carried colourful towels, handkerchiefs and wet clothes.

Some people noticed Laolao and me standing by the door. They talked to Laolao. A moment later, I saw a tall and slender woman with short hair walking towards us. Her bare feet were in a pair of muddy sneakers and her blue pants were rolled up to her knees. Before I saw her clearly, I heard her astonished voice: "Oh! Mother! How did you come? Why did you come? And, with her...!"

Laolao was struck dumb for a few seconds. She then said in a low voice, "I haven't heard from you for so long. They said you might be missing the girl..."

"What? Missing her? Do I have time to miss her in my present situation? Well, come this way with me!"

Laolao's words were cut short by the woman's angry reply. I did not understand why the woman was so upset to see us.

It was arranged that we would spend the night in a small office which was the supervisor's room. I fell soundly asleep as soon as I was put into a single bed.

I did not know how long I slept but I was wakened by hand claps. In the darkness, there was talking in lowered voices, sobbing, and more claps to kill buzzing mosquitoes.

"...So, you see, I simply can't keep her with me... I'll give her to someone... Maybe a childless couple..."

I recognized this as the woman's voice.

"...I just cannot believe how weak and timid you have become! Why couldn't you try to bring up the girl by yourself? I wish you would be as courageous as you have always been in facing difficulties. There will be a day when everything turns better..."

This was Laolao's voice. I didn't understand what they were talking about and fell asleep again.

٭   ٭   ٭

LIFE WAS HARD AND THE WORK INCREDIBLY HEAVY ON THE farm. Brought up in a wealthy family, Qin lacked the necessary skills and physical suitability. But, having a strong will, she tried her best to endure all this hardship and never complained. She hoped that by performing outstandingly well she might be able to atone for her 'crime' and win back trust from the Party.

Qin never questioned whether this sort of punishment was right or whether human souls could really be salvaged by toil. For years, the Party used labour as a punishment to remould 'imperfect' people. The irony lay in the paradox: in Marxist theory, labour and labourers were always highly valued and appreciated, whereas in communist society the authorities used labour as a punishment!

The female and male Rightists, about five hundred on this farm, lived in separate rows. Qin and nineteen other women occupied a large room. Each woman had her own space, two feet wide and four feet long, on the huge plank bed. All the Rightists were supervised by a dozen farm workers who lived in smaller rooms with single beds.

Everyday, the Rightists got up at five o'clock before the sun rose and returned to their rooms after dark. There was little machinery on the farm and all work had to be done by hand. Qin got arthritis since she had to stand barefooted in chilly muddy water while transplanting rice shoots in early spring. Her delicate fair skin peeled off several times and weeks of cutting wheat with a sickle under the burning summer sun made her thin fingers become thick and rough like old carrots. She suffered lumbago from having to carry heavy baskets of mud on her shoulders the whole winter, as they built river dams and dug irrigation canals.

After working in the fields for more than twelve hours during the day, she hardly had any strength to wash herself and would throw herself in bed as soon as possible, allowing unscrupulous mosquitos to attack her furiously. When arthritis tortured her, and she felt her muscles aching, she lay with her teeth clenched and eyes wide open till day broke.

The hardest time was in September that year. The rice paddy was ready for harvest in a month. It was at the time when the government was calling on people to create 'miracles' in production. The authorities on the farm therefore decided to create a miracle in the rice fields.

Now the rice paddy in sixty mu of fields must be pulled up and transplanted into one mu of land. As time was crucial to this daring enterprise and everything had to be completed within a week, the Rightists were obliged to work day and night continuously to enable the success of transplantation. With their two hands, Qin and five hundreds others pulled out the rice paddy from sixty mu of fields, peeled off the leaves, put the stems with heavy ears into baskets, carried them as fast as possible to the new field, and squeezed the stems tightly into a single mu of land.

There was no time to sleep. Meals were sent to the fields and eating was the only time to have a rest. One night, Qin was sitting by the fields and eating a piece of steamed cornbread. She fell asleep halfway through, her head leaning back against the basket filled with stems behind her. The bread dropped into the muddy field. She had not slept for two and a half days.

Qin was not the only one. A few other women sitting beside her rested their heads on their knees and slept soundly. Some men simply flattened their bodies in the muddy fields to have a better rest.

"Phee... Phee..." A supervisor blew a sharp whistle and said loudly, "Get up, everyone! This field is finished. We'll move to a new field!"

Qin was wakened by his voice, but she felt too weak to raise her heavy body. When she finally managed to stand up, she saw the team was already marching on the trail between the fields. She quickened her steps and caught up the end of the team. She and two other women formed the last row.

"Let's walk arm in arm, so we can all close our eyes at the same time." Qin had the idea and suggested it to the other women. They were eager to accept this idea and linked their arms at once.

As soon as they closed their eyes, drowsiness came back to them again. So the three women walked under the moonlight in a half-sleepy way. They had no idea how long they had walked until all of them woke up together suddenly. "Splash!" They opened up their eyes and found they were standing in water. They had walked into the small canal alongside the trail! They all laughed, their drowsiness completely gone.

The transplantation project was completed in time. A couple of days later, Qin and the other Rightists noticed some visitors arriving in jeeps. They were officials from the city, escorting foreign friends from East European countries to observe the miracles created by the Chinese people.

In the fields tightly packed with rice stems, the foreigners gasped, and exclaimed in admiration. Qin and her friends watched from a distance. They could hear the visitors' laughter and see the cameras lifted in their hands. "Would they believe the rice stems grow naturally this way?" Qin wondered.

A few days after the visitors left, all the rice stems in the new field died. The new task facing the Rightists on the farm was to remove the dead plants from the field and make them into compost. Qin, like everyone else, did this silently, without complaint. Though many had doubted the viability of the transplantation project from the very beginning, no one dared to voice contrary opinions any more.

Despite all these trials, Qin always volunteered to do the heaviest, dirtiest and least wanted assignments and never asked for a day off. Perhaps the most despised assignment on the farm was the monthly cleaning up of the toilets, ditches dug into the ground and circled by mud walls. Whenever the supervisors called for volunteers to clean the toilets, many women's faces would turn pale and they would try to hide themselves in the crowd, pretending not to be aware of the matter at hand. At this moment, Qin would always step out with a pleasant smile.

When she was ladling human waste into a bucket with a long-handled dipper, the terrible odour almost made her faint. She held her breath and partly closed her eyes to avoid the numerous flies buzzing around. When her sneakers stepped on top of the maggots crawling around the ditches, she felt sick and almost vomited. But she told herself to persist and not to show any sign of disgust.

Qin looked down upon some of her roommates who often grumbled at the coarse meals and heavy work and always tried to find excuses for sick leaves. She regarded these women as the 'real' bourgeois Rightists, who were basically different from herself, a totally 'wronged' one. And she wanted to prove this with her actions!

From 1959 to 1961, China suffered from a serious depression, a direct result of the Communist Party's radical policy.

With the Anti-Rightist Campaign over, Party Chairman Mao decided to usher the nation into "the paradise of communist society" — the first one in the world. The motivation was his ambition to become communist leader of the world following Joseph Stalin's death in nineteen fifty-three.

People's communes were set up in rural areas. Every commune had twenty-some villages, owning their land, farm tools, grain, and animals collectively. There was no more private land and all people worked together in the now public fields. 'Big Public Canteens' were created as one feature of the ideal society. All people stopped cooking at home and ate in free public canteens instead.

With the slogan "to catch up with Britain and America in industrial growth", people, both in urban and rural areas, went all out to produce iron and steel. Rough furnaces were built everywhere. Anything made of iron, including cooking pots, scoops and door knobs, was thrown into the furnaces to make steel. Without necessary technology and basic experience, of course, all the 'steel' turned out to be garbage, despite people's zeal.

This sort of situation did not last long, however. Internally, the failure of the mass production of steel and the neglect of farm land paralyzed the nation's economy. Externally, relations between Russia and China began to deteriorate and the Russians withdrew all their economic and technical aid and started to call in debts.

In many provinces, especially underdeveloped rural areas, millions of people died of hunger during these years, after all edible stuff, including the bark of trees, wild herbs, and fungus, had been consumed.

The situation in Beijing was generally much better than in the rest of the country. Though people could not get enough food, at least no one died of hunger. Each Beijing resident was guaranteed a monthly quota of three ounces of meat and a half pound of fish, as well as a limited amount of vegetables and grain.

People's daily activities were reduced to ensure that they would need less energy. Most political meetings in the evenings were cancelled so as to let people stay at home. Many primary schools had classes only in the morning and let the children stay at home in the afternoons.

On the labour farm, however, the Rightists had no right to reduce their daily heavy work. Hunger, therefore, seemed harder to ignore. At lunch time, they would quickly swallow up the coarse, meagre food in their bowls, and their stomachs would be empty again long before dinner time.

Fragrance, Qin's best friend on the farm, died miserably during this period. Fragrance was a mother of three teenagers. Her husband, a nationalist army officer, had followed Chiang Kai-shek to Tai Wan in 1949 and left his family behind. A primary school teacher, Fragrance 'became' a Rightist simply because she had offended their school principal by a careless remark.

When she saw her skinny and hungry children at home during holidays, the loving mother was heartbroken. Returning to the labour farm, she started to save her daily food from her own mouth. At every meal she would put aside one of the two pieces of steamed bread given to her. When the weather was fine and there was sunshine, she would dry the bread on the roof of their flat. In this way, she was able to take a bag of dried bread to her kids at the next holiday. There was nothing that made her more happy than looking at her kids eating the food joyfully. But Fragrance was badly undernourished and fainted several times as she worked in the rice fields.

One autumn day, as the Rightists were having their lunch break by the fields, Fragrance heard some people talking about the castor oil plants growing along the canals. They had been planted around the resident huts and beside the fields in spring. The people mentioned that the castor beans were soon to be ripe for harvest and would be made into lubricant oil for industry.

"Are these beans edible?" Fragrance looked at the plants with broad palm-like leaves and asked. Ever since spring time, she and many others had learned how to recognize edible wild herbs and mushrooms growing in the fields and woods, and she was enthusiastic about knowing all edible plants in the wild.

"To eat a few beans is OK, but not too much. They are poisonous," said one man, a former agricultural researcher.

Fragrance took his words to heart. That night, when every one was in bed, she pretended to go to the toilet and came to the castor bush planted behind the kitchen house. She looked around and saw no one. Then she reached out her hands and picked a few beans off the stem. She put them into her mouth and tasted carefully. They were rich in fat, something she had not consumed for months. She thought the small shining black and white beans were so sweet and delicious and she really wanted to pick more. But, remembering the beans were poisonous, she restrained the desire.

The next evening, Fragrance said secretly to Qin as she was washing some wild herbs under the tap, "The castor beans are just — just delicious! You can try some. They won't hurt you. I have already tasted them."

Qin thought for a while and smiled at her, "You'd better not pick the beans again. They are planted by the farm, not growing in the wild. If your action is ever spotted by someone, there might be trouble."

Fragrance's face turned red. She simply nodded her head.

A few days later, at midnight, Qin and her roommates were woken up by horrifying moans growing louder and louder in the darkness. They turned on the light bulb and found the noise was from Fragrance. She was crawling on her sheet, twisting her body with painful effort. She was pulling her short hair hard with her fingers, her face greenish-pale, her eyes opened wide with the look of a dead fish.

Qin rushed over by her side and asked hastily, "What's wrong with you, Fragrance? Hold my arm and try to sit up!"

The rest of the women were all alarmed at the sight of Fragrance. They tried clumsily to hold her up and found her limbs were stiff and her hands cold. She was murmuring a few words, "Pain, pain, deadly pain..."

Qin quickly put on her coat and pants while she said to the rest of the women, "I'll go and get the supervisor. You'd better all dress yourselves!"

The supervisor soon came with Qin. He looked at Fragrance and said haltingly, " She looks... like she's been poisoned..."

Qin was struck by his words. Castor beans? She almost spoke the words out loud, but she was sufficiently quick-witted to swallow them. Instead she asked the supervisor, "What shall we do if she is poisoned? Shall we wash out her stomach? Force liquid down her throat?"

"...I am not sure what is really wrong with her. She has to be sent to a hospital for a check up," the supervisor said, and left the room to look for help.

Half-an-hour later, Fragrance was lying on a wheelbarrow being pushed by a few men towards a small town.

The next evening, the supervisor came back from the hospital in town and brought the news of Fragrance's death. Everybody except Qin was shocked to learn the cause for her death. An autopsy was performed on her body and her stomach was found filled with castor beans.

A death notice was sent to Fragrance's home in Beijing. Her children learned that their loving mother chose to remain as the enemy of the people till the last minute of her life, for she died from having stolen and eaten public plants.

Qin's sorrow over the miserable death of Fragrance was soon diluted by a new event on the farm. Another roommate, the young woman turned in by her fiancé, made a mistake at this time which brought her lifelong humiliation.

The pretty young woman was sent to clean the farm's hen house one day and she happened to see a newly laid egg in the straw. Her eyes lit up and, without a second thought, she picked up the fresh egg and put it into her pocket.

Her action, however, was spotted by someone. A public meeting was held that evening and everybody criticized her for this 'shameful behaviour'. In addition to her Rightist status, she was set down in her file as a 'thief'.

As former colleagues from the same institute, she sobbed and complained when she was alone with Qin: "Qin, you understand, I am not a thief. The egg was too attractive and I forgot everything. I just thought how happy my old mother might be when I brought it back home at the next holiday... And now, I am so worried that I can never exonerate myself..."

Of course, Qin understood the horrible shadow of hunger haunting everyone. She had been suffering from dropsy for months, but she made no complaint. The only thing she could do was to follow the other Rightists to search for edible wild herbs in the fields during their breaks. In a short period of time, she had learned to distinguish quite a few wild herbs.

She wiped the tears from her friend's face with her own handkerchief, comforting her. But deep in her heart, she could not help feeling contempt for the young woman's behaviour. "She is weak," Qin thought. "I will never become degenerate in this way even if I die of hunger."

On October 1, the National Day, the farm workers killed a pig in celebration. At dinner time, the canteen was crowded. Everyone waited happily in line to get a bowl of roast pork. As they hadn't tasted meat for a fairly long time, this was certainly a most-wanted delicacy for everyone.

After Qin got her share, she quickly found a seat. She was ready to finish the pork and a full bowl of steamed rice in a few minutes! Before she started to enjoy her dinner, however, she noticed a farm worker sitting beside her. He was gobbling up his share and his bowl was almost empty. Qin's mind turned over quickly for a couple of seconds. She then said to the farm worker with a smile: "I have never been fond of pork. It's too greasy." Her voice was low. "Would you help me finish this?"

"Ah..." The worker was too glad to say anything and Qin quickly poured most of the pork from her bowl into the man's. She did all this inconspicuously.

Qin's effort was effective. She was praised several times at public meetings held by the supervisors. These supervisors were originally farm workers and had their own way of making judgements. They did not seem to understand fully or care too much what kind of political disgrace these men and women had made. They tended to judge these Rightists by their attitude towards labour and life on the farm.

At those moments, Qin's heart always beat faster, though her face remained calm.

"Qin is hard working."

"Qin is not afraid of dirty and heavy assignments."

"Qin never asks for sick leave."

"Qin has no bourgeois haughty manners."

These praises would linger around her ears for days and she would naturally remember again the words of her institute's leader: "...Those who are proved properly remoulded may have their Rightist title removed."

The cost of her health and everything else, she thought, was worthwhile.

Qin wished the day would soon come when she would finally be forgiven by the Party and the people. She imagined how surprised and happy Tian-zhi might be when she returned home as a normal citizen once again. Then he would know he had made the correct decision to stay with the marriage.

Qin was no longer a proud woman, but rather a guilty wife, when she thought about Tian-zhi. The fact that he had not divorced his Rightist wife had already had an impact on his career. Tian-zhi had been appointed as a chief engineer for a big project aided by the Soviet Union. But he was asked to leave that position without any explanation shortly after Qin became a Rightist. Qin had not seen Tian-zhi for more than a year now and was naturally concerned about what his life was like as well as what his plans were, but she was too nervous to get in touch with him, not sure if the wound in his heart was healed yet.

However, it was at this time that Laolao brought Qin's daughter back to her. Qin felt it extremely hard to present her daughter to Tian-zhi when their relationship was still unstable.

"He has already made a sacrifice. Would he be willing to make another by accepting the little girl into the family?" She didn't know. "If not, could I keep her on the farm? No. When I have to work more than twelve hours a day in the fields, who is going to take care of the little thing? And who knows how long the labour punishment is going to last? Perhaps the best way is to find a couple to adopt her."

But Laolao was strongly against the idea of adoption. She lingered on the farm for a few months. Because the supervisors had a good impression of Qin, they agreed to let Laolao and Qin's daughter stay for a temporary period. They made space in a small tool room and laid a bed there for the two. In return for their kindness, Laolao often found time to help as a volunteer in the kitchen, and to clean the public area.

Gradually, Laolao made the little girl understand that the slim woman was her mother, and Lin was only her aunt.

Laolao and Qin had finally arrived at a decision to send the girl to a kindergarten in Beijing. There were numerous kindergartens in the big city, but finding one for Qin's daughter was a tough task, since there was a limited number receiving kids to stay overnight and they all required reference letters from the parents' employers.

Qin got a letter from her institute leader, but she would be too embarrassed to present this sort of letter to anyone. The letter went like this:

"To whom it may concern:

This letter is to confirm that Rightist Qin, an employee of our institute, needs to find a kindergarten for her daughter..."

The title put in front of her name was to remind everyone of her present status, something she would rather die than acknowledge. What made the letter more unacceptable was the fact that, during that period, no kindergarten would have been willing to admit the child of a Rightist!

Fortunately, a woman labouring on the same farm learned about the dilemma Qin was in and introduced her to a small kindergarten run by a few housewives who, fortunately, did not insist on reference letters.

*　　*　　*

ONE AFTERNOON, LAOLAO AND I WERE CARRIED BY tricycle to the kindergarten which was situated in a narrow lane in Beijing's busy shopping centre.

As the women there took my luggage and asked me to say "Bye" to Laolao, I suddenly sensed that I was going to be separated from her and to have to stay in this strange place by myself! I was horrified and burst out crying as I reached my arms towards her. Laolao comforted me and said she was going to buy an ice cream for me and would return soon! She knew I was fascinated by the first-time-taste of ice cream during the day. I certainly liked the idea of having an ice cream once again. But I found Laolao's wrinkled eyes moist with tears as she tried to smile at me. The fear in my heart became deeper. I held her legs and would not let her go, crying even louder. The women came up together and grasped me from Laolao and gestured for her to leave quickly. Laolao rubbed her eyes and walked away. At the yard entrance she turned around and waved to me, then she disappeared. I cried miserably for a long time until I no longer had any strength. I knew Laolao would never again return to me.

When the first Saturday came, all kids were supposed to go home and spend Sunday with their parents.

I was playing with toy blocks alone in a big room. This was a small kindergarten composed of only two flats in a narrow square courtyard. All the kids were taken home one by one by their parents. Two women were sitting by the door knitting something with their hands and waiting for someone to come and get the last kid, me. It was late in the evening. Still, no one came to get me. The women became impatient. They were anxious to go home, too. I saw them stretching their necks every once in a while to check the street outside of the yard entrance.

My mind was concentrating on my toys when I heard one of the women shouting out happily: "Peace! Your father is coming to take you home!"

I raised up my head, and found it already dark outside. A tall man standing by the door in a black fur hat and a dark grey long coat was smiling at me. He came over and reached out his arms: "Peace, come home with Dad now."

I withdrew a little bit in natural fear of a stranger.

"Isn't this your Dad?" one of the two women questioned me.

I stared at him. He smiled kindly at me and his eyes behind the thick glasses were nice and trustworthy. Laolao had never returned since she left that day, and I knew she wouldn't come back to me any more. "This 'Dad' looks nice," I thought, and nodded, "Yes, he is."

He held me up clumsily in his arms. I felt warm against his broad chest and did not protest or cry. He carried me towards the bus stop by the busy street and tried to get me to talk on the way. I was serious and silent all the time, wondering where he was going to take me.

As we passed a candy store beaming with bright colourful lights, he stopped at the door and looked at me gently: "Call me Dad, and I will buy some honey preserved oranges for you... OK?"

He waited for my answer, a shy smile on a face full of expectation.

I gazed at the warm vapour coming out of his mouth in the cold night air.

Maybe I did not call him 'Dad' that night. I can no longer remember this detail for sure. But I have never forgotten his words that night in a busy Beijing street, nor the honey preserved oranges he bought for me. The way he talked to me, with a little embarrassment but with sincerity and loving care in his eyes and voice, is as fresh today as it was decades ago.

This was the first time I met Tian-zhi, my father. His sincerity somehow instilled a stream of warmth in my heart and I did think he was my father from that moment on.

As I learned later, before Laolao returned to her hometown, she found Tian-zhi and told him about my situation, hoping he would reach out to help. Tian-zhi agreed without hesitation. He felt, as he was still Qin's husband, he should be responsible for the innocent little girl, so he had come the following Saturday.

Tian-zhi found that the accommodation in the small kindergarten was not ideal, and later sent me, in the name of his own daughter, to a first-class one. My new kindergarten was originally the home of a chief eunuch who served the Empress Dowager in court and built his own home like a palace. After the Liberation, his home had been confiscated and turned into a kindergarten. I stayed at this school until I went to grade school, three years later.

6

A Boarding School and
the Clouds Overhead

"YU XIN" (IN CHINESE IT MEANS "TO TRAIN A NEW generation") Primary School was one of the few very good primary schools among five hundred in Beijing in the early nineteen sixties.

First of all, it was a boarding school with dormitory buildings, canteens, neatly trimmed gardens and a spacious auditorium. All pupils — around six hundred — lived in the school on weekdays and stayed at home on Sundays. Secondly, this school had well qualified teaching staff and strictly planned courses, so its graduates could have a better chance of passing entrance exams to first class high schools. Its higher costs prevented many low income parents from sending their children here, so the majority of the pupils were children of higher-ranking government officials.

I entered Yu Xin in 1962, shortly before my seventh birthday. I was the shortest one among the thirty-six kids in my class and always sat in the first row. In a departure from the provision in ordinary schools, in addition to our Chinese teachers, arithmetic teachers, painting, musical, and physical education teachers, each class also had a couple of 'life teachers', who looked after our daily lives.

Regulations at the school were strict. We got up at six in the morning as the bell tolled and then lined up in the sportsground to do our morning exercises before breakfast. We had four classes in the morning, and two in

the afternoon. At nine in the evening, we went to bed. The campus was circled with iron fences and we seldom had a chance to see the outside world
during the week. Except at the times when we were led to a cinema half a
mile away, about once every other week, no one was allowed to step outside the iron gate.

I lived with four other girls in one room in the girls' building. Our
clothes were taken to the school laundry once a week, where a few women
did the washing with their hands. To train them, the school required all
girls to start washing their own socks and handkerchiefs at grade four, and
encouraged them to wash their own underwear at grade five. But there
were no such requirements for boys of the same grades. However, by grade
six, the graduating year, all pupils, both male and female, had to wash their
own clothes.

I felt puzzled as to why girls should start their own washing earlier than
the boys, and I asked the laundry women. They looked at me with their
eyes open wide, their expressions telling me how silly my question must be.
"Why..." they replied with sarcastic voices, "don't you see that you girls
sooner or later will get married? If you don't learn washing, how can you
wait on your husbands and children in the future?"

This was an idea which I had never heard from our 'life teachers'. Most
of our 'life teachers' were caring and nice women, except Zhu, a young
woman about twenty-five years old. She was harsh and strict to the kids,
and full of shrewd and tricky methods.

In the evening after supper, we had a reading class during which we were
allowed to read cartoons and novels. The forty-five minute class was very
precious to us since we all wanted to read as much as we could during this
short period. Quite aware of our anxieties, Zhu always took advantage of
this to indulge her own ego.

She usually sat in a chair on the platform, with the books spread on the
desk in front of her, declaring that only those who sat most straight in their
chairs would be allowed to read. We all tried to sit as standardly as we
could, with our hands behind our backs, squaring our shoulders and staring
forward, in the hope of being the first one to be picked by Zhu to come to
the desk and choose a book.

But she would usually wait about a minute before she called a kid. She
would observe seriously one kid after another, and shake her permed short

hair slightly at intervals, as if she was really having difficulty in finding a qualified kid. The waiting period seemed to be unbearably long. Usually by the time the last kid got his book, fifteen or twenty minutes would have passed.

Sometimes if one pupil was absent, she would refuse to begin our reading class. She would send one of us to look for the absent pupil while she told the rest of us that if the absent one did not come within five minutes, this evening's reading class would be cancelled. You could imagine what an ordeal we experienced during these five minutes, as Zhu glanced at her wrist watch and announced coldly: "One minute has passed! ...Two minutes have passed! ...Three..." At each report delivered in her threatening voice, we gasped and watched the door in desperation.

No one liked Zhu, but we were afraid of showing this, as she often reprimanded those disobeying her. Everybody had to raise his or her hand to get permission to talk in class, and she would draw a cross with a piece of chalk on the lips of anyone forgetting to raise a hand first. She would seize the ear of a disobeying kid and pull the child around in the classroom until he or she was in tears, or she would punch a stubborn boy's back against the wall several times to make him yield.

I must have been a mischievous one when young. One evening in my third year at the school, I directed a prank in my dormitory. We knew Zhu would inspect all the dormitories after the 'bedtime ring' sounded, and she would eavesdrop outside of each door and rush in to punish those who were still talking.

The girls in my dormitory had decided to teach her a lesson. At nine o'clock, the bell rang. I quickly arranged the five girls into the following scene. One girl was lying in bed with a white sheet covering her whole body, pretending to be dead. Two others, dressed like Buddhist monks with printed sheets around their chests as long robes, were kneeling beside the 'corpse' and mumbling something as if praying for the dead. I and another girl were standing against the wall by the door, with our faces buried in the hoods of cotton-padded overcoats. In this way, I imagined we must look like the Ku Klux Klan we saw in cartoons depicting the evil white Americans who persecuted poor black people. In the minds of nine-year-olds, corpses, Buddhist monks, and the Ku Klux Klan were all terrifying subjects which we hoped might shock and frighten Zhu.

However, our naive revenge ended quite unexpectedly in failure. Zhu had noticed the unusual noise in our room and eavesdropped outside the door for quite a few minutes. She suddenly kicked the door wide open and stepped in. It was not Zhu, but us, who were actually shocked and we stopped our performance at once.

Zhu lifted the sheet abruptly off the 'corpse', harshly removed the hoods from the Ku Klux Klan and sternly announced: "Since you do not want to sleep, go outside now!"

The five of us were put to stand in a line along the corridor, barefooted and clad only in our underwear. We were not allowed to move or make any sound. Zhu stayed in our room with the door open and came out to inspect us once in a while to see if somebody was not standing straight. Hours passed and we felt sleepy and tired in the cold corridor. We tried to lean against the wall or squat on the ground but were frightened back to our old position when Zhu rushed out. At that point, we were sorry for our prank.

After this event, the girls became quite disciplined, but the boys were not tamed by her artifice. One evening before the reading class started, the boys were excited and alert, not sitting in their chairs but moving about in the classroom anxiously. The bell rang and Zhu entered the classroom with the usual serious look on her face. Before she had time to shout at the boys running around, several of them sprang at her with brooms in their hands. Some quickly locked the door lest she should escape. Some knocked at their desks and booed loudly to boost the morale of her attackers, while the girls watched with great surprise. Zhu fought back bravely, her hair getting messed up and the buttons on her coat being torn off. A few minutes later she managed to unlock the door and run out.

Zhu disappeared for a few days. One day when all of us had almost forgotten what had happened, she returned to our evening class and bad farewell to us. She was going to transfer to another school, she said, and was going to tell us a piece of news before her departure. According to Zhu, the school principal had been considering awarding our class the honour of being a 'best disciplined collective' as a result of Zhu's effective supervising. But the 'inhumane incident' took place and the decision was naturally cancelled. "Now you see the cost of your prank?" She ended her speech with an ironical smile.

We did not feel sorry for Zhu's leaving, but we all felt it a great pity that we narrowly missed the chance of becoming an honourable 'best disciplined collective'.

"The boys were certainly wrong. They were responsible for losing our class honour. What a pity!" We blamed each other while no one ever thought about whether Zhu's words were true or not.

During my years at the school, my arithmetic marks were just so-so, while my Chinese was always the best in the class, my compositions often being put on display on the school wall's columns. In my third year, I was selected as the school's broadcast announcer. Together with a few other kids, under the leadership of an art teacher, we ran a literature program on the wireless.

My real interest, however, was in acting. At grade three, I had the idea of creating and performing some plays. I talked to seven other pupils in my class and set up a 'Mini Drama Group'. At first, our activities were secret. In the afternoons, when other kids were playing on the sportsground, we hid in my dormitory to rehearse the mini dramas created by my imagination.

I directed our plays without any scripts. The scenes and plots were all in my mind. Therefore the actors' lines and actions were different each time we rehearsed. That didn't cause much confusion, however, as I was always the hero or heroine in the plays.

Our plays reflected the propaganda and political education children received at that time. One of the plays was about how the Viet Nam people fought against the American invaders. In 1965, America had seriously involved itself in the Viet Nam war. Besides anti-American and support-Viet Nam movies and performances in theatres, we learned from cartoons, pop songs and dances about the crimes the Americans had committed in Viet Nam and about ways to kill the Americans efficiently. Our play, based on these clues, described how the Viet people lured the drunken American soldiers to a trap filled with sharply pointed bamboos.

Another play, "The Monkey King", was based on a Chinese classical novel. Party Chairman Mao wrote a poem in 1962 praising the Monkey King's unyielding courage in fighting with various demons in the world. This poem was actually a metaphor for the new conflicts between China and the East European Bloc, headed by the Soviet Union. China was largely isolated from the outside world in the 1960s because of its old hostility to the West, headed by the Americans, and also because of the new split in the communist world. Mao's poem expressed his determination to lead the Chinese people on an independent path through the long, arduous journey to the ideal communist society. Impressed by the colourful and fantastic movie about the Monkey King, I tried my best in our rehearsal to dress up myself with sheets, pillow cases, and towels, to personify the hero.

Our play about Lei Feng was definitely influenced by the nationwide propaganda at that time. Lei Feng was a young soldier who liked to read Chairman Mao's works and often volunteered his own time and money to help the needy. After he died in an accident in 1962, Chairman Mao gave instructions that the whole nation should learn from him. For a while, many people tried to act selflessly and were eager to help others. Children of my age were encouraged to do the same. If I found a coin or a pen on the road, I would immediately hand it in to the nearest police station, or to the teachers' office if I had found it on campus. If I was sitting on a bus while a senior citizen had no seat, I would quickly give my seat to the senior. If I saw someone pulling a heavy cart on the street, I would come over to help. I did these things happily, believing I was a Lei-Feng-style good child. Since Lei Feng was also praised for his hard work and thrifty life style, we all regarded dressing in old, worn-out clothes as an honourable thing.

The group's activity was discovered by the teacher who taught us Chinese. He was happy that we children could create so many mini plays and asked us to perform in our classroom first before it was arranged for us to do it in the school's auditorium.

But an unexpected event occurred which spoilt the teacher's plan. On the day of our performance in the classroom, I led my friends to start with "The Story of Lei Feng", followed by "The Monkey King", and then, "The Viet People Kill the Americans." It all went on well until shortly after the last play began.

Rainbow, my best friend, who acted the part of a Viet girl trying to lure the American soldiers out of their camp into the jungle with a bottle of liquor, was reciting her lines in front of the classroom. I and the rest of the actors and actresses were standing by the wall and waiting for our turn, while the other pupils and the teacher were watching attentively in their seats. Suddenly, a stout boy sprang up from his seat and rushed towards Rainbow. He pushed her harshly down to the floor and rode on top of her, while shouting aloud to the boys sitting in their seats, "Come on! Let's rape the Viet girl!"

Three more boys rushed over and joined the stout boy's attack. They laughed and tried to pull off Rainbow's pants, while she struggled hard to protect herself. Lying on the floor, Rainbow used her hands to grasp her belt desperately and her legs kicked the air vehemently. The boys' attempt was thwarted by her kicking but they kept shouting, "Rape her! Rape her!"

I was horrified by the scene and stood against the wall, seized with terror. Our teacher, who had been sitting at the back of the classroom, didn't understand at first what had happened and thought the fighting was part of our play. But it didn't take long for him to figure out the oddness and quickly come over. He found Rainbow lying on the floor, all tears, and understood everything at once. He pushed the boys back and helped up Rainbow. He then pushed the stout boy against the wall and questioned him angrily, "Where did you learn that dirty word and shameful action?"

The boy looked at the teacher boldly and stated: "I am only playing the role of the American soldiers! I got this idea from a book I read in our evening class. It tells how they raped Viet women!"

The teacher frowned. "Remember, never do this again!" he said simply, letting the boy return to his seat.

Our mood was totally destroyed. I went back to my seat and didn't want to perform any more. I knew what book the stout boy was talking about. I had read the book, *Letters From the South*, too. There was detailed depiction in the book of the various crimes the Americans were committing in Viet Nam. There were descriptions of Americans stripping off women's clothes, and so on. The first time I met the word "rape" in the book, I had asked our life teacher what it meant. She curled her lips and replied, "A bad word. Don't learn it!"

Her refusal to tell me aroused my curiosity. On Sunday when I returned home, I asked my mother the same question.

My mother pondered for a few seconds and replied, "This is a word used to describe women being bullied by bad men."

"How do they 'bully' women?" I was still confused.

"Well," my mother hesitated, "by saying dirty words and... beating them up. When you are older, I will let you know more."

That day, the boys' effort to pull off Rainbow's pants further explained the confusion in my ten-year-old mind in a horrible way.

＊　　＊　　＊

I WASN'T A HAPPY CHILD MOST OF THE TIME, ESPECIALLY when I had to go home on weekends.

By the time I started to go to grade school, my mother, Qin, had returned to Beijing and resumed her work in the educational institute. (After labouring on the farm for three years, most Rightists, except a few very stubborn ones, had been allowed to return to their previous jobs.)

She had three children now. As kids might interfere with her work, she sent me to Yu Xin School, and my brother and sister to boarding kindergartens. The whole family could get together only on Sundays.

My mother was the centre of the family, because she took care of everything. My father, Tian-zhi, seemed to be studying all the time and paid little attention to the kids. Nainai, Tian-zhi's mother, a silent woman in her sixties, stayed inside her own room all the time and came out for meals and washroom only.

On Sundays, my mother always tried to arrange a happy tour for the family. Perhaps she felt that the children had been closed in their school and kindergarten for a whole week and they needed to go out. My father, though unwilling to put down his books, was always dragged to join us. He brought back a camera from Russia and my mother asked him to take snapshots for us each time we went to the palace parks, historical museums and the various famous scenic spots in Beijing.

My mother was active in sports, too. She was a good table tennis player. On some Sundays, she would take the kids with her to watch her playing. My father would never come with us to these events.

Once, my mother won the second place in a district competition and she decided to celebrate it with us kids. She took us to a small restaurant in the centre of the shopping area and we had a few typical Beijing snacks: pea flour cakes, meat balls, and shrimps wrapped inside thin pastry and steamed in oil and water on the pan, jellied hot tofu soaked in thick soup made from vegetables, and bean sauce.

After the meal, she took us to the largest store on this street. Entering the store, I found it was composed of about one hundred small stores selling different products at different corners. My mother told me that these small stores in this area were originally owned by different private capitalists. After the Liberation, the stores were gradually nationalized and they were combined into one large state-owned store. After her explanation, I came to understand why this large store looked so strange in shape: separate small or large sized stores, each with its own roof, but without doors and front walls, all spread around many tortuous narrow alleys.

We came to a counter selling candies. There was only one shop assistant, an old bald-headed man, standing behind the counter. I was immediately drawn by the bright-red-coloured sugarcoated haws linked by two-foot-long sticks. My mother bought one stick and said to me, "Share it with your brother and sister. You cannot finish the whole thing on your own."

I felt excited as I accepted the long haw stick the old man passed to me. Suddenly, I remembered something and asked him, "Where is the capitalist now? I mean, the one who owned this candy store before?"

The old man seemed unhappy to hear my question. He murmured in a low voice: "Who is a capitalist? This was my store before. But I am a state employee now."

My mother thought that my question had offended the old man and blamed me for being talkative. "You will make a lot less trouble if you learn to shut your mouth!"

When I was in grade two, I noticed that the relationship between my parents had changed and there were now constant disputes between them. The kids were not allowed to go into their room at those moments. But outside of the door, I could hear my mother's angry voice. Most of the time she was complaining about Nainai, our grandmother.

I had long felt the tension between my mother and Nainai. From my observation, Nainai was an old-style rural woman and expected her daughter-in-law, my mother, to respect and obey her unconditionally. She felt that an educated and economically independent daughter-in-law like my mother was too difficult to be controlled. Nainai avoided fighting with my mother openly, but she had her own way of expressing her resentment.

One Sunday afternoon, when we came home all tired after spending a whole day in a park, Nainai brought out some dirty clothes and soaked them in cold water. She did this silently, without saying anything or looking at anyone. My mother understood that Nainai was forcing her to wash the clothes at once. There was no washing machine in the household in the 1960s and all laundry had to be done by hand. Though my mother was tired, she could not leave the wet clothes for the next day.

One Saturday evening, my parents were going out. They explained to me that they were going to a meeting where children could not go. I agreed to stay at home with my brother and sister. But Nainai came to us after they were gone and commented ironically: "Do you know where they have gone? To a meeting? Nonsense! They went to an opera!" Looking at our confused faces, she grumbled to herself, "She is simply not a woman!"

Once, through the closed door, my mother's angry voice resounded: "This is the new society, not the old feudal society! I won't tolerate her bullying any more! Why don't you ever talk to her about this? I understand you are the filial son of a widowed mother, but you have to be fair! She wants to occupy you totally and she is jealous of all other women! Could you understand my grief a little bit? Are you listening?" Her voice was soaring. My father remained dumb the whole time.

When the door was finally open, I saw my mother packing up her suitcase with a stern face, while my father sat in his chair reading a book. Her movements were not fast, as if she was expecting my father to plead with her to stay. But until she put her milk-coloured gauze kerchief around her neck and was ready to go, my father's eyes stayed stubbornly fixed on the book on his knee and not even a single glance was thrown in her direction. Obviously irritated by his icy manner, my mother lifted her suitcase abruptly in one hand, and grasped my hand in the other.

"Let's go!" She tried to sound calm, but the coldness in her voice and her trembling hand made my heart sink. I followed her downstairs, leaving my brother and sister behind crying aloud.

Each time my mother would end her dispute with my father by leaving home with me and staying in her dormitory in the institute for months. The longest time lasted about a year. On Sundays during these periods, I would come to stay in her dormitory instead of going back home.

During the time when I had to spend Sundays with my mother in her institute, I felt extremely lonely, with no kids there to play with me and no one talk to me. As all married couples could get a residence from the government, those who stayed in the institute dormitories were singles only. My mother shared a room with another woman who was divorced. That woman was suffering from arthritis and often groaned with pain. My mother would always ask me to massage her legs at those moments. "Peace, go over to help Auntie Lan!" she would say. And I would stand by the groaning woman's bed and hit her legs with my fists for a long long time.

Sometimes, my mother would let me practice calligraphy with a brush pen by the desk in her room, while she would lean against the blanket in her bed, reading a book.

She seldom talked about my father or the younger kids. When she did mention them, I often felt very uneasy. "Is your father a nice person?" she once asked me, putting down her book and looking at the ceiling.

I thought for a few seconds but failed to fish an appropriate answer from my tangled mind. "I... I don't know."

One Sunday morning, she asked me to go home and spend the day with the rest of the family. "You can come back after supper," she said.

I felt nervous as I knocked at the door. My father opened the door. I saw the same kind-hearted smile but I felt the distance between us, though it was only a few months since I had seen him. He asked about my life at school, but was careful not to mention my mother. His honest eyes behind the glasses looked tired and depressed.

The home was very different from the days when my mother had been there. It had lost its sweet and warm atmosphere and seemed dull and grey. My little brother's and sister's clothes were dirty and their hair was tangled in a mess. They must have become used to the status quo at home, I thought, for they were attentively playing with toys on the floor. The white silk flowers in the vase, the oil paintings hanging on the wall and the lamp shade were covered with dust. The books in my mother's bookcase looked as neat as before, but those in my father's were carelessly laid.

At lunch time, Nainai made some food typical of her hometown: corn porridge, pancakes made with small pieces of green onions and deep fried pork, and stewed bean noodles with green cabbage. With an apron around her waist, she happily served everyone at table and washed the dishes afterwards. She talked pleasantly to my father and the younger kids. She was acting as the centre of the family now. I was surprised that Nainai was eager to do household chores and was not dumb any more — quite a different person from the one she had been before.

My father finished his meal quickly and went back to his reading again. My heart was heavy at being in the home without my mother. Every minute seemed to be like an hour. I left early, despite my father's efforts to convince me to stay for supper.

Back at my mother's dormitory, she asked me all details about home, including every word my father had said. She then stared through the window with a pensive look.

I didn't understand why my mother only took me with her and always left my brother and sister with my father at home. I tried to explain to myself that I might be her favourite child. This seemed to be the only reason. However, she did not talk much to me when we were together, and I could feel she was actually very disappointed with me. She would sometimes watch me for a few seconds and then say in a depressed tone: "Well... How could you become so plain looking? When you were born, you were a beautiful little girl. But look at you now! You are short and skinny. Your nose is flat and your complexion is not as fair as mine..."

Always at this moment, I would lower my head with a strong sense of inferiority and not know what to say. But I still loved and relied on her as much as ever, because she was my mother. I tried to study harder at school and get good marks to make her happy and proud of me. But, out of class, I often felt miserable and sad. When my classmates were playing cheerfully on the sportsground, I preferred sitting with Rainbow by a stone table in a quiet corner in the well shaded garden, appreciating the smells and shapes of the flowers and leaves on the trees, and observing ants busying themselves with human-like activities.

Rainbow's mother, a high-ranking government official, divorced her father after he became a Rightist. Rainbow told me that her father used to be the manager of a large plant, but he was presently staying somewhere outside of Beijing. She didn't know where he was or what he was doing, for her mother refused to say anything about him. Her mother had already re-married, her new husband being a young factory worker.

Most other kids in the school would go home on Saturday afternoons and return to school on early Monday mornings. But Rainbow and I were among the few students, five or six in number, who always returned to school on Sunday evenings. I didn't know what obtained in Rainbow's case, but my mother said she didn't want me to be squeezed in buses during rush hours on Monday mornings.

On those Sunday nights, we could always stay up late chatting because the teachers would not return to school until the next morning and no one would come to stop us. One Sunday night, as Rainbow and I were in our beds, she suddenly raised her upper body out of her quilt and reached towards me. Her eyes were shining in the moonlight and she said excitedly, "Peace, I saw my father today!"

"Where did you see him?" I asked her curiously.

"In a shopping centre near my home. I was buying a pencil when I saw a man walking towards me. He reached out his hand and called me 'Rainbow'. He was with me for about an hour in the shopping centre. He asked me about my school life and what I liked to eat." Rainbow reached her hand into the bag hanging from her bed head and brought out a roll of dried haw jelly. She put it into my hand and continued, saying: "He bought me a whole bunch of this after I told him I liked it. I didn't dare to tell my mother after I returned home. Do you think I should let her know, or not, Peace?"

I thought for a while and replied: "I don't know either... But, Rainbow, have you ever seen your father before? No? But then, how did you know that man was your father?" I wondered.

"Well, I don't know." Rainbow looked at the window from which the moonlight was shedding onto our blankets. "I just feel he is very different from my step-father."

"Oh, Peace!" Rainbow suddenly asked me. "Do you think your mother is going to find a step-father for you as well?"

"...I don't know." My mood changed. It was always sad to think about the future of my mother and me.

✳   ✳   ✳

MANY A NIGHT, WHEN THE OTHER GIRLS IN MY DORMITORY were fast asleep, I could not close my eyes. My bed was by the window. I would gaze at the moon, the stars, and the willow trees waving in the breeze outside. My mind floated among the scenes I had touched upon in books and in reality: the lonely beautiful woman living on the moon for thousands of years in the old legend, the palace-like underground tomb of the emperor buried five hundred years ago in the suburb of Beijing...

When my thoughts fell upon death I felt frightened. I imagined the miserable situation my mother or I would find ourselves in if one of us died. It would be terribly lonely to live in the world without Mother. Where could I go then? If I died, Mother might feel very sad and cry every day. She might regret having blamed me all the time. My nose quivered and I began to weep. "So, it might be better that I die first," I resolved.

*　　*　　*

EVER SINCE QIN'S RETURN TO BEIJING FROM THE FARM, she had felt that the relationship between Tian-zhi and herself was an unequal one. He stayed in the marriage out of sympathy, but Qin's political status reminded him all the time that he must keep his distance from her. It had reached the point where there was no communication and understanding between them. The warm, cordial and trustful intimacy between the couple was gone forever. At home, she was no more than a nanny and housekeeper. Tian-zhi wouldn't say anything to her about state affairs, his work, or hers. Their conversation was strictly limited to food and clothing, if ever she mentioned those. She was greatly disappointed at her new role in the family. This was not what had motivated her to endure the hard years on the farm!

At first, Qin made every effort to warm up their relationship. She took care of Tian-zhi in every possible way. She learned to cook the food he liked, made him clean and neat, and never let him touch any housework. Still, Tian-zhi's attitude remained the same. Qin's mind was tormented like this for years and she found such a relationship unbearable. She wanted to give voice to her grievance, but the political inequality between the couple had deprived her of the right and she simply could not complain about anything to Tian-zhi!

Gradually, she convinced herself that the whole problem actually originated with Tian-zhi's mother, Nainai.

Qin knew that Nainai had not been in favour of Tian-zhi's decision to marry her at the very beginning. Nainai had urged Tian-zhi to give up Qin, a "devalued" woman who had married before and had a daughter! "What a shame! Aren't you afraid of being laughed at by people!" Nainai was quoted as saying to Tian-zhi. Qin learned this from a neighbour, an old lady who enjoyed telling Qin everything Nainai told her. But Tian-zhi had ignored the traditional values and convinced Nainai to accept Qin into the family.

A year after their marriage, Nainai learned from the gossip of the neighbours that Qin had become a Rightist. At first, the word 'Rightist' puzzled Nainai, an illiterate who never cared about political affairs. When Qin was sent to the labour farm, however, Nainai figured out immediately that the word 'Rightist' must be a shameful title and that Qin must have done something bad, or she would not have been punished this way by the government. Once again she grumbled to Tian-zhi about having married such a woman and brought endless trouble to the family: "What's the point of keeping her any more? You have already had a son, anyway!"

Qin would never forget the insult Nainai threw at her one summer night. It was on a holiday, four months after Qin had been sent to the labour farm. After the all-out effort of finishing the wheat harvest, the Rightists on the farm were given one day off.

That evening, Qin finished her field work at eight o'clock. She cleaned off the mud on her body in a hurry and set out for the long-distance bus stop, three miles away. When she reached there, she found a few hundred people already waiting at the stop, all Rightists from the farm. It was the first time they had got a day off since coming to the farm and everybody wanted to go home immediately. But there was only one bus to Beijing every thirty minutes. The first bus took more than fifty people, packed like sardines inside the small old-style vehicle. Qin squeezed hard and was lucky enough to get on the next bus, half-an-hour later. When the bus arrived in Beijing, it was already close to midnight. Qin got off the bus and shot like an arrow towards the last city bus leaving that night in the direction of Tian-zhi's home.

One hour later, Qin stood outside of the apartment on the third floor and knocked at the door. She knocked and knocked, but no one came to answer the door. She wondered whether Tian-zhi had gone on business to another city, as he often did, but thought that at least Nainai should be at home. She called Nainai and knocked again for ten minutes. "It's Qin. I am back. Please open the door for me!" She said repeatedly. Her voice was not loud, but the neighbours on the same floor, upstairs, and downstairs, were all woken up by her in the middle of the night. They stretched out their heads and watched Qin in silence. Qin felt embarrassed under their gaze. "Tomorrow, everybody in the building is going to know that I came back from the labour farm and was not allowed to get into my own home!" She stopped knocking, staring at the dim light bulb hanging on the ceiling in the corridor.

At this moment, the old lady living next door came out. She had observed that Qin was forced to leave the home as a pregnant woman, and was sympathetic to her situation. She knocked at the door and called Nainai. "I am your neighbour! Your daughter-in-law is back! Please open the door!"

This time, the door opened quickly. Nainai stood inside the apartment, no surprise on her calm face. When the neighbour left, Nainai said coldly to Qin, "Aren't you on the farm? Why have you come back?"

"I have a day off and I am back to see my son," Qin forced herself to smile.

But Nainai wouldn't let her in easily. "Your son is in the nursery on the western suburbs, not in my home." Her voice was not high, but Qin felt the stab of the last two words.

"Yes, I know. But there are no more buses running at this hour. I need to spend the night at home." She repressed her anger and walked towards the bedroom.

Nainai's voice followed Qin's back. "I have locked up that room. Tian-zhi is on business in South China."

Qin turned around and forced herself to speak calmly, "I am not divorced from Tian-zhi yet. This is still my room. Please give me the key!"

Nainai was stunned at Qin's firm attitude. Without any more argument, she passed the key to Qin.

Qin walked into her room and locked the door from inside. She threw herself into bed weakly. Her tears soon soaked the pillow.

*　　*　　*

TIAN-ZHI ALWAYS TOOK HIS MOTHER'S SIDE IN CONFLICTS between Qin and Nainai. He had his reasons. Stories about Nainai's sacrificial jump off the cliff in order to have a son, her hard life with an abusive husband, her painful efforts to raise three kids on her own, threw a shadow over Tian-zhi's childhood life. When he came back from Russia, he brought Nainai out of the small mud house on the bank of the Yellow River to Beijing and made up his mind to compensate her sorrow and suffering with as much as a pious son could provide. He had expected Qin to be obedient to his mother just as he always had been. That was why he became truly unhappy when he noticed Qin's unyielding attitude to Nainai.

When Qin left home with Peace, she meant to give a lesson to Tian-zhi. She was not a traditional housewife and submissive servant to his old fashioned mother! She hoped he would be oppressed by the heavy housework she left behind and therefore realize her sorrow and sacrifice over all these years.

However, Tian-zhi didn't plead with her to come back as she had expected. To him, her headstrong behaviour was annoying and unforgivable. They had reached a deadlock. Qin was fully aware of the situation jeopardizing her marriage. Of course she was afraid to lose Tian-zhi and she would do anything to save their relationship. But what?

Upon returning from the farm, Qin was told that she could live a normal life as an ordinary citizen, except that her Rightist status would still remain on her file for future reference. Though disappointed that her Rightist title was not removed, she was happy that at least she was able to do her research work again. She had determined to re-establish her reputation and recover her past honour. She planned to try again to win trust from the Party and become a Party member. She knew very well that only by being accepted as a Party member could her innocence be finally proved and a prominent future become possible.

Now she realized, when alone in her dormitory room, that her Rightist status, not Nainai, might be the major factor in her losing Tian-zhi's favour. "If I become a Party member, he will no longer feel regret at having stayed with the marriage," Qin concluded.

To her dismay, however, the Party leader of her institute told her that there was little chance of her application being considered, as her Rightist status still remained on her file — a requirement of the government. Since the definition of a Rightist was "anti-Communist Party and anti-socialist"as well as "enemy of the people", even a fool could see that there was an insurmountable barrier between being a Rightist and being a Party member.

Qin's face turned pale as she learned this. Her eyes were expressionless and her voice was full of disappointment as she murmured: "So, there is no political future for me now..."

The Party leader might have been touched by Qin's desperate expression. He thought for a while and comforted her. "Don't think that way! There may be one day when Chairman Mao and the Central Party Committee see fit to remove the Rightist status from some of you. If you keep on being active and close to the Party, you may have a good chance of being among the first to get rid of the title, when the day comes..."

His words undoubtedly served as motivation for the hopeless woman. Qin set herself the goal of trying to be among the first ones to get rid of the disgusting title hanging over her head. But how should she be active and close to the Party? she asked herself. Of course she would never again be silly enough to answer the Party's call to criticize its work. She had learned enough from that! Qin figured out that the Party was represented by the leader in her institute and it would not be wrong to have a good relationship with him — all the time.

*　　*　　*

DURING THE SUMMER HOLIDAYS WHEN THE SCHOOL WAS closed, I stayed in my mother's institute every day and night. Gradually, I became familiar with Sunshine, the Party leader in the institute.

The man in his mid-forties had a pair of slender eyes which often gleamed with a tricky light. Below his tidily combed grey hair was a well nourished pink face. He was always dressed neatly in dark wool suit and shining leather shoes. Though he was gentle with me, his smile had a slick and mysterious aspect and I often felt strangely uncomfortable looking at his face.

When my mother and I were having our meals in the institute's canteen, Sunshine liked to join our table with his dish and, while eating, always made my mother laugh heartily with his humour. At those moments, I would feel uneasy, for I noticed my mother's frequent laughter was drawing other people's attention to our table.

Sunshine sometimes came to our room to see if we were in need of his help and he would talk with my mother in a low voice. From some of their words, I could see they were talking about my father and it sounded as if Sunshine was trying, on behalf of the Party, to solve my mother's family problem. My mother's attitude towards him was respectful and trustful. She regarded Sunshine as the embodiment of the Communist Party, which was her source of power and support.

One Sunday evening, Sunshine invited my mother and me to have dinner in his home. His wife, a small woman with hair braided into two hip-long pigtails, made noodles, fried black bean paste, and finely chopped cucumber salad for us. I watched silently as the small woman moved around the kitchen and the dining room table, picking up noodles from the boiling water with a pair of chopsticks, and passing filled-up bowls into everyone's hands. It was a very common simple food, but my mother praised her cooking skill again and again. After the meal, the wife stayed at home to wash the dishes and take care of their three kids, while Sunshine took my mother and me to watch a new opera.

The beautifully shaped crystal pendant lamps reflected softly on the refined mirror-like marble pillars, and my mother's happy laughter sounded like silver bells in the spacious hall of the theatre. I looked up and found she was particularly beautiful this evening. Her rosy cheeks, the sparkling black eyes, the pearl-like shining teeth, the graceful line of her nose, the neatly trimmed short hair, the elegant ivory gauze kerchief around her smooth neck, and the fashionable dark blue corduroy jacket — everything about her was charming and elitist. She was already in her mid-thirties and had three children but she was generally acknowledged as the most attractive woman in her institute, though there were many younger women there.

I seated myself on my mother's left side and Sunshine sat on her right. It was a touching opera about a group of underground communists fighting with the Nationalist Government before nineteen forty-nine. Close to the end of the opera, as the revolutionary heroine was brought to the execution ground with her male comrade-in-arms, the actress on stage stepped up to the guillotine, fearlessly singing a solemn and stirring song. I was deeply moved by the communist martyr's heroic deeds and my cheeks were wet with tears. As I looked for my handkerchief in my coat, I was surprised to find that Sunshine had reached out his hand and grasped my mother's, saying in a low voice, "We are revolutionary comrades alike, aren't we?"

My mother seemed embarrassed. She tried to withdraw her hand quietly. He didn't lose his grasp, however, and my mother gave up her effort. She squeezed out an uneasy smile and her eyes stayed fixed on the stage. I watched all this going on with an inexpressible feeling and forgot totally about what was taking place on the stage. As a girl, I had been told many times that a man and a woman were not supposed to touch each other unless they were in the same family. Sunshine's action was certainly impolite and offensive!

The crimson velvet curtain descended slowly to the stage and the lights over our heads were turned on one by one. As my mother started to clap her hands together with the rest of the applauding audience, my breath returned to normal.

At the bus stop, when Sunshine waved "goodbye" to me, I nodded my head, my eyes avoiding his. My mother was dissatisfied with my impolite reaction and urged me to say "goodbye" too.

On the bus, we got only one seat and my mother let me sit on her lap. As soon as the bus moved off, she whispered into my ear, an uncontrollable joyfulness in her tone, "You know, Peace, Sunshine told me tonight that the Party is now seriously considering my application to join it! I may become a Party member very soon! Are you happy to hear this?"

As a ten-year-old, I couldn't understand the importance of being a Party member, but I knew it was an honourable thing, since all the heroes and heroines in movies, operas, cartoons, novels, and news reports were Communist Party members. I knew my father was a Party member, too. He was a nice and respectable man. But... I asked my mother if Sunshine was also a Party member. She was surprised that I could ask such a silly question.

"Of course he is!" she said smilingly. "He is the Party's secretary in charge of the institute."

"But, I think he is not a... not a..." I stopped to find a suitable expression, but found my mind quite confused by the pictures of Sunshine's cunning smile, his hand grasping my mother's, and the big characters, "Communist Party Member..."

I imagined what it would be like on the day when my mother became a Party member. Would it be the same as when we were admitted as members of the Young Pioneers at school, wearing our red scarves and taking an oath in front of Chairman Mao's portrait, accompanied by loud drums and gongs? Remembering how excited I was at that moment, I wanted to see my mother happy, and I looked forward to that day for her.

But that day didn't come as the months went by, and I gradually forgot about it.

My mother's self-started separation ended abruptly. She got a phone call from the kindergarten that my four-year-old sister was infected with encephalitis (a brain disease) and was in hospital. She rushed to the hospital and found my father there as well. Looking at the poor little thing lying in bed with her life in danger, she felt regret immediately. She stayed in the hospital for a whole week, praying in her heart that the little girl would resist the threat of death. It was a miracle that my little sister finally recovered from the dangerous disease, as many other patients with the same disease died at that time.

My mother returned home together with my sister when she was able to leave the hospital. She had no time to contend with my father for her position in the family any more, for the storm of the Proletarian Cultural Revolution was now thundering overhead.

7

*The Storm of the Proletarian
Cultural Revolution – Upheavals in
Nineteen Sixty-Six*

EVER SINCE THE FOUNDING OF THE NEW CHINA, POLITICAL campaigns had been launched every couple of years to accelerate China's progress. In 1966, an extraordinary campaign, the so-called "Great Proletarian Cultural Revolution", began to prevail in this land. It was a notorious movement which lasted for ten years and brought nationwide death and upheaval.

In the early 1960s, after a series of radical campaigns had put the country in difficulty, some Party leaders, headed by Liu Shao-qi, the President of China, and Deng Xiao-ping, the Party's General Secretary, began to adopt milder policies that stressed economic development rather than class struggle. Mao was vexed when he found his orders could no longer be executed without question. He thus resolved to ruin his political rivals and maintain his own power by starting a nationwide revolution.

Mao had observed Soviet leader Khruschev's betrayal of Stalin after his death. He understood that his radical policies and iron hand control of China had created numerous enemies who he feared might try to negate his deeds as China's greatest leader after he died, just as Khruschev had done to Stalin! Starting a Cultural Revolution would wipe out all potential Khruschevs in China and Mao's name would then go down in the annals of history as a hero forever...

Of course Mao was aware of the chaos and huge loss of life which such a revolution might bring about in the nation. But to him, life was the last thing China needed to be afraid to lose. And chaos? "Big upheaval throughout the world leads to great order across the land!" That was Mao's philosophy.

Early in 1966, the revolution was still confined to academic circles and nothing violent took place. School children like us were not totally involved and we still had normal classes and life, except for the additional requirement of writing some prose pieces to criticize a few writers who were alleged to have written poisonous works attacking the Party. We learned from our teachers and from newspapers that these writers had attacked the Party with their pens and that we must attack them back in order to safeguard our beloved Party. When I read their 'poisonous' articles, however, I could not figure out why they were poisonous. Perhaps a ten-year-old's mind was still too simple to understand some of the ambiguous lines: our teachers had to try hard to help us find the poisonous stuff in their works.

As summer began, *People's Daily*, the Party newspaper, which had the largest circulation in the country, put out an editorial with the title, "Wipe Out All Monsters and Devils"! The editorial called on all revolutionary people to take action to wipe out landlords, rich farmers, counter-revolutionaries, Rightists, and capitalist line-carriers. As always, the function of the media was to act as the voice of the Party and tool of dictatorship. That signal having been sent out, the nation was soon in a mess.

Like groups of bees, organizations of 'Red Guards' emerged spontaneously in all universities and high schools to safeguard Mao's 'revolutionary headquarters'. Like snowflakes, big-character posters covered almost all the buildings in schools, factories, and government offices. Most people stopped their work to engage in ferreting out hidden counter-revolutionaries and to debate day and night over issues such as who was and who wasn't a revolutionary, and how to correctly carry out the Cultural Revolution.

The atmosphere changed dramatically in my school as well. Classes could no longer be conducted undisturbed. As the students were too young, revolutionary actions were mainly taken by the teachers. The school's principal, a middle aged woman, was attacked as a capitalist line-carrier, and several teachers were exposed as counter-revolutionaries.

We were excited to be able to run around the campus and read posters on the walls of corridors, canteens, auditorium, and outside the classroom buildings. New posters came out everyday and quickly covered up old ones, and we felt there was not enough time to go through them all before they were replaced by still newer ones, so we would only read those attacking somebody we were familiar with.

One teacher charged that the father of a nurse working in the school's clinic had served in the Japanese Army during World War II. A laundry woman reported that the school principal had once asked her to make a cup of tea for the principal's daughter who was already thirteen years old and should have been able to help herself. One teacher exposed another for poisoning students with bourgeois ideology in his teaching. A grade six student announced his discovery of two young teachers, a male and a female, dating in a park one Sunday. Fight-back posters would immediately appear defending those attacked and seeking to win understanding from the revolutionary masses, and the focus of attention would shift to new discoveries thereafter.

The staff of the school gradually formed into different factions. They were so caught up in attacks and counterattacks on posters that the students were totally neglected. For children as young as we were, the chaotic situation and the flourishing posters on campus were exciting and satisfied our curiosity to know all about our teachers.

On one hot day after lunch time, when everyone was taking a nap, we heard a noise growing louder and louder in the sportsground. We jumped out of our beds and rushed to the centre of the noise, despite our life teacher's efforts to stop us.

On one corner of the large sportsground, two young teachers were debating in loud voices on behalf of different factions in the school. I listened attentively and found they disagreed about whether the principal was a revolutionary or a capitalist line-carrier. The woman, we recognized, was the master in charge of grade six, and the man, our painting instructor. Gradually more and more people, both students and adults, were attracted to their argument, and the two fighters had to climb on top of a one-metre-high concrete platform to let more people have a better view of them.

With flushed faces and voices gradually hoarser and hoarser, the two teachers waved their arms vehemently, beside themselves with anger.

Eventually, their argument drifted away from the theoretical discussion into abuse, and they tried to push each other off the platform. I was deeply shocked to see our painting instructor becoming such a rude and harsh man, with dirty words from his mouth pouring over the female teacher. He used to be a loving and gentle teacher who sponsored our school's broadcasting station and many times he taught me how to read a poem with emotion over the microphone. But look at his twisted face now!

Oh! The female teacher was pushed off from the platform! She fell on the ground and tried to get up, while shouting revolutionary slogans at the same time. With the help of some onlookers she climbed up on the platform again. At this time, some spectators who were sympathetic to the woman joined the argument on her side. The man, too, had his supporters. Their argument continued for two hours and gradually drifted away from its original controversy to a vulgar quarrel. They were clearly tired and losing interest now, but none of them was willing to be the first one to retreat, with so many watchers still observing attentively.

At this embarrassing moment, someone phoned a high school nearby for help. Soon an excited voice from the loudspeaker was talking at the sportsground: "Attention, please! Here come the young revolutionary Red Guards from No. 4 High School! They were in their swimming pool when they heard about the crucial struggle in our school. But they have quickly come over to support our revolutionary actions."

I turned my head and saw about two dozen male Red Guards, still in shorts, running in two lines towards us. The two fighting teachers seemed to have found their rescuers and the woman was immediately in tears. The head of the Red Guards, a boy about sixteen years old, came over and questioned the two adults soberly, as if he were a judge. The man and the woman vied with each other to explain to the Red Guards what was going on, and their argument returned to its rational shape. With nothing violent going on, most onlookers lost interest and quickly left the spot.

The next day I had almost forgotten the event when I heard that the female students in grade six were going on a hunger strike in support of their teacher, the woman who argued for the principal and was judged as wrong by the Red Guards. However, their actions were mocked by the male students in the same grade. Big-character posters appearing over the following days revealed that the strikers actually had their meals regularly, not in the canteen, of course, but sent to their bedrooms by the female teacher.

On one side, Mao was trying to set fires in the whole country, and on the other side, the moderate Party leaders who were afraid that the whole nation might be trapped in disaster, secretly tried to put out the fires.

Mao felt the time was now ripe. In June, he posted his famous "My Big-Character Poster: Cannonade the Headquarters!" He announced that there was a bourgeois headquarters within the Party Central Committee which was trying to suppress the revolution, instead of supporting it.

In July that year, the situation became tenser, and no classes could be conducted. Leaders at all levels — school principals, factory managers, institute directors, high-ranking government officials — all were denounced as 'capitalist line-carriers' and criticized and tortured at the whim of the revolutionary masses.

All schools in Beijing stopped classes to go enthusiastically all out for the revolution. Our school was ordered closed, with the reason that this sort of boarding school was cultivating bourgeois aristocrats, not revolutionary successors. Children of my age were too young to take part in adult actions and were asked to go home.

That summer, I stayed home with my eight-year-old brother, five-year-old sister, and Nainai, watching all the horrifying changes going on in Beijing everyday.

Red Guards, who were fully supported by Mao and were feared by all people, frequently issued new orders. These orders were created by different factions and many of them sounded rather absurd. Among them were orders such as: no one should wear black; people should walk on the left side, a symbol of revolution, rather than on the right side, a symbol of revisionism; and those whose surname was Chiang should have it changed to show their hatred towards Chiang Kai-shek.

A pedestrian would be abruptly stopped on his way by Red Guards and questioned about his class status. If the answer was 'landlord', 'capitalist', or any other category listed as a bad element in the society, he or she would receive a beating right on the spot. If the answer was 'poor peasant' or 'worker', he would be released with a "sorry".

Women's hair styles were taken into consideration, too. Young girls wearing long pigtails all cut their hair short to be in step with the 'revolutionary fashions'. Middle aged women who permed their hair were urged to straighten it since permed hair was regarded as the 'bourgeois style'. Old women who had their hair worn in a bun or coil, a traditional style for married women, were urged to cut their hair short to the ears.

All the old women in my neighbourhood were called to a meeting by the Red Guards one evening. Nainai went there, too. When she came home, she told me: "The Red Guards told us that the coiled hair style was a remnant of feudalism and should be eliminated." She spoke with difficulty, trying to use the words she had just learned at the meeting.

The next day, I saw her cut her sparse grey hair with a pair of scissors. A few old women who lived in the same building did not cut their hair in time. They were caught by Red Guards waiting on the sides of the streets with scissors in their hands. I heard their screaming and reached my head out of the window, only to find these old women trying in vain to run away while the Red Guards were laughing loudly.

Not only hair styles but fashionable dresses also became something forbidden. Though it was in hot summer, no women were wearing skirts or dresses in the streets, but long pants instead. Everyone was in plain-coloured clothes — white, blue, and grey.

One day, as a young woman wearing a pair of high-heeled shoes was passing by our building, she was caught by the Red Guards who nailed one of her shoes on the outside wall of the building and let her go home with one foot bare. A notice was put beside the nailed shoe: "Look! Here is the outcome of wearing bourgeois paraphernalia."

The hiring of housekeepers and nannies was also regarded as the bourgeois life style and all domestic workers were ordered to leave forthwith. Old men and women with the class status of landlords and capitalists were ordered to leave their children's homes in Beijing and return to their hometowns, where they would labour in the fields under the supervision of the revolutionary masses. One day I watched the old woman next door moving out with her luggage while her small grandson held her legs and cried loudly.

The first violence I had ever seen since the revolution started took place on a hot summer day. I heard noises coming from the sportsground of a nearby high school and saw people running towards it.

I followed and found a middle aged woman, who was said to be the principal of the school, being tortured by the students. The woman was forced to kneel on top of a platform with her hands bound up at her back, while some young boys swished her with leather belts. The boys were dressed neatly in white cotton shirt, blue pants, and four-inch-wide red armbands inscribed with "Red Guard" in golden characters. They waved the leather belts at the woman for a while, and stopped at intervals shouting, "You must confess to the revolutionary youngsters all the crimes you have committed during your rule of the school! Tell us! What actions did you commit against our great leader Chairman Mao! Tell us! In what ways did you implement bourgeois educational policies!"

More and more people gathered. Many watched with sympathy and some whispered to each other, but no one dared to help the poor woman. She was sweating under the scorching sun, her messy hair sticking to her blushing face and her black short-sleeved shirt all wet at the back. She spoke in a low voice: "Revolutionary youngsters, I have made mistakes in my work, but I did not do anything against Chairman Mao..."

Her words were cut short by more swishing. "You slimy snake! We will make you honest! Confess! Confess!" The Red Guards waved the belts in time with the shouts, while one of them led the crowds to shout slogans: "Smash in her dog head!" "Down with the stubborn bourgeois pig!"

"Oh, blood!" The word burst out from someone. It made my heart shrink to see red blood oozing out of the skin on her face and arms. Her eyes kept looking at the ground and her lips were tightly closed. She remained silent and wouldn't speak at all now. The boys were seemingly irritated by her attitude and kicked vehemently at her. One of them picked up a stool and hit her head. With a flop, she suddenly fell on the platform. The boys did not stop their kicking, though, declaring to the crowd that the cunning woman was pretending to be dead. I was terrified at the scene and left quickly.

The next day I heard that the woman died right on the spot and her husband, shocked by the cruel news, killed himself with a large dose of sleeping pills that very night.

Violence escalated fast. Red Guards rushed into Buddhist and Taoist temples hundreds or thousands of years old and smashed all the statues. Monks and nuns were ordered to move out of the temples and get married like ordinary people. Anything which belonged to the 'Four Olds' category, namely, old ideas, old culture, old customs, and old habits, as listed by Chairman Mao, was to be destroyed.

Murders and lynchings were heard of constantly, mostly done by teenage Red Guards. Since Chairman Mao, then worshipped by the Red Guards as their 'Red Commander', had stated that "rebellion is righteous", these youngsters were so intoxicated by the freedom to rebel granted to them that they created all kinds of 'rebellings' of their own.

Thorough searches were carried out in the homes of those people who were newly in trouble or belonged to the old category of 'class enemies'. The properties of these families were either seized right on the spot or taken away by the revolutionary masses. Confiscation, torturing, lynching, and raping were common during the searches, and no one would come out to stop what was going on. The victims, who did not dare to show any dissatisfaction or resistance, had to welcome these revolutionary activities and sometimes had to join the smashing and destroying of their own homes to prove their cooperative attitudes. Many were beaten to death simply because they refused to cooperate. Some victims, despairing of finding justice and unable to bear the mental and physical suffering, committed suicide together with their spouses. Some hanged themselves, some drowned themselves in the imperial lakes and city rivers, and some threw themselves off highrises...

Thousands of lives had been lost in Beijing during the terrifying 'Red August'. But that was only a small number, compared with the city's population of four million. A popular slogan in those days went, "The day that a small group of class enemies feels miserable is the day for the large number of proletarian revolutionaries to feel happy." Indeed, there were people suffering from tears and deaths, while there were also people, comparatively a much larger group, greatly satisfied...

The Communist Government had ruled China for seventeen years by then. Many of its officials of various ranks, from the central government to the grassroots level, had been corrupted and had used their privileges to bully the ordinary people. The revolution now put workers and peasants in the highest social position, 'the leading class', as Mao claimed, to lead everything in the country. Such honour had successfully encouraged the members of the largest group of the nation's population to throw themselves into the chaos. The common people finally had a chance to express their hatred towards corrupt officials, and to feel themselves the real masters of the country for the first time in their lives.

During this time, we heard about a horrifying massacre carried out in a village twenty kilometres south of Beijing. The morale of the peasants in this village was boosted by the revolutionary flames burning in large cities. They decided to carry out some revolutionary activities, too. Within a day, all the family members of the people who held the class status of landlords in this village were arrested. After a public denouncing meeting was held, these families, men and women, children and adults, all together more than thirty in number, were buried alive in a big pit.

As the news spread to the city, all people 'imperfect' in this way or that were terrified. In my home, since there was no adult around, we kids felt extremely insecure. My mother came home always late at night. My father had transferred to Xi An shortly before the start of the revolution. That was a large city about a thousand miles away from Beijing and we seldom heard from him. As the situation turned violent in Beijing, Nainai left us and went to her daughter's home, a small town two thousand miles away in the North.

We felt isolated from other children in our neighbourhood. Once during an argument with a girl, she accused me of being "the daughter of a Rightist". As a ten-year-old, I didn't fully understand what a 'Rightist' meant, yet I could feel it was a bad word, and that there must be something wrong with my mother. To avoid being insulted, during the day we tried our best not to go out unless we had to buy our groceries or dump the garbage.

One evening around supper time, a six-year-old girl, a friend of my brother, sneaked into my home and hid herself in the shade of the corridor. When I found her, she told me while shivering with fear: "I dare not go home. Some Red Guards are searching my home and beating up my parents there..." I learned that her father had just become a 'counter-revolutionary' because he used a piece of newspaper to wrap noodles bought in a store and someone noticed that Chairman Mao's photo happened to be printed on the paper. This was reported to the Red Guards and he was accused of insulting our great leader.

My mother feared that a search might be carried out in my home at any moment. She started to go through our belongings. She tore up many of the family photos which might arouse suspicions, including Laolao's and other relatives' pictures taken before the Liberation, and my father's photos taken in Russia in the early nineteen fifties.

She first intended to burn these photos on the coal stove in the kitchen, but fearing that the smoke and smell might alert the many revolutionary neighbours in the same building, she changed her mind and brought them to the washroom. She was about to flush them down the toilet, but stopped, and thought again. There were reports in those days that some Red Guards and revolutionary masses had searched the sewerage and found gold rings and necklaces flushed by scared owners. My mother took the photos back to her room again.

The next day, my brother and I, feeling perturbed, sneaked out of our apartment. We carried the torn up photos in a bag and came to a park two miles from home. We wandered to the stream, passing through the weeping willow woods. I looked around and saw nobody. There were hardly any people in the park nowadays. Then I took out one photo and tore it further into fine small pieces and threw them into the floating stream. I moved to a new spot and repeated the same action. A few hours later, I had finished the task according to my mother's instructions.

The large collection of books at home had to be disposed of as well, for most literature books and almost all foreign language books were declared to be 'poisons', and keeping them at home would occasion unexpected disasters.

For the following few days, my brother and I were busy carrying all the books to the salvage station about one mile away from home. The salvage station in those days was extremely busy, always with hundreds of people waiting in a long line to sell their belongings, mostly books. Hundreds of thousands of clothbound books, technological texts or literary classics, were sold at one or two cents per kilo. To our dismay, many of the books we had brought there were not accepted because they were printed in foreign languages — Russian, English, Japanese, and German — which my father had used... Why? The station worker told us cockily: "All books in foreign languages are products of capitalism, bourgeoism, and revisionism. They are useless and poisonous and cannot be recycled."

These unacceptable books were therefore piled up and set on fire right in the square outside of the station. Watching the dark smoke carrying pieces of book ashes up to the sky from the raging flames on the ground, I felt it a pity that so many fine books were destroyed in this way. But on second thought, I felt better: these books would no longer poison people, as they said.

I was deeply impressed by a young man during the days of our book selling. He was about twenty years old, with a pair of glasses on his delicate face, and dressed in an old blue suit. He came to the station everyday, not to sell anything, but to stay around the burning books and try to pick out some books before they became ashes. I found that he had taken quite a few books I had brought there. His fair face would blush whenever the station workers shouted to stop him and he often murmured something to cover his embarrassment: "What a pity... What a pity... So many books..."

With the blowing of the autumn wind came the flood of millions of Red Guards from cities all over China. To show his support of and trust in their revolutionary activities, Mao received the Red Guards for the first time on August eighteenth. He smiled and waved his hand while standing on top of the Tian-an-Men tower, the grandiose golden-red entrance of the Forbidden City, while half a million revelling and tearful Red Guards jumped and hailed from the extensive Tian-an-Men Square. Though they could not actually see Mao's figure clearly owing to the great distance, these excited young people tried their best to voice their wish, "Long live Chairman Mao! Long live Chairman Mao! Long live..." as they pushed one another on their way through the Square.

With the zealous wish of seeing their Great Leader, millions of young people came to Beijing. While waiting to be received by Mao, they went about the city to learn new ways of how to carry out the revolution. To satisfy the desires of the young people, Mao had to mount the Tian-an-Men tower eight times in the last few months in nineteen sixty-six. His receptions attracted more and more people coming into Beijing. Within a short time, the big city was packed with Red Guards who, not able to find a place to stay, simply rested in Tian-an-Men Square and along the streets, determined to see Mao before they would leave. As they were regarded as the guests of Mao, they were not required to pay anything on their travels all over the country and, within a short period, hundreds of millions of Red Guards were running around all corners of China like sparks of fire setting the whole country burning!

The Red Guards were actually tools used by Mao to get rid of people unwanted by him. When Mao found that a Party leader, either in the Central Committee or in a province, was not satisfying him, Mao would let his men pass a message to the Red Guards' organizations. The out-of-favour Party leader would soon be attacked by the Red Guards, and lose his position.

News was released everyday about high-ranking Party leaders found guilty by Red Guards and revolutionary mass organizations. Government ministers, army marshals, even the President of China, were brought to public meetings to be criticized and denounced by tens of thousands of people. The mayor of Beijing committed suicide with his wife one day, and in a short time they were followed by many other prominent people.

The situation in my home continued to worsen. Hooligans and rascals, pretending to be Red Guards, frequently dropped in to search and take away whatever they liked. We had to lock our door from inside all day and avoid going outside.

But a horrible thing took place, despite our caution. I went shopping with my sister one day and came home to find our door wide open. A big dark faced boy, about fifteen years old, was kicking my brother harshly with his leather shoes, while my brother was rolling on the floor and crying. The room was in a mess, with drawers open and all their contents littered around. The big boy was mad that he did not find any money and poured his anger out onto my brother. I was shocked to see this and screamed with fear. The boy, tired of his savage action or afraid that more people would come in, pushed me down on the floor, and went out.

No one could protect us. My mother still came home very late, long after we were fast asleep. She always left home before dawn and we usually judged if she had been back or not the night before by checking whether or not her blanket had been touched.

It was September now. The weather was getting colder, with the autumn wind blowing, but the fighting spirit of the people was more intense. Various combat groups of different factions — either students, workers, or peasants — were organized throughout the country. They were armed with big sticks, broad knives, rifles, grenades, machine guns and cannons seized from the state arsenals. Hundreds of thousands of people were dying in conflicts in other cities. Beijing, as the capital city, witnessed less serious casualties, and the conflicts were mostly on a smaller scale.

A heavy rain which lasted for seven days and nights finally washed away the last warmth of the summer.

My mother had not been home for three consecutive days. This was very unusual and I became extremely worried. On the fourth day, I went to the public phone installed on the first floor of this building and tried to call my mother. A man's rude voice talked with me on the line: "Who are you looking for? Qin? Is she your mother? She cannot go home! Why? She has to stay at the institute to confess her crimes!" He hung up.

I called a few more times that day, but each time after I said I was looking for my mother, the line would be cut off. I hung up the phone and stood for a long time inside the building entrance watching the heavy rain pouring out from the grey sky. It gradually got dark, but I still did not want to leave, in the hope that my mother's figure would appear in the rain at the last moment.

✳ ✳ ✳

THE MOMENT QIN HAD BEEN FEARING FOR MANY DAYS finally came.

The commencement of the Cultural Revolution once again smashed her dream of becoming a Party member. As a Rightist, she had been ordered for months now to confess her crimes to the revolutionary masses everyday and to receive their criticism. This was not a new experience, as she had been subjected to this procedure many years ago when she was first denounced as a Rightist.

Though extremely upset at being put on trial yet again in her life, there was a deeper fear inside her this time. She was concerned that a certain 'encounter', for heaven's sake, should ever be discovered!

Her heart sank, when Sunshine, the Party leader of the institute, was declared a 'capitalist line-carrier' one day by the revolutionary masses. As the number one enemy in the institute, the once dignified man was now facing attacks from the revolutionary masses who vied with one another to expose the 'crimes' he had committed when he was in power. The 'encounter' Qin had been concerned about for quite a while was finally to come to light.

The scene took place during a routine criticism meeting held in the big conference hall. Qin was not alone. A few other people in this institute, either Rightists or counter-revolutionaries, were being criticized along with her.

As the criticism meeting was half way done, a man jumped onto the plat-form where all the 'criminals' were standing in a row, with their heads bent low. Qin quickly glanced at him and found he was a junior clerk in the institute's administrative office. He had been working there for a few years and had a reputation for keeping close track of the institute leaders. That was how he came to be sarcastically nicknamed "The Adopted Son of Sunshine" by some people.

Qin was wondering what the junior clerk was going to do when she heard a crisp sound. She squinted her eyes and found that he had slapped Sunshine in the face and spat ferociously into his grey hair. He then laughed grimly and began his exposition: "Sunshine, you old dog! Now you must confess your dirty affair with the Rightist Qin!" He stopped for a few seconds to enjoy the sensation his words had created in the big hall. His pimpled face looked greasy and purple with excitement. "Aha, you thought no one knew what you did? But I saw it! Last summer when I was on a night shift one day I peeped into the window of your office…"

Qin felt as if someone had hit her head with a club and she almost fell on the platform. The crowded hall suddenly became deadly quiet and every-one listened with great interest to the young man's vivid description. Qin closed her eyes, but she could feel the sneers from the people sitting below like hundreds of needles pointing into her. Her back was suddenly covered with cold sweat and her mind was empty. The floor beneath her feet seemed to be slanting terribly in one direction and she tried hard to keep her balance. The young man's sharp voice sounded like a duck crying from a faraway distance and she could no longer hear what he was saying…

…That summer day? She certainly remembered. It was during the last time when she had left home in a fit of pique to live in the institute dormi-tory. She wanted to give Tian-zhi a lesson and let him realize her impor-tance in the family. But, to her disappointment, the stubborn man simply would not give in, however awkward his life had become. A year had passed during which their cold war of separation had endured…

As leader of the institute, Sunshine offered to help break the deadlock. Qin was truly grateful that there was such a warm-hearted leader and trust-ed him with all the family disputes. Though it seemed strange that the leader's efforts at mediation helped not at all, but just made things worse, his big-brotherly attitude towards Qin did comfort her lonely heart. He encouraged her to wait patiently for the day when she would get rid of her Rightist status and join the Party. He always told her that the Party's organization was considering her application now. He invited her to dinner and the opera on the lonely weekends...

She recalled the spring night in the theatre, when Sunshine took her hand in his unexpectedly, as if he was carried away by the scene on the stage. Her instinct told her to draw her hand away immediately. Yet since they had been nice and friendly to each other for so long, and especially since he had just told her the good news that the Party was considering admitting her, she felt it hard to respond with annoyance. To avoid embarrassment, she tried to withdraw her hand in a natural and inconspicuous way. But he didn't let her hand go until he had tasted the full range of her nervousness.

After that, Qin told herself that she should keep a distance from him. But, considering his careless behaviour, as though nothing had happened, she felt puzzled.

"Perhaps he was really moved by the opera and forgot himself at that moment. And, if I react too strongly, he might think I am too sensitive and squeamish, still a petty bourgeois-minded woman..." She tried to comfort herself. "Maybe it is simply wrong to think of our Party leader as a low and mean man." With this in mind, she quickly removed her suspicion of the man and behaved with him in her usual friendly fashion.

If that 'encounter' had not take place, Qin might still regard him as a nice leader and caring big brother! Her mind fell reluctantly upon the summer evening she would have preferred to forget forever.

It took place shortly after supper time when most people had left their offices and gone home. Qin planned to go out for a walk since the dormitory, located on the top floor of the building, was hot and suffocating. She had a bath, put on her short-sleeved white shirt and light grey skirt, picked up a folding fan and walked out of her room. On the staircase, she was stopped by a young man, a junior clerk in the institute. He told her that Sunshine had just hurt his foot and was staying in his office. The young man had been sent to ask Qin for help.

"What can I do to help him?" Qin wondered.

"He wants you to spread medicine around his foot," the young man said with a faint smile.

Though it seemed odd, Qin still went to his office to help. Sunshine was sitting on a sofa, with one foot bare. Qin felt the air in his office was stuffy, and she looked around. It was not dark yet, but the curtain at the window was drawn, and the light turned on.

Sunshine smiled as he saw Qin and showed her the cut on his foot. She looked at it and found it was only a minor cut.

While she squatted on the floor and spread the medicine on his foot, she felt uneasy, as they had never been so close to each other, and the smell from the man's foot made her sick.

She was unhappy and kept silent. "He shows no respect for me at all, or how could he let me do such a mean thing. Why didn't he ask that young man to do it!" she grumbled in her heart. But, remembering Sunshine's position and the care he had given her all the time, she forced a smile to her lips and pretended she was willing to help.

"It is OK now! You won't feel the pain any more!" she said, as she was fixing the last piece of tape on the cut. At this moment, Sunshine suddenly reached out his hands and caught her shoulders tightly. She did not expect this to happen at all and was not sure how to react. She raised up her head and looked at him in great panic. The man's face changed dramatically, all his dignity gone. Now humble, staring at her with his eyes burning with desire and hands trembling with lust, he ventured some words in a suppressed voice: "Qin, I have loved you, ever since the first time I saw you! It has been for so many years! I felt happy when you left Evergreen, but mad when you married again so quickly! I've always felt jealous of Tian-zhi and I wish you would divorce him. We two are the best match in the world! Of course, you understand this — I can't wait any longer! Please... let me..."

Now Qin realized what was happening. "No! This is not right! You are doing something unfair to your wife..." She said hastily while trying to stand up and get rid of the man's hands. But he moved his hands like the chela of a crab, holding tightly onto her neck now. Qin's face blushed with anger and embarrassment, but she was still alert enough to know that she could not cry for help. Her Rightist status and Sunshine's position as a Party leader would make the scene too complicated to be explained.

Without making a noise, she struggled hard to push him away, and they both stood up. The chela around her neck made her breathless. Her neatly combed hair was in a mess and her white shirt was twisted around. The man breathed heavily and forced his lips onto Qin's face, the greedy light in his eyes making him a horrifying monster.

"Let me go! Please!..." Qin squeezed out the words in a subdued voice, trying to move her face away from the man's hot lips. All of a sudden, Sunshine pushed her onto the sofa and quickly rode on top of her. "Wham!" Qin slapped at his face and pushed hard at his chin. His head was shoved backward but his hands were tearing up her skirt vehemently.

At this moment, there was a sound by the window, as if something had hit the window glass. Sunshine was seized with alarm and restrained his hands immediately. "Who is it?" He turned his head to look at the window. There were footsteps moving away quickly outside of the window. Qin was struck dumb for a couple of seconds. She pushed Sunshine off her body, raised up from the sofa, and rushed out of the door.

She returned to her dormitory and threw herself in bed heavily. Thank heaven her roommate, Lan, had gone out, and no one would notice her horrified expression. The dusk was falling and the light in the room was dim. Her heart was still beating fast but her hands were cold.

"What a fool I have been!" She was totally lost in regret and covered her face with her hands. "I have always regarded him as the representative of the Party and trusted him as a selfless man, as all Party leaders should be. But... But... What a fool I have been."

She realized that her suspicion a few months before had been correct. His action in the theatre had been planned purposely to test her reaction. Her naive trust in him as a Party leader led him to create today's scene. "He is such a dirty man! He is taking advantage of my anxiety to remove my Rightist status and to join the Party." Qin's mind was extremely sober now.

"But what should I do next?" She knew that she could not tell anybody what had happened today, not even her husband. The couple had not seen each other for almost a year now and Qin couldn't expect Tian-zhi to be more understanding than any other stranger. But no one in the institute would help her. Sunshine had always behaved as a respectable and dignified leader and it was quite possible that she herself, once she dared to complain, would be labelled as a 'bad woman' who tried to seduce the innocent Party leader! Yes, it was quite possible. She had heard many news reports that 'bourgeois-minded' women who had seduced and 'corrupted' Party leaders were seriously punished. And who would believe her innocence as a Rightist?

Qin felt heavy-hearted. She understood that the best policy for her was to keep silent. As for Sunshine? She decided to maintain a peaceful but distant attitude towards him. "If I don't spread this story, it is reasonable that he will be grateful and not do anything harmful to me," she thought. But when she remembered the footsteps leaving the office window, her heart almost stopped beating! Who could it be? Did this person see everything? Would this person also keep quiet? What if he didn't...? She shivered.

✳　　✳　　✳

"BANG!" SOMETHING HIT THE FLOOR HEAVILY. QIN COLLECted her thoughts and found Sunshine had been kicked on his back and had fallen on the floor with a flop. The young man had finished his exposé and now Sunshine was ordered to confess everything. A strong built man, a representative of the revolutionary masses, came on to the stage and lifted up Sunshine by his collar: "Now confess! How did you harbour Rightist Qin in our institute over the years? How deep is your relationship with her? Did you have intercourse with her? How many times have you had it? Where and when?"

"Confess!" "Confess!" some people shouted loud in their seats. Their enthusiasm was kindled. They expected to hear a salacious story which would season the dull criticism meeting which was held daily.

"No, we had no affairs," Sunshine's voice was low, but clearly heard in the quiet big hall.

"Shut up! You, dishonest old dog, are trying to slip away! I tell you, you are dreaming! You really need more beating to tell the truth!" The young man slapped Sunshine in his face a few times and kicked at his legs. Sunshine almost fell again but managed to stand on his feet. As the young man stopped his beating, everyone in the hall listened attentively to what Sunshine was going to say.

"No... to tell you the truth, I never have... Owww!" He was kicked so harshly from behind on his leg that he kneeled on the platform all of a sudden, his two hands supporting his body. Qin glanced at him from the corner of her eyes. His usually neatly combed hair fell down and covered his eyes. His pale face was twisted with pain and a stream of blood was running from his lips to the chin. A complicated feeling welled up in Qin's heart.

At this moment the young man came in front of Qin and questioned her about whether she had sex with Sunshine that summer evening. Everybody in the hall held their breath and stretched up their ears. Qin felt all her muscles became stiff. She looked at her feet and shook her head numbly. The young man then ordered her to confess when and where else she had had dirty liaisons with Sunshine. She shook her head again. "Never!" she said firmly.

"Do you want me to make you honest?" the young man raised up his hand over Qin's head and threatened.

"Nothing is nothing! I can't lie!" Qin was irritated and shouted in a loud voice.

The young man's hand fell on her face with a sharp sound. A red print immediately appeared on Qin's fair cheek.

A lanky man who worked in the same office with Qin stood up from his seat and shouted: "You snake! Who can believe you! Everybody knows that you are a Rightist but have always dreamt of joining the Party! It is not surprising that you would try to seduce the Party leader! You'd better confess everything honestly!"

The young man who had been standing on the platform all this time came over and kicked Qin on her leg and shouted, "Confess!"

Qin staggered and almost fell on her knee. A flame of rage was burning in her chest. She understood that the lanky man had always been jealous of her work, but she had never expected that he would take revenge on her in this mean way! She felt trapped in a totally helpless situation!

"Let me have a chance to expose!" A woman stood up in her seat suddenly. Qin looked down and found it was Lan, the woman who shared the same dormitory with her. They had got along well. Qin wondered what she wanted to expose. Was the current revolution distorting people's relationships completely?

"I can prove that there was a close relationship between Qin and Sunshine!" the woman said. "I have seen Sunshine come to our dormitory to talk with her a few times to solve her family problem. I know she had been invited to have dinner at his home and to watch an opera during that period. But that is all. I've never seen Qin have any dirty affairs with Sunshine. Qin was wrong in that she maintained a good relation with Sunshine because she has always wanted to join the Party. But she is dreaming! Our great Party would never admit a Rightist like her!"

Qin now realized that Lan was helping her to get out of the swamp in an indirect way. She knew Lan had already done her best, in this dangerous situation. No one in the institute dared to show sympathy to her nowadays. Everyone was afraid of being attacked as friend of a class enemy! Her nose quivered and her eyes were moist. She felt grateful for Lan's braveness.

Time was up and the meeting was over. The 'enemies' were not allowed to leave the institute. Qin was locked in her dormitory room on the third floor of a building. Representatives of the revolutionary masses watched Qin in turn and questioned her on the same annoying topic.

Qin was not allowed to sleep for two nights. She was utterly exhausted and refused to answer any more questions. She begged them to let her go home, for her children were too young to take care of themselves. They threw some papers at her and said: "We will, after you confess everything honestly in writing!"

Sunshine was locked at the other end of the corridor on the same floor. He must have been undergoing much more serious trial there, for Qin could hear the constant sad cries of the man during the day and night. The tortures must have been extremely savage, for his crying sounded like the noise of an animal being butchered. Quite a few young people were overcome with revolutionary enthusiasm and volunteered to interrogate the enemies with torture.

One afternoon, as Qin was writing her self-criticism report, she chanced to hear, from the open doors, the conversation in the next room between the two women supervising her.

"Have you ever seen what people look like after they have been beaten to death?" asked one.

"No. What do they look like?" The other one showed interest.

"I went back to my home village in the suburbs last week. I was horrified to see the villagers had killed six men with sticks and shoulder poles. All the six men had been Beijing residents, but were charged as 'undesirable people' by the revolutionary masses in their work places and therefore sent to this village to become peasants. The peasants in my village felt that they were already suffering from the shortage of arable land and were unwilling to accept the six men as new villagers. They finally decided to kill them. The six men's hands and feet were bound, and the villagers rushed over with sticks and shoulder poles and beat them to death right in the yard! I saw their bodies. I was shocked to see that their bodies shrunk so much, they looked as short and soft as tree worms..."

Qin's hair stood on end. She closed her eyes and covered up her ears with her hands.

That night Qin had a nightmare. She dreamed she was with Laolao in Han Zhong when the mob rushed into their old house waving sticks and knives in their hands. She saw Laolao beaten to the ground and dying and she screamed out miserably... Qin was woken up by loud voices. The two women rushed into her room, turned on the light, and questioned her harshly: "What are you doing in here? Are you trying to commit suicide? You cannot die before you confess all your crimes! Do you understand?"

Qin said nothing. She was still haunted by the nightmare. The two women exchanged eye expressions and ordered Qin to stand against the wall. They started to search the room, and left with a pair of scissors, a small cutting knife, and a handful of metal kneading needles which they found in the drawers.

On the fifth day, the head of the revolutionary masses came into Qin's room. There was a dry smile on his lips as he said: "Sunshine has confessed everything now. There was sex between you and you are the one who seduced him! Besides that, you had intended to seduce a couple of other higher-ranking officials as well! You did all this because you want to have your Rightist title removed and join the Party! You are a snake dressed up like a beauty to corrupt innocent men on our revolutionary team!" He paused for a second and continued, "The Revolutionary Committee has decided to give you one more week. You can go home in the evenings now, but you must confess all your crimes conscientiously before the revolutionary masses lose their patience! If you keep on with this stubborn attitude, you will be punished with a shaved 'devil head' and paraded in the streets!"

"No! No! Sunshine is lying! He slanders me just to protect himself! He is mean!" Qin burst into screams. She was sure that Sunshine must have been forced to lie to save himself from the savage beatings. But didn't he know what his irresponsible words were going to cost a poor woman?

The Chinese society tends to judge a woman's value exclusively by her sexual attitudes. Once a woman was disgraced in this respect, she would lose everything a normal woman could have — her reputation, her career, her husband, her friends, and even the respect of her children! Qin could imagine the horrified eyes of her children when they saw her in a 'devil head', and she could foresee the severe reaction from Tian-zhi when he learned this!

"Oh, heaven! Where is justice!" She leaned on a desk and cried aloud in despair.

✻   ✻   ✻

ON THE FIFTH EVENING AFTER MY MOTHER'S ABSENCE, SHE came home with an extremely stern and pale face. I was terrified by her cold expression but dared not ask her anything.

At night, my brother and sister soon fell asleep in their small room. But I stayed awake in my single bed in the large room. I watched my mother secretly from the shadow of the desk beside my bed.

My mother sat still in front of the dresser. She was looking at herself in the mirror. The lamplight fell on her face, and she looked cold and pale as a marble statue. She took out a comb and started to comb her shoulder-long hair. Her dark brown hair was soft and shining and she combed carefully, slowly. I held my breath lest I startle her. But suddenly I noticed streams of tears running on her cheeks! Then she murmured in a low voice, as if she was talking to someone in the mirror, "...Do you know? They are going to put a devil head on me... and display me in streets... Oh, I am so scared... What can I do? What can I do? No! I won't let them do it! I won't!" her voice trembled with sobbing.

I was stunned and felt miserable to hear her words and sobbing. Tears ran out at the corner of my eyes. I bit my blanket tightly lest my weeping be heard by my mother.

Then I saw her stand up. There were no more tears in her eyes. She looked stern and cold once again. She opened the drawer and took out a pair of sharp four-inch long scissors. She stared at the scissors for a few seconds and then wrapped it with a piece of handkerchief. She walked to the door and put the wrapped scissors into her handbag which was hanging on the hook of the glass and wood screen.

With a clatter, my mother turned off the lamp light. The room became dark. Cold rain drops blown on the window glass added grief to my heart and I stared in the darkness with my eyes wide open.

...Oh, what has happened, Mother? I asked silently. My thoughts fell upon a scene I had witnessed in the streets during the days as some 'bad women' were displayed with their scalps half-shaven, an insult created by Red Guards to punish women and called 'devil head'. Those women looked horrible — indeed, like devils, with half of their scalps bald. Many onlookers laughed and spat at them as they were forced to walk slowly in the middle of the streets...

Oh, no, how could my mother be treated like that! Was that the punishment for a Rightist? Oh, no, no... Who could help my mother? Who could come to help us? I covered my mouth with my hand, trying hard to force back my crying which was ready to burst out any moment.

When I opened my eyes the next morning, my mother had already gone. I was anxious the whole day, waiting for her to come back safely. In the evening she came home and told us that Beijing was no longer suitable for us kids to stay and she had to send us somewhere else.

Where could we go? My mother knew it was difficult to find a safe harbour on the broad land of China in those days...

Since the revolution had started, Laolao, with the class status of 'landlord', was forced to clean up the streets everyday with a group of 'enemies of the people' under the supervision of the local revolutionary committee. Uncle Honesty, as a school teacher, was charged as a counter-revolutionary and put into jail. His crime was a serious one. He declared in public one day that all human beings might make mistakes. He was then questioned: "How about our great leader Chairman Mao?" He replied: "As a human being, he also may make mistakes." Uncle Honesty was almost beaten to death by the angry masses who were irritated by Honesty's malicious attack on the great leader.

It was impossible for us to go to Han Zhong. My mother would not feel safe sending us to my father in Xi An, either. He had not written any letter home for months and who knew what sort of situation he was in!

At this urgent time, my cousin, Aunt Lin's son, came to Beijing from Xi An. The fifteen-year-old student was not a Red Guard but he came to

Beijing with a group of students wishing to be received by Mao. From him we learned that Aunt Lin was also in trouble at her school. The students in her high school had prepared a paper-made, two-foot-long chimney hat for each 'problem' teacher and forced those teachers to kneel on the sports-ground for hours as a punishment. Aunt Lin's crime was her family background as a landlord.

When my cousin learned about my mother's anxiety, he volunteered to take my five-year-old sister to his home in Xi An. He assured my mother that his home was safer than Beijing, since the courtyard they lived in held the provincial government's offices and was always guarded by armed soldiers.

After my sister was taken away, my mother decided to send my brother and I to the home of Uncle Golden-birth, my father's younger brother. He was a worker in the forestry area near the Soviet-Chinese border in Northeast China. As the working class was regarded as the most honourable and revolutionary minded class during that time, Uncle Golden-birth might be the only relative who could provide a safe shelter for us, my mother thought.

Our luggage was quickly packed. Besides our daily clothes, my mother bought a long, thick, cotton-padded overcoat for each of us, as she knew the temperature in that area was often between minus 20°C and minus 40°C in winter and the ground was snow-covered most of the year. My brother and I, having stayed at home for so long to avoid the violence outside, were excited about our trip to a far away place and forgot to think about how long we were going to stay there or whether we would be able to come back home one day.

At five o'clock on a cool morning, we left our home to catch the train. The station was packed with Red Guards from all over the country and it was difficult to get a seat. After we finally squeezed our luggage on the shelf and found a space beside a big middle aged man, my mother got off the train.

The siren sounded. There were only two minutes left. My mother stood on the platform outside of our window, trying to smile at us. I came to the window and reached out my head, guessing she wanted to say something to us. Yes, her smiles faded away and she started to talk to me in a low voice: "Mom has no choice but to send you away. You might have to stay there for three, five years, or even forever..." She hesitated for a few seconds as she saw my surprise, but bit her lips and went on with difficulty. "I have acquired a fatal disease... a tumour... in my stomach... and may not live in the world for long... If I die, you must be obedient to your uncle and his wife, respect them, and regard them as your parents, their home as yours..."

She started to weep and gazed at me with tearful eyes. I was seized by an ominous presentiment and could not utter a single word. At this moment, the train moved slowly, leaving my mother standing on the platform behind.

The sound of her last words and the sight of her tearful face deeply upset me! I remembered her sobbing in darkness and the horrible words "devil head" and "displayed in the streets" and I sensed that she might commit suicide. Though not knowing exactly what had happened, I knew it must have been too much for her to be attacked again and again, and she must have lost any hope of gaining understanding from people, and atoning for crimes in her youth.

"My mother is a good woman," I could no longer control myself and cried out from a broken heart. "She always loved the Party and Chairman Mao and she always urges me to do the same... How can she be treated like that..."

My eight-year-old brother had kept quiet all the time, not speaking a single word. I knew he was sad, too, but as a man he was forcing himself not to cry in public.

The middle aged man sitting beside me wondered why I was so sad and comforted me: "Don't keep on crying like this! You will see your mother again, won't you?"

"No... I am afraid... I'll never see her again..."

8

Hiding in the Forestry Area

IT TOOK THREE DAYS AND NIGHTS ON THE TRAIN TO GET to Yi Chun, a forest city close to the Soviet border in Northeast China. The further we went, the colder it was. But revolutionary fever was high all the way.

Slogans and big-character posters appeared at all railway stations and Red Guards filled almost every space on trains coming and going. Most of them were dressed up in the most fashionable way, green-coloured army uniforms, green caps, leather belts, and red armbands. They sang revolutionary songs eulogizing Chairman Mao and read aloud Mao's quotations to encourage themselves and everyone passing by. By that time, *Chairman Mao's Quotations,* a small red book, was in free circulation all over the country and almost every Chinese, illiterate or not, had a copy.

On the last day of our trip, I had recovered from my grief and was infected by the optimism of the Red Guards in the same carriage. They were a group of high school girls from a border town and had been received by Mao at the Tian-an-Men Square a few days ago. All the way back home they tried to share their happy experience with people on the same train.

Finding that I could sing more revolutionary songs than they could, they invited me to join in their propaganda activities. I felt it a great honour when they called me a "young revolutionary militant". I felt relieved that, outside of Beijing, no one was aware of my family background and therefore I had no fear of humiliation any more.

I stood on top of my seat and read Mao's quotations aloud with emotion. The Red Guards hailed me and clapped their hands, and asked me to lead all the passengers in singing popular revolutionary songs. I did, but found that only the Red Guards sang passionately. Many other passengers either sang with their lips only, or simply looked at us indifferently.

Yi Chun, a new city built after the Liberation in 1949, was in the centre of China's largest forest area. The virgin land was opened up when the government decided to explore its rich resources and transferred tens of thousands of workers from inner China to here. When the Korean War ended in the mid-fifties, large numbers of ex-soldiers were also sent to this scantily populated district.

My first impression of the city was wood, wood, everywhere. In the railway station, logs were piled up waiting to be delivered. Along the streets, over the wooden fences, you could see factory workers processing logs into boards in the open.

In the residential areas, hundreds of flats were lined up along the dam of a big river that almost circled the city. Five or six families were put in a flat and each family had two rooms with a front yard encircled with a wooden fence. Within the yard, short logs to be used for fuel were piled up like a wall, usually three or four metres high. Public toilets were also made of wooden boards, appearing here and there like small cabins among the flats and by the streets.

Uncle Golden-birth, my father's younger brother, used to be a poor farmer in central China. In 1953, he was selected by the people in his village to be a soldier. The Korean War had been on for three years then, and China had sent three million people to the battlefields. In rural China, very few people were willing to go to Korea and quotas had to be forced upon each village. The villagers were not blind. None of the young men who left for Korea had come back — only their belongings. When new quotas were assigned to the village, the villagers selected Golden-birth, an honest and shy man who seldom opened his mouth in public.

A horse-driven cart came by the village on the day of departure. Five young men from other villages, with their hands bound behind their backs, were sitting on the cart. Golden-birth said to the people approaching him with a rope: "Don't bother! I won't run away." Silently he climbed onto the cart.

As soon as the driver raised the whip in the air to urge the horses to run, Plain-pearl, Golden-birth's wife, rushed onto the road with her one-year-old son in her right arm and three-year-old daughter in her left hand. The driver withdrew his whip, startled. Plain-pearl lay down about five feet away in front of the horses and shouted angrily: "I won't let my husband be killed by the Americans! If you want to take him away, crush me and my kids first!"

Of course, the villagers dragged away Plain-pearl, and the horses dragged away Golden-birth.

Fortunately, when Golden-birth was waiting for his turn at the front on the China-Korea border, the Korean War ended. But, instead of being sent home, he and many soldiers were asked to stay in North China to open up the wildness. When I saw him, he had already worked in a local motor repairing plant for fifteen years and was the father of six children, aged from three to eighteen.

His home was two rooms in the middle of a flat, one a kitchen and one a bedroom. The bedroom was whitewashed, with two large wooden trunks standing against the wall, and a large mirror hanging above the trunks with its frame full of family snapshots. Because of the cold weather, there was no bed, but instead, a 'kang', a brick-laid platform connected to the cooking stove in the kitchen. When firewood was burnt for cooking, the smoke and the heat would go all the way through the inside of the kang to the chimney. Beneath the wooden floor of the bedroom was a cellar where thousands of kilos of potatoes were preserved as the sole vegetable for winter.

The bedroom was rather small, with the large kang taking up about half of the space. Actually, the kang was very important for residents living in this cold area. At night it served as a bed for the whole family. During the day, blankets and pillows were piled up on one end, and people could sit on the kang mat, as there were no chairs in the room. At meal times, a small, square, short-legged kang table was laid in the centre of the kang and all people sat around it.

In the kitchen, beside the one-metre iron pot on the clay stove, there were a waist-high water vat, a shoulder-high jar of salted vegetables, a cupboard, and a small kang newly built by Uncle Golden-birth because of the increasing number of family members.

In each room, a bare bulb hung from a twisted electrical cord. The light was dim at night, but no one was supposed to read anything, anyway.

This was the typical furniture for a worker's family in this area. In home after home of our neighbours, I saw the same few furnishings, arranged exactly the same way.

Uncle Golden-birth was a solemn man, quite different from my father by virtue of the stubborn look in his small eyes, and the always tightly-closed lips in his long face.

He worked hard six days a week in his plant and would go into the mountains on most of his holidays. In summer, he would work in his vegetable fields, opened up in the wildness when he came to Yi Chun many years ago. In autumn, he would harvest his field products, pick wild fruit, nuts, and mushrooms, and go hunting. And in winter, he would cut down fuel trees in the woods and drag them home in the snow. Most people living in that area had the same lifestyle, for their income from the factories was never enough.

The women here, unlike women in Beijing, stayed at home to cook, wash, take care of the kids, and feed the pigs and chickens. The majority of the workers' wives were illiterates. Wife abuse was common when the husbands were drunk or tired.

Because the flats were close to one another, any quarrel or beating in a family would easily attract the attention of crowds of people in the neighbourhood. People would gather at the doors and windows and watch with great interest. Quarrels between neighbours would also draw a large crowd of observers who enjoyed hearing family secrets exposed by adversaries, and seeing women's hair torn out, and men's faces scratched. This was understandable, for a quarrel might be the only recreation in their dull daily lives.

Uncle Golden-birth's wife, Aunt Plain-pearl, had a quite different character from her husband. She laughed loud, talked fast, and worked quickly. Her parents chose Golden-birth as her future husband when she was only seven. Luckily, the couple, despite their different personalities, proved to get along well after their teenage marriage.

Aunt Plain-pearl was about thirty-six when I first saw her, but the hard life she had had dealing with six children, two pigs and a dozen chickens had carved deep wrinkles in the corners of her large dark eyes and thin cheeks. Most women in that area had six or seven children, not because they liked a large family, but simply because they did not know any methods of birth control.

Although about three thousand miles away from Beijing, the sparks of the Cultural Revolution did not miss this quiet forest area.

One morning shortly after our arrival, children and housewives in the neighbourhood ran around excitedly, telling each other that the mayor of the city had been ferreted out by the revolutionary masses as a capitalist line-carrier, and was to be paraded in the streets.

Aunt Plain-pearl was feeding the pigs in the yard when she heard the news. She quickly washed her hands clean, combed her ear-long short hair neat, and changed into her best costume — a brown and beige plaid corduroy coat. Then she led four of her younger children, and my brother, and me, to watch the parade.

In the main street downtown, curious people stood in the chilly early winter wind, waiting anxiously for the parade to come through. Aunt Plain-pearl waved and talked loudly to her acquaintances in the crowd every now and then, and proudly showed my brother and me to them as her guests from the capital city, Beijing.

I was surprised to notice that all the women here were dressed up as if they were going to the theatre. I could see that they seldom had a chance to go outside of their homes and the parade obviously provided a good break from their dull lives.

The noise of a loudspeaker approached us more closely and the people pushed one another to have a better view. Finally we saw a truck carrying a group of people moving slowly towards us.

The mayor and several other officials of the city stood along the two sides of the truck, with their arms bound behind their backs and two-foot-long, chimney-like hats made of white paper on their heads. Their names and titles were written with black ink on the hats. Wooden boards about two feet square were hanging from their necks. Words describing their titles were written on the boards: "capitalist line-carrier", "counter-revolutionary", "double-faced man", "traitor", "spy", and so on. A group of revolutionary representatives stood behind these criminals. They held thick clubs in their hands to supervise the movement of the criminals. On the body of the truck were posters such as "Smash the mayor's dog head" and "Fry the mayor in boiling oil"!

The mayor, a man about sixty years old, with his head bent low, a running nose, and an expression in his eyes like that of a dead fish, looked apathetically at everything around him.

The representatives of the revolutionary masses, also standing on the truck and identified by the red armbands around their left arms, shouted slogans through the loudspeakers in their hands: "Revolution is innocent!" "Rebellion is righteous!" "Down with the black mayor and his dog followers!" "Long live the victory of Chairman Mao's revolutionary line!" "Long live our great leader Chairman Mao!"

Their shouts were accompanied by revolutionary music played on a gramophone to add drama to the scene. As a rule, all members of the audience were supposed to shout the same slogans after them, but very few people responded.

Most of the audience's attention was drawn to the only young woman bound up on the truck. The crowds pushed over to her side to see a 'female criminal'. From the words written on the board hanging on her neck, I learned that she used to be the secretary of the mayor and was accused of having an affair with him. She was in her twenties. Her black hair was partly shaven off from the centre of her skull. Her eyes and lips were tightly closed. She looked pale, ugly, and numb, like a chicken scalded in boiling water with a portion of its feathers removed.

The watching women did not understand the words on her signboard, but a broken shoe hanging from her neck explained her status to those who were illiterates.

"Oh, she is a broken shoe!"

"She is not pretty at all!"

"Pah! This evil seductress!"

"Serves her right!"

I heard the crowd's comments. Some spat at her, for they knew a broken shoe was the symbol for an adulteress. People vied with each other to have a better view of her, and kids screamed with excitement as the truck advanced. My mind was suddenly struck by something.

"Do the revolutionary masses treat all accused women this way? What might happen to my mother in Beijing?" I shuddered at the thought, and moved my eyes away from the young woman on the truck.

The parade soon lost its novelty, for numerous parades were held afterwards, not only for government officials of various ranks, but also for real criminals such as thieves, murderers, rapists and sodomy practitioners. The category, 'sodomy practitioner', puzzled many children including me, but adults simply refused to explain.

Near the end of 1966, large-scale fighting, that is, a resort to violence in debates and disputes, began to prevail in China. Different opinions had eventually created numerous factions among the Red Guards and other revolutionary organizations.

Violence escalated gradually, from sticks, spades and knives, to rifles, grenades, and guns. Many of these weapons were acquired from the People's Liberation Army, whose different troops supported different factions.

Many people, mostly young Red Guards and workers, died heroically shouting the slogan "Long live Chairman Mao!", believing they were sacrificing their lives to safeguard Mao's revolutionary policy. Imitating heroic figures in movies, some Red Guards even killed themselves with their last grenade, or jumped out of the window on the fourth floor, after all their comrades had been killed, to show their determination to fight to the death.

In rural areas, ironically, the significance of the revolution was linked with, or utilized, in parochial and patriarchal disputes in many parts of the country. The feuds between villages and family clans were usually led by persons whose class status was 'hired farmhand' or 'lower-middle and poor peasant', as those two categories of people were regarded as the most revolutionary in nature and met with no suspicion about their purity of mind. Large numbers of peasants, including women and children, died without knowing anything about the real intention of the Cultural Revolution.

The violence lasted for two years. No specific statistics about the deaths were calculated, but rough estimations put the dead and the wounded all over the country in millions.

In the small city, Yi Chun, there were two major factions. One was the "August 28th Students' Union", so named because some of the students had been received by Mao on August 28, 1966. Its members were students from the city's three high schools. The other was called "The Red Rebellion

Regiment", an organization of the industrial workers in the city. The students seemed to be more radical than the workers, for they insisted on smashing the old municipal government, while the workers regarded the government as not bad. Skirmishes took place now and then, but never on a large scale, and so casualties were few.

Despite his dumbness where political issues were concerned, Uncle Golden-birth became a member of the "Red Rebellion Regiment" simply because everyone else in his motor-repairing plant had taken part in the organization, and he did not want to be regarded as a coward. However, his eldest daughter, Jasmine, a dark-skinned, large-eyed eighteen-year-old high school girl, was active in the "August 28th Students Union". The two sometimes would have debates at home, but these often ended up with Uncle Golden-birth stumped by the annoying issues, and rendered tongue-tied and red-faced. Of course he was not the equal of a high school student in debate.

Anyway, we benefited a lot during the period of violence by keeping two different factions at home. On one night, Uncle Golden-birth would come home warning us not to go to a certain area where the workers, with large sticks in their hands, were ready to beat up August 28th Students coming through. On another night, Jasmine would hurry home, telling us the password for the students' patrol.

Housewives were not forgotten by the revolution, either. Women in this area were constantly called to attend criticism or self-criticism meetings. They were used by the factions in their conflicts, too. Once when the students planned to get manpower from other cities, the workers asked all the housewives to come to the railway station and lie down on the rails, preventing any train from moving. Though unwilling to leave their children and chores unattended, the women were too scared to refuse, since no one wanted to be criticized as inactive in political struggles.

Self-criticism meetings were held about once a week and the women of every three flats were required to come together to study Mao's Quotations. I was often invited to read Mao's works for them and lead them in reciting three articles Mao wrote in the nineteen thirties and forties. "Old Man Moving the Mountain" said that if the Chinese people worked hard and continuously, like the legendary Old Man, there would be no difficulty they could not overcome. "Serve the People" called on every

Communist Party member to serve the people wholeheartedly and selflessly. "In Memory of Dr. Norman Bethune" praised the Canadian doctor who died while helping the Chinese people during World War II, and called on all Chinese people to learn from his internationalist and communist spirit.

In those years, these three articles were required to be recited by heart by all Chinese, including children and illiterates. After studying these articles, the women were required to do self-criticism and check their own behaviour in accordance with what they had just learned. Illiterate as those women were, their life experience had taught them how to avoid being fooled when under the pressure of hypocritical politics. Many times I couldn't help but laugh at the women's humorous self-criticisms.

One women who had seven kids said: "I have recently been sterilized because I want to serve the people better, as Chairman Mao told us to do."

Another woman said: "If it were not for learning from Dr. Bethune's communist ideology, I wouldn't have married a crippled veteran back from the Korean War." I knew that the purpose of this sort of study was to make them criticize their own mistakes and wrongdoings, but the women talked only about their merits, and no one would touch upon mistakes.

January was the coldest month in Yi Chun. Temperatures often fell to minus forty degrees. My brother and I were both suffering from chilblains. There were a number of coin-sized festering spots on my hands, wrists, feet and ankles. The biting pain made me restless but I knew there was nothing the adults could do to help us. The family never had extra money to seek medical treatment. If anybody was ever sick, he or she would just wait for a natural recovery. Aunt Plain-pearl looked at my hands and said: "Once you have chilblains, you are going to have them every winter. My kids have suffered this for years, but there is nothing we can do about it."

Jasmine was not afraid of the freezing weather at all. She and four other girls in her class decided to take a 'Long March' to Beijing. It was a fashionable activity then. In 1935, Chairman Mao and his communist troops were chased by Chiang Kai-shek's Nationalist Army for a whole year. Mao and tens of thousands of communists ran zigzag from South China to North China for thirteen thousand kilometres, on foot, to avoid being wiped out. This Long March became the symbol for the communist struggle afterwards. Many pious Red Guards were following suit in those days, carrying out Long Marches of various distances to show their revolutionary determination.

I was excited to hear Jasmine's decision. I admired her and the other girls for their braveness. But I worried for them, too. I knew it had taken us three days and nights to get here from Beijing by train. How long was it going to take these girls on foot?

Uncle Golden-birth and Aunt Plain-pearl were more worried about where to find money for Jasmine's expenses on the road. For a few days, they tried to convince her to stay, but Jasmine was stubborn.

"It won't take much money for the march. We will sleep at railway stations at night," Jasmine insisted.

"The pig in the shed is still too small to be sold. Where else can I get money for you?" Aunt Plain-pearl grumbled.

Jasmine was in a low mood for a few days. She didn't speak to anyone at home, but kept her hands on the move, knitting a wool sweater that had been my rosy-coloured sweater. Jasmine had unravelled and re-knitted it at least three times since I had come here. No one in her family ever had a wool sweater. Jasmine had long felt jealous of her classmates who had something to knit. Every time she was trying to create a new pattern for my sweater, she would ask whether I liked it or not. To tell the truth, I would rather have kept my sweater in its original pattern, for it was knitted by my mother. But I didn't want to pour cold water over her zeal, so I just nodded agreement with every square or triangle she created.

Jasmine was a lucky girl. One day the mailman's bicycle stopped outside of Uncle Golden-birth's home. He was delivering a money order from my father in Xi An. Every other month, my father would send eighty people's dollars to cover living expenses for my brother and me. Uncle Golden-birth's monthly salary was eighty people's dollars too, which had to support his eight-member family.

Jasmine took the eighty people's dollars my father had just sent here and started her Long March with the other girls. On the day of their departure, she put on my brother's light blue sweater and my navy blue cotton-padded overcoat. My mother had bought an oversized sweater for my brother and two oversized long coats for us before we left Beijing, not knowing how long we were going to stay in Yi Chun. Now the sweater and the overcoat were just fit for Jasmine's grown-up body. She put on leg wrappings and a pair of leather boots. On her left arm was a 'Red Guard' armband. She packed a blanket and some clothing into a bundle and carried it on her back. With the little red book, *Mao's Quotations*, in her right hand, Jasmine waved goodbye to everyone and left home.

In spring, different forms of showing loyalty to Mao were introduced into people's daily life by travelling Red Guards who constantly brought new inventions from big cities back to Yi Chun. Worship rituals including 'Loyalty Dances', 'Quotation Songs', 'Morning Salutes' and 'Evening Reportings' became the compulsory daily routines for everyone.

In early mornings, people in every three flats would come out of their homes and gather in the streets to practise their worship rituals. In our neighbourhood, we all came to the passageway outside of the fences on which we hung a portrait of Mao. I would lead all the people, each holding Mao's little red book in hand, to do the 'Morning Salute'. First, we would pray in one voice to "wish sincerely our great leader, great teacher, great commander, the most, most red sun in our heart, Chairman Mao, to live forever!" The next step was to sing two or three 'quotation songs' composed by some revolutionary musicians. The third step was to read aloud five or six paragraphs chosen from Mao's little red book. The last step was the 'Loyalty Dance'.

Problems often loomed here as the adults felt clumsy, or too embarrassed to dance, having never danced in their lives before. At this time, the children would tutor them with great patience in each movement. Uncle Golden-birth always pulled a long face and looked mad, when his stiff movements were corrected by the kids.

Since there were some very old and sick people who could not come out of their homes to practise worship rituals, three other young girls and I in this neighbourhood volunteered to do door to door services for them. We went to the home of one old lady to sing and read Mao's quotations for her, and her sick husband lying on the kang.

After our services, I asked whether they understood anything of our propaganda or not. The skinny old lady quickly nodded her head like a chicken pecking at rice on the ground: "Yes. Yes. We understand everything you read. Oh, what beautiful voices you girls have!"

All the other girls left her home contented except me. I doubted that our serious performance was effective, for I clearly noticed that the sick man had his eyes tightly closed and his brows knitted all the time, and the skinny lady looked at the floor indifferently throughout our performance.

Medals with Mao's portrait or famous quotations inscribed on them became the most popular and fashionable ornaments in the country. Everyone had at least one medal on the front of his coat and many kept dozens at home. The shapes and materials of the medals changed rapidly from small-sized ones, simple in design and low in quality, to large, refined ones with exquisite workmanship. The largest one could be the size of a tea saucer, and the owner would attract jealousy if he appeared in public with that. Wearing these medals was regarded as a symbol of loyalty to Mao, and absurd behaviours were observed now and then.

One day, two workers at Uncle Golden-birth's factory argued about which one of them was more loyal to Mao. One of them, a man in his forties, took off his clothes and pricked the sharp pin of a large-sized medal with Mao's portrait into the flesh of his chest to prove he was the more loyal one. Pained and bloody, this man paraded himself in the streets for hours, and felt proud when people were shocked at the sight of him.

*   *   *

THE BIGGEST DIFFERENCE BETWEEN LIFE IN YI CHUN AND life in Beijing was the way we slept at night. As the city was snow-covered for seven months of the year, the whole family would sleep in one heated kang instead of on separate beds like we did in Beijing.

With our arrival, Uncle Golden-birth constructed a small kang with bricks and mud for him and his wife in the already crowded kitchen. The rest of the family, eight children from three to eighteen years, slept on the old kang, about six square metres large.

It was really uncomfortable, with every two children under one blanket, and one's head facing another's feet. What embarrassed me was that I had to take off my clothes in the presence of a sixteen-year-old boy, Uncle Golden-birth's first son. When I was only a seven-year-old girl, my mother told me a story, dramatized with exaggerated facial expressions and gestures, to instill into my mind the conception that my body should not be looked at by any man. But the boys in the family were all timid and shy. They would avoid looking at us girls when we went to sleep. It didn't take long for me to accept this way of sleeping with ease.

Uncle Golden-birth wanted to train all the kids to be diligent persons and every morning at five o'clock he would get up and shout to the whole house: "Get up everyone!" It was hard for us to get up so early when the sky outside the window was still dark on cold snowy winter days, and it usually took about half-an-hour before the last one got out of his blanket amid the increasingly fierce scolding of Uncle Golden-birth.

I was afraid of getting out of the warm blanket, too, but after I found the benefit of getting up earlier, I always tried to be the first one. Since it was hard to get water in winter, the family members would often use only one or two basins of water to wash their faces in the morning. Knowing that the last one would have to wash his or her face in unbearably filthy water, I always tried to get up as quickly as I could, so as to wash my face in clean water.

About nine years old then, my brother felt deeply frustrated by the cold weather and the harsh rules in the family. One snowy morning about two months after our arrival, he insisted on hiding under his blanket, despite the fact that all us others had gradually got out of the kang, impelled by Uncle Golden-birth's angry voice.

Aunt Plain-pearl came over to talk to my brother, but he still kept silent with his eyes tightly closed. Seeing this, Uncle Golden-birth could endure no more and suddenly took his leather belt off his pants, pulled my brother out of his blanket, and began to lash him. My brother cried out in horror. We were all frightened, but no one dared to stop Uncle Golden-birth, for he would beat anyone who tried to stop him when he was in a rage. My brother's attempt to resist the harsh rules failed and after that he never dared to delay too long in the kang, though he was still among the last ones to get up.

A few days after we arrived in Yi Chun, I felt very itchy everywhere on my body. The kids in the family told me that I must have lice now. They asked me to take off my shirt and found some rice-shaped insects on it. It was the first time I had ever seen lice and I was horrified. The kids comforted me: "Don't be afraid! Everyone has lice, more or less!"

Every night, I took off my shirt and caught all the lice. But the next morning, I felt itchy again. I suspected the new lice were from the clothes of the other kids, since we slept so close to each other on the same kang and all our clothes were laid on top of our blankets at night.

One day, Uncle Golden-birth brought home a small bottle. It was a strong poisonous pesticide. He emptied the pesticide into a washing basin and diluted it with about two litres of water. A strong irritating smell quickly spread in the air. Uncle Golden-birth asked all the kids to take off their clothes, except for their underwear. He then dipped the water with a towel and wiped the towel through every kid's hair and body. I closed my eyes and lips to keep out the liquid running over my face. Soon I felt dizzy, found it difficult to breathe, and experienced a painful pressure over my chest. All the kids complained of the same uncomfortable feelings. "You won't die!" Uncle Golden-birth said briefly.

The lice disappeared for a few weeks, but they came back just after we had recovered from the poisonous symptoms. "The new ones must be from our neighbour's home, through the crevices of the walls. That woman is filthy and lazy and her seven kids are all lice-ridden. They have never adopted any hygienic methods!" Aunt Plain-pearl commented, feeling proud of herself at the comparison. Therefore, every four or five months when the kids complained about the itching, we would have another pesticide bath.

Although a woman herself, Aunt Plain-pearl often complained that it was a money-losing business to raise daughters, as sooner or later they would marry into other families. Therefore, she held, it was not necessary for girls to study too much, but instead they should do as many house chores as possible and learn all the kinds of skills required for a housewife. I didn't agree with her at all and tried to explain to her a girl could perform functions equally important to a boy's when she grew up. I was surprised that my argument aroused fight-backs not only from my aunt, but from her daughters as well. Gradually, I started to learn cooking, tailoring, and some other heavy housework, accepting these as natural tasks for a female.

Every other day, Endurance — the second daughter of the family, a girl one year older than me — and I would go to the public well about a hundred yards away from our flat, to get drinking water for the family. The windlass was very heavy, with iron chains attached to a bucket of water. The two of us would stand face-to-face to wind it up together, and carry it home with a shoulder-pole. Five large buckets of water, each containing about thirty litres, were needed to fill up the big water vat, and I would breathe heavily upon finishing this task. What really made me tremble was getting water in winter times when the area around the public well was covered with thick slippery ice and we had to work with great care, lest we fall into the well.

Chopping logs into small pieces of firewood for cooking was another daily task but I found it a pleasant thing to split a thick round log, usually one foot in diameter, into fine pieces, just with an axe.

Washing clothes for the whole family was also a job for the girls. I liked doing the washing in summer, for we could carry all the clothes to the riverbank, about a mile away from home, wash them on the rough stones appearing out of the broad, fast-floating water surface, and spread them on top of the grass on the bank to dry.

Tending the two pigs raised in the corner of the yard also occupied some of my time. In spring and summer when the snow had melted and the green grass grew, Endurance and I would go to the fields, the riverside, and the marsh land, to pick up edible wild herbs for the pigs, as there was never enough grain at home, even to feed people. We collected a whole bag and then carried the heavy load home on our shoulders. Half of the wild herbs we got would be laid on top of the roof to dry for the pigs' winter consumption.

Labouring in the forest left me the most wonderful and deepest impressions. Though the work was extremely heavy for an eleven-year-old girl, it was there I started to learn the beauty and strength of nature, and the hardship of life.

Starting in May when the snow finally melted, Uncle Golden-birth would take four of the elder children in the family into the deep mountain every Sunday when he did not have to work at his repairing-plant.

Many years ago, he had secretly opened up the wild in the prairie far away from home, since all land was owned by the state, and individual ploughing was illegal. The one-acre piece of land cost him his health, and made him spit blood seriously for he had opened it up with his two hands only. He knew very well that, once discovered, what he had been doing would be regarded as 'Capitalist Practice', and arouse big trouble. He had no choice, however, as his salary was not enough to feed the family, and he had to grow food on this secretly-opened land.

In early morning, we took a mini-train, a special transportation tool in the forest area, for two hours, and got off at a station with only four or five small houses around. In the floating mist of the surrounding valley, the mysterious forests revealed their charm. I could smell the fresh leaf-buds of the oak, maple, birch and pine trees, in the air. A narrow trail wandered in the quiet valley and led us into the vast reed marshes, where the illegal field lay.

We walked on the trail for half-an-hour and then stepped into the marshes at the sight of a hazelnut wood. The yellow dry leaves of the reeds left over from the winter before were taller than an adult man, and we had to follow one another closely, lest one of us should miss the road. At the same time, we had to pay attention to each of our steps on the ground, making sure to lay our feet on top of small grass mounds and avoid falling into the muddy water. The smells of the crushed newly grown weeds and the splashed dark muddy water preserved in small patches, and the singing of birds startled by our sudden intrusion, reminded people of the coming of spring in the isolated wilderness.

Right in the centre of the marsh land was the hidden field. We turned over the thick black soil with spades and hoes and planted pieces of potatoes. For a few hours, everyone bent over working and no one talked. As the sun reached the middle of the clear blue sky, we stopped for a while to have our lunch. Food was simple — steamed cornbread or boiled sorghum brought from home and washed down our throats with cold spring water from the running stream in the birch woods nearby.

In the summertime when the potatoes were growing, we would come to remove the weeds under the scorching sun and swarms of attacking mosquitoes. In the golden fall, we would dig up the crop, about a thousand kilograms in all, and carry it on our backs to the small railway station two miles away.

Autumn was the happiest season. Hunting and wild fruit picking were conducted at this time. In the splendid valley, the forests displayed gorgeous colours ranging from jade green, through orange gold and ruby red, to violet purple. When the hunters, usually adults, carrying their rifles and ropes, disappeared into the dark woods, the children would start picking up wild fruits along the outskirts, not daring to drift away too far for fear of wild animals. We collected hickory nuts, hawthorns, blackberries, hazelnuts, birch-leaf pears, and mushrooms.

But our major task was to collect pine nuts, an expensive delicacy. Boys would climb up on the pines and, with long bamboo poles, knock down cones to the girls below. We pounded the cones with wooden clubs and extracted nuts from the pulp. Tens of kilograms of pine nuts could be collected by the kids during the fall. The hunters usually could carry home a deer, or a couple of hares and ring-necked pheasants.

In winter when the whole world turned white and the ground was covered with thick, solid, icy snow, our lumbering work would start. Armed with axes, handsaws, and sledges, we came to the woods in the eastern hills about five miles away from the city. This was one of the few lumbering lands preserved for the local residents to get fuel from. A government supervisor stood at the entrance of the trail leading into the hills, checking all the logs drawn out of the woods and taking precious species, such as northeast China ash and so on, off of the sledges.

After selecting a suitable tree, two of us would sit face-to-face in the snow with our legs stretching forward, and start sawing it. Many times we had to work when snow was falling in big moist flakes and fierce wind cut our faces like sharp knives. Our brows and eyelashes were quickly frosted up, and our lips could not move. With chilblains on hands, wrists, feet and ankles, our limbs became numb in the freezing temperatures. But we managed to move our seesaw back and forth mechanically, knowing that a pause would make our frozen limbs worse. By the time we got ten trees down, it would be dark, and we would load them on two sledges and go home.

The big river encircling the city was now quiet and smooth with thick ice and snow on top of it, and it served as the best road for the lumbering sledges. One night Uncle Golden-birth and I were in one sledge, with him pulling in the front and me pushing at the back. It was a windless night. The moon was bright, shining softly on the silver river bed and on the solemn hills along the bank. Besides our footsteps and the squeak of the wooden sledge in the snow, I could also hear Uncle Golden-birth's heavy breathing as he bent over, his head close to the ground, to pull the heavy sledge. With the other children left far behind with their sledge, it seemed our sledge was the only object in the vast world. The scene reminded me of a famous Russian folk song I learned in primary school in Beijing a couple of years before.

The icy snow is covering the Volga.
A three-horse carriage is running along the river.
I heard someone singing a melancholy song
and found it was the young driver.
Why are you so sad, young guy,
with your head bending low?

My heart was filled with an unspeakable sorrow, for what, I could not tell. Nature was beautiful but you simply were in no mood to enjoy it when life seemed to be so hard and miserable.

Uncle Golden-birth's steps slowed down. We stopped for a rest. He stepped into the untrodden snow and cupped a clean clump in his hands and swallowed it up with haste. With a long sigh, he felt his burning throat relieved somewhat. He then climbed up on top of the logs, spread his limbs flat there and stared at the mysterious night sky. After a while, he talked slowly in a unusually soft tone.

"Peace, you see, life is so hard, and I have lived like this for forty years now. It seems that sufferings never end, and I sometimes feel life is really meaningless... But I have to go on — the kids need to be fed... Of course, you are different from my children. You still have hope that one day you may go back to Beijing to live with your parents. But my children, well, have no hope at all, and this is the sole life style waiting for them..."

This was the only time I ever saw him show his emotions and I suddenly felt a strong pity for this seemingly stern and silent man. I searched my mind for a while but could not find any words to comfort him. He was right. My brother and I always cherished the hope of reuniting with our parents one day and leaving this sort of life, full of hardship, poverty and hunger.

Aunt Plain-pearl often compared the kids to the two pigs she raised. "If you have one pig, you have to feed it. If you have ten pigs, you also have to feed them. What's the difference!" she said with a resigned tone, as if there was no way out.

I understood that she was implying that the children, eight in all, should be fed just like pigs, with whatever food was available.

It was really hard for her to find enough food for everyone in the big family. First of all, the government had set a grain quota for everyone according to age. But the eight kids were all in the growing period and the ten kilograms of grain per head each month, with very little vegetable and meat kind to go with the daily meal, could hardly fill our stomachs. Meat could be had only once or twice a year, except during the traditional New Year's Festival when there was meat for a few days.

The two pigs in the shed were not fed for meat but, when big enough, would be sold to the state for money. What was more, Aunt Plain-pearl was trying to save money to buy a wrist watch for Jasmine, a bicycle for her first son, and a sewing machine for herself. Together, these three 'luxuries' would cost around four hundred people's dollars. That was a big sum for the family, and she could only reach this goal by putting aside part of the money my father sent to us every other month.

Therefore, Aunt Plain-pearl could only guarantee enough food for Uncle Golden-birth, the family's breadwinner, and had to ignore the needs of the children. For many days, at lunch time, when Uncle Golden-birth had gone to work, there would be no other food except a bowl of boiled potatoes. Eating potatoes everyday for two years made me sick at the sight of them but I had to swallow them up to fill my empty stomach. I envied the pigs in the shed because they had wild herbs to eat daily. As I watched Aunt Plain-pearl boiling the fresh, green leaves of the wild herbs I had picked up from fields, I felt a strong desire to eat some of these. But she would say with humour: "That is for pigs, not for you. Pigs can be sold for money when big enough. But what are you good for?"

Once a month, in the evening, when Uncle Golden-birth got his salary, Aunt Plain-pearl would prepare a special meal for him, usually a dish of fried eggs and a cup of sixty percent liquor. With all the kids watching beside him, however, he often felt uneasy about enjoying the dish alone, and he would give each child a mouthful of the eggs with his chopsticks. There would not be much left in his dish after this distribution. He would then look at his dish and heave a heavy sigh.

One day in early spring when the last potato in the house had been consumed, we were facing the problem of what to have for lunch. Aunt Plain-pearl had to buy five pieces of steamed bread from a restaurant. With nine people at home to share the bread, each person was supposed to have only half a piece, about one ounce. I felt happy and looked forward to lunchtime anxiously, for it was rare for the family to eat steamed bread made of wheat.

But when Uncle Golden-birth's elder son, then seventeen years old, came home with an empty stomach, he was annoyed to see there were only five pieces of bread available for so many people. He grumbled for a while and took two pieces away angrily. I watched him and wondered if his selfish behaviour would be reprimanded by the adults. However, Aunt Plain-pearl only sighed in a helpless way. The rest of the family had to share the three pieces left on the table, and each of us got only a mouthful. I chewed my share carefully and slowly, a fingertip large piece each time, and found that even plain bread could taste sweet if it remained in your mouth long enough.

Despite the hunger we suffered constantly, none of the children in the family ever tried to get food illegally. It was Uncle Golden-birth's life philosophy that "poor as we are, we should always cherish lofty aspirations." Indeed, all his children, including my brother and I, behaved honestly and never did any disgraceful thing.

Uncle Golden-birth's pride was badly wounded one day when a neighbour told him that two of his youngest kids were seen eating leftovers in a small restaurant downtown.

At night, when everyone was at home, Uncle Golden-birth conducted a public trial of the two family traitors. He tore off the clothes of Little-sea, a boy of seven, and Little-phoenix, a girl of four, and ordered them to kneel down in front of the portrait of Chairman Mao hanging on the wall.

"Now, ask forgiveness from Chairman Mao for your sinful behaviour," Uncle Golden-birth shouted out to the naked little figures on the floor.

It might be that the kids were too nervous at the situation or that they did not know how to ask for forgiveness. Anyway, they simply twisted their bodies a little bit, looking at the people with their big black eyes full of fear.

Uncle Golden-birth was irritated by their lack of response and suddenly started to beat them in their heads and backs with a leather belt. Blood was running out of the boy's ear and dropping on his shoulder. The little girl's smooth back was bruised with bloody welts. Their endurance was short and before long they crumbled on the floor and started to pray, sobbing: "Chairman Mao, we are sinful. Please, please forgive us…"

*   *   *

THE DRIVEWAY IN FRONT OF THE HOUSE WAS LIT UP BY the lights of a car. Mrs. Thompson was back from her party at a friend's home. Her Cadillac had been sent to a garage for rust at the rear and she had to take a taxi tonight.

I stood up to open the door. Max jumped up from the sofa and rushed ahead of me. His front paws scratched the door impatiently.

Mrs. Thompson came in. She bent over, held Max in her arms, and poured numerous kisses onto his skinny cheeks and around his mouth.

"Hello, my dear! I am back. Have you been missing me? Oh, darling, you have been!"

Max jumped up and down excitedly around her. She hurried into the kitchen, fumbled to take out a couple of dog biscuits, and put them inside Max's mouth.

"Now, you've got your treatment!" She watched Max gobbling up the biscuits with a loud noise. She always felt guilty for leaving Max a few hours at home. "Have you fed him tonight, Lilac?" she asked me.

"Sure, I won't starve him. He had half a can of beef, half a can of chicken, plus his cereal."

"Oh, good!" She smiled, looking satisfied at my report.

Max ate much better than many people in the world, I thought. Just the artificial bones he had daily cost more than five dollars each.

With the dog settled, Mrs. Thompson started to take off her coat. I looked at my watch. It was eleven pm. I stood up and prepared to go upstairs.

"Lilac! Are you ready to go to bed?" she called to me.

Her voice sounded lively. I returned to the small sitting room and looked at her. Her face was pink, her lipstick fresh red, and her eyes were glittering with a youthful light. She must want to talk to me. I sat down in the soft chair beside the fireplace. "No, I am not sleepy yet."

"How was your evening?" she asked casually.

I could see she actually didn't care how I spent my evening. She wanted to talk about her own evening. I had no idea how often she would go to a party for this was the first time she had ever been to one since I had come here.

"Nothing interesting," I replied. I didn't want to tell her that I had just talked with my mother on the phone. A couple of months before, I received a letter from my mother. She told me that Uncle Golden-birth was seriously sick, a liver problem that had tortured him for many years. I wrote a letter to him immediately and slipped a one hundred US dollar note inside the envelope. "Please use this small amount of money to buy some nutritious food for yourself," I wrote. Tonight my mother had told me that Uncle Golden-birth was in hospital now. He wept for a long time after reading my letter... But what was the use of telling Mrs. Thompson all about this? It had nothing to do with her life.

" ...How was your party?" I asked her.

"It was wonderful!" The youthful light was still in her eyes. She didn't look like a woman in her seventies at that moment.

"The food was ordinary. There were only four people at the party — the host, the hostess, I, and another man." She paused for a while, her expression telling me she was still immersed in some sort of happy memory.

"Do you know him? I mean, the male guest?" I asked, just to show I was following her.

"Yes... but I haven't met him for more than twenty years... He was a friend of my husband, also a banker." She was not looking at me, but staring at the candle in its holder above the mantlepiece.

"So, you knew each other when you were young?" I asked.

"He is so handsome, and so well informed!" She might not have heard my question, fully indulged as she was in her own exclamation marks. "He just knows everything going on in the world! There are not many men like him nowadays... Oh, Lilac, it was such an interesting evening!"

"You look great tonight. The dark green dress suits you very well," I looked for a topic to please her.

She stood up and turned around to look at herself, and asked me with uncertainty: "Do you think this dress is too tight? I must look fat in this!"

She felt at her waist and touched her belly, perturbed. To her horror, those parts of her body all seemed unforgivably enlarged at the moment. Her face was overridden with regretful clouds now: "Oh, yes! It is too tight! I shouldn't have worn this dress tonight! I must have looked fat! Oh, my God!"

She threw herself heavily into the sofa and leaned against the sofa back. With a helpless moan, she covered her cheeks in her hands and closed her eyes.

I watched her silently, the youthful light disappearing, the young girl shrinking into an old lady once again.

The next evening, as usual, I made separate meals for the two of us. She preferred to have baked meat everyday, so I prepared beef, mutton, chicken and fish for her in turn. When I first came to the house, I ate the same food as she did, to avoid double work. But I became satiated with meat after a week and returned to my old habit, plain rice and stir-fried vegetables everyday.

When I brought her food into her room, Mrs. Thompson was watching TV and smoking in her chair. The room was filled with smoke.

"Oh, the air is too bad! Why not open the windows?" I asked as I laid the food on the small table in front of her.

"I have been used to this and I don't notice it." She smiled.

"But, I do feel you should change some of your habits, if you want to keep healthy," said I, deciding to tell her my opinion.

"Yes? What are they?" She showed interest.

"You always want to be slim, but you insist on eating a lot of meat everyday. You are afraid of cancer and heart attacks, but you smoke a whole package each day. Besides, you don't do exercise but sit in front of the TV all the time... What can you expect?"

She listened to me with an embarrassed smile. "I know you are right. But... I am just lazy."

"If you want to change, let's start from today!" I suggested. "Finish your dinner and let's go out for a walk! There is an old Chinese saying, 'Walk a hundred steps after each meal and you will live to be ninety-nine years old.' "

"OK. Let's start today!" she agreed happily.

Dusk was spreading over the woods on the eastern side of the driveway. The remaining light in the western sky was quickly fading, leaving a blurred view of the stretching lawns. The fallen leaves of the oaks and birch trees were blown up by the autumn wind and piled up at the feet of the thick trunks. The air was fresh and humid, soaked with the sweet breath of trees and grass.

"Some old Chinese people believe that the best time to do outdoor exercise is after sunset and before dark. Trees are supposed to release their essence into the air at this moment," I told Mrs. Thompson. "According to this theory, we should be out a little bit earlier tomorrow."

"I haven't seen you doing exercises. How do you keep slim?" she asked.

"I practised Tai Chi and sword dancing for years in China. But that was not the only reason. You are what you eat. I have told you many times it is not good to take too much meat and sweet, but you won't listen."

"Oh, Lilac! I was brought up this way. It is difficult to change now."

"Yes, I can understand," I nodded.

She had tried a few times to go without meat for a few days, but every time she ended up by taking double amounts of meat or other greasy stuff. Once, she surprised me by finishing a two litre jar of ice cream in a single evening. The other time she shocked me by emptying a one pound bottle of peanut butter at breakfast. I gradually gave up my efforts to turn her into a semi-vegetarian.

*　　*　　*

TO ME, HUNGER WAS COMPARATIVELY EASY TO TOLERATE. What I felt as a great loss in Yi Chun when the first novelty of the forest-style life had vanished was the shortage of cultural life. There were no books, there was no music, there was not any sort of recreation. Only two Chinese movies were shown in the downtown theatre for two years: "The Landmine Warfare", and "The Tunnel Warfare". There were also two Russian movies, "Lenin in 1917" and "Lenin in 1918". Those movies were usually shown free every couple of months. We saw them so many times that we could recite every line.

At night when everybody was in the kang, Little-sea and Little-phoenix enjoyed playing the game, Seeing a Movie. They buried their faces deeply in the pillow and after a while they would claim that they were seeing pictures going on in front of their eyes. I tried once to do as they did but found it did not work at all. After a while, I understood it was only their imaginations.

As there were no books in Uncle Golden-birth's home, I often went to visit our neighbours in the hope of finding something to read. However, I only found one book in one neighbour's home. That was the very famous classical novel, *Dream in the Red Mansion*, written more than two hundred years before. The owner of the book, a high school graduate, smiled at me and said: "You are too young to read this book. I am afraid you cannot understand it." But thirsty for any books available, I begged him to lend it to me.

The four-volume book brought me into a world full of brilliant palaces, wonderful gardens, and beautiful poems. I read it at times when I was not working, and often when everyone else was asleep on the kang. I sobbed sometimes over the miserable fates of the hero and the heroine. Often at those times Aunt Plain-pearl would look at me and say, "Peace must be crazy! I've never seen anyone reading and crying at the same time."

One summer night as I was lying in a shed in the courtyard in which a temporary bed had been made for me and Endurance to spend the hot summer night, I heard the radio in my neighbour's house playing a piece of fairy-like music. I listened attentively and realized it was the famous piano concerto, "The Yellow River". I was completely saturated with the beautiful tones and my mind was soon carried away. All the wonderful memories of life in Beijing came back to me!

>...I was playing the role of a little bird with black satin hanging from my arms on the ancient opera stage in the house of an eunuch whose grand and luxurious home had been turned into a kindergarten.

>...I was standing in front of the music classroom and singing my favourite song to my classmates, while my music teacher was playing the piano and smiling at me now and then.

>...I was reading novels with Rainbow by the stone table in the school garden where neatly trimmed rows of ilex, blooming pink roses on the sharons, bushy shadows of the old peach trees, and winding wisteria vines separated us from the noisy sportsground.

>...My classmates and I were learning Chinese chess, calligraphy, paper cuts... were seeing popular science movies in the Beijing Children's Palace which used to be part of the emperor's garden palace.

>...My brother, sister and I were running and laughing joyfully around the lakes and rockeries in Beijing parks on sunny Sundays.

...My mother and I were watching classical operas and modern plays in brilliantly illuminated theatres.

The music ceased and I fell back to reality. I stared at the dark wall of the shed and my heart was filled with loneliness. How was my mother now? Almost two years had passed since we had come here and we did not hear from her often. In her letters she never talked about herself, but always encouraged my brother and me to study Mao's works conscientiously, to labour vigorously, to be obedient to Uncle Golden-birth and his wife... Her tearful face at the Beijing railway station loomed before my eyes once again. Was she still in trouble? When would she be able to get us back to Beijing? And how was my father now? He wrote letters to us once in a while and sent money to Aunt Plain-pearl regularly. Was he also in trouble? If not, why couldn't we join him in Xi An? How I wanted to see them all! But I had to be careful not to show my homesickness during the day, fearing that might offend my uncle and aunt.

When I picked wild herbs for pigs in the marsh land, when I cut twigs from the chaste trees overgrown along the river bank, I would stand still and look towards the south, in the direction of Beijing, for a long, long time. The endless hills outside of the city blocked my view farther south. I looked at the torrential river beneath my feet and felt the water was cold and detached, because it was not floating to Beijing, but to the Amore River at the Russian-Chinese border up in the north. I envied the wild geese flying south in rows over the hills on clear autumn days. They were the only ones who might have a chance to see the city and the people in my dream.

Every time I came close to the railway station and saw the engines breathing white smoke heavily, I would feel thrilled and stop for a while. I knew the train had carried me from Beijing to this forest area and it would be the only thing that could take me back to my mother again.

I started to keep a diary, writing in it about my homesickness and my daily activities, and recording my naive poems. I regarded this small hard-covered notebook as the only place where I could talk openly. As there was no place in the two-room home for me to put the diary, I kept it in one corner under the mat of the big kang.

One afternoon when I came home, I smelt tension in the house. My cousins were standing around the room, all looking at me with cold eyes.

Aunt Plain-pearl was sitting in a lotus position on the kang, with an iron hard face. My eyes caught sight of the diary notebook in front of her on the kang. I suddenly understood what had happened: my diary had been read by them when I was not at home!

Seeing me stand on the floor numbly, Aunt Plain-pearl struck the diary hard with her palm and poured out a stream of abuse. Her words were those used by the shrews during their street quarrels and I trembled when I heard these dirty words used against me. What made her so mad at me? Through her scolding, I gradually learned that what made her so vexed was my account in the diary about one of the serious beatings I had received from Uncle Golden-birth. It was a detailed record, including the unhappy conversations between my cousins and me, which caused the beating, and even how many bruises I had on my body. Clearly, Aunt Plain-pearl was afraid that one day these details would be exposed to my parents.

I was embarrassed that my secrets were revealed to the public, but I kept silent, not knowing how to explain my record to them. Gradually Aunt Plain-pearl's scolding attracted more and more neighbours, who hurried over to watch by the door and window. Her morale was boosted and the abuses escalated. She called me "an ungrateful thing" and claimed that she had raised me for two years in vain.

At this moment, I felt that I had to talk, or the observing neighbours would be fooled by her words.

"You should not talk like that, Aunt," I said. "First, my father sends you money regularly for our living expenses and I have worked hard to help in the house. Second, I am grateful to you and my uncle for your kindness to me. You have already read my diary and you know that your loving care was also recorded in it. I have only written the truth..."

This explanation somehow irritated her even more, and she began to scream and curse vehemently. I was surprised when she shot out the following words: "Who do you think you are? You fucking little thing! Do you know your family name? If it was not for the sake of showing due respect for my brother-in-law and sister-in-law, I would never allow you to step inside this door!"

My family name? Of course I knew. Her brother-in-law and sister-in-law? She should be referring to my parents. But wasn't it strange that she talked as if I were not a member of my own family and not a relative of hers? What did she mean? I felt puzzled, but I didn't have time to think as more dirty words were poured into my ears.

I was irritated by her endless scolding and cried: "I will write down everything! I will remember who is nice to me and who is not!"

She waved her arms towards me and looked for the handy broom on the kang. She then struck me on the shoulder with that broom. At this point, a few watching women came over and tried to hold down her arms, advising her not to be angry with a child. Suddenly she fainted on the kang. The women gave out whoops, some pulling the hair at the back of her head, some trying to bend over her rigid limbs.

I was already tearful, but seeing her in such terrible shape, I was scared. I felt regret almost immediately for my fighting-back a moment before and knelt down in front of her to plead for her forgiveness.

A couple of minutes later she came to, and the first words out of her mouth were: "Wait until Golden-birth comes home in the evening! I'll ask him to beat you to death!"

I was frightened. I knew when Uncle Golden-birth beat the kids, he would pick up whatever was close at hand, whether belt, pieces of china, stools, and never think about the consequence of using his weapon.

Just at this moment, one of our neighbour's boys shouted to me from the yard: "Peace, your uncle is home! Run away quickly!"

I was startled at his warning and rushed towards the doorway. It was too late. Uncle Golden-birth had leaned his bicycle against the fence and entered the room. Seeing his wife lying on the kang sobbing and many neighbours watching with great interest, his long face turned stern and he asked: "Who?"

Aunt Plain-pearl said to him weakly while glancing at me out of the corner of her eyes: "Golden-birth, I can't live in the world any longer..."

Before she finished her words, he had noticed that I was trying to sneak out of the room and he quickly came over to me.

I rushed out of the room, but half way out into the yard he caught me and kicked me down on the ground. I tried to stand up, but under his continuous kicking, I failed. Two neighbours came over and held his arms and told me to run away. I struggled to stand up and rushed to the streets outside despite the pain in my knees and back.

I ran, ran, until my last strength was consumed, then I found myself in the empty sportsground of a high school. I walked to the central heating house where there was a tall chimney. I sat down at the foot of the chimney and leaned my back against it. This was a quiet corner. I would not be found by them.

There was no one around, except one or two crickets singing in the nearby open space overgrown with weeds. I looked up in the sky. It was getting dark. Stars were twinkling in the early summer dusk. Trains whistled from the railway station a couple of miles away. The sound was so familiar and warm... Yes, I should go back to my own home, to my parents. Mom did not know what kind of life I was having here. If she knew, she would certainly not let me stay here any longer. But how could I get on the train without a penny in my pocket? Tears ran out of my eyes and wet my cheeks. I wept and wept until I dozed away.

I didn't know how long had passed when I was wakened by a soft voice. Two school girls found me huddled up against the chimney and led me to their bedroom. They were active students who stayed in the school to continue the revolution when many others had got tired of it and left for home. I spent the night with about ten girls in the big kang in their large bedroom and my sorrow was quickly banished by their joyful laughter and funny chattings.

Early next morning, they escorted me back home and pleaded for me in front of my aunt. Uncle Golden-birth had already cooled down after the night. I felt guilty for what I said to Aunt Plain-pearl the day before and tried to do more house chores to make up for it.

It was true that I did not hate them. I understood they were poor people. Life was really hard for them and sufferings seemed endless, with so many kids to be brought up and the constant worry about their next meal. It was reasonable that they had bad tempers and often wanted to punish the kids.

A few months passed and the desire to see my mother grew stronger and stronger in my mind. When I saw the mailman once again bring the money from my father, I collected up my courage and told Uncle Golden-birth that I missed my mother dearly and wanted to use this money for my trip to Beijing. My voice was calm, but my heart was trembling, afraid of being rejected by them.

They looked at me with suspicious eyes and said nothing. "Do you also miss your mother?" Aunt Plain-pearl asked my brother. He hesitated for a couple of seconds and replied: "...No..." I understood he was afraid of offending them. He was clever enough. Aunt Plain-pearl smiled at him and then commented to me sarcastically: "I have mistreated you, right? No wonder you are missing your mother!"

I waited anxiously for a few more days and finally the adults told me that I could make the trip. My brother was surprised to know their decision and immediately asked to go with me. "I miss my mother, too!" he cried out.

We changed three trains in the three-day-and-night trip. The trains were crowded as before, but we were lucky enough to have a hard seat. Although I was twelve years old, I was so skinny and short that I looked like a nine-year-old. My brother, with his large head, thin neck, and bone-showing body, looked even more fragile. We carried bags full of pine nuts and dried mushrooms on our backs and squeezed with exhaustion among the passengers packing up the platform. The sight of our small figures roused pity from station workers and they let us get on the train before the others.

After sitting on the hard seat three days and nights, we felt extremely tired. At last, my brother crawled underneath the seat and fell asleep on the floor. I had to look after our luggage. Aunt Plain-pearl had warned me again and again not to sleep on the train lest people should take away our luggage. I tried hard to keep my eyes open but still I dozed off sometimes. When I suddenly woke up and found my head leaning against the shoulder of a man sitting beside me, I felt horrified and immediately apologized to him. The middle aged man, who looked like a worker, smiled at me kindly and said: "Don't worry. Just lean against my shoulder and sleep, poor child!"

When the train finally arrived in Beijing, it was eleven o'clock at night. We got out of the station and felt enveloped in a home-like atmosphere. The broad streets, the grandiose buildings, the magnificent squares, the clean buses, the numerous stores, the official Mandarin dialect, everything seemed friendly and familiar to me. I became excited and wanted to talk to everybody on the road.

We took buses and an hour later we came to my mother's institute. It was midnight and the big iron barred gate of the institute was locked from inside. I climbed over it. That was a skill I had learned in the past two years when I often had to collect wild fruits on trees. Before my feet touched the ground, however, the light bulb over my head lit up. The door keeper came out from the reception house beside the gate. I quickly recognized him as the old door keeper who had been working there for more than twenty years. He recognized me, too, and shouted towards the building at the back of the yard.

"Qin! You are wanted!" His shouting echoed in the quiet, deep night.

We watched the dark building standing quietly against the dark sky and waited nervously for the reply.

One window on the third floor lit up and our hearts started to beat fast. As soon as my mother's figure appeared at the window, my brother, who had been silent all the time, burst out with a sharp cry: "Mom..."

I was shocked to see, under the bright light bulb in her bedroom, that the dense, dark brown hair of my mother had turned grey in just two years. She was only thirty-eight but she looked like an old woman now.

Receiving no information from us beforehand, my mother was very surprised at our abrupt arrival. She was even more surprised to see that the two kids had not grown a bit after being away for two years, and that we were so skinny and had lice hiding in our dirty hair and shabby clothes.

We were very tired and soon slept soundly in my mother's clean bed, unaware that she had a sleepless night.

The next morning, my mother got up very early and asked us to stay inside the room and not to go outside. She came back a couple of hours later and gave us the address of a man whose home was a few miles away.

At that time, the violent fighting between factions in Beijing had ceased and normal life was returning. The revolution was largely carried out by criticisms of individuals and it was therefore safe for us to go out alone.

In early September, nature had already displayed its fall glory in Yi Chun, but it still kept its summer features in Beijing. It was a fairly long distance from my mother's institute to our destination, but we chose to walk there instead of taking a bus, having been used to walking long distances in the mountains and being keen to look at the changes in Beijing. Having been absent from the vigorous and busy city for two years, I hesitated when I had to cross the streets with floods of bicycles. I felt that I was truly a girl from the deep country.

At the corner of a small lane, we found a quiet courtyard. That was the home of the man we were looking for. He and my mother used to be comrades-in-arms in the air force when they were young. He trusted my mother as an innocent woman and agreed to let us stay at his home during the daytime.

For fifteen days, we arrived at his home early in the morning, spent the day there, and came back to my mother's institute at night. Every night when I was lying beside my mother in the same bed, I would tell her something about our life in Yi Chun. I narrated everything in a peaceful voice and did not feel sad at all. I had become used to life there and took everything for granted. But my mother cried, secretly, after turning off the light. When I noticed her pillow wet one early morning, I felt regret about what I had told her.

One morning, I got up too late and therefore bumped into a woman in the washroom. I lost no time in recognizing her as a pretty, sweet young woman who used to work in the same group with my mother. I was happy to see her again after two years and volunteered to help her carry her washed clothes back to her bedroom. In her room, she asked me why I had come to Beijing, still with the same sweet smile and gentle voice as before. I replied, "I miss my mother". She then told me, "You should not miss her at all. She is a bad woman!" As if someone struck me in the head, I suddenly realized something I had long forgotten and I left her room awkwardly.

It was late, so my brother and I hurried out of the building. In the courtyard, I found many adults were doing the routine morning exercises. I stopped beneath the grape vines a few yards away and watched them. I recognized most of them, all of whom used to be fond of joking with me a few years before, when I stayed in the institute with my mother.

They finished their exercises and noticed me, too. They certainly recognized me, for I had not changed a bit. I was expecting them to burst out smiling with surprise and come over to hold me as they had done many times in the past. But strangely, none of them moved towards me; instead, they looked at me and whispered to each other with an ambiguous expression. A couple of them nodded to me slightly with faint smiles. My heart shrank. I felt my self-esteem badly hurt. I came to realize that these familiar old friends were pretending not to know me, or fearing to talk to me, simply because of my mother. I couldn't stand there any more and rushed out of the grape vines and ran into the street.

That evening, I came back earlier than usual, leaving my brother in a small barber's shop by the street. I sneaked into the building and, on the second floor, found my mother standing in a row with a few men in a large hall. They stood with their bodies straight but their heads lowered, looking at the floor. Among the men I recognized the familiar figure of Sunshine. They were receiving criticism from a man, who I guessed might be the head of the revolutionary committee and who was talking in a harsh voice to them.

I withdrew silently, disturbing no one. It was still early and my mother would feel bad if she knew I had come back earlier and found out her secret. I went to the backyard to pass the extra time. There I met a boy whose father was the head of the revolutionary committee. The boy told me proudly: "I have seen your mother cleaning the yard and toilets everyday. She was also ordered to wash the dirty coats for the old door keeper. She must obey my father's orders."

It seemed that the most difficult part of my mother's situation had already passed. She survived, swallowing all the humiliation and torture, for the sake of her kids. She was put into the group with a few others, called 'the monsters and demons', and worked as a sanitary woman every day under the supervision of the revolutionary masses. My mother was afraid that we might be hurt to see her situation and that was why she let us stay away during the day.

Fifteen days passed quickly. It was time for us to return to Yi Chun now. My brother had been pleading with my mother for quite a few days not to send us back. She really felt the dilemma: it would mean throwing us back into the suffering if she let us go back, my accounting of the hunger and abuses in that home having tortured her heart very deeply; but it was impossible to let us stay with her this way...

Finally, she made up her mind to send us to our father in Xi An, a decision she would have preferred by every possible means to avoid.

My brother and I felt relieved that we did not have to go back, and were happy that we would soon join our father and little sister, but my mother's face looked serious. She tried to speak as gently as she could to us: "When you arrive in Xi An, you might find that people are not friendly to you... because of your father... I hope you will be prepared for that."

Why? Was there something wrong with my father, too? My mother's warning sounded very strange. But I was too excited about the idea of seeing my father and sister again in Xi An and did not think too much about the hint in her words.

My mother looked at us with a complicated expression. She seemed to have something more to tell us, but she hesitated for a while, and finally swallowed whatever it was in her mind.

9

A Home Without Mother – Father's Diary and the Secret of My Birth

XI AN SERVED AS THE CAPITAL OF CHINA FROM THE SIXTH century to the ninth century. As one of the ten largest cities in China, and the key city in the northwest, it was a miracle that it had survived factional fighting with its rich historical relics still preserved.

The ancient city wall, about thirty metres tall and wide enough for six buses to run abreast on its top, with four magnificent city gates, enclosed the old city in a square. Outside of the southern gate of the old city was the well-planned 'academic area', where a number of universities, colleges, and research institutes were located.

At the end of the academic area was the seven-storey Wild Goose Pagoda, a temple built at about the time of the sixth century for a Buddhist monk who spent twenty-six years on his journey and study in India, brought back the first complete set of Buddhist sutra to China, and translated them into Chinese.

The research institute where my father worked was very close to the Wild Goose Pagoda. After a day and night on the train and bus, my brother Wei and I finally reached the entrance of the institute on a late September day.

We put down our luggage by the door of the reception house and talked to the doorman. He looked surprised to know whom we were looking for. The man asked us to wait outside and he went into the courtyard.

I was anxious to see my father and stretched my neck to follow the man's trace. His figure disappeared at the turn of the line of ilex bushes. The courtyard was well shaded by tall poplar trees and I could see two three-storey grey-coloured buildings behind the trees, and a flat with a big roof and windows like that of a canteen, between the two buildings.

Suddenly, I heard a sharp whistle. A minute later, many people came out of the buildings and quickly formed into rows in the courtyard. A young woman stepped out and started to sing and dance at the very front. The people behind her, men and women, young and old, followed her immediately.

> Beloved Chairman Mao, the red sun in our hearts,
> we have so many intimate words to tell you
> and so many passionate songs to sing to you...

I understood they were practising the 'Loyalty Dance' and I giggled as I saw some of them moving their limbs awkwardly, trying hard to catch up with the young woman's graceful movements.

But all of a sudden I stopped my giggling. A familiar figure was walking towards us, in hasty but limping steps. The first thing which came into my eye was a big piece of cardboard about two-feet-square hanging from his neck, with certain characters written on it and a big red ink cross over them. This was something I had become familiar with over the last couple of years. A red ink cross over the name was the treatment given to a criminal when he was given the death penalty and brought to the execution ground. This was applied to all 'problem people' nowadays as a punishment. I was struck numb for a few seconds. Could this man be my father? He had always remained a tall, strong, nice-looking, gentle and respectable person in my mind. But the bending back, the worn-out grey jacket and pants, the old shoes and the crippled steps of this man were by no means familiar to me! The man came closer and I caught the familiar gentle smile on his face. Oh, this was my father!

I dropped the bag in my hand and rushed towards him. He reached out his hands from behind the big cardboard sign and held my shoulders. I looked up and found he had become much older, his broad forehead carved with deep wrinkles, his hair turned grey and overgrown like weeds, his honest-looking eyes behind the thick glasses full of small bloody veins. He tried to smile at me, but what a miserable smile! I realized at once that my father was no more a respectable leader of the institute, but a 'criminal'!

Tears streamed down my cheeks. I sobbed weakly in his hands, my head against the hard cardboard. Wei didn't come over. He stayed by the door of the reception house and watched us silently. My sobbing had interrupted the dancers in the yard. They all stopped their movements and watched us in curiosity.

My father wiped off the tears on my cheeks with his hands and said gently: "Stop weeping, Peace. Let me ask permission from the Revolutionary Committee to take you home."

Out on the street, the cardboard hanging on my father's neck attracted the attention of many children. They spit and threw stones at him and read aloud the characters written on it, "Tian-zhi, Capitalist Line-Carrier and Counter-Revolutionary".

I lowered my head, my heart pierced by a deep sense of humiliation. My father seemed to be used to this. He went on at the same limping pace, totally ignoring the stones beating on his body and on the cardboard like hail.

But ten-year-old Wei found the insult unbearable. He picked up a stone from the ground and threw it back at the kids. My father quickly stopped him: "No, you cannot do this, Wei! They have the right, but you don't."

Fifteen minutes later, we came to a yard entrance. A few large four-storey red brick apartment buildings circled an open space. This was the dormitory yard for all the employees of the research institute and their families.

In front of one building entrance was a little girl squatting on the ground playing with mud. Seeing us, she stood up, threw away the stick in her hand, and rushed towards me.

"Sister! Brother! I knew you would come!" She spoke in a tender voice and reached out her little hand to hold mine. I saw a pair of large almond-shaped black eyes in a sharp-chinned face. Her hair was divided in the middle and combed into two pigtails behind the ears. That was my sister, seven-year-old Little-red.

"How did you know that we were coming?" I asked and looked her up and down. She had become very skinny over the two years, pale and fragile like a bean sprout.

"I have been missing you all the time. I miss Mom, too... Why is she not coming?" she asked.

The image of Mom standing still with her grey-haired head bending low flashed into my mind. "She is not able to come with us this time..." I told Little-red.

We went into our home, a three-bedroom apartment on the third storey. I saw a young woman with glasses cooking in the kitchen and asked Little-red who she was.

"That's our neighbour. She and her husband are both engineers in the research institute. After Father was denounced as a capitalist line-carrier, the revolutionary committee arranged for the couple to move into our apartment. They take the largest room and share the kitchen and washroom with us."

There were only two rooms left for us. My father and Wei shared one; Little-red and I shared the other. There was a double bed in each room. My father's room was crowded with a large cabinet, a desk, a chair and two bookshelves. My room was larger, with a door to the balcony. At one corner was the double bed for Little-red and me. A table and four chairs occupied another corner. A desk was lined up against the wall beside a few trunks containing all the family's clothing. There were no decorations in either of the rooms, and everything was arranged in a careless way.

I missed the home we had had in Beijing before the Revolution. It was clean, comfortable, and cordial, because Mom was with us then. But now, at thirteen, I became the hostess of the family.

When I woke up early the next morning, I found Little-red was staring at me, her upper body resting on her elbows.

"When did you wake up?" I asked her.

"Sister, I have been watching you for a while." Her dainty face looked serious. "From the side, you look just like Mom!"

"...Do you still remember what Mom looks like?"

"Yes, I remember her very clearly." She lay down on her pillow and looked at the ceiling. I could see she was trying hard to catch something buried deep in her memory. "And I remember the time I lost my way when Mom took us to the emperor's Summer Palace... She found me crying under a rockery... and she bought me a large ice cream... It was a strawberry ice cream... I have never had it again since then..."

I moved my eyes away from her face. The light in her wide-open almond-shaped eyes made me miserable.

Different from me, Little-red was often praised as the most beautiful child wherever she went. Her large black eyes, small cherry-like lips, soft smooth brown hair, and faultless fair skin were undoubtedly inherited from my mother.

Two years before, she had been brought to Xi An by Aunt Lin's son. Since then, she had stayed mostly at Lin's home, the place where I had spent my earliest years of life. Little-red was able to spend Sundays with my father when he was not working.

"Last summer, Father didn't come to take me home for a long time. I didn't know what had happened and I missed him every day."

Little-red told me how she came to know my father's situation. "One day I heard Aunt Lin and Uncle Virtue talking with their children about how funny Father looked when he walked in the streets with a big cardboard sign hanging from his neck and two watermelons on his back. I was deeply hurt by their description. But they were eagerly talking and didn't pay any attention to me. I left their home secretly and ran for three miles in heavy rain to get home. I have stayed with Father since then."

My father had been 'ferreted out' by the revolutionary masses in his institute shortly after the start of the Cultural Revolution. He had simply been unlucky enough to be the head of the institute. When most leaders at all levels of government organizations became 'criminals', it was impossible for him to avoid the same fate. He had been locked in a room for days and nights to force him to 'confess his crimes'. He had been criticized numerous times at public meetings, and the revolutionary masses would beat him up whenever they felt dissatisfied with his confession. His ankle was badly hurt when a man hit his legs with a big club to force him to kneel down.

At one of the criticizing meetings, a group of young workers beat him to the floor, smashed his eye glasses to prevent him from moving away, and threatened to hit him to death with big clubs.

"Why did you refuse to increase our wages and benefits? Today it's time for us to get revenge!" shouted one worker. "Come on! Comrades! Let's beat him to death today!" He raised up the thick stick in his hands and hit at my father's head. At this crucial moment, he was held by a few people sympathetic to my father. They all knew that wages and benefits were set by the government and that my father should not be blamed for those.

The revolutionary masses racked their brains for ways to humiliate my father. They made the cardboard sign and ordered him to put that on whenever he stepped out of his room. The function of the sign was to remind all people in the city to keep him under surveillance, and it proved effective. Shop assistants, barbers, bus conductors, kids and some pedestrians never missed a chance to bully him.

My father's hair was overgrown like weeds because the barbers refused to serve a criminal, exposed by the cardboard sign hanging on his neck. The third day after my arrival, I bought a pair of hair-clippers and tried to cut his long hair at home. My fingers were all thumbs and I was all sweat, and my father's hair turned out funny. But he comforted me: "It looks good. I like it."

Every morning, I got up early and cooked a potful of cornmeal porridge and warmed up a few pieces of steamed bread on the small coal stove in the kitchen. After breakfast, my father would put the big cardboard square on his neck and go to the institute to receive criticism from the masses. Wei, Little-red, and I would go to the primary school nearby. Little-red was in grade one, Wei in grade four, and I, in grade six.

A couple of months later I started to go to a secondary school. When I finished school in the afternoon, I would go shopping at grocery stores on my way home. Our supper was simple, always rice porridge, quick stir-fried vegetables and steamed bread. It was difficult to find any meat or eggs in the grocery store. Even if there was meat available, I would not know how to cook it. Life in Yi Chun taught me how to distinguish edible wild herbs and fruits, but not how to cook meats.

By the end of 1968, primary and secondary schools in China had gradually resumed classes. As the old school system had been destroyed and the new one had not been created yet, we were learning nothing except Mao's works every day in class.

I found an interest in reading after school. As most books were forbidden and no libraries were open, it was hard to find books. Some of my schoolmates had secretly preserved books they could not bear to destroy and I bartered with them to satisfy my thirst for reading. I would lend one book to them, and borrow one at the same time. I would finish reading the borrowed one quickly, and barter it with another friend before I returned it back to its owner. We did this in a secret way, for fear of being criticized as reading 'feudalist and bourgeois contaminated publications'. Though fully conscious that what I had been reading were 'poisonous' works, I simply couldn't restrain my craving for those Chinese and European works of literature.

My father came home very late each day. He would first come into our room to see if Little-red and I were fine, and then return to his own room. Though already late at night, he would sit by his desk and read Marxist and Leninist classics for a long time before he went to bed. Gradually he noticed my indulgence — reading 'poisonous' works. He worried that my reading might be discovered by the revolutionary masses and cause trouble for the family, therefore whenever he found those books beside my pillow, he would take them away. The next morning, when I found the books disappeared, I would plead with him to give the books back to me, as they belonged to my friends. My father would warn me repeatedly not to do it again before he gave the books back to me reluctantly.

One Saturday night, my father did not come home. I waited and waited until I fell asleep. The next morning, I met our neighbour in the kitchen. By then, I had learned that the two engineers had the task of supervising my father. Once I dumped some used papers in the garbage can at the kitchen corner. As soon as I turned away, the young wife stopped her cooking and searched the papers to see if I had destroyed some important evidence about my father. I always avoided talking to that couple with their special task, but this morning I was anxious to know the whereabouts of my father so I broke the silence.

"He was locked in a room by some of the revolutionary masses yesterday. They were trying to educate your father..." the young wife replied. A faint smile flickered across her lips that deepened my anxiety.

"...Please tell me, Auntie, what has really happened to my father? He didn't return home last night," I begged her.

She glanced at me, hesitated for a moment, and finally said: "Yesterday was pay day. Some people locked up your father to force him to hand over his salary to them."

"Why should they do that? We need money to buy food as well!" I was shocked.

"Why?" the young woman sneered. "Your father's salary is too high!

He makes more than two of us ordinary engineers do!"

I was puzzled at her words, not sure who was right. At this moment, I heard my father's uneven limping steps. I went out of the kitchen and saw my father coming into the apartment. He looked utterly exhausted. He nodded to me wordlessly and went back to his own room.

Soon after this incident, the Revolutionary Committee of the institute made the decision to reduce my father's monthly salary to forty people's dollars, a quarter of his original pay. After buying our monthly quota of grain, there was little money left to buy vegetables. I had to arrange to buy the cheapest things in stores to keep the family having three meals a day. Most of the time, we could only have salted pickles instead of fresh vegetables on our table.

As most people stopped working to attend to the Revolution, there were scarcely any goods you could buy in stores. Each resident in Xi An was assigned a quota of half-a-pound of pork monthly, but no eggs or other kind of meat was available. By paying higher prices, people could get some poultry and eggs from peasants on the black market.

Our family had to make do with whatever the state quota provided, for there was no extra money to buy stuff from the black market. To save money, I had to make all the steamed bread and wheat noodles with my own hands instead of buying them ready-made. Everything had to be made from flour, and the procedure took hours daily. Little-red always helped me in kneading the dough. She was too short to reach the kitchen counter and would stand on top of a stool for half-an-hour each time. By making all foods on our own, we were saving but a few cents every day.

Besides the heavy burden of cooking, I had to wash the clothes for the whole family. There were no washing machines then in Chinese households and people had to do all washing with their two hands. By that time, I had heard from my school friends that there was a certain kind of insect hiding in an adult man's underwear and if a woman washed it and didn't clean her hands thoroughly afterwards, the insects might come into her mouth when she ate her food. The horrible result would be unexpected pregnancy!

After I heard this theory, I was scared. The next time I washed my father's underpants, I felt nervous to touch them. Who would be the one to wash them safely? I looked around and thought hard. Then I noticed Wei.

"Wei, come here and help me wash Father's underwear!" I told him.

"Why can't you do it on your own?" he replied unhappily. His experience in Yi Chun had taught him that washing was the job of women and a man should never be expected to do it.

But I was too embarrassed to explain my reason to him, for sex was never talked about in my family. All I could say was: "You will understand that when you grow up."

He refused to cooperate, however, and I had to rely on myself. Afterwards, I rubbed my hands under running water with such great care that they became red.

I sometimes received notes delivered by the children of the plumber, the carpenter, the cook, or other revolutionary workers, to my father. I read them and found they were asking my father to give them some money. I knew there was no money in my home and I hated to pass these notes to my father. I discussed with Little-red about what to do, but we both felt weak and helpless. Fearing that these members of the revolutionary masses would torture my father for revenge the next day, I suppressed my impulse to tear up those notes, and passed them to my father anyway. My father would then squeeze out some money from our meagre daily budget to satisfy these demands. And in the following months, fresh vegetables disappeared from our table totally.

In the research institute, there were a few other men also in trouble. One was a senior engineer who was suspected of being a spy for the Nationalist Government in Taiwan. Proud man as he was, the man could not tolerate the insult and torture poured on him and threw himself off the balcony in his home on the third storey one day. He died immediately, leaving his jobless wife and five kids unattended. The wife started to support the family by mending clothes for people, but that did not earn enough to feed the whole family. Two of her older kids, Jade, a girl of my age, and Six-finger, a boy of my brother's age, helped the family by hooking carts, a special profession embraced by school-age poor kids.

In Xi An, some people specialized in carrying earth from the suburbs into the city for households using earth to make coal cakes for fuel. Dragging a whole cart of earth for a few miles on foot was an arduous journey, even for an adult. We often saw men dragging carts with their heads almost bent to the ground, sweating all over, breathing heavily on their way. A poor child who wanted to earn a few pennies would stand beside the road, holding a rope connected with a hook. When an earth cart was passing by, the child would ask the carter if he wanted a hook or not. Once permitted, the child would hook up the cart and drag along with the adult. If the carter was paid one dollar for one trip, he would give five cents or ten cents to the child, depending on the child's size.

One day, a friend told me that she found my brother Wei had joined the 'hooking gang' with Jade and Six-finger in the streets. I was shocked and felt very sad. Wei was only eleven. He looked skinny and undernourished, with a large head on his thin neck, and a narrow chest. How could he pick up this exhausting and also embarrassing profession without telling me? I concluded that he must be hungry, having had no good food in his stomach for months, and that he intended to earn a few cents to buy some extra food.

That evening, Wei came home looking tired and in dirty muddy clothes. I asked him not to do it again. He said nothing. The next morning he went out again with his self-made hooked rope.

One night Wei came home very late. I and Little-red were already in bed. I heard Wei's footsteps going directly into his room and they didn't come out again.

"Wei, you haven't had your supper yet!" I spoke loudly from my own room.

There was no answer. I felt it odd and got out of my bed. I pushed his door open and turned on the light. Good grief! I was at once horrified by the sight.

Wei was lying in bed, with his mouth tightly biting on his quilt. His face, his shirt, and the quilt were stained with blood all over! His eyes were closed, his brows frowned in a knot. He was trying hard not to cry out.

I brought a wet towel and wiped away the blood on his face and found two of his upper front teeth gone! Blood continued to ooze out from the wound in his mouth and stain the quilt. I asked him what had happened. He made no answer; his eyes remained closed, but tears were running down his cheeks...

The next day, my friend Jade told me what had happened the day before. "Wei and I and Six-finger met a team of carts yesterday. We each got a hook and went on the road together. When we were climbing onto a stone-laid arch bridge, Wei's rope broke and he fell on the stone surface all of a sudden..."

Except for Jade, I didn't have any other friends in the same courtyard.

We both understood that girls in our courtyard didn't want to befriend us because they despised our parents. Jade was still haunted by her father's suicide and became a very timid girl. She always walked with her head lowered and never dared to look at anybody straight in the eye. If she ever spoke to a stranger, her voice would start trembling at once.

But I was different from her. No matter how painful and nervous I felt internally, I always tried to walk with my head looking up and my voice never trembled when I talked to someone, including the revolutionary workers.

The confident, or perhaps obstinate, attitude on my face had irritated some of the children of the revolutionary masses and they planned to teach me a lesson by shaming me.

They deliberately talked in front of me about the situation in the criticizing meetings, going into detail about how my father was tortured, and then laughing loud. At those moments, I would give them a sharp glance and turn away immediately.

One day, I was called into a girl's home, without being told what for. After I sat in the room for a while, I found that the atmosphere was quite unusual, with all those present (about fifteen girls in all) looking extremely quiet and serious, as if they held some sorts of secret in their minds. I asked them what we were going to do. One of them said that we had to wait for the coming of Jun. I knew Jun was a strong built sixteen-year-old Red Guard, the daughter of a revolutionary worker. She was always the girls' ringleader and was often invited by the Revolutionary Committee to lead the masses in shouting slogans at criticizing meetings because she had a loud voice.

When Jade arrived a moment later, I was still doubtful about the purpose of the meeting so I only nodded to her. After she sat down on the edge of a single bed, she blinked at me inconspicuously and signalled for me to go to the washroom. I understood she wanted to tell me something in secret so I went to the washroom two steps away from this room. As soon as I entered, Jade came in too.

"They are planning to criticize you today. I just learned this," she whispered into my ear. "You should leave here quickly!"

I was shocked by the news and rushed out of the washroom to go back to my home upstairs. As soon as I stepped onto the staircase, however,

Jun's strong figure appeared beneath. She was a little bit too late. The rest of the girls had rushed out of the meeting room and wanted to chase me, but I quickly ran into my own home and locked the door of my apartment.

"You dog girl! Don't ever disguise yourself as a revolutionary! Don't you see what material you are made of! Now stay at home to criticize your Rightist mother and capitalist line-carrier father!..." I leaned my back against the apartment door and heard Jun's mad, loud voice firing from the staircase. That might be what she planned to tell me at the meeting, but I didn't give her the chance to let it out into my face.

I closed my eyes. My mind was agonized. I did not understand exactly what my parents had done to make them be regarded as enemies of the people. However, I never believed the titles put in front of their names were justified. Right from my childhood, I had received instructions from them to love our great leader Mao, to love the Party, to love the country, to love socialism and the communist system, to love the people, to be selfless, to be active in physical labour, to help others at your own cost, and to study hard for the purpose of serving the society better — all the doctrines of the communist ideology. Who could believe that such faithful people as my parents would turn out as enemies of the people? And why was their loyalty and sincerity not understood by the people?

One day on my way home, I passed a few gossiping housewives by the staircases. One of them was Jun's mother. As they noticed me, the focus of their conversation shifted to my parents.

"Do you know, her father is now trying to divorce her mother!" Jun's mother spoke in a loud voice with a dramatic look, as she glanced at me from the corner of her eyes.

"Oh, really?"

"Why?"

"Tell us more..." The rest of the women quizzed Jun's mother eagerly.

The word "divorce" struck me hard. What? Father was trying to divorce Mother? I almost collapsed. My legs felt heavy as lead lumps, but I braced myself to climb upstairs. Back home, I sat helplessly in a chair and considered what I had heard with a horrified feeling.

Yes, I realized, for quite a long time now my father had avoided mentioning my mother to us. And when we talked about my mother, he would keep his mouth shut and remain silent. It might be true that he was thinking of a divorce.

I was so fearful that we would lose my mother and I wanted to prevent it, but I did not have enough courage to discuss this matter with my father. Wei was still going out every day and coming home late every night. He had become an extremely silent boy, not even talking to me and Little-red. The only one I could now talk to about my worry was Little-red.

Little-red was also frightened to hear the news about divorce. We figured that my father might loathe my mother because of her Rightist status. But we didn't care about that! We needed our mother dearly! And the family could not function without a mother! We must try to influence my father to go along with our thinking.

In the following days, we frequently mentioned my mother in front of my father. We suggested at every possible opportunity how important mother was to our family and said that we missed her very much. At dinner time, I would blink my eyes at Little-red and we would deliberately recite aloud Mao's quotation about uniting as many people as possible to carry out the revolution. But my father looked unmoved, except that sometimes he fixed his eyes on us for a few seconds, pensively. Perhaps he simply did not see through our naive tricks and did not understand our intention at all.

One day as we were affixing a stamp to the letter we wrote to my mother, my father's eyes were attracted by the pretty-looking sportswoman printed on the stamp, and, to our surprise, he said gently: "Don't you think she looks like your mother?"

A spark lit up in our hearts, and I quickly exchanged glances with Little-red who was bright enough to respond immediately: "Yes, Mom is as beautiful as this woman, isn't she?"

But my father seemed to have just wakened up from his dream. He looked at us, sighed, and returned to his own room without saying anything.

Day after day, my worrying grew. Then I learned everything in one lonely summer evening.

My father and the other 'problem people' had been sent to a village fifty miles away to help the peasants for their summer harvest and he was to stay there for a whole week. Wei was not back yet. Little-red had gone to bed and soon fell asleep .

I came into my father's room and started to examine the stuff on his desk, hoping to find out some clue about what was in his mind. Among the hard-covered works of Karl Marx and Lenin, there was his diary. I hesitated for a moment, and finally opened it. I quickly scanned the pages and my eyes were caught by the following lines:

> ...It is hard to believe and painful simply to think that, having joined the communist cause wholeheartedly for more than twenty years, I would finally become a counter-revolutionary! How did all this happen? What have I done? Have I really changed? Perhaps all these years I have concentrated too much on technological works and lost my grip on the remoulding of my political outlook. But anyway, I can't accept the charge that I am a counter-revolutionary and a capitalist line-carrier! Chairman Mao said that the masses are the real heroes. Therefore, I cannot blame the masses as being wrong, but find fault with myself... I am totally confused! I must study the original works of Karl Marx and Lenin carefully once again to find out the right answers for the proletarian revolutionary theory and to keep pace with the developing situation.

The following pages were my father's analyses of his work in the institute and the criticisms from the masses. I quickly turned over the pages and looked for the words in my mind. There! My eyes were caught again by the paragraphs.

> The pointed question is once again brought out by the revolutionary masses today: how can you prove that you are a revolutionary when you are still married to a bourgeois Rightist wife after so many years?

> They won't believe that I know nothing about how she became a Rightist in nineteen fifty-seven. They questioned me: 'As you were sleeping in one bed during that period, how could you know nothing?' I didn't know how to answer this question.

> The head of the revolutionary committee talked to me today. He mentioned Chairman Mao's early instructions that bour-

geois Rightists are bourgeois reactionaries and therefore should be regarded as our class enemy. He wanted to help me realize my petty bourgeois sentimentalism in dealing with serious political issues. He emphasized that actions must be taken by me to demonstrate my determination to break with my past mistakes so as to gain forgiveness from the revolutionary masses and, eventually, to be 'liberated' from the present situation.

I came home very late again tonight. The kids watched me with their large eyes wide open when I came in. They were still waiting for me, afraid mishaps might take place... Children's hearts are always innocent and beautiful. Looking at their delicate, skinny bodies, I felt guilty. They need better food when they are growing, but there has been no extra money at home for months now, not even a few pennies to buy a bottle of cooking vinegar Peace asked for yesterday.

I came upon a paragraph in the biography of Karl Marx tonight, which described the hardships Marx used to go through in London. There was no food for days and no money to send his sick little son to hospital. The poor child died miserably. His tiny body lay still in the cold coffin... I couldn't control my tears as I read to this point.

Yes, it's time to make up my mind. I must hate her, hate her, as a class enemy! Right, a bourgeois Rightist is a bourgeois reactionary. And there is no difference between this type of class enemy and any other type. They are all enemies of the communist society and of the people.

...I should think about the fact that she is the daughter of a rich landlord and she grew up in a family in the exploiting class. I should never forget that my father laboured hard all his life and died in poverty! I should never forget that my poor mother was forced to jump off the cliff to find her hope in life! I should never forget that millions of communists have sacrificed their lives to overthrow the dark old society and to create the new! I should never forget that there are still billions of people suffering in the world and waiting for us to liberate them! The task is heavy and the road in front is arduous for our communists! My own suffering is nothing compared with the holy cause of communism!

....Still, I feel it's so hard to make a decision. Though theoretically I understand I must, when I imagine that I pick up the knife and point it at her, her tearful face reappears in front of me and all my guts leave me at once! Oh, who can tell me what I should do!

Today, the head of the revolutionary committee read to me the official document issued by Qin's institute. She was not only a Rightist, she was proved to have had an affair with the institute's former leader, too. The revolutionary masses in her institute have exposed everything and she is under punishment now. The rumour I heard a long time ago is finally proved.

I have never felt so calm and firm as today. I don't feel guilty any more...

My dear children! You are all sound asleep now, in this deep night. I hope you are all having sweet, sweet dreams. You are not aware what kind of life is waiting for you... Your father is going to lead you on a hard, arduous journey alone! Your childhood will be spent on a path overgrown with thistles and thorns... But, please, don't blame your father! It is also for your own fortune that your father makes this decision. I will take all of you with me wherever I go in the future and give you all the love and warmth a father can give...

I felt a lump in my throat and tears blurred my view. I closed up the diary and returned to my room with total despair. It was hopeless now... It was all finished...

I closed my eyes, but could not sleep for a long time... Then I saw my mother coming into the room... She cooked a good meal for us, but watched us with a sad smile... I held her hand tightly, fearing she would leave us alone again. I wanted to tell her something, but my throat was choked all the time... My mother brought some new clothes for us and started to wash the dirty ones we took off, but I noticed blood was dropping from the end of her ear-long grey hair... I was terribly scared at the sight, and then I heard her saying that she had contracted an incurable disease and would die soon. I rushed to her, but found she had diminished... Her figure had dissolved into a pile of snow right on the spot where she had been doing the washing a moment ago... I grasped the snow in my hands and cried out sadly and my heart split into pieces...

Someone was pushing me. I woke up and looked around. It was deep in the night and I realized that I had had a horrifying dream. Under the soft moonlight coming through the window I saw Little-red push her delicate upper body out of the blanket and saw her hand shaking my shoulder.

"What happened, sister? Why are you crying?" she asked, her large black eyes looking at me anxiously.

Still sobbing, I told her about my dream in broken sentences. Mom died! Little-red suddenly burst out with a miserable crying and embraced me with her small arms. I held her shivering fragile body and we wept together in the large bed.

The autumn wind was blowing away the dry hot summer air in the highland. The noisy and monotonous chorus of cicadas hiding in the dense leaves of the poplar trees in the backyard of our building had eventually faded. As the weather turned cooler, my father was pronounced 'liberated', a special term used to describe government officials who had gained the initial forgiveness from the revolutionary masses. His work was not yet resumed, but the eye-offending cardboard hanging from his neck was finally discarded.

We were thrilled to hear this, of course. With that damned cardboard removed, we could now walk together with my father in the streets without fearing to be attacked by stones or sneered at by anybody. Though my father was not a leader of the institute any more, nothing could satisfy us more than being able to live like the ordinary people.

On the first Sunday after my father was 'liberated', we got up early in the morning and went to the famous Princess Park, an old garden named for the most favoured daughter of the emperor who lived in the sixth century. We stayed in the park the whole day, appreciating joyfully for the first time in years, the big-roofed pavilions, the zigzag stone bridge on the lake, and numerous historical tablets surviving from over a thousand years ago. As my father asked us to stand still while he smilingly took snapshots of us, scenes flashed into my mind of the days in Beijing a few years before when my mother used to take us kids out to parks on Sundays. My heart seized up and my mind became vacant. The white clouds above the golden-and-red-painted pavilion, the willow branches swaying gently in the breeze by the lake, everything turned grey and dull. Mom's appealing laughter, the kids' sorrow-free laughter, had all gone. A century seemed to have passed.

I didn't mention my mother to my father any more. I understood he had already made up his mind. I knew his own sorrow was no less than mine. From the letters my mother wrote to us children, I couldn't see what was going on between her and my father. And my father, as usual, always avoided any conversation concerning my mother.

The discussions between Little-red and me now often focused on which of us three was going to be sent to my mother in Beijing and who was going to stay with my father in Xi An, when the day finally came. Based on my experience in the past, I believed that I was the one going to be sent to my mother, and Little-red and Wei would undoubtedly stay in Xi An. Little-red worried about my prediction, for she too, wanted to stay with Mother, if she could have a choice. Then I remembered the words in my father's diary and told Little-red: "Perhaps we don't have any choice. Maybe we will all go with Father, for he is politically out of trouble now."

But before I had enough time to think about that, a quite unexpected event took place and threw me into the abyss of endless inner suffering ever after that.

One day after lunch, I sat on the balcony to mend my father's coat which was worn out at the collar and the sleeves. The autumn sun was warm and comforting. Sparrows were twittering on the wire poles in the yard. Some kids were playing hide and seek around the building entrances. Little-red and Wei had gone to their friends' homes after lunch and I was alone at home.

A girl's sharp voice suddenly broke the peaceful atmosphere. I put aside the coat in my hand and looked down over the railings. It was Jun! And she was looking at me!

Finding me watching her, Jun sneered. With one hand on her hip and the other pointing at me, she said in a loud voice: "Peace, you dog girl! You'd better behave yourself! You'd better not think that your father is now liberated and that no one dares to criticize you any more!"

I felt it strange that she should act like this when I had not offended her at all. I questioned her about what she was saying. I never dreamed that she would utter the following words: "You are simply not Tian-zhi's daughter!"

What? What was she talking about? I felt as if my head had been struck hard by a club, and the blow had made me dizzy. My heart was beating fast and my legs were shaking. I caught the railings and tried to stand still. More and more people gathered below and watched the event with curiosity.

Jun's sharp voice became higher and higher with excitement, her triangle-shaped eyes emitting a vicious but triumphant light. But I just couldn't understand a single word.

"What are you saying? You are lying..." My voice was weak and trembling. My legs were shaking so vehemently that I could not stand there any more. I turned my back, moved inside the room and fell on the bed, paralyzed.

The door to the balcony was opening. Jun was still screaming in the yard, "Go and check the truth in the institute yourself!"

I lay in bed motionlessly like a dead person. "I am not Tian-zhi's daughter! Am I an adopted child? Is this what Jun meant to say?" My heart was filled with an impending terror.

Wei walked silently into the room. He didn't look at me, but searched for something in the trunk.

I braced myself to raise up, but I felt weak and sat back on the bed. "Wei," I stared at him and asked him in a nervous voice. "Am I your sister?"

"Yes, of course." he replied briefly, glancing at me carelessly. Clearly he knew nothing about the horrible event in the yard a moment before.

"But, but why did she say I am not Tian-zhi's..." I almost shouted out, but stopped, not knowing how to continue. "Tell me, Wei! Am I your sister?" I repeated my question.

Wei must have been frightened by the desperate look on my face and the strange question I asked him repeatedly. He walked towards the door and threw the words: "I don't know either..." behind him.

That afternoon, I went to the research institute. This was the first time I had dropped by since my arrival in Xi An a year ago. I had always avoided coming here for fear of seeing my father's miserable situation.

The grey-coloured buildings inside the courtyard looked as mysterious as before. There was a long line of big-character posters on the outside wall of the canteen and some people were standing in front of them, reading silently.

I went over and found that was the 'final appraisal' made for my father by the revolutionary committee. It accounted to the public for the personal history of my father and the decision to 'liberate' him.

My eyes quickly caught the lines on the first page:

"...In 1957, Tian-zhi married Qin, a Rightist and ex-wife of a counter-revolutionary clique member..."

I stared at the word 'ex-wife'. For a while my mind seemed to have stopped working and rusted over. What did this strange word mean? I simply could not imagine that. What? What? My mind became completely vacant at this moment...

Some people standing by were looking at me and whispering to each other. I was startled, and left the institute in a hurry.

I moved slowly on a road. The autumn wind was blowing, cooling my head, and I gradually realized that 'that word' referred to my mother. But what was the connection with me then?

I had come by the rough idea by then that a baby would only be born after a woman married a man. If my father married my mother in 1957, which was two years after my birth date, then I could not be the child from their marriage. If I was not the child of Father, then whose child was I?

All the suspicions in the past now loomed into my mind like ominous icebergs in the sea.

...In Beijing a few years ago, after each dispute between Mother and Father, she would leave home with me, but not with my sister and brother.

...I had heard quite a few times people's comments that Little-red and Wei looked different from me.

...In Yi Chun when Aunt Plain-pearl abused me, she sometimes would make strange remarks such as: "Don't feel too good about yourself! You really don't know what your surname is!" and "If it were not for the sake of my brother-in-law and sister-in-law, I would not bother myself to take care of a mean thing like you!"

I didn't understand her real meaning then and felt confused by the way she talked. But now I understood. "I don't belong to my father's family," I said to myself.

However, it puzzled me that my parents had never mentioned anything to me all those years. If Mom was married to someone else before, why did she avoid mentioning even a single word to me, for many people had married twice and it was regarded as normal... Perhaps... perhaps I was an illegitimate child? I shuddered at this thought, for an illegitimate child had no status and dignity at all in Chinese society. Then who was the man who had created my life? Was he as handsome and respectable as Father was? Was he still alive in the world? Perhaps he had already died a long time ago, and Mom would feel pained at the mention of him?

It also puzzled me why Father treated me exactly the same as he treated my sister and brother, not at all as the kind of step-father appearing in so many novels and fairy tales. I still remembered the first time I saw him in Beijing, when he smiled at me so kindly and stretched out his warm arms towards me as if receiving a long-lost daughter... And the Saturday evening many years ago, when he took me home from the kindergarten and asked me to call him 'Dad', was still a fresh painting in my mind... Was it possible that I was actually the illegitimate child of Mother and Father before they got married? No... No.

I suddenly remembered a few sentences in the letter he wrote to Mom, which he quoted in his diary: "...After our divorce, I will support and take care of all the kids, including Peace." There was no doubt that I was different from my sister and brother, who were the real children of Father, or he would not have written in that way in the letter.

Now that it was clear that I was not the child of Father by birth, I felt extremely frightened and insecure. A short time before when I learned the inevitable fact of divorce between Mom and Father, I was heartbroken, but I understood Father was forced to choose this way for the sake of his future as well as the kids'. He wanted to protect us and never let us live in difficulty again, once he was 'liberated'. And I couldn't hate him at all, though he pushed Mom out of our life. I had cried a lot but deep in my heart, I understood clearly there was no way but to follow Father in my future, whatever kind of life was waiting ahead.

Now with the shadow of my birth mystery overhead, I suddenly felt that I was like rootless duckweed floating in an abandoned pond, or a small boat on the endless sea, lonely, unsecured, with my past and future full of mystery...

"Oh, I wish Mom would come to get me! I won't mind whatever status she has! I need you, Mom..." Tears could not be controlled any more and I squatted weakly on the ground at the corner of a building and buried my face in my hands.

At the dinner table that evening, I looked secretly at Father, Wei, and Little-red. Their peaceful manner proved that they knew nothing about what had happened during the day. The food was still the same as usual, rice porridge, steamed bread, and stir-fried cabbage. But they tasted different to me today, with a raw, unfamiliar flavour.

I filled up a bowl with porridge and passed it to Father. He smiled amiably to me as he usually did. However, I felt the smile was different today and my heart shrank. Under the soft orange-coloured light bulb and amid the warm steam of the food, Wei and Little-red were gobbling up their meals. I told myself that everything was still the same. No one knew the secret in my heart, and the family was harmonious.

Yes, Father had always been nice to me and he was really a loving and beloved Father. Little-red and Wei trusted me and had become used to relying on me. How could I ask or tell them something which would make everybody sad? I had no right to disturb them with any more sorrow and disturb the peace and relief barely secured in the family. I must keep all the mysteries, all the doubtful questions, all the sorrowful feelings, everything, locked in my heart.

I was about fourteen years old then. The decision to keep the secret of my birth deep in my heart began to torture me from that year. When I was alone, I often wondered who could be the man who gave me life and what kind of man he was, a man so mysterious that all my relatives avoided mentioning him. It was quite possible that he was no longer alive. But how had he died?

Gradually I became a very sensitive and sentimental girl. The slightest implication, a suspicious sneer or a careless comment made by people, would disturb my over-sensitive nerves and throw me into tears and agony and sleepless nights...

10

Living among the Peasants

AS 1970 DAWNED, WE LEFT METROPOLITAN XI AN TO RESETTLE in a rural area a thousand miles away.

Mao had given new orders recently. He required all government officials and intellectuals in higher learning and research institutes to go to rural areas and mix with workers and peasants — the labouring class.

Mao thought it was necessary for intellectuals, who had stayed in big cities and been long separated from the reality of Chinese society, to become familiar with the situation in the country's broad rural area. He intended to have their minds remoulded through physical labour, so as to prevent the growth of bureaucracy, corruption, a new bourgeoisie, and capitalists. To answer the call of the great leader, many government agencies set up 'cadre schools' in the poorest regions of China.

All the intellectuals and their families in my father's research institute had to go to the 'cadre school'. Cooks, carpenters, repairmen, janitor, doorkeepers and drivers were allowed to stay in the now empty institute, because they belonged to the working class and their minds needed no remoulding.

An exception was my friend Jade's family. As her father had killed himself, and her mother was a housewife, there were no more intellectuals in the family of mother-and-five-kids. But the family could not be categorized as working class, either, as Jade's father was a suicide 'criminal'. The Revolutionary Committee reached the decision to send the family to a mountain village five hundred miles south of Xi An.

Jade's family was horrified by the decision. They understood that, once sent to the mountain village, they would become peasants forever and never be able to come back to the city. Jade's mother pleaded to the Revolutionary Committee, in the hope that the family could go to the 'cadre school' with the rest of the intellectuals. She was refused. A deadline was given to the family for moving away.

On the day of their departure, I went to Jade's home to say goodbye to her. A big truck stopped outside of her home. A few men jumped off and put a long poster on the wall under their window: "A warm farewell for you as you go into a spacious world"! The men helped the family move their stuff onto the truck. As I waved to Jade, she buried her face in her hands and started to cry. Her mother had been weeping for days. She wore a long face, not looking at or talking to anyone. The truck moved away.

Three days later, we packed up all our luggage in haste. We chose only the most necessary things to take with us. The heavy furniture, cabinet, desk, bookcases were left to the working class families staying in Xi An.

We were on the train for a day and then on a truck for hours. Our destination was a small village on a large plain in central China. Henan was one of the poorest provinces in China, because the constant floods from the Yellow River passing through it had left nothing to the people living on its banks but impoverished soil on thousands of miles of the barren plain.

Our family and four others were assigned to go to a village on one truck. As the truck bumped along a winding dirt country road, I watched the scenery in the winter fields. There were a few trees with naked branches standing in the bare farm land. A thin layer of snow barely covered the light brown salinized soil. Here and there, shivering in the fierce cold wind, were a couple of dried corn poles left from the autumn harvest.

The road was rough and the truck jolted us badly. Everyone on the truck was either wrapped in a blanket or shivering in the cold air, and felt so sick, they knotted their brows and closed their eyes.

Before dark the truck arrived at a village named 'Slope Lu' where about one hundred mud houses were scattered around, each separated by mud walls. As we descended in the truck to the centre of the village, many villagers, informed of our coming days before, came to help move our luggage and take aged people to their own homes for a rest. The children and many women who had never been more than two miles from their village were excited to see the truck, and the 'city dwellers', as they called us.

A group of young girls about my age, that is, around fourteen or fifteen, soon surrounded me.

"Oh, look! This girl is wearing a jacket buttoned in the front!"

"She has two pigtails instead of one."

"How does she make her teeth so white?"

These were the comments they made about me.

I noticed with surprise that all the girls in the village had kind of yellowish-brown spots on their teeth, perhaps a result of the heavy fluoride in their drinking water. Their clothes were made of hand-woven rough cotton cloth, either dyed black or russet, narrowly cut to fit their relatively robust bodies. Obviously, the clothes were made by the girls themselves, from spinning the raw cotton into yarn, and then weaving the yarn into a whole piece of material, to tailoring the material into coat or pants in an awkward way. Not only was the style of their clothes old fashioned, buttoned on the right side of the body like a seventy-year-old woman would do, but their hair style, a long pigtail dangling at the back of the head, was also something I had seen only in movies about the China of a few decades before.

The location of the 'cadre school' was a piece of barren land on the bank of a dried up river. The river bed was full of stones and reeds, with here and there a waterlogged depression, and the only residents in it were hares and wild geese. The task facing the newcomers was to build houses for their families, open up the river bed and turn it into farm land, with their two hands. The intellectuals were expected to be remoulded through these basic life activities, therefore everything had to be done from scratch. But before the newcomers built their shelters, they would live in the nearby villages with the peasants.

We were assigned to move into the worst house in Slope Lu. It had been a public horse stable since 1958 when the commune system was set up in rural China and all private land and farm animals became collectively owned. Outside of the house, a few steps away, was a large manure pit about four metres in diameter. The villagers were required to dump their night soil there to make fertilizer for the public fields.

Inside the house, about sixty square metres in area, there were no separate rooms and no ceiling. The purlins on the roof were connected with sorghum stalks, darkened over the years by smoke, and ridden with dusty spider webs. The mud floor was damp. We spread cinder and slag on top of it to make it drier. There was a door in the mid-front of the flat and two small windows, about one square foot large, on each side. The windows were glassless and we put old newspapers on them to stop the cold wind coming in.

When it got dark, the whole house seemed horrifying, as mice squeaked and ran about among the stalks on the roof. There was no electricity in the village so we lit up the oil lamp bought in the village store and sat around a newly-built mud stove in the centre of the house to keep warm. The dim light from the lamp cast our shadows on the walls in strange shapes.

There was no chimney connected with the stove and the smoke of the burning coal filled the air and made us dizzy. Our neighbour, a smiling middle aged peasant who helped us to build the stove in the day, comforted us: "Don't worry! A little bit dizzy in the head is nothing serious. You will get used to the smoke in a few days."

We got some cornmeal, dried beans, rice, turnips, carrots and cabbages from a large village two miles away. In the following months, this stuff became our daily food.

The living conditions of the peasants in this area were incredibly poor but they never complained and never blamed nature's stinginess. They accepted everything silently and tried hard to harvest corn, sorghum, cotton and yams from the poor soil. Vegetables and meat were luxuries — only for festivals. In autumn, they would dry the yam leaves in the sunshine and preserve them as vegetables for winter.

At meal times, the villagers would bring, in one hand, a large bowl of dark-coloured soup made from dry yam leaves and bean noodles, and in the other hand, a few pieces of steamed yams, to visit each other. Usually, three or four of them would get together, standing or squatting on the mud floor, exchanging news while eating. In the first few weeks after our arrival, there were always villagers, both young and old, coming to our home for a chat at meal times.

The villagers got their drinking water from wells with their water lines only about two yards below the ground. I quickly learned how to get water from the well with only a rope connected to a pail.

Except for young girls, all the villagers wore black or dark blue home-made cotton clothes and shoes. Young girls were sometimes in a reddish-yellow colour, or, every couple of years they might get a piece of colourful machine-made material, a gift from their fiancés. The traditional practice was that a fiancé was chosen by the girl's parents when she was four or five years old. Besides some money paid to the girl's parents at their engagement, the fiancé was expected to send her a piece of cloth every year until they got married in their late teens.

After the founding of Communist China and the announcing of the new marriage law in the early 1950s, young people were granted the right of free choice of their spouses, so the old tradition in the rural area had to be modified to a certain extent. If the girl grew up and found she did not like the chosen fiancé, she might try to reject the marriage, but in doing so, she and her family had to pay back all the money and gifts received from the fiancé over the years. On the other hand, if the boy disliked his fiancée and wanted to retreat, he had no right to ask for the return of the paid-out money and gifts.

Clearly, the village was not influenced much by the blazing fire of the on-going Cultural Revolution. Situated in one of the poorest regions in China, it was a corner forgotten by the Red Guards.

The village school continued its classes in the normal way. Unlike in big cities, teachers here were still highly respected by everybody and I was shocked to see a teacher slap the face of a lazy student. There were seven grades in the brick, mud, and straw made school at the outskirts of the village. Little-red, Wei and I soon started our education in different classrooms.

Not long after our arrival, the traditional lunar calendar's New Year Festival was close at hand. As the biggest event in the year, it was warmly celebrated. The villagers would put on their best clothes and eat the best food, usually braised pork with bean noodles and steamed wheat bread. In every village there was an open-spaced clay platform, a stage for the performance of local operas. As a rule, each village in turn would sponsor a whole night's performance to entertain visitors from other villages.

Slope Lu enjoyed the reputation of having the best performing group in this area. The local operas were based on legendary stories, embellished with colourful silken costumes and head decorations and accompanied by traditional musical instrument like the ban hu (a two-stringed instrument), the bamboo flute, the sheng (a multi-tubed instrument), and noisy drums and gongs. The performances were the most exciting recreation for the peasants, as most of them had simply no opportunity to see a movie. This year, however, the village school teachers, who were the natural organizers and also the musicians for each year's performance, were worried about what they should play.

The teachers had heard, perhaps from the newcomers, that traditional operas were forbidden now because they were feudalist relics, mostly stories about how ancient generals fought bravely for the emperors, or how young people longed for free choice in their marriages. They had also heard that Mao's wife, Jiang Qing, had allowed only eight modern dramas to be performed in the country, five of them being Peking operas, two being ballet dances and one, a symphony. These eight dramas were labelled as the "Eight Revolutionary Model Dramas" and people all over the country were encouraged to learn the performance or at least sing pieces of the music.

After serious discussions, the school teachers had made up their minds to rehearse one of the Peking operas, a story about how a group of wounded communist soldiers was helped by people in World War II. However, the local people had difficulty in mastering the music of the Peking opera which was from quite a different school. They decided to try to combine the two things — local music, but the original content.

I was invited to play the role of the heroine, a young hostess of a tea house and an underground communist. The teachers were confident that my appearance, my voice, and my acting skills, would win new fame for Slope Lu in this year's competition. I had no interest in the strange music of the local opera and it was hard to learn, but encouraged by the village girls who had become my friends, I accepted the challenge and started to rehearse.

Every night after supper time, a few village girls and I would go to the school. Little-red often came with me, for there was no other place she could go. All the actors were girls. They played all the male roles in the opera. I asked them why.

"The villagers don't like teenage boys and girls being together every night, for that may create scandal," one of the girls replied.

The teachers quickly found my voice was different from the vocal sound they were familiar with and they tried hard to correct me. I made an effort, too, but I was impatient about learning something I did not like.

Practising continuously for hours in cold winter evenings often made us sleepy and shivery. The girls would find some dried sorghum poles and set a fire on the mud floor of the classroom. We warmed our cold hands and feet over the fire and in the thick smoke. The girls were eager to hold Little-red high in the air and she would start to sneeze and cough from the smoke. At those moments, they liked to ask me about the big cities. They were interested in everything I told them, and the coldness and sleepiness were soon driven away.

One night, after our practice, we left the school yard and returned to the quiet, sleeping village. To save lamp oil, people would go to bed as soon as it was dark so the whole village was quiet except for the barking of one or two dogs, now and then.

The girls were still excited from the rehearsal and did not want to go home. One of them, Pretty-twig, suggested that they should treat me to the game, 'Listening at the foot of the wall'. All the other girls felt excited at her idea and were eager to show me the game. I felt puzzled at what they wanted me to do, for I could not understand the meaning of the game they mentioned.

Pretty-twig asked if I had ever seen how a rooster helped a hen to lay eggs. I shook my head, still puzzled. She then gestured with one palm pushing hard on top of the back of the other hand, and asked again: "Now, do you understand?"

I felt stupid, for I still could not figure out the meaning of her gesture. She was very disappointed at my stupidness and was about to lose her temper: "How could you understand nothing at your age? Aren't you already fourteen years old!"

The other girls stopped her and said: "Well, Pretty-twig, don't be annoyed. We will show her what it is, right?"

They explained to me that one of the school teachers, a young man who played the bamboo flute, had been married about a month ago and we should go to listen secretly at the foot of the wall outside of his house.

I told Little-red to go home to sleep and I followed the girls. On the way to the teacher's house, I didn't ask the girls any further questions, fearing they would laugh at me for knowing nothing. But my mind worked hard to try to understand the significance of our activity. Then I suddenly remembered a short story I had learned from my primary school textbooks years ago.

It was about an event in old China. A rich but greedy landlord had hired a few farmhands to work for him. Every morning before dawn he would imitate a cockcrow outside of the window where the farmhands lived, and then urge them to get up and work in the fields, as a cockcrow was the sign of daybreak. The farmhands wondered why the cock always crowed when it was still dark outside. They finally discovered the landlord's secret and served him his own sauce. They caught him outside of the chicken shed, pretending not to know who he was as it was dark, and they beat him with clubs and sticks as they would a thief.

Oh! I had it! Yes, the girls must want to fool the teacher to get up by imitating a cockcrow! I also felt excited about the idea and quickened my pace.

When we reached the young teacher's house, we all shut up our mouths and sneaked one after the other into the yard shed by moonlight. We held our breaths and stayed outside of the window of the bedroom. I was a little bit nervous but the other girls only had a surreptitious look on their faces.

It was quiet and dark inside the room. I waited anxiously, and wondered why the girls were not doing anything yet. A few more minutes passed and I lost my patience. I decided to take action of my own. I cupped my mouth with my hands and imitated the crow of a rooster — "Cock-a-doodle-do..."

The sound broke the silence both outside and inside the house. The young teacher's voice came from the window: "Don't be silly, Peace! I know it's you. Go home to sleep. It is already midnight."

All the girls felt dismayed. They dragged me out onto the street and blamed me for spoiling their game. I was confused. Didn't I do what they had planned? The only pity was that my imitation of a cockcrow failed to fool the young teacher!

We were still arguing about the failure of our scheme when I saw a torch moving towards us. As it came nearer, I discovered it was my father! During the day, he went to the site by the river bank to build the 'cadre school'. After supper, there were often villagers coming to our home to chat with him by the fire.

Tonight at midnight, my father found Little-red coming home alone and asked her my whereabouts. Little-red told him that I had gone with the other girls to play the game of 'Listening at the foot of the wall'. My father was shocked and set out at once to look for me. He went around the village until he heard the noise outside of the young teacher's house.

My father looked very unhappy, but he didn't explain anything to me and only warned me not to stay outside as late as this any more.

Not only was I too slow to appreciate many of the local customs, I proved to be quite stupid in imitating the vocal sound of the local opera. Three days before our public performance, the teachers, after failing to correct my 'foreign tune', as they described it, gave up their effort and asked another girl to replace me. She was short, timid, and plain-looking, with a pair of small eyes on her narrow yellow face. But when she acted on the clay-made stage, lit up by two large gas lamps and circled with colourful red and green silk curtains, I was surprised by the sonorous voice coming from her thin, narrow chest. There was no microphone, but her singing could be heard clearly by the audience at the far back of the square.

※　　※　　※

ON THE SECOND DAY OF THE LUNAR NEW YEAR'S FESTIVAL, my mother appeared unexpectedly at our dark, damp house at lunch time. As the door was very low, she had to bend a little bit to come in. She was in a dark brown cotton-padded jacket, black pants, and black shoes.

We kids were extremely happy to see her and sprang over to the door, while my father stood up from his seat and forced an awkward smile on his face. His eyes behind the thick glasses looked embarrassed.

My mother looked even older than a year ago, with her grey hair almost white and a few more wrinkles on her forehead and at the corners of her eyes. She quickly opened the big bag she brought from Beijing and took out many delicious foods. There were beef and mutton cooked in soy sauce, skin of soy bean milk, bean curd cooked in spices, dried shrimps, mussels, and fish — things we had not tasted for a fairly long time.

That evening, our house was full of a good smell coming from the stove. We changed into the new clothes my mother bought for us and helped her in preparing a big dinner.

When I was alone with my mother, she asked me in an unhappy tone: "Why didn't you write me a letter and tell me where you were moving to?"

I was struck dumb. Why hadn't I thought about writing her a letter? It might have been that I was so involved in my new experience with the peasants that I had forgotten the most important thing. How silly I had been! It must have been difficult for my mother to find us in this out-of-the-way place, for my father didn't tell her when we left Xi An.

At night, my mother shared the big bed with Little-red and me. For the first time in the last couple of years, I felt like a child again, with a mother beside me to take care of me. How I wished that she would stay with us and the family could be like a family once again!

She and my father talked in the fields a few times. Every time they would come back with stern faces. Little-red and I observed, and guessed secretly what was going on between them, and expected, though with little hope, that they might become reconciled.

A few more days went by amid our anxiety; Little-red and I secretly analyzed all the indications and felt there was nothing encouraging.

One day after lunch my parents went to the fields again. A long time passed before they came back with an angry air. As they entered the house, we all looked at them nervously. My father said to my mother: "Now you can explain to the kids what are your problems..." Then he turned around and left again.

My mother stood by the door for a few seconds and then came to the bed. She leaned against the pillows and blankets piled up on one side of the bed and asked us to come closer to her.

"I am sure you have already heard something about Mom. But I must tell you what mistakes I have made." She looked at each of us and talked slowly and clearly, her eyes looking cold but her voice calm.

"Mom said something wrong in the year nineteen fifty-seven. Whatever I said was against the Communist Party, and against socialist ideology. I have since then been labelled as a bourgeois Rightist, the enemy of the people... You all must understand: it is necessary that you draw a clear line between you and me and be careful not to let my wrong ideas poison your innocent hearts... You are not supposed to obey me, but to follow the Party and Chairman Mao in whatever they require... I am your mother, but politically, I am an enemy..."

We all remained silent. I did not know what was in my brother's and sister's minds. but I felt my heart crumpled by a powerful hand. Though my mother was trying to stay calm and talk gently, I could feel the grief and reluctance in her eyes and tone. How I wanted to tell her, "We love you and cannot live without you, Mom!" How I wanted to tell her, "You are a good mother, and not an enemy!" I was sure my brother and sister wanted to say the same thing. But we all remained silent. The humiliating title, "bourgeois Rightist", which we had learned a long time ago but for the first time now heard in her own voice, was like a huge rock pressing on our chests and preventing us from uttering any sound.

The day came when my mother had to leave, taking me with her. I wasn't surprised at all, with the mystery of my birth buried deep inside me. Despite my mother's confession, I still felt it was much better to live with her, the source of love and care.

But as my eyes fell upon my brother and sister, especially Little-red, I felt sorrow for them. It seemed they understood that they had to stay with Father, so they didn't try to beg or complain, but accepted the fact sadly and silently.

My father borrowed a handcart from our neighbour and carried our luggage to the railway station thirty miles away. Little-red accompanied us for two miles along the winding country road. She walked beside me silently, but I knew she was feeling miserable. Again and again, we asked her to return home but she insisted on walking with us for more time.

At the intersection of a broader road, we urged her once more. She stopped reluctantly, looked at Mother and me, her eyes full of expectation, and asked in her tender voice, "Mom, Sister, are you going to come back and get me?"

A shadow came over my mother's eyes and she replied, "Yes... Be a nice child..." Little-red waved to us. My mother took my hand and turned away abruptly. She walked very fast and I found it hard to keep up with her pace. A few minutes later, I looked back. Little-red was still standing alone in the barren winter fields, staring at the handcart moving farther and farther away from her.

"Poor Little-red, please turn back and go home..." I said silently and waved to her again. My nose quivered and my eyes were blurred by tears. I felt that I had abandoned her.

The small delicate figure and the striking colour of her red cap gradually vanished from my sight.

❊   ❊   ❊

I FOLLOWED MY MOTHER TO A SMALL VILLAGE, ON THE ridges of the mountains outside of the rising and falling Great Wall, a relic of the five thousand kilometre long wall serving as the Chinese border more than two thousand years before.

There were about thirty households scattered around the slope and foot of a hill. Rich stones from the mountains were used to decorate the village with grey-tiled rooftops, rock walls, rock cisterns and rock terraces.

On the slope of the hill, a flock of sheep was moving slowly and searching for the newly-grown grass. A boy in a long old black coat sat on a large rock, silently watching the herd, with a long switch in his hand. The setting sun's orange-coloured rays shone on his young face.

At the end of the winding trail leading to the village, a blindfolded donkey was dragging millstones in endless circles. The monotonous sound of his hoofs falling on the ground was matched by the heavy and depressing music of the millstones.

A woman came out of her fenced yard and climbed on top of a stone terrace. "Lo—-Lo—-Lo—-Lo—-" she shouted loudly in all directions, calling back her pigs from searching for food in the wilderness.

That was the scene I saw when I walked into the mountain village where my mother was assigned to stay.

Besides my mother, there were three other people, one woman and two men, assigned to settle in the same village. The local people arranged for the 'Beijing cadre', as they called them, to stay in the village's public houses. There were two flats, an office room for the village heads to hold meetings in, a classroom for the school-age kids, a storeroom, and a guest room.

The two men, one a college teacher and one an English translator, used the office room as their residence. My mother and the other woman, an official from Beijing's Public Security Bureau, moved into the guest room where a mud wall separated the sleeping quarters from the kitchen.

My mother sent me to a secondary school in a small town about five miles away and I came to the village only on the weekends and during vacations.

The four 'Beijing cadre' members were in their late thirties and early forties. Every morning, they got up as early as five o'clock and followed the peasants to work in the fields all day. They were always in their worst clothes, with holes and patches, to make themselves look more like the local people. Each month they would get their grain supplies from a state-owned store in town. They decided to eat together for convenience's sake. Every week, one of them would be responsible for cooking and would come home half-an-hour earlier from the fields to prepare lunch and supper.

They were supposed to be re-educated by the peasants, who, as Mao stressed, had much cleaner brains than those of the intellectuals, despite their dirty hands and their feet stained with cow droppings.

Some members of the Beijing cadre were 'problem people', but the good-natured peasants never bothered to care what kind of political status they had in Beijing. Instead, the peasants thought these Beijing cadre members were all well educated and knew everything in the world. They often consulted them on whatever problems they had, including public decision making and family quarrels.

When my school closed during the time of spring ploughing, summer and fall harvesting, and winter vacation, I came back to the mountain village and stayed with my mother. She asked me to work as a volunteer labourer in the fields every morning and to study at home or teach the village kids how to sing and dance in the afternoons.

Getting up early in the morning was not a hard thing for me; life in Yi Chun had already trained me. As the day broke, the head of the village, a man selected by the peasants, would strike a piece of iron bar hanging beneath the eaves of the public house, and the sounds would gradually draw all the people to him.

The village head would then assign farm jobs among them. At the end of the day, the peasants would come to the village accountant who would take down how much they had worked, and, at the end of the year, grain would be distributed to them according to their contributions.

As I was a volunteer labourer, I was always assigned to work with the females. They did the less heavy work such as flattening the fields, smashing the hardened and impervious soil, hoeing weeds and cutting wheat. Our tools included hoes, spades, sickles and a hammer-like, long-poled wooden tool.

There were not many plain-fields in the mountain area. The peasants had terraced mountain slopes as well as they could into beautiful ladder-shaped crop fields.

During their breaks, the women would sit around the fields, stitching the soles of cloth shoes for their family members and gossiping about news in the village. Most of the news was about 'sex'. The women often laughed loudly with their backs bending forward. I noticed there was a middle aged woman named Little-bound who seldom joined in the women's lewd conversations.

She was a small figured, timid-looking mother of three. I wondered how it was that she had such a strange name. One day, an old woman told me the history of Little-bound.

She had been only fourteen when she was married by her parents to a husband fifteen years her senior. On her wedding night, the poor girl was frightened and screamed loudly to avoid her husband's advances. The villagers who had been eavesdropping outside gave the stupid husband the advice that he should bind her up in order to carry out this activity smoothly. The husband followed the advice, surrounded by the poor girl's sharp, shrill cries. This practice lasted for quite a long time, in fact, until her first child was born, and the binding and screaming stopped after that. But she had gained the nickname 'Little-bound', and her original name was forgotten by the villagers.

In the mountain areas women were scarce and men had to save for ten years or more before they could get a wife. Although ever since the early 1950s the law had forbidden mercenary marriage, it was hard to stop people in the backward areas where economic conditions, rather than love, was the consideration in marriages.

One morning, the women were smashing the hardened soil in a field near the peak of the hill. During the break, I felt thirsty and wanted to find water to drink. My friend Yellow-hair took me to the nearest house on the slope of the hillside. She told me this was the home of Lucky-smooth whom I knew to be a simple-minded, awkward-looking peasant about forty years old.

Yellow-hair was one year older than me and a nice looking, kind-hearted girl. Her hair, unlike most Chinese, had an unusual light brown colour, which had occasioned her name.

We approached the small stone house. A dish-sized mirror was hanging on top of the roof and reflecting the dazzling light of the sun. Yellow-hair said it was the villagers' belief that the mirror on the roof would prevent evil spirits from coming into the house when there was a sick person inside.

"Who is sick?" I asked curiously.

"The wife," Yellow-hair replied briefly. She gestured to me to stop talking as we entered the dark house.

It was dirty and smelly inside. I looked around and found a young woman sitting on the kang. I was surprised to see a man like Lucky-smooth could have such a pretty young wife! She was a good-looking girl with neat white teeth, large black eyes and thick black hair braided into two pigtails at the back of her head. Yellow-hair introduced me to the wife and she nodded happily. Her delicate pale face blushed when she smiled shyly at me. As I was still wondering why she would become Lucky-smooth's wife, she started to move with difficulty on the kang made out of mud and stone. She took an old hand broom and crawled inch by inch over the kang to sweep it. I realized immediately that she was paralyzed in her lower body! I quickly stopped her attempt to make a clean place for me, and sat on the kang. I tried to start a conversation, but it was in vain. She was apparently too nervous to say anything.

There was no chair in the room. An empty bowl and a pair of chopsticks were on one end of the kang and a few other things like bags of grain and clay-made jars were scattered on the dirty floor. Yellow-hair found an empty bowl and filled it up with water from a vat by the wall. She passed the bowl into my hands. I didn't look at the water and started to drink. The wife watched us silently with an embarrassed smile. I had already figured out that she was also dumb.

When I waved goodbye to the wife and left the depressing house, I asked Yellow-hair how Lucky-smooth married this girl.

"She is from another village, and is only twenty-one years old," Yellow-hair told me. "Since she has congenital malformation in her lower body and is dumb, her parents married her off to Lucky-smooth without any bargain last year. Anyway, Lucky-smooth paid her parents all the savings he had made over the years."

Yellow-hair's voice was serene, but I felt an unbearable noise in my chest.

When news spread among the villagers that the paralyzed wife was pregnant, many people congratulated Lucky-smooth, for they all knew that his purpose in getting married was to have a son in order to pass on the family's surname. But I heard my mother say with worry to her roommate that it would be dangerous for the paralyzed woman to give birth to a child.

One night, shortly after I fell asleep, I was awakened by a rapid knocking on the window. I got up and opened the door. Lucky-smooth stood at the door in heavy rain. Under a large straw hat, his usually expressionless lean face looked alert.

He stuttered in excitement that his wife "is in red", that is, was bleeding, and he asked for help from my mother and the other Beijing cadre members. Unfortunately, the Beijing cadre and the village head had gone to a major town that morning for an assembly meeting and would not be coming back for two days.

What could we do? I felt pressured by the anxiety in his eyes and the expression on his thick partially opened lips. Obviously, he was waiting for an answer from me. In the absence of the adults, I felt the responsibility to help. I rushed to Yellow-hair's home. She got up from the kang and talked with me at the door. We decided to fetch a doctor from a major village two miles away, and set out immediately.

We had to climb over a mountain on our way. The sky was starless and as dark as black ink. Though the rain was not heavy, I shivered with cold under my thin jacket. I staggered on the narrow winding trail and stumbled all the time over the naked roots of bushes and small rocks.

Yellow-hair was familiar with the mountain trail and walked rather fast, but she stopped and waited for me once in a while. The hillsides were overgrown with bushes of wild jujube and their thorns tore up my pants and jacket when we began to climb towards the summit.

The summit of the mountain was strangely-shaped, with steep cliffs on both sides. My legs began to shake as I approached it. I had to grab the crevice on the slippery cliff surface tightly with my fingers and lean my knee against it as I crawled over it nervously. Yellow-hair reached the summit first. She perched on the tip of the cliff and reached out her hand to me.

Over the summit, the rain ceased and I came upon a scene of utter tranquillity. I felt a little bit nervous at the silence in the deep valley beneath my feet, which seemed mysterious in the misty darkness. I talked loudly to

Yellow-hair, who walked a few steps ahead of me. Then I heard the cawing of black crows, startled by human voices and reeling across the valley.

Yellow-hair looked back and said to me, "Oh, do you hear the cawing of the black crows? This is not auspicious. I am afraid Lucky-smooth's wife may not be able to survive her trials…"

We were dismayed when we reached the clinic in the major village. The young doctor, who had been assigned by the government to work in the mountain area for a few years, was angry to be woken up at midnight and refused our request to come to help the labouring woman. He knew too well that, as one of the few doctors in this backward area, he was treasured greatly by the peasants who never dared to show any resentment, whatever he did.

I explained to him that the woman was paralyzed and could not come here and it was necessary for him to come with us. He replied sarcastically: "A paralyzed woman should never get herself pregnant! Don't you understand?" With a backward glance at my stunned face, he returned to his room and shut the door behind him.

Back in the village, we learned that the poor woman had already fainted a few times. Hearing our bad news, the few villagers who had gathered in Lucky-smooth's house decided to carry the woman to a small town hospital five miles away. They laid the woman on a stretcher made of poles and strings and set out at once. Yellow-hair followed the stretcher to the town. I was tired and sleepy and returned home.

I got up the next day. It was almost noon and the sun shone brightly in a blue sky thoroughly cleaned by the rain. The whole village was silent. There were no people walking around and no barking dogs. What had happened? I wondered, looking around. Then I found that far above on the hill slope, around the small stone house, there were dozens of people, children as well as adults. I remembered what had happened the night before and quickly walked up to the house.

Outside of the door, a few women were wiping their eyes and hooting at the kids hopping around. Men with numb faces were squatting in the shade of a big jujube tree in the rock-fenced yard and smoking at their pipes quietly.

I hesitated at the door, fearing what I might see inside the dark house. At this moment, Yellow-hair stepped out of the room, her slender eyes swollen. She led me to the back of the house and we both sat on the edge of a stone terrace.

"She died." Her voice was low and exhausted. "The doctor said that the baby's head was filled with water and too large to get out of the woman's body. It was a difficult labour and the woman lost consciousness. We waited outside of the delivery room for hours. I looked through the door when it was opened. I saw pools of blood and the iron pincers in the doctor's hand... Then the doctor came out and asked Lucky-smooth which one he would want, the wife or the baby, since only one of the two could survive. Lucky-smooth replied, he would prefer the baby. The doctor returned to the delivery room and a moment later brought the news that a baby boy was born. Lucky-smooth was exhilarated, even though it was a blue baby. He begged the doctors to make all efforts to save the baby, for he would be the only son in his life. But the baby lived for only two hours and the wife died as the sun rose in the morning."

The stone terrace where we sat was surrounded by thick bushes of the wild jujube. They were full of small bean-like red fruits, a rather striking colour under the clear autumn sky. I had no mood to collect them today as I used to. I walked back to the front yard with a sunken heart. Then I heard two women sighing and talking in low voices.

"What a pity! It was such a big-sized boy."

"No doubt it would be. Didn't you see how Lucky-smooth took care of her and fed her with all good food he could get!"

I didn't feel any pity for the death of the baby, but I couldn't forget the shy smile of the pale-faced young woman. Anyway, it was she, not the baby, who had lived with Lucky-smooth for two years.

"Why didn't Lucky-smooth ask the doctor to save his wife first?" I questioned the talking women.

"Why? He married the paralyzed woman to have a child. Of course he would prefer the baby to the wife!" they answered, sounding as if this should have been obvious to me.

I walked into the house. On the cold, hard, small mud kang, was a human figure covered with a dirty, colourless cotton-padded quilt. The figure looked as small as if it were a child. I lacked the courage to look at her face under the quilt. My mind was crowded with the pictures of a large head blue baby, a woman's bloody body, a pair of shining pincers, and a pair of large black eyes in a pale face...

Squatting on the ground was the motionless Lucky-smooth, his head sunk deeply in his hands. I watched him for a few seconds, but could not find any suitable words to comfort him. I left the house silently.

* * *

MY MOTHER SEEMED TO ENJOY HER NEW ROLE IN THE village. The peasants were very impressed that my mother was not behaving like a 'spoilt city dweller', since she often chose to do the heavier work usually assigned to men.

Through the years, all the tenderness and gentle manner expected from a woman had left my mother. She looked like a man, dressed in a blue jacket full of patches, waved a spade or sickle vigorously and laughed heartily just as the peasants did.

My mother was always in high spirits when any peasant came to her for consultations. The young people liked her especially. They often came in the evening to talk about their sorrows, their hopes, or just sit on the kang and watch at my mother silently. I found that my mother's attitude towards these people was always warm and cordial. It was among them that she felt the respect and equality she had long lost, I perceived.

Old Chen, the former English translator, was quite another type. His fair-skinned face, which wore a pair of glasses, never showed a smile. When working in the fields, he was quiet and slow, and very cautious not to hurt himself. Looking at him, I always felt that he was like a prisoner forced to work. Frequently, he would find various excuses, a hurting back, a painful ankle, or a serious headache, to ask for sick leave. When it was his turn to cook for the Beijing cadre, he always left the fields much earlier than others would do.

One day when Old Chen was cooking dinner in the kitchen, I was keeping a diary in my mother's bedroom. He came over and chatted to me gently.

"My daughter is about your age. She loves to write poems." Old Chen took out a black and white picture from his wallet and showed it to me.

It was a family picture. Old Chen, his wife, and four kids.

"Are the kids staying with their mother in Beijing?" I asked.

Old Chen's eyes stayed fixed on the picture, and nodded.

After a period of silence, he asked what sort of literature I liked most.

"Would you show me your favourite of all the poems you have ever written?" He looked interested.

I found he was not a cold, emotionless person, but someone who enjoyed talking about literature and art, which had long disappeared from my mother's daily concerns. I stopped my writing, showed him the naive poems I wrote, and helped Old Chen in his cooking. When I found the large water jar was empty, I offered to fetch water from the well half-a-mile away. He was glad and nodded continuously, "Thank you very much for doing so, very much..."

When my mother came home and found I was breathing heavily after fetching water twice to fill up the big jar, she looked unhappy and asked: "Did Old Chen ask you to do this for him?"

"No, I volunteered." I replied hesitatingly, trying to guess why she was unhappy. "He was interested in reading my poems..."

"Poems?" She sneered and shook her head faintly. "Funny..."

I failed to understand what was "funny" — my naive poems? Or Old Chen?

Besides labouring in the fields, the Beijing cadre were also responsible for leading the peasants in studying any documents the government had issued.

In 1970, when China was preparing to hold a National People's Conference, the list of candidates for the conference was given to all people for discussion. All the peasants, about a hundred in number, were gathered in the village's classroom one evening. After the long list of the names of the candidates was read to them, the Beijing cadre pushed the peasants to voice their opinions. But they continued to keep silent, apparently showing no interest in these strangers on the list. Their lack of interest in the democracy granted to them was displayed once again when China was making its Constitution a few months later.

But enthusiasm was displayed when they came upon familiar topics. Once, the county government had caught a group of criminals, and documents were issued to the village to canvass public opinion about the criminals' proper punishments. Everyone in the village listened attentively and commented eagerly.

When a rapist's case was touched upon, an old woman's husky voice exploded abruptly in the air: "Cut off his cock!"

Fang, the former college teacher, who had been taking notes, was puzzled at the slang the woman used and asked a peasant beside him what a 'cock' was. Though his voice was low, it was heard by all people and they all burst out laughing.

"You are a Chinese teacher, Fang, but you don't understand the Chinese language!" someone in the corner teased him.

"He is still a virgin. No wonder!" a peasant said loudly. People laughed again. Fang's face turned red.

Fang was thirty-eight, the youngest one of the four Beijing cadre members. Though handsome, tall, healthy and well educated, he was still single. No woman wanted to marry him, for he was like my mother, a Rightist.

The friendly and casual atmosphere between the Beijing cadre and the peasants became tense a year after their arrival. In 1971, China started a new campaign to crack down on all bad elements in its rural areas. The Beijing cadre received orders to go all out to ferret out bad people in the village.

The intellectuals stopped working in the fields, and started talking to the villagers individually and collecting information. During the day, I saw men and women coming one by one into the public flats to confess their own wrongdoings or expose those of others, while my mother and the other three Beijing cadre members questioned them with a serious demeanour and took down notes. I didn't know much about what they were doing, for most of the time my mother would let me go out when somebody came in.

One night, I was woken up by my mother's conversation with her roommate.

"This is such a poor, small-sized village, with only a hundred and three people, including kids. There are no landlords and rich farmers to be targeted." This was the voice of Auntie Pay, a Party member and head of the Beijing four. "We have worked hard for so long and the only things we have discovered so far are dirty adultery stories…"

"….Yes," my mother said in darkness. "It is shocking to know that almost everyone in the village has had an affair with somebody else. I am surprised that they could still live peacefully together for all these years!"

"This is a culturally very backward area. The peasants don't regard adultery as something serious…" said Auntie Pay.

"We are supposed to come here to learn from the peasants. But I doubt how we could do it when almost everyone in the village has some problem…" My mother's voice sounded like an immature girl's.

"You are not supposed to think this way!" Auntie Pay's voice suddenly turned harsh. "Do you remember Chairman Mao's words on principal and secondary aspects? The principal aspects of the peasants are good, and their weaknesses are only secondary."

"Yes, you are right. I should remember Chairman Mao's words. I was wrong to say that." My mother hurried to agree with Auntie Pay, as if she was afraid of offending the woman lying on the other end of the kang.

As their investigations went further, the Beijing cadre discovered a 'big' case in the village.

Rich, the head of the village's militia, was a man in his early thirties, six feet tall, with the face of a horse. His class status was 'poor peasant', the most honourable class in rural China in those years. Rich had never been to school and didn't know even how to write his own name but he had impressed the Beijing cadre deeply with his eloquence and the loudness with which he told dirty jokes in the fields and at public meetings. My mother and Auntie Pay secretly called him 'Horse-face' instead of 'Rich'.

A secret concealed for years was revealed. Horse-face's woman was not his wife, but a well-to-do peasant's wife. Five years before, the pretty woman had been married into the well-to-do peasant's home in this very village. Horse-face became very jealous and eventually forced the woman to move into his own home, with the excuse that "poor people should have priority in everything in the communist society." The well-to-do peasant's class status was the lowest one in the small village which had only thirty households. He was too scared to argue or fight with Horse-face, the head of the village militia, and had to swallow his agony. Now, encouraged by the Beijing cadre, he let out all his sorrow.

The Beijing cadre felt what Horse-face had done was totally against the state's marriage law and that justice must be done. In an afternoon, Horse-face was called into my mother's place, where the four members of the Beijing cadre had a serious talk with him. I stayed in the kitchen room and prepared supper by the stove. Their talking could be heard clearly through the mud wall.

I heard Auntie Pay ordering Horse-face to return that pretty woman to her original husband. "As what you have done is totally against the law!" Her voice was stern.

Bang! "Nonsense!" Horse-face hit the wooden kang edge with his large palm. I sneaked to the door between the kitchen and the meeting room and peeped through a hole on the wooden door. Horse-face's suntanned skin became red, his large round eyes flaming with irritation. "As a poor peasant, I had no money to marry a wife. But I wouldn't want to be single all my life! I took her because her husband's class status was the worst one in the village. I have done nothing wrong! I simply want a wife! And that is the right we poor people are entitled to under communist rule!"

The Beijing cadre must have been stunned by his philosophy, and must have felt the difficulty of communicating with such a man! They looked at him and frowned. No one said anything. I held my breath. Then, suddenly, I saw Fang point his finger at Horse-face and say: "You are not a poor peasant! Your behaviour shows you are simply a hooligan, one of the "lumpen proletariat" as Chairman Mao says in his work *Class Analysis in Chinese Society*. You must send the woman back to her husband, or we will force you to do so!" Fang hit his fist loudly on the edge of the kang to show his determination.

There was silence in the room. Auntie Pay stood up from her chair. I quickly went back to the stove side.

The door opened, the four members of the Beijng cadre came out with serious looks. Horse-face followed them out, too. But he stopped by the stove. He laughed as he looked at me and said loudly: "It smells good! What are you cooking, Peace?"

Before I could say anything, he stepped forward and lifted up the heavy wooden lid covering the two-foot-wide iron pot. "Well, steamed white bread!" he exclaimed. "Can I have supper here?"

My mother, I, Fang and Old Chen all looked at Auntie Pay to see what she might say.

Auntie Pay was clearly vexed by Horse-face's provocation. She said coldly to him: "We have only enough for the five of us. You'd better go home and think about what we have talked about."

Horse-face laughed loudly again, then stopped all of a sudden. His black round eyes now looked like a pair of plums. He shouted out angrily: "You Beijing cadre have white bread to eat, while we poor peasants have only cornbread! Is it fair that you eat good food everyday but speak for the rich peasants and not the poor? What did Chairman Mao send you people here for? To bully us poor peasants? I won't go home! I'll stay here!"

He reached out both hands and picked up four pieces of steamed bread from the pot, sat on the threshold, and started to wolf down the food.

The Beijing cadre members looked at each and then came to the pot one by one and picked up the bread left on the bamboo steamer. My mother passed me half of her share. Fang and Old Chen returned to their room in the other flat. Auntie Pay, my mother, and I went into the room inside, sat on stools, and ate our meal silently. I wished Horse-face would be satisfied and go home after supper. My mother and Auntie Pay must have been thinking the same way, too. I could sense the nervousness in their cloudy eyes.

As Horse-face stood up from the threshold, however, instead of going outside, he stepped inside, walked into our room and threw himself on the kang! With a comfortable burp, he stretched out his limbs and his huge body occupied the whole kang!

My mother and Auntie Pay whispered and got up from their stools. "Get up!" Auntie Pay's voice sounded upset. "Don't you know it's impolite for a man to lie in a female room!"

"Please go home, Rich! We need to rest now." My mother tried to repress her anger and sound gentle.

"What! Why can't I rest here?" Horse-face's countenance now looked longer than a real horse face. "This room belongs to the village people. I am a poor peasant and I have more right than you to sleep on this kang!"

It was clear Horse-face was deliberately provoking the Beijing cadre for their 'unfair' treatment of him. For the first time since they came to the village, the intellectuals found they were at their wit's end in dealing with a peasant, a tough one.

After dark, my mother, Auntie Pay and I had to spend the night in a peasant's house nearby. For the following days, Horse-face came in to eat with us at meal times and slept on the kang every night.

The women's nerve broke down on the fifth day. They gave up their intention to do justice. And Horse-face didn't show up the sixth day.

※　　※　　※

MOST KIDS IN THE VILLAGE HAD RECEIVED A FEW YEARS' education in the small classroom on one side of the public flats. Here there were about twenty-five kids taught by one middle aged woman at the same time. She taught from grade one to grade four, and would give lectures to a few of them at a time, while arranging for the rest to do exercises. She had been here for years and had no difficulty handling the class this way.

She was a sick woman, and had been suffering from a women's disease for years. She often asked the kids to catch baby owls from the mountain, baked them to ashes on the stove, and ate them up with rice wine, a folk prescription to cure her disease. When my mother asked me to teach the kids how to dance and sing, the sick teacher agreed happily.

"It's wonderful! I am too sick to sing or dance, but the kids need to learn these things," she said to me smilingly.

I taught the kids quite a few of my favourite songs and invited other teenagers, who were about my age but had long stopped going to school, or never gone to school, but to the fields instead, to join us in the evenings. I led them to practise some basic gymnastic skills I learned in my primary school years.

Every evening after they finished their supper, the young people would automatically gather in front of the public flats, some practising the skills I taught them, some watching happily. It seemed this activity brought some excitement to the dull lives of the young people, and they were eager to come.

I was glad to see that Change, the prettiest girl in the village, had got permission from her parents and also came to learn handstands and leg splits and so on. She was the eldest daughter in the family and her parents gave her the name, Change, with the hope of having boys after her. However, there were four more girls born after her and the disappointed parents did not allow her to go to school but sent her to work in the fields instead. She often came later than others since she had to finish all her household chores.

On the evening of the National Day, October 1, I organized a performance for the villagers as a celebration. When the sky turned dark, people started to come to the small square in front of the public flats. A stone terrace was lit up with two gas lamps. All the kids were dressed in their best clothes and waited anxiously beneath the terrace. The village head and

Auntie Pay gave speeches of congratulation because this was the first time in the village's history that they had had an artistic event.

Just before I led the kids onto the stage, the audience shouted out: "Wait, wait a moment! More people are coming!"

I looked up towards where their fingers were pointing and saw the lights of about a dozen torches beaming and moving from different directions along the slopes of the hillsides, towards us. They were peasants living on the other side of the mountains, usually four or five families as one village. They must have heard about the event tonight and travelled for miles to see it.

Both the kids and I were touched by people's enthusiasm and the performance that night was very successful. Although there was no musical instrument to accompany them, the children's singing and dances were unusually beautiful and the mini-play aroused hearty laughter from the peasants.

When the performance was over and everyone had left, I sat together with Yellow-hair, Change, and two other girls. Their faces were still shining with excitement. We tried to recall details of our performance and commented on them happily. I told them that they all looked graceful and pretty on the terrace under the gas lamps, especially Change, and that it was a pity I did not have a camera to take a picture for them. Hearing my words, however, they stopped laughing and their faces looked pensive.

When the fall harvest vacation finished, I returned to the school in town and forgot whatever I had said to them. One morning a few weeks later, someone knocked on the door of my dormitory.

I was surprised to find that Yellow-hair and two other girls were standing outside on the doorsteps. They did not want to come into the bedroom, since they were too shy to meet the other students. I led them to a corner and asked what they were here for. They poked at one another and compressed their lips into sweet smiles. I noticed that each of them was carrying a small basket covered with towels. They were all in their best coats, made of crimson corduroy, and straw hats hung on their backs.

Yellow-hair finally told me that they wanted to have a snapshot with me, the way we had been in the dance. I remembered that the straw hats were something I used as props in the dance I taught them.

After I left the village to go to school, the girls had saved by collecting chicken eggs and pear-leaved crabapples from their own backyards. They hoped these would sell for enough money to have a picture taken. Change was not able to come with them, because her mother had castigated her: "Forget that crazy idea of picture-taking! These eggs will be sold to buy table salt."

I realized what kind of dream it must be in the minds of these girls to have a picture taken, something I had been so used to from my childhood. We went downtown and sold the eggs and fruits to the state-owned supply and marketing store, the only place peasants could legally sell their products to.

We went to the small studio in town and took the picture, posed as in the dance, the way they wished. We discussed for quite a few minutes as to what to write on the picture and finally agreed on the most popular slogan then, "Forge a Red Heart in the Vast Field!"

11

The Path to 'Revolution'

MY LIFE IN THE SECONDARY SCHOOL, IN THE EYES OF
Yellow-hair and Change, was paradise. It was true that as a student, you
did not have to toil in the fields all day, but the suffering I experienced
there was something Yellow-hair and her friends would never understand.

As the scorching fever of the Cultural Revolution gradually faded near
the end of 1969, China faced the problem of how to dispose of millions of
unemployed Red Guards. The function of the Red Guards, as the tools for
fighting, smashing, and grabbing, were no longer applicable, once most of
the old system and old traditions and behaviours had been destroyed.

Mao then gave the instruction: "It is a good resolution to send the educated urban youth to work in the countryside and mountain areas where
they can be re-educated by the poor and lower-middle-class peasants."
These former Red Guards, therefore, were sent to the poorest regions and
border areas as 'new peasants'. It became a rule after that that all secondary
school students should become peasants upon graduation.

In 1970, new school systems structured according to Mao's ideas were
introduced. Besides the heavy emphasis on learning Marxism, Leninism,
and Mao's thought, the curriculum was made to fit the needs of the greater
population of the country, namely, workers, soldiers, and the peasants.
New courses like militia training, agricultural knowledge, machine tool

handling, and acupuncture skills were added to prepare the students for the society.

The school I went to was the sole secondary school in the small town. There were about a dozen flats on campus. In addition to classrooms, offices, and the canteen, there were two dormitory flats, one for single teachers, and one for students whose homes were too far away from the school.

I shared a large bedroom with eleven other girls. There was almost no other furniture in the room except a large, wide plank bed. Each of us occupied a space about three feet wide in the bed. At meal times, we all stood around a table in the centre of the room.

Most students of the school were the children of peasants. They could only afford to buy the cheapest foods at the canteen. To meet the financial needs of the students, the cooks prepared turnip soup, boiled with soy sauce and water, and cornbread for us every day.

The school's forty teaching staff were mostly university graduates from Beijing. Beginning with the Cultural Revolution, they were categorized into several kinds — some as revolutionary teachers, some as neutral conservatives, and some as monsters and demons. The last category was not allowed to teach in class, but forced to do manual labour around campus.

All of the teachers were under the leadership of the school's Revolutionary Committee, headed by a dark-faced man with tobacco-tarred teeth. He used to be a peasant, then a cook in the school canteen. During the Cultural Revolution, he was made director of the Revolutionary Committee to symbolize the leadership of the working class.

At first, my class was taught by a revolutionary teacher. He used to be a physical training teacher, but he was asked to teach our Chinese class because of the shortage of trustworthy teachers. In class, this robust man liked boasting about his pure family background, in the hope of getting respectful reactions from the students.

"I am a hundred percent revolutionary in nature, because my father was a coalminer!" he would say proudly, smiling from ear to ear and observing our reactions. I didn't like him at all, for his favourite program in class was to lead the students in reading Mao's works.

At that time, we had four classes in the morning, each lasting forty-five minutes. Before each class began, everyone would stand up from his seat and face Mao's portrait hanging above the blackboard. The teacher would then lead all students in wishing that our great leader would live ten thousand years long. The students would wave Mao's little red book in their right hands and repeat three times: "Ten thousand years! Ten thousand years! Ten thousand years!" After that, they would sit back in their seats and sing a revolutionary song before the teacher started his lecture. Every morning we had to repeat the ritual four times.

The ritual was tedious but I found the class of the coalminer's son even more boring. I was the one responsible for leading the students in singing, so, each time the self-labelled revolutionary teacher came to teach, I would choose a song which had many paragraphs. One song was selected from a revolutionary opera eulogizing Mao's activities in his early years as a guerrilla leader.

> The Plough on the sky is bright.
> The water of the river ripples with silver light.
> The people in the mountain raise their heads to watch.
> The light from the Octagon Building beams in the dark night.
> Our leader Mao is writing articles under the oil lamp.

It took ten minutes to sing the whole song. The robust teacher had to stand by the door waiting for us to finish.

In April 1969, China and the Russians had a border war in the north, and the whole country was in a panic. The war was widely regarded as the signal of the Third World War. Mao soon issued instructions: "Dig deep underground tunnels. Accumulate enough grain..." as preparations for the atomic war close at hand.

A nationwide mass fervour of tunnel digging then started. People went all out to dig tunnels in their yard, in public squares and in sportsgrounds. The scales of the tunnels were different. Private tunnels at home were usually a few metres deep and only big enough to keep the family members. Public ones like the one built in my school's sportsground were deeper, strongly-constructed (with bricks and cement), and well furnished, with toilets and kitchens.

Besides taking part in the diggings everyday, the students were also taught the skill of how to shoot down an enemy airplane with a rifle by range estimation. For days we lay on the sportsground for target practice.

We also learned all the possible protection methods in case an atom bomb fell.

Half a year after I entered the school, Tong, an excellent math teacher, was assigned to our class. He was thirty-seven years old, tall, strong, with bright sharp eyes, a high nose bone and clear-cut lips. He was a Rightist, and had belonged to the school's 'monsters' group for years. Owing to the shortage of teachers, he had been recently allowed to reappear in class, with the precondition that he must not try to poison the students with bourgeois ideas.

Tong was cautious but he still made slips of the tongue once in a while. One day when he was trying to explain the circle in geometry to us, he drew a circle in the blackboard and then said: "Suppose this is a big water melon and there are six peasants to divide it among..." Suddenly, he seemed to remember something and quickly changed his words, "Oh, no, how could poor peasants be able to eat luxurious stuff like a water melon? Now let's suppose there is a full bag of beans..."

It seemed that the whole class, except me, did not notice his quick change. I thought he might be too cautious about the warning given by the school authority and I felt sympathetic to him, because he, like my mother, was also a Rightist. I visited him in his dormitory after class.

He lived with two other 'monsters' in one room. They were all single men, as no woman wanted to marry them. Their room was dirty and smelled bad. The oldest monster, in his mid-fifties, used to be an English teacher. He was suspected of being a spy because he had received letters from abroad. He looked glum all the time. When he was not labouring, he would lean against his pillow in bed, smoking one cigarette after another and staring blankly at the ceiling. He never paid attention to me when I came to their room.

Tong was nice to me and helped me to solve my problems in math studies. After he became our teacher, my class, forty-five students in all, rose to fame quickly in the school for our excellent performance in almost every aspect of math. Most of my classmates became enthusiastic in math and geometry, including me, one who always frowned at math.

A song and dance group, a martial arts group and a table tennis group were organized and tutored by Tong alone. Our performances were warmly welcomed. I was selected as head of the song and dance team of the school when it was set up later, and I often led the students in performances at big events in the town hall.

In 1971, there was no more violence in China. Big-character posters and criticizing meetings were the major means of reminding people of the ongoing Cultural Revolution. 'Red Guard' became an youth organization in every school under the leadership of the Party. Students who were considered morally sound and politically pure were admitted into the organization.

Five most active students in my class had become Red Guards. I envied them. I wanted to join the organization, too. A Red Guard was not only the symbol of your political virtue, it was also the necessary first step in your life, if you wanted to have a better future.

Besides the Red Guard organization, there were also the Communist Youth League, which admitted applicants from fourteen years up, and the Communist Party, which admitted applicants from eighteen years up. If you became a member of these organizations, you would enjoy priority in almost everything — employment opportunities, promotion in careers, further educational opportunities, and many other benefits.

Like secondary schools, universities in China resumed classes too. Under the new rule, no more entrance exams were held to enrol students, and secondary school graduates were not allowed to go to universities directly. Universities admitted only young people who had been working as factory workers, peasants, or soldiers, and who were recommended by the Party's organizations in areas where the young people had stayed. The standard held by the Party's organizations in recommending the young people was not based on their academic performance, but their political behaviour.

I wanted to have a good start in my political life, as a Red Guard first, then, a member of the Communist Youth League, and eventually, a Communist Party member. To climb up the social ladder, you had to follow the path designed by the Party. But I hesitated to hand in my application to the Red Guard organization in my school. I knew that on the application form which would be discussed among the Red Guards, there were questions like:

"What is your family background?"

"Are there any political smirches in the history of your parents and your relatives? What kind of smirches are they?"

I was too scared to answer these questions. My family background, according to the standard used then, should be my Grandma Laolao's class status. That was landlord, an exploiting class and a very bad category.

My parents' history? Oh, just forget it! I did not want anybody to know! My mother was a Rightist. My father had been a capitalist line-carrier. And the man who had created my life, dead or alive, might have an even more horrible title! At a time when one's political background was emphasized in every situation, I undoubtedly belonged to the bottom of the society.

I never dared to ask my mother anything concerning the secret of my birth. She always looked dismayed when she was with me. As she worked in the fields with the peasants or talked with the other Beijing cadre members, she always smiled and even laughed heartily. But I felt her smiles were unnatural and there was a hollow sound in her laughter.

I couldn't make her happy either. She wished I would act like a revolutionary-minded girl, always enthusiastic at political issues and pleasant to everyone all the time. But I wasn't that type at all.

One Saturday afternoon, the four Beijing cadre members and the village head were studying Mao's works and official documents in my mother's room. I came back from school and nodded to everyone silently, not daring to interrupt their political studies. I then sat at the corner inside of the kang against the wall, listening to what they were reading.

I knew my mother wished me to show enthusiasm in political studies, but I could not pretend long: the dull documents and Mao's quotations, which I had read thousands of times in the past few years, soon made me fall into a doze. I tried hard not to close my eyes and lower my head, but all in vain.

As my head knocked against my knees abruptly, I heard giggles in the room and I was embarrassed that my absent-mindedness was noticed by the other people. The meeting was soon over and the people left. When there were only my mother and I in the room, she was terribly angry.

"You disappointing thing! You always fail to live up to my expectations! Why did you fall asleep during the political studies? Don't you see how the other people were laughing at you? You make me lose face and let me down! They might think I taught you this way! And they might think you are influenced by my bourgeois ideas! Who knows that I never forget to urge you to be active in political studies and be a revolutionary youth!" She shouted angrily and put a newspaper in front of me and asked me to read the editorial on the front page.

I glanced at the newspaper and grumbled unwillingly: "There is nothing new there. Clichés stressing class struggle again... "

"What! How could you be so bold and stupid as to say that? You... You... You are genuinely the seed of a bad man!" She was obviously irritated by my attitude. Her face turned pale and her voice quivered, and she suddenly slapped me harshly on the face. I was shocked at her violent action and burst out crying in a few seconds.

She had been talking in a repressed low voice but her words, especially the last sentence, like a sharp knife, had deeply cut my heart.

What? I was the seed of a bad man? It was obvious that she was referring to the mysterious man who had created my life. It was clear that Mother hated him very much... And the man must have been a shame for her, in every respect!

She had never talked to me about the existence of such a man in her life and she thought I didn't suspect anything either. I never had the courage to ask her anything about the man, fearing the issue might hurt her deeply, but for years I had been weaving various dreams in my mind about the mysterious man and his relationship to my mother, and, to me. The dreams, though different each time, had always been beautiful, emotional and miserable. Many times I was deeply moved by my own imaginings and would secretly weep for a long time under my blanket.

But today my mother, my only dependable person in the world, totally destroyed all the secret illusions I had woven.

...Oh, he was a bad man! And I... the seed of a bad man! The last mysterious wish in my heart was smashed! I felt so weak, so overwhelmed by a flood of great disappointment. I buried my face in my hands and sobbed in heartbroken grief.

My mother was stunned to see me so sad. Knowing nothing of what was in my mind, she thought that I was only feeling hurt by her harsh slap. She asked me to shut up immediately, fearing my cry would be heard by somebody passing by the window.

But my mind was filled with the sad memories of the past and the long over-pressed secret sorrows and I couldn't stop at once. She was certainly in a panic, or perhaps she felt regret for her violence when she found my nose bleeding heavily. She took a towel and wiped my face hurriedly while she started weeping, too.

"Stop crying, OK? I beg you... Stop... Oh... Don't torture me this way, OK? What do you want me to do? Let me know..." she whimpered, shaking my shoulders desperately.

My heart split to pieces as I saw my mother full of tears. She looked a real old woman now, her messy grey hair hanging by her cheeks, her loose skin lined with wrinkles, and her eyes, withered and turbid now, full of despair. I suddenly felt a strong guilty sense for my own behaviour. I reached out my hands and grasped her cold hands and tried my best to swallow up my sobbing. I looked into her eyes and said:

"Forgive me, Mom... I will never make you angry again...."

Before I finished my words, we were in each other's arms and crying again.

☆   ☆   ☆

MY MOTHER WAS VERY CONCERNED ABOUT THE FACT THAT I was not a Red Guard yet. To her, being a Red Guard would not only make a good start for my future, it would weaken her guilty sense as a Rightist as well.

"If you don't become a Red Guard, people may think that you are a backward-minded youngster because I am a Rightist and I have brought you up this way," she said unhappily. "Why haven't you written an application until today?"

"I..." I hesitated to choose a proper expression. "I'd like to. But... Mother, may I conceal the facts of my family background as a landlord and your status as a Rightist when handing my application up?" I finished my words with difficulty, my face flushed.

"No! No! You should never conceal anything from the Party's organizations." She looked horrified by my daring idea; her eyes opened wide and her brows raised up.

"If you do that, it means you are not loyal to the Party. And, once your deception is discovered, you will receive more punishment!" My mother warned me. She insisted on my confessing everything frankly in my application, ignoring the bitterness in my heart.

Back at the school, I went to the dormitory of the revolutionary teacher who was in charge of the Red Guard organization. But at his doorsteps, I trembled.

What were people going to think about me once they found my secret? Oh, that was unthinkable! I had always behaved like someone from an innocent family and, if the truth was exposed, everyone was going to regard me as a hypocrite! Oh, no... I turned my back and quickly left.

Waking up early the next morning, I realized, however difficult, it was something I must go through. Once again, I plucked up my courage and came back to the teacher's door.

With a trembling voice, blushing face, and broken sentences, I confessed everything. I begged the teacher to keep my secret in a smaller circle, to let as few people know as possible.

I loosened my breath after the confession and wiped off the sweat on my forehead with my handkerchief. The teacher had been looking at me motionlessly throughout my talking. He commented finally: "It is good that you can trust the Party and be honest. But whether you can be accepted into the organization or not depends on, first, how you continue to prove your loyalty to the Party and to remould the bourgeois influence in your mind, and second, whether the Red Guard Committee will pass your application through their discussions."

A few days later, all the students in my class were making bricks in the sportsground, as one of the subjects in the new curriculum. I took off my shoes and socks, and jumped into the cold muddy water to mix the mud with my bare feet. This hard process was usually done by male students. But I wanted to show my determination to remould myself. I moved with difficulty in the cold, knee-deep muddy water. Though the coldness of early spring made me shudder, I felt happy when I noticed the other students standing by looking at me with appreciation.

Suddenly, I saw a male student walk towards me and shout out in a loud voice: "Peace, I heard that your grandmother is a landlord and your mother is a Rightist! Is this true?" There was a faint smile hanging at his lips but his voice was full of malice.

I stopped and looked at him. I felt dazed and almost fell into the muddy water. The other students were all looking at me with surprise. I stepped out of the water and rushed back to my dormitory. I threw myself on my bed, buried my face in the blanket and cried miserably.

What could I do? Everyone knew it now. I could no longer feel proud of myself in front of others, because I was not equal to them. I was inferior to all of them, because I was born into such a dishonoured family!

Laolao's class status was landlord. But her life today was worse than the lives of many poor peasants, with poverty plus humiliation. I couldn't forget the situation described in Aunt Lin's letter after her visit to Han Zhong not long before.

As Aunt Lin was politically free of trouble, she was able to get a few days off from her school in Xi An during the New Year's Holidays. She kept her stay in Han Zhong as short and quiet as possible, for Laolao's family was under close supervision, from the neighbours, and from the local government. Uncle Honesty was expelled by his school and jailed for four years because of his frankness in stating that all human beings, including Chairman Mao, might make mistakes. After he was released with the title, 'active counter-revolutionary', he was not able to find any job and had to stay at home with Laolao. Laolao was in her seventies, with poor health and troubled eyesight. She relied on the money my mother and Aunt Lin sent to her in turn and there was no extra money to support Uncle Honesty.

At this time, a concrete bridge was being built on the Han River. Large amounts of broken stones were demanded for the construction. Some people earned their daily bread by smashing the cobblestones on the river bank into small pieces. Laolao urged Uncle Honesty to take this as a temporary resolution.

Uncle Honesty went there one morning and returned home early in the afternoon. Laolao was surprised when he came home so early. But he locked himself in his own room, aggrieved. He had never expected that he, a well bred, decent gentleman, would be reduced to mixing himself with those uneducated rude people, men and women he regarded as the worthless elements of the society. He worked silently, to protect his pride. But his self-built pride proved fragile on the cobblestone-laid river bank. He was slow and inefficient at breaking the stones with a hammer. After a whole morning's work, his wrist was too sore to lift the hammer any more, but the small pile of stones he had created was not even enough to change for a piece of bread. While sitting on the ground and eating the cold riceball Laolao prepared for his lunch, he doubted whether he could ever support himself this way. To make things more unpleasant, as he returned from the toilet, he found the small pile of broken stones, the result of the day's effort, was stolen!

He could no longer keep his silence now and said loudly to the people around: "Don't you feel ashamed to steal!"

"No more ashamed than being a counter-revolutionary!" The reply was like a slap in Uncle Honesty's handsome face. He lowered his head, his power all gone.

Uncle Honesty would have stayed at home and died of hunger, had it not been for Laolao. From the next day on, Laolao prepared lunch for two, lifted a hammer in her hand, and went to the river bank together with Uncle Honesty. She was the oldest woman on the site — her grey hair waving in chilly wind, her small bound feet moving with difficulty among the cobblestones, but her confident attitude to the people around encouraging Uncle Honesty to stay by the river bank.

My mother and I felt sad to know their situation. But what could we do to help, when we ourselves were trapped everyday!

Someone came in and sat beside me. A warm hand patted on my shivering back. I heard the gentle voice of Tong.

"Stop crying, Peace. I have learned what has happened."

I stopped sobbing and listened quietly.

"The world is complicated and so is human nature," he went on. "You are very young and you cannot understand it now. But you will understand when you grow up. You have a long way to go and you will meet more unexpected events. How can you be so upset and behave like a coward in face of such a minor problem? Get up now and come back with me! Be courageous!"

I stopped crying and sat up. I stared at my bare feet stained with mud, thinking about Tong's words. I stood up and walked with him back to the sportsground again.

With Tong beside me, I felt braver. I looked at the students and the boy who had insulted me a while before. Somehow, they all avoided my eyes and no one talked. Without a word, I jumped into the muddy water again.

Months passed after I handed in my application. I watched two more students in my class become Red Guards and my application was still not discussed. I became quieter now, with less laughter and less talking. I felt deeply hurt when some of my roommates deliberately boasted about their Red Guard armbands to make me jealous. I never felt I was inferior to them in any aspect, except that they were offsprings of poor peasants and workers.

I visited Tong more frequently, since he always tried to make me happy. Besides helping my math studies, he taught me to practice high kicks and play sword. I pretended to kick his nose with my toe and pointed the sword to his face, and he pretended to be frightened and tried to hide. Our funny jokes made the other two 'monsters' in the room laugh, too.

Once, as I was running after Tong with a sword in my hand, he jumped out of his room and hid himself among the thick bushes in the yard. I searched in the bushes and laughed out in triumph when I caught him.

My laughter drew the attention of the revolutionary teachers living in other rooms on the same flat. One of them, a thirty-odd handsome man, our music teacher, called me into his room and warned me seriously: "You should not come into that room and be close to those people. Not only because they have political smirches, but also because you are a grown-up young girl and you should be cautious of men, especially those men! Or your reputation may be ruined."

Though already fifteen then, I had not had my first menstruation yet and my chest was flat as a boy's. My mind was still too far away from thoughts of sex and I regarded any implications concerning sex as an insult to my respected teacher. I told Tong about those warnings. He did not say anything, but I saw him grit his teeth, and blue veins stood out on his temples.

*　　*　　*

AS WE CROSSED THE BRIDGE AND CAME CLOSE TO THE PROPerty entrance, it was already dark.

"Shall we go back?" I asked Mrs. Thompson. For the past week, she had kept on taking a walk with me outside of the big house after supper.

"Let's come to George's house and see what he is doing!" She looked towards the direction of the stone house on the edge of the property.

I turned my head and noticed the bright lights from the windows of the small house about a hundred yards away. The old house looked mysterious among the dark woods in the night air, like a scene in a fairy tale.

We walked slowly towards the lights. The leaves rustled under our feet.

As we came close to the two-storey stone house, I saw through the window that two figures were moving around under the bright lights. One was George, the gardener, his upper body naked. The other one was a big-boned woman, with a bra narrowly holding her heavy breasts. They had not drawn up the curtains on the kitchen window and I could see clearly they were preparing food.

I felt embarrassed to see George and his new girl friend half-naked. "I don't think we should visit them now," I said to Mrs. Thompson.

She stopped under a birch tree and looked into the window. "Oh, gosh!" She was taken aback at the scene. Without any words, she turned around.

"I just cannot believe George has changed totally into another person!" she commented angrily, when the stone house was far behind us. "His wife has just passed away a few months ago, and he is already flirting with other women!"

"I saw him dating an old lady in the garden early in the summer. What happened to her?" I wondered.

"I don't know. That woman looked cheap in my opinion. But George sent flowers to her, and the flowers were from my garden!"

"This big-boned woman looks a lot younger than the old one."

"She is too young for George, and too big. I cannot imagine how George got to know her. His taste!" There was a sour flavour in her voice.

"I am quite impressed about the attitude when people are in love here. The Canadians seem to be quite open-minded. Look at George, he is already in his seventies, but he changes his girlfriend freely, without the fear of being condemned by public opinion."

"Would people in China condemn this sort of thing?" she asked curiously.

"Oh, not only this, a lot of other things which would be regarded as completely normal in the eyes of a Canadian!"

*   *   *

IN THE HOT SUMMER OF 1971, A NEW ROUND OF CAM-
paigns was started to expose hidden class enemies on campus. All students
were encouraged to expose and criticize wrong ideas spread by their teachers.

I had become used to the frequent political campaigns. To rule China
successfully, the government had to launch political campaigns constantly.
The campaigns were very effective. First of all, those who were dissatisfied
at the Party's rule could be singled out through the nationwide mass movement. Secondly, all other people would be scared by observing the cruel
measures applied during the campaigns and so would behave themselves
and submit to the Party's rule unconditionally.

Within one week, all the building walls on campus were filled with big-
character posters. Unexpectedly, the majority of the posters were attacking
the 'revolutionary teachers', and only a small number were criticizing the
'monsters and devils'.

For instance, the chemistry teacher was charged with spreading a bourgeois life style in class. The reason was that when he taught the students
how to remember the element symbol 'Hg', he said, "Just remember Ai Chi
Ji. That will be easy." The sound of Ai Chi Ji, in Chinese, meant "love to
eat chickens".

It might sound absurd, but the love of good food was regarded as a sign
of the bourgeois life style when hardship and plain life were valued as
virtues, during the revolutionary years.

Another revolutionary teacher, the Marxism Theory teacher, a member
of the school's Revolutionary Committee, was attacked for sexual harassment of girl students in his class. He fondled a girl Red Guard, promising
to admit her into the Communist Youth League as soon as possible.

To my surprise, the music teacher, the man who had warned me not to
be close to the 'monsters', was exposed as having an affair with a young
shop assistant in town some years before.

"They were caught in bed one night," that big-character poster declared
in detail. "The music teacher knelt on the floor and begged pardon from the
revolutionary masses..."

Many students who had read this poster exclaimed in surprise. The
music teacher had always put on an arrogant air and it was funny to imagine the way he knelt on the floor!

The music teacher's handsome figure disappeared for quite a few days.

He was certainly hiding somewhere, shamed by the scandal flying around campus.

I met Tong. He smiled at me confidently. Not a single poster had criticized him, the Rightist, because he was adored by all students. The other 'monsters and devils', attacked or not attacked, continued their daily manual labour indifferently. To the students, they were 'old enemies' and there was nothing new in them to be exposed. To the monsters themselves, they had been criticized numerous times over the years and they had long became numb to criticisms in the campaigns.

As the movement developed, more and more 'revolutionary teachers' were attacked and there was chaos among them. They suspected each other for manipulating students in these attacks. Some classes had to be cancelled, for the teachers attacked claimed sick leaves.

The school's Revolutionary Committee found that the campaign was distorted and developing in a disadvantageous direction: the real class enemies were still in hiding and the revolutionary teachers were trapped. They started to take action.

One afternoon an assembly meeting was held for all students and teachers in the school yard. Sitting in the middle behind the desk laid at the front, was the former cook, the present director of the school's Revolutionary Committee. Everybody understood that the man with tarred teeth was only a symbol at the meeting, as his simple mind didn't provide him enough tactics to deal with the shrewd teachers. As usual, he sat in his seat silently smoking cigarettes throughout the meeting.

The Vice-Director of the school's Revolutionary Committee, a teacher with a pointed nose and a pair of sharp round eyes, gave a speech over the microphone on the desk.

"Revolutionary teachers and revolutionary students, let's be alert! The class enemies of the people are trying to fish in troubled waters! They are inciting the revolutionary masses to struggle against each other, so as to hide themselves deeper.

"As we all know, some of our revolutionary teachers have been attacked by rumours over the past few weeks. They are all trustworthy comrades of our revolutionary teaching staff. You should not believe in rumours spread by our enemies.

"Revolutionary teachers and students! Let's open our eyes wide and see through the tricks of the real class enemies! Let's unite together to carry out the campaign successfully!"

In the following days, a shocking piece of news spread quickly. A fifteen-year-old student was denounced as a counter-revolutionary. He was charged for writing a slogan against Chairman Mao.

A public denunciation meeting was held. The young boy was brought to the meeting with his arms bound behind his back. The Marxism theory teacher came in front and criticized him first. His speech explained how the boy became a counter-revolutionary.

After learning the Marxist philosophy of 'the negation of negation', the boy wrote a slogan, "Down with Down with Chairman Mao"! He showed the slogan to the Marxist theory teacher, and asked naively: "Isn't this an example of the negation of negation?"

His question was not answered at that time. However, when the school's Revolutionary Committee felt the need to punish one as a warning to hundreds, the boy's creation was brought out as a deliberate attack on our great leader Chairman Mao.

Following the Marxist theory teacher, a few students also came in front to expose the boy's crimes. The boy was said to have written posters attacking the revolutionary teachers, including the Marxist theory teacher and the music teacher.

As the denunciation meeting ended with everyone shouting slogans, a few police officers came over, handcuffed the boy and took him away in a jeep. I watched with the crowds as the jeep left the campus. I was totally confused. It was hard to figure out who was and who wasn't a real revolutionary.

I was called into the office of the Revolutionary Committee one afternoon. The dark-faced former cook was sitting in a chair and smoking. He saw me come in and pointed me to the Vice-Director with a languid gesture.

I went to him. The man with a pointed nose and sharp round eyes reminded me of an owl. He smiled at me cordially and asked if I could expose any wrong ideas spread by Tong.

"No," I said. "I don't remember if he has ever said anything wrong."

The man looked at me for a while and went on: "Some people have noticed that you often come to the monsters' room. We have reason to worry that you may be influenced by Tong's bourgeois ideas."

He paused for a little while to observe my reaction and went on. "We know that you have a strong wish to join the Red Guards organization. Although you are from a rather complicated family background, and the Party's policy is that there is a principle of stressing the importance of family background, we do not stress on that exclusively. Your political attitude and performance are also included in our consideration."

Eventually I understood that the Owl was giving me a chance to prove my loyalty to the Party and my qualification to become a Red Guard. But how? Could I do what he had asked me to do? Expose Tong in my posters? No, I couldn't do that! He had always been nice to me...

But, if I did not do as he asked, it would mean that I was not loyal to the Party since I was standing on the side of a Rightist. And I might lose the chance to become a Red Guard forever. Being a Red Guard was not only my wish but also my mother's. I did wish I could wear that striking red-coloured armband and walk around proudly on campus! But how about Tong then? There was no doubt that he would be badly hurt if I did that.

In the following two days, I was tortured by serious inner struggles. When I saw the figure of Tong from a distance, I would try to avoid him, as a guilty feeling was already forming in my mind. In the end, I could not get rid of the strong appeal of the red armband and I convinced myself that Tong was indeed a class enemy.

In the evening, I found the few Red Guards in my class and told them that I was going to expose Tong. They all agreed, for they had felt pressure for not exposing their Rightist teacher. I thought hard about what to expose. Of course, Tong had talked a lot to me, but none of it seemed to be wrong ideas in my mind.

Suddenly, I remembered his mocking one revolutionary teacher in class.

"He can only lead you in reading Mao's works in Chinese class. Of course, we cannot expect more from him when he is actually a graduate from a sports school," Tong said.

I decided to choose this instance and wrote it in my posters. After the other Red Guards signed their names after mine, I pasted it on the wall outside of our classroom and waited in a fidget.

The next morning when I went to the classroom, my eyes fell upon the posters I put out the day before. I suddenly felt a sense of guilt in my heart. I sat in my chair and looked around; some students were having discussions about the posters in low voices.

The bell rang, and Tong entered. I dared not look at him. He stood silently in front of the blackboard for a few seconds. The few seconds seemed to be unbearably long. Then I heard his voice, as gentle as before.

"My students, if you ever find I have any errors, please tell me. I will accept whatever is correct... But, I swear that I have been doing my best, based on my conscience, in teaching this class and protecting your young and innocent hearts. I will never cheat any of you... Please trust me... Now, let's start our class..."

Oh, I felt regret almost immediately for what I had done and I almost wanted to rush out and tear off the damned poster! I raised up my head and tried to look for his eyes.

He looked calm, as if fully involved in his lecture. The whole class was extremely quiet today and everyone was listening attentively. My heart sank. Throughout the class, Tong's eyes never fell on me even once!

The campaign ended a few weeks later. Tong was ordered to stop his teaching and return to manual labour with other monsters and devils. His teaching position was filled by the coalminer's son.

The music teacher and the Marxism theory teacher were as active as before, as if nothing had happened to them. The girls in my dormitory questioned the Owl about why the immoral teachers were still allowed to teach in class.

"As they are revolutionary teachers and they both came from working class families," explained the Owl, "the so-called affairs or sexual harassment, rumours or truth, are but minor problems and do not devalue their principal good nature."

A few more students in my class were admitted into the Red Guard organization, as a reward for their active behaviour in the campaign. But I was once again forgotten.

This was not fair! I found the revolutionary teacher in charge of the Red Guard organization and asked him why. He hesitated for a while before he told me: "Peace, you should be able to understand this. As someone from a bad family background, you have to be prepared to go through more trials before you can be fully trusted by the Party."

His words were just like a bucket of icy water pouring on me, making me cold from head to toe. I stared at him in despair, not knowing how to respond. I wanted to tell him that I had sold my soul in exchange for this glorious symbol, that I had lost the precious friendship and the warm, caring, brotherly love of my teacher forever, and that I could never look at him with innocent eyes again! All for this precious red armband! But how could I tell him these things? He would definitely conclude that I was a speculator in the revolution!

It seemed he could see through my mind, for he smiled slightly and patted me on the shoulder: "Don't indulge in the unhealthy sentimentalism of the petty bourgeoisie. You should trust the Party and its organizations and keep on remoulding yourself..."

I became satiated at these sorts of clichés and all my patience left me. I stood up and left him wordlessly.

The most difficult thing was to face my mother. I knew her anxiety and disappointment would be much greater than mine, for she had always placed her hopes on my progress. But I had let her down once again.

On the way home that weekend, I walked alone in the boulder-strewn gully that zigzagged towards the small village in the hills. As the stone houses up on the hill slopes came into view, I stopped and sat on a rock in the bushy grass beside the road.

There was no one else in the gully and the whole universe seemed to be in tranquillity.

I looked up into the cloudless sky. There was not even a bird flying over. The green grass under the hot sunshine was sending out a thin aroma. I breathed deeply. It would be nice to hide in this peaceful place forever, never to have to see anybody.

The grass started to shake. Why? There was no wind! I gazed at the grass. A turtledove moved out slowly towards me. I was surprised to see her and leaned forward to reach her. But she turned away abruptly and suddenly became traceless. I looked around and wondered at her whereabouts. Where had she gone? Did she have a safe place to hide herself? Did I scare her away? Would she come back to me again? I looked at the dense grass and felt at a loss.

I walked slowly towards the village, its stone houses visible under the bright sun. My eyes kept on searching the grass alongside the trail. "Where is the turtledove? Where is she hiding?" I murmured to myself, deliberately slowing down my pace.

Quite unexpectedly, my mother was calm after she learned my bad news. Though I could see the disappointment in her eyes, she spoke gently: "That is nothing serious. You are still young and there are plenty of chances in the future... "

Her voice sounded pale and weak, and I knew she was only trying to comfort me, and herself.

Someone was singing a sad melody. His loud and sonorous voice was clear from the other side of the yard in the public flat. I looked at the window and listened attentively. It was Old Chen singing in English.

"He is singing 'The Last Rose of Summer'... I haven't heard this song for more than twenty years." My mother's voice sounded behind my back. I turned around to look at her. She was gazing at the window lattice covered with rice papers. There was an unfamiliar sentimental look in her eyes.

"What does this song say?" I asked curiously.

"Old Chen has become insane recently." My mother didn't answer my question. "He drinks alcohol every evening and then sings alone in his room. When he couldn't get alcohol, he would beg the village women to give him a bowl of the sour pickling water from their jar..."

"How does it happen?" I was surprised, remembering his discussion with me about poems a couple of years before.

"Who knows! He often talks about his wife and kids in Beijing... Perhaps he feels lonely, especially since Fang has gone."

"Where has Fang gone?" I was surprised.

"Oh, Fang got married two months ago and moved into the bride's home. Someone introduced him to a peasant girl on the other side of the mountain. She is only eighteen, more than twenty years younger than Fang, but an illiterate and hunchbacked. Her parents are very poor and didn't mind Fang's Rightist status. Anyway, Fang has a fixed salary each month, and that is a very desirable factor for them."

"But how could a well educated man like Fang agree to marry an illiterate?" I was shocked by the news.

"Fang has his own understandings. He told me that his children, if he has any in the future, would benefit from his marriage into a poor peasant's family. He was satisfied at the thought that at least his children would inherit their mother's good family background, and not his. Isn't he wise?"

*   *   *

THE SMALL OVAL-SHAPED LEAVES ON THE OLD SCHOLAR trees turned yellow and started to fall. The thick bushes on campus where I used to play hide and seek with Tong became bare branches with sparse little red fruits and could no longer hide anyone any more.

It was my final year in the secondary school and, in a couple of months, I was going to graduate and be assigned to a village as a new peasant, like almost all my classmates.

At this time, my mother received a letter from Lan, her roommate of a few years ago in the institute dormitory in Beijing. The divorcée had got married again, to a navy officer who worked in western China. My mother remained grateful for her help at the denunciation meeting and they had been writing to each other over the past few years.

"I have learned that the regiment my husband works in is going to enrol more people to strengthen its propaganda team. I know Peace likes to perform, sing and dance from her childhood. Why not let her try her luck in the navy force?" Lan wrote.

When the personal cult of Mao had reached its peak during the Cultural Revolution, numerous propaganda teams were set up in schools, factories, and army regiments to eulogize Mao.

Students who could sing and dance well, or were able to play musical instruments, often had the chance to enrol in such a propaganda team and avoid becoming new peasants after graduation from secondary schools.

My mother had been worrying about my future, too. Lan's suggestion lit up a fire of hope in her heart.

"Yes, it is a good idea," she said excitedly to me. "You should go to the West and try to enrol in the navy force."

A few days later, I returned to school and talked to the head of the Revolutionary Committee. I asked him for a reference letter to prove my student status at the school.

"I am going to move to the place where my father stays," I lied to him.

"That's fine." The former cook nodded his head carelessly. His dark rough hand slowly took out a red stamp and he stamped the lower right corner of the simple letter he wrote for me. Passing it to me, he gave a yawn and fumbled in his jacket pocket for cigarettes.

As the day broke, I carried my simple luggage on my back and walked towards the long-distance bus stop quietly. I wanted to leave the school secretly and not to tell anyone. As I walked through the campus, I bid farewell to it silently.

I had spent two years here, but not in vain. Life had taught me what were the true, the good, and the beautiful, and what were the false, the evil, and the ugly.

The bus stop was at the foot of the broken ancient town wall. The autumn breeze blew up the fallen leaves on the ground. The paved road beneath my feet disappeared somewhere far away in the hills.

A cart drawn by two horses moved slowly towards me. The driver, an old peasant, was huddled up in his dirty sheepskin overcoat with his sleepy eyes half-closed. The clear sounds of the hoofbeats of the horses were distinct in the early morning. I watched their slow moving until the sounds faded.

Suddenly, I found someone riding on a bicycle and rushing towards me in haste. It was Tong! My heart beat fast now and I felt fear, an indescribable baffling fear. For two months, I had avoided him on campus and he seemed to forget my existence, too. I felt ashamed to see him again after that event.

The red-painted bus emerged from the turning of the road and I felt rescued. I grasped my luggage and jumped onto the bus.

Tong got off of his bicycle and looked anxiously into the bus.

He looked older now. Under the messy hair was a pair of pained eyes surrounded by dark circles and printed with numerous small blood veins. His face was pale, with more wrinkles in the corners of his eyes and on his lean cheeks.

The bus moved and he reached out his hand, as if he wanted to wave "goodbye" to me.

The sun appeared from behind the hills, its orange-red rays shining on the complicated expression on his face…

12

The Man in the Riddle

I WALKED ON ONE OF BEIJING'S MAIN STREETS. IT WAS HALF a mile away from the city's centre, the Tian-an-Men Square. The glazed tiles on the magnificent buildings surrounding the square were dazzling under the sun. It was shortly after eight o'clock in the morning, but the midsummer's hot air had already driven away the coolness of the night before.

It was nineteen eighty-four. History had turned a new page. China had officially announced the end of the Cultural Revolution after Chairman Mao died in nineteen seventy-six. The whole country was engaged in economic reforms launched by the new leader, Deng Xiao-ping.

In Beijing, private enterprises became legal and small commercial businesses were filling up 'holes' left unattended by the state. Tens of thousands of small-scale restaurants and thousands of fashion pedlars had sprung up like mushrooms in all corners of the city. In busy shopping areas, snack food carts lined up in long rows, selling delicacies from all over the country. There was barbecued lamb from the far west, boiled fishball soup from the eastern coastal area, spicy cold beef noodles with apple pieces from the north, fresh seafood dishes from the south, hot bean curd cooked with minced pork from central China, plus many traditional Beijing pastry snacks.

In large state-owned stores, imported goods like Japanese coloured televisions, cameras, recorders, washing machines and refrigerators were strikingly displayed to attract attention, and crowds of people shouldered one another, talking in loud voices to compete with the noise of pop songs. Coloured televisions and automatic washing machines became popular household furnishings and there was always a shortage of supply. A bride in the 1970s would wish her groom to have three 'turning items' ready for her in the new home: a wrist watch, a bicycle, and a radio. In the 1980s, the rapid development of the economy had bolstered many brides' appetites. The three turning items had now become a television, a washing machine, and a refrigerator.

A beauty salon, the first of its kind in the city, had been opened the previous month in the busiest shopping centre, beside the Imperial Palace. When the news was widely carried by the media, people swarmed in to have their eyes enlarged, nose bones raised, freckles removed and pimples flattened. Most customers in the salon were young women, sitting stiffly on long benches, nervously waiting for their first-time experience. When a young man finally stretched his head into the door after making up his mind perhaps a dozen times, his pimple-covered face would turn even redder with all the female customers eying him and, in most cases, his courage to step in would vanish at once.

Women were more daring and took the lead in the fashion world, too, dressing as dazzlingly as they could to catch up with the world. Foreign movies and magazines provided them with unlimited boundaries for their imaginations. Colourful shirts, silk dresses, high-heeled shoes, earrings, necklaces, lipsticks, and permed hair reappeared after more than a decade's absence. Fashion shows were held frequently and always drew big audiences. One show put on by a group of women aged between sixty and seventy-two had recently become a hot topic.

The large grey-coloured brick city wall, big-roofed city gates, and the willow-lined city river, after being in existence for more than five centuries, were flattened amid the noises of construction machines. Erected on their sites were miles of high rises and elevated multi-level highways.

Dozens of luxurious hotels were built for foreign tourists and business people. Foreign made taxi cars replaced the traditional manpowered tricycles and competed with millions of bicycles in the streets. Outside of theatres were large colourful posters of movies from America, France, England, Japan...

I watched everything with a relaxed feeling. The day before, I had just received an admission letter from the Graduate School of the Chinese Academy of Social Sciences. It was a hard-won success. I had prepared for years to pass its six strict academic tests, and then narrowly passed its political background investigation. I was lucky to be one of the twenty selected from a few hundred applicants to study at this famous school.

The future in front of me was promising. To be a journalist in the largest news agency in China was a profession dreamed of by many young people. The only pity was that I was already twenty-eight, and the best time of my life had slipped away.

I looked back at the three years spent in the navy force, another three years in a hospital, four years in a university, and then two years in a company... What eventful years! It seemed that I had always been plagued by politics and always lacked the necessary tactics to protect myself. Was it because I had been too naive, or was I simply a fool? If I could have a second life, would I become more clever and make correct choices?

I came to a grocery store by a busy intersection. Many bicycles were squeezed into rows outside of the store. People were waiting in line in front of the counters to be served by the shop assistants. No one looked worried. With the present economic policy, there were plenty of goods and many more varieties on the shelves.

I bought some wild rice stems, a few cucumbers, a handful of green onions, a bunch of spinach, a piece of lean pork and five half-foot-long crucian carps. These were enough for lunch and dinner today, I thought. My mother would be happy to see there was steamed fresh fish with ginger and green onion when she came home for dinner in the evening. She always liked this dish.

With the groceries in my hands, I walked back along the broad street, its many high rises lining up on one side. My home was on the ninth storey of one of the high rises. After years of separation, my parents had finally returned to Beijing and had been reunited.

*　　*　　*

THE DAY, SEPTEMBER 9, 1976, HAS ALWAYS REMAINED CLEAR in my memory. That day, Chairman Mao died at the age of eighty-three. I was then working in the dispensary of a hospital in a small city in West China.

Everybody was called into a meeting room to listen to an important news bulletin at three o'clock that afternoon. People were chatting casually while waiting for the news to be announced by the radio on the table. I thought there might be new instructions released by the great leader, perhaps a stress on class struggle again. At three sharp, the radio announcer read slowly in a mournful tone that "Our great leader Chairman Mao has passed away." Everybody in the room stopped talking and looked stunned. Then, with the radio sending out heavy-hearted funeral music, a fat woman, who was about twice my weight, burst out into loud crying, and some others started to weep, too.

I was seized by a horrible feeling — "The sky is going to fall over our heads soon!" There were no tears in my eyes, but my heart beat vehemently like a drum. I had been used to pray that Mao live to be ten thousand years old and I had never thought that he might also die like ordinary people. "What is going to happen, to China, and to us, without Chairman Mao?" I kept on asking myself. There was no answer and my mind was numb.

"Oh, Chairman Mao! How can we live without you! Oh..." The fat woman shrilled loud and tearfully while patting the table in front of her with her fist. I knew how sad she must feel. She was born into the family of a poor mountain peasant. Her father became the head of the village after the communists came. With the newly acquired power in his hand, he was able to live a much better life than the rest of the villagers. His daughter, the fat woman, was 'recommended' by the villagers to study in a medical university during the Cultural Revolution and became a doctor. The whole family were grateful to Mao and the Communist Government for all their blessings.

The thought suddenly came into my mind: How would my mother feel now, at Mao's death? She had always claimed that she loved Mao and the Communist Party and urged me to do the same. Would she feel heartbroken now? I had to go home and stay with her, in case she might become too sad.

At five o'clock, I left my dormitory in the hospital for the train station. As I passed the state-owned grain store in the main street, I was surprised to see many people waiting in long lines to buy rice, flour, millet and beans.

"Why are you all buying grain now?" I stopped to ask one woman who often came to the hospital for her sick kids and had got to know me well.

"Now, with Chairman Mao dead, who knows what upheavals China is going to face? Maybe the Americans or the Russians will invade us, knowing the head of China is gone. We won't starve to death with enough grain stored at home, once the war starts…" she replied with exaggerated facial expressions, waving several empty bags in her hands.

During the one-hour train ride home, I could not stop worrying about my mother. She had left the small mountain village a couple of years before. When I started to work in the hospital, she asked the authorities for permission to work in the same city with me. It was then arranged that she would work as a school teacher — the least wanted job in those years — in a secondary school in a small town one hour by train from my hospital. But not long after her arrival, she found that all the staff in the school, and almost every student's parents, had learned about her unspeakable past. Her Rightist status and the accusation of adultery were both recorded on her file, and followed her wherever she went. My mother was deeply hurt, and she noticed every subtle change in the attitude of her colleagues and of the students' parents. She tended to be suspicious of people's remarks, carelessly or deliberately made about her, and was easily irritated at the 'cold stones and hidden arrows' hurled at her. She was on bad terms with some of her colleagues, who made her angry to death by boasting about their own 'pure backgrounds' and vilifying her with invidious language.

My mother worried that the humiliation in her background might affect my progress. I had worked hard in the hospital to try to become a member of the Communist Youth League. I had sacrificed many Sundays to volunteer in the hospital and was always active in doing the dirtiest work, cleaning the toilets and mopping the corridors, plus coming half an hour earlier, and leaving half-an-hour later than everybody else, every day. The Youth League admitted people aged from fourteen to twenty-five, and the majority of young people in China were members. My mother was very anxious that I was still not a Youth League member at the age of twenty-one. She was clear that her background constituted a negative factor in my application, but she was too proud to admit this and only blamed me constantly for not acting appropriately enough.

"You never learn to shut up your mouth, a bad habit you were born with!" she would say, mentioning once again my stupid behaviour in the navy force.

My heart would sink whenever she mentioned that. That event took place in the summer of 1974, when China was launching a nationwide campaign to criticize Confucius, a scholar who lived more than two thousand years ago. All officers and soldiers in the navy regiment stopped their daily work and studied the government documents everyday. After the documents were read to everyone, people were assigned to small groups to further digest them. The group I was with had about ten people and we were required to talk about our opinions one by one at those meetings. Most people would just repeat the same sentences in their speeches: "I am in full support of the wise decision made by our great leader Chairman Mao and the Party's Central Committee. I promise to carry out the campaign wholeheartedly."

These words had been repeated over the years whenever there was a campaign against someone or something. Everybody had learned them by heart and no one would bother to think of something different to say. I watched the people in my group murmuring those clichés in dull voices out of numb faces. I felt disgusted and remained silent until I was the only one left.

"Peace, it's your turn now." The head of the group looked at me and spoke in a sleepy voice.

"...Well, what I should say?" I moved my eyes away from the birds jumping on the branches of a peach tree outside of the window and glanced at the motionless, statue-like figures sitting around the room. I knew I was not supposed to respond this way, but somehow I felt the boring situation was too much to bear that day and I just let my true thoughts flow out.

"I simply don't understand why we should criticize Confucius after all!"

Everyone in the room seemed to wake up from general anaesthesia and they looked at me and each other in excitement. The dead atmosphere in the room became alert all of a sudden.

"Indeed, I don't even know who Confucius was..." one girl giggled and said to me. She was a simple-minded girl, the same age as me, nineteen. I wasn't surprised that she didn't even know who Confucius was. We shared the same dormitory and I had never seen her reading a single book in the past three years.

"Confucius was a thinker and educator who lived more than two thousand years ago. He was the one who created China's earliest educational system..." I tried to explain to the girl in my own words.

"Shut up!" My talk was cut off by a girl with two thick brush-like eyebrows. She pointed her finger at me in a fierce manner. "How dare you say that Confucius was a thinker and educator? The documents we just studied have pointed out clearly that Confucius was a conspirator with aggressive ambitions! And a hooligan! A traitor! And should be criticized thoroughly from his skin to his soul! But what you have just said was totally against the decision made by the Party's Central Committee!"

I was irritated by her deliberate provocation. The brush-browed girl was twenty-five years old and had finished grade nine before the Cultural Revolution started. She should have read enough to know what kind of historical person Confucius really was. She was very clear about the fact that I was telling the truth, though it was different from what the documents said. If she wanted to play dummy and lie as everyone was doing, let her go ahead! I wouldn't care! But why did she break her silence to flare up at me? Of course, I could see through her trick at once. She used to be a famous Red Guard leader in her school in Beijing years before and she had boasted a few times about her 'heroic activities' in dealing with teachers in the crazy years. Now, as head of the Youth League branch in our company, she was trying hard to join the Communist Party so as to be promoted to a higher position. She seized my words as an opportunity for her progress.

"Whatever the documents say, I don't think my explanation concerning Confucius was wrong." I insisted on having my opinion and tried to find support from Mao's words. "Chairman Mao's Quotations says that 'Everything divides into two'. Why shouldn't Confucius be divided into two and possess both negative and positive sides?"

She was stunned. No one dared to say Mao's words were wrong. But this former Red Guard had acquired a well trained eloquence. Her eyeballs moved fast and in just a few seconds she found a suitable Mao quotation from her brain bank.

"But, don't forget that Chairman Mao has said 'Make a concrete analysis of concrete conditions!' In the case of Confucius, it is a concrete matter and no positive analysis should be applied!" She announced this loudly, word by word, the brushes above her eyes dancing triumphantly.

I was stuck. Mao's words were full of dialectical tricks. Everyone could use his words as a weapon to attack others. I was no match for Brush-brow.

A few days later in an assembly of all the people in the navy regiment, the political commissar gave a two-hour report. I had turned a deaf ear to his tedious speech until the following words made their way into my ears: "...The campaign to criticize Confucius has been carried out successfully in our regiment. All officers and soldiers in our regiment have been in full support of the Party's wise decision and have responded actively so far. However, there is one person among the regiment's fifteen hundred staff, who stupidly wanted to reverse the verdict on Confucius! She — we will not name her — has gone so far as to say that Confucius should be divided into two sides, too! What silly nonsense! If the Party started the campaign to criticize Confucius, how can you say that he had some good points!"

I didn't hear what else the commissar was talking about. Many people sitting in the front rows in the big hall were turning their heads back in search of me and whispering to one another. I felt ashamed at being the object of the curious eyes and mocking smiles shooting at me from all directions in the big hall. I heard someone in the back row talking in a low voice to his friend: "...a fool. Why did she speak it out?" I lowered my head and gazed at my shoes, my face hot to the point of bursting.

When the commissar finished his report, representatives of each company stepped onto the stage one after another to read loud articles criticizing Confucius. The one reporting on behalf of our company was Brush-brow.

After the assembly, I became a well known person in the regiment. Brush-brow became well known, too. When almost everyone else was shunning me, she approached me openly and warmly as if nothing had happened.

"You have been applying to join the Youth League for a long time." She talked with a full smile, the two brushes parted widely on her forehead. "As head of the Youth League branch in our company, I have the responsibility to help you become a qualified youth so that you can be admitted..."

Though confused at her unexpected friendly attitude, I still thanked her for her kind offer.

In the following weeks, Brush-brow asked me to go out for a talk every other evening after supper time. The regiment was housed in the mountains for security's sake. In the evenings, most people in our company would gather at a small sportsground, a flat ground opened up by the hillside, to play or watch basketball and badminton before it got dark. Brush-brow always led me to a spot on the hill, where we would sit under an apricot tree and have a fine view of the sportsground underneath. Brush-brow often recalled her splendid days as a Red Guard in Beijing, while a cool breeze swept through the hills, fading slowly as the dusk climbed up the trees.

The campaign ended two months later with five more people in the regiment admitted as new members of the Communist Party. It had become a rule that the Party always drew some new blood testified to be 'pure enough' through frequently held political campaigns. As one of the five new Party members, Brush-brow had fulfilled her wish. I wasn't surprised at her success, but I felt I had once again been fooled.

One evening, the loud speakers, installed at many corners among the hills to allow everybody to hear, announced a dispatch introducing the excellences of the new Party members. Brush-brow was described like this: "She has been active in the campaign to criticize Confucius, keen and sharp in struggles against wrong ideas and behaviours. She is also a warm-hearted person who never looks down upon backward-minded youngsters, but instead, sacrifices her own precious time to have repeated talks with them and help them improve…"

I never had a chance to ask Brush-brow when the Youth League branch would consider my application. She did not bother to talk to me any more.

Auntie Lan, my mother's former roommate in Beijing, invited me to come to her home one Sunday. Her husband was a head officer in the regiment's Office of Political Affairs. The dormitories for married officers were flats lined up at the foot of the mountains. Since I had come to the navy force, Auntie Lan had rarely invited me to come to her home, and I knew there must be something important. I hurried up my lunch in the canteen and came down the hills and found Auntie Lan's home behind the large assembly hall.

Auntie Lan was alone at home. She poured me a cup of jasmine tea and talked in a soft voice. "My husband attended a meeting yesterday. At the meeting, the case of your wrong ideas about Confucius was brought up for discussion, among other affairs. Don't be upset! Have a drink of the tea now, or it will be cold... They tried to analyze your motivations. Somebody at the meeting suggested carrying out an investigation into your background, since you are the only one in the whole regiment to have a Rightist parent and the only one to voice a different opinion in this campaign! They suspected that your mother might have influenced you to do that..."

"No, my mother has never talked with me about Confucius." I was in a panic. How could they suspect my mother for the mistake I had made! I regretted my thoughtless behaviour.

"Auntie Lan, you know very well that my mother is still labouring in a small village outside of the Great Wall in the north. We don't write to each other often..."

"Don't be nervous, Peace!" Auntie Lan smiled at me. "My husband tried his best to protect you. He told the others that you are only a nineteen year old girl and have not seen your mother for three years. 'In the navy force,' my husband insisted, 'she is trained and educated to become a perfect person. It may only be that she has not yet got rid of her petty bourgeois ideas, and she is still so naive that she said the wrong thing.' The others were finally convinced by my husband and a resolution was reached that you are exempt from punishment, except that an oral warning is going to be given to you by your company leader."

I felt relieved and thanked Auntie Lan and her husband for their help. "I will be very cautious and never say wrong things again. I will study Chairman Mao's works harder and make every effort to join the Youth League soon."

Auntie Lan then frowned and said in a serious voice: "To be honest, both my husband and I feel that the navy force is no longer a suitable place for you to stay any more. I am sure your mother will agree with us, too. You see, as you are the only one with a problematic family background, each time there is a political campaign, you will be in a vulnerable position, and there is little hope that you can progress, as hard as you have tried..."

I kept silent. I thought about a few other political events, on a relatively minor scale, where I had become a target because of what I had said. I also thought about the painstaking efforts I had made during the three years — all in vain, since I was again and again closed out of the holy door of the Youth League, while I watched some people who had records of theft and sexual harassment being admitted into the door. Auntie Lan was right. The navy force was not a good place for me. I should leave it before it became too late!

When the first snow of that winter was whitening the hills and the roofs of concrete buildings scattered in the gully, I left the navy force and started to work in the hospital.

After two years of acting as a 'perfect youth' in the hospital, I was twice selected as the annual 'model worker' and made speeches in the city's public assemblies. To gain this honour, I had to cover the 'real me' deep inside, and always be prepared to respond actively to the Party's calls, whatever criticism campaigns were started. I drew political cartoons, wrote criticizing articles and poems, and made public speeches, always playing a leading role in the hospital. I didn't question 'why' any more. What was the good of understanding 'why' anyway? I felt tense all the time, as I was living so hypocritically, so much against my nature! But I knew I must grit my teeth and endure with dogged will, for I was very close to the door of the Youth League now. The head of the Youth League branch in my hospital had informed me that a two-person investigation group would be sent to the navy force soon as part of the admission process.

✻   ✻   ✻

THE TRAIN ARRIVED IN THE SMALL TOWN AT SEVEN o'clock in the evening. There were a few buses in the square outside of the train station. I approached the bus going in the direction of my mother's school. I looked at the old bus covered with dust outside and stuffed with people inside. It was already as packed as a can of sardines, but several more people with luggage on their shoulders were still at the door pushing hard at each other's backs, trying to squeeze themselves inside. I turned away and started the three mile trip on foot.

The school was surrounded by corn fields. My mother had one room and a kitchen in a flat at the back of the school yard. I stepped into the home and glanced at the small room with a desk, a double bed and a book-shelf. My mother wasn't here. I called cautiously, with a perturbed feeling: "Mom! I am back."

She reached her head out of the kitchen. "Oh, Peace! Why have you come home today? It is not Sunday." To my surprise, there was no trace of the sadness I had expected to see in her face. Instead, there was only a dull coldness in her eyes.

"....Mom, did you hear the news that Chairman Mao passed away? I was afraid you might be too sad..." I replied hesitatingly.

"Sure I have heard the news... But it's funny that you worry about me this way," she said, while bending her back slowly to search the bamboo basket underneath the kitchen cabinet to find some eggs.

I stood by the kitchen door, confused. The cold indifference in her voice, the numb expression in her eyes and the languid movement of her body was far from what I had imagined. Hadn't she required me to love and obey Chairman Mao more than love and obey her all those years? Didn't she always tell me that Chairman Mao was the greatest man in the world and the emancipator of all Chinese people? Why was she not feeling upset at all, and acting as if a stranger had just died? Of course there was no smile on her face, but still, her reaction to Mao's death didn't conform.

My mother steamed a big bowl of egg custard, put some soy sauce, black vinegar, and sesame oil on top, and brought it to the table.

"Let's have supper now." She passed me a piece of steamed bread. "You should catch the ten o'clock train back to the hospital tonight. Remember to start your work as early as usual tomorrow morning. You know the Youth League branch is considering your application now. Don't let any careless negligence spoil it at the last moment."

We did not say anything else during supper. After we finished eating, it was totally dark outside. My mother wanted to accompany me to the train station.

"No, Mom," I tried to stop her. "I don't want you to walk back alone so late."

"It doesn't matter to me. I am used to walking alone at night," she said, and found a flashlight.

We walked silently along the pavement towards the train station. There was hardly any vehicular traffic on the night country road, only a couple of people riding on bicycles passing by. There were no street lamps, but two lines of big Chinese scholar trees on both side of the pavement, their branches with thick small oval-shaped leaves reaching high over our heads, leaked out spots of soft moonlight.

I felt uneasy at my mother's dumbness. Usually, when we were walking together, she would ask me every detail about my behaviour in the hospital, anxious to know if I had made any progress or any new stupid mistake. But tonight she was just silent, looking heavy-hearted. I searched in my mind for some interesting topic to stimulate her.

"It's interesting, Mom." I said. "I saw many people lining up to buy grain this afternoon after hearing of Chairman Mao's death. Is that really necessary?"

"Oh!" My mother sighed weakly. She seemed not to have heard my question. After a long pause, she said slowly, her voice full of despair: "Now, with him dead, there will never be a day to prove my innocence! I will have to remain guilty forever! Till the day of my death..."

I knew she was referring to her Rightist status.

"But how can it be?" I asked, my voice not confident at all.

"...Who else in China do you think would have the guts to reverse the decisions Mao has made?! For nineteen years, I have been waiting and dreaming of the day when Mao would finally realize that he had wronged many innocent people like me, and thus issue an order to correct the decision he made in 1957, for he was the only one who could correct his own decision. But who knew that he would die before he realized that!"

I suddenly understood what kind of impact Mao's death had had on my mother! Right until this moment, it had never hit me that my mother had carried this secret wish in her heart, and that it had supported her in enduring all the hardships and the inhuman treatment over the years.

I shuddered. The cool air in the September night gave me gooseflesh all over. The moonlight was blocked by thick clouds and the road stretching in front of us looked dark and mysterious. I turned away my face to look at my mother secretly. Her expressionless eyes and the tightly closed lips made her face a pale, hard mask. I took the flashlight from her hand and turned it on. The light was dim and the road under our feet became even more blurred and depressing.

The fate of a person and of a country, however, is always unpredictable. Just one month after Mao passed away, when most Chinese people were still wondering and worrying about their future, Mao's widow, Jiang Qing, and her three close friends were arrested by their political rivals during a successfully planned coup.

After that, China started to move at an unusually fast pace, with exciting news and changes almost everyday.

I became a Youth League member a few months after Mao's death. The investigation of my political behaviour had been done. The head of the hospital's Youth League branch told me: "At the navy force, we were shocked to hear that you had been a 'youth with a backward mind' and 'always voiced opinions different from the Party's ideology'. We felt this kind of comment very old fashioned and decided to ignore it. Anyway, we have observed you for two years and we know very well what kind of person you really are."

A few days later, I took the oath in front of a red flag and was formally admitted as a Youth League member. However, as I repeated the oath to be loyal to the cause of communism and to fight for the emancipation of mankind, I felt a huge emptiness in my mind and the membership suddenly seemed not so desirable after all. Nowadays, with a freer political atmosphere and less mind control, more and more people were talking about things which could definitely have put them into jail just a year before.

My mother was happy and excited to receive one good piece of news after another. She was facing a turning point in her life. My father had asked her to reunite with him in Beijing.

In April 1976, five months before Mao's death, tens of thousands of people in Beijing had gathered for days in the Tian-an-Men Square in memory of Premier Zhou En-lai who had passed away in January that year. People gave public speeches and read poems to express their sorrow for the dead and their hatred for the living rulers of China, while floral wreaths piled up like hills in the square.

My father was visiting friends in Beijing in those days. He went to the Tian-an-Men Square to present a wreath to the dead premier, and listened to the speeches and read the poems pasted on the huge monument in the centre of the square. He was deeply touched and cried when he felt the strong current flowing and trying to burst out from the chests of millions of Chinese people. He felt pained and heartbroken, too, to realize that the holy cause of communism he had been devoted to for decades was, in the end, so hated and so opposed by the people! He could foresee that China and its one billion people were faced with a severe trial, a test even more rigorous than the Cultural Revolution launched ten years before!

He was greatly shocked when the government cleared the Square with armed forces on the night of April fifth, and followed this with a nation-wide purge of people who had been involved with the event or felt sympathetic towards it. As a faithful Party member and an honest person, he was unwilling to suspect the Chinese Communist Party of any evil intention. But then, who was wrong? Could it be hundreds of millions of the Chinese people? Or the beautiful Marxist ideology aimed at extinguishing exploitation and oppression and bringing happiness to all mankind?

He had a heart attack and was sent into hospital.

A few months after Mao's death, my father was asked to go back to Beijing. He was assigned to head a foreign affairs department in a government agency. Since coming back from Russia, he had never had a chance to leave China. But this new position required him to travel frequently to foreign countries, as China was opening its doors to the outside world now. He visited Japan, Europe, North America. He opened his eyes wide and tried to learn as much as he could, as if he were a visitor from Mars.

It was at this time that my mother received a letter from my father.

In late 1977, Deng Xiao-ping, the man twice driven out of power by Mao, returned to China's political arena again. An exciting news item was announced in October that year: universities in China would resume their old practice of entrance examinations; the recommendation system adopted during the Cultural Revolution was to come to an end.

My heart almost jumped out of my throat at the news. To study in a university had been my dream for years, but something I didn't have the right to dream for, when recommendations were available only to politically sound people. Now, after ten years of the Cultural Revolution, all people who had missed the chance to go to universities from 1966 to 1976 were given the right to take the national entrance exams on the same two days in December.

There were only two months for preparation. I spent all my spare times reviewing politics, Chinese literature, history, geography, and mathematics, courses required for all arts candidates. My brother, Wei, and my sister, Little-red, had at that time finished their secondary school education and settled down in different villages as new peasants. They had both decided to take the science exams. Though the three of us were not in one place, my mother wrote to each of us constantly to boost our morale.

More than two thousand people, aged from fifteen to thirty, took part in the exams held in a school in the small city where I lived. One month later, the results came out. Forty people had passed the minimum scores required by the exams. I was one of the forty. I rushed home that afternoon to tell my mother the good news.

As I came into the yard of my mother's school, I saw her all smiles, talking to a few people in a happy voice. As she saw me coming over, she stopped talking and turned toward me. I didn't wait for her to ask.

"Mom, I have passed!"

My mother's face shone with excitement but she tried to look calm. "Excellent! I have got phone calls from your brother and sister today. They both have passed, too! And now the three of you will become university students at the same time!"

The people standing by congratulated us and praised my mother for her success in raising three children who now brought credit to her. My mother thanked them while she commented that her three children were all stupid, and passed the exams only by good luck. I listened to their talking happily. I knew my mother was trying not to vaunt her pride lest she might hurt those who had failed the exams.

"It's still too early to get carried away!" A cold voice was flung at us from the other end of the flat. We all turned our heads to look for the voice. A woman of stout build, the wife of the school principal, was dumping garbage in the corner. She was famous for her sharp tongue and bad temper. Knowing that everybody's attention was on her, she threw another stone: "Don't forget there is still a political background investigation to be passed!"

Her words were like a bucket of cold water pouring over our heads. We all became silent. The neighbours departed one by one, leaving my mother and I standing alone in the yard.

That evening, my mother gazed at the lamp on her desk and said with a solemn look: "I am so fearful that my status will stop you all from entering universities. Now, you three have passed the exams. If you fail to pass the political investigation, if I become the blockade on your way of success once again, I will see no point in continuing my life any longer..."

"Oh, no, Mom!" I stood up from my chair and tried to comfort her. "There have been rumours that the government will no longer stress the candidate's political background. The investigation will be carried out only routinely..."

"If that is true, if you three... No, even if only one of you could be admitted, I promise I will kneel on the ground and kowtow to Deng Xiaoping!" My mother's voice trembled.

The stout woman's threat proved a thing of the past. In March, after two months' waiting in heart-exhausting anxiety, my brother started to study physics, my sister, medicine, and I, English, in three different universities. My mother packed her luggage and returned to Beijing to join my father.

My mother's Rightist status was removed in 1979 when the Communist Party Central Committee decided to re-evaluate each of the cases of the half million Rightists in China. The majority of the Rightists who had survived were declared to be 'the wronged ones'.

My mother was deeply grateful when her innocence was finally confirmed. The Party's organization had sent letters to the schools where my brother, my sister and I were studying, requiring my mother's Rightist status to be cleared from our files.

During the summer vacation, when the three of us gathered in Beijing, my mother asked us to write letters of thanks to the Party's organization. She had already written such a letter to express her own thanks.

"Why should you feel so indebted to them?" I was extremely reluctant to write this sort of letter. "It should be them, not you, to feel that way! They have wronged you for twenty-two years and they acknowledge your innocence now without even feeling sorry. But you are already old! And time won't return! What are you thanking them for?"

My mother shook her head. "You don't understand..." She wanted to convince me, but she found it hard to find any good reason.

Looking at the sparkle in her eyes, I knew she was seeing the light in her life again. It didn't surprise me a few days later, when I saw my mother writing an application to become a Party member, something she had lost the right to do for so long!

In 1979, the whole country was discussing a theoretical topic: 'Practice is the sole criterion of truth.' The purpose of the discussion was to criticize the late Chairman Mao from a realistic point of view and break his image as God. However, intellectuals, especially university students, started to explore the discussion further and brought up many new issues unexpected by the authorities. 'Democracy', 'dictatorship' and 'freedom to vote in elections' were topics warmly debated on campus. Some universities held strikes in their fight to gain rights for free elections in the student associations. A 'Democratic Wall' appeared on a main street in Beijing, with frequently renewed big-character articles commenting on and attacking China's political system. The 'Wall' had attracted millions of readers and shaken their already unstable faith in the Communist Government. The authorities smelt danger and banned the 'Wall'. About a dozen people notorious for their leading roles in the 'anti-communist' movement were arrested and sentenced to ten or fifteen years in jail. Though the students became quieter, they were no longer as obedient and submissive as they used to be.

I felt puzzled about how my mother could still be so faithful to the Party when she had endured such a horrible life. Didn't it ever occur to her that her life was totally destroyed because of her blind worship of the Party? She might never have thought about this! It was also possible that she would rather cheat herself to keep faith with the Party, and not allow herself to think otherwise, since she had paid such a high price to gain favour from the image of them she had in her heart. Sometimes it was too cruel to face reality.

On second thought, however, I didn't think my mother was that simple. She had her worries, perhaps. I remembered an unhappy encounter not long before.

One morning I went to my mother's institute at which she had been working ever since she returned to Beijing. As I was talking with her in the yard, her face suddenly turned stern. Before I could understand what had happened, she had turned her back and walked away with hasty paces, leaving me standing alone in the yard.

I was surprised and looked around, but only found an old man standing a few yards away from me. He was watching me with a smile. I glanced at him and didn't know who he was. But as soon as I turned around to look for my mother, a long forgotten image sneaked into my mind. Oh, was it him? I turned my head again.

A careful second look proved my memory. The old man was Sunshine! He looked much older now, with silver-white hair, and a body twice as round as twenty years ago. Strange! How could he become such a short and fat man? The memory left in my childhood mind was quite another one. Time had changed everything about him, except the elusive smile and the frivolous look in his slanted eyes.

He watched me attentively. It was apparent he realized who I was and was waiting for me to show my surprise. I stood there hesitating. My mind told me that he was also a victim in the last political campaign, but my instinct would not allow me to show my recognition of him. A few more seconds went by, and I finally turned away, quietly.

My mother was still in a bad mood when I found her. She said with strong resentment: "I simply don't know why such an immoral person was not punished by the Party's organization, but instead has been promoted to a higher rank! And I still have to work under his leadership! Where can I go to find justice?"

I also remembered my mother's comment after she read some sharp articles on the 'Democratic Wall': "The atmosphere of those days smells just like it did before the Anti-Rightist Campaign in nineteen fifty-seven. Actually, some of the opinions on the wall are much much sharper than what people said in nineteen fifty-seven. I don't think the Communist Party will let them go so easily this time..."

I wrote the thank you letter, as my mother desired.

*   *   *

WHEN I APPROACHED MY HOME BUILDING, I FELT MY BACK sweating. "I need to take a shower back home," I said to myself.

In front of the building entrance was a fenced green field. In the middle of the field stood a pine tree. An old woman, my neighbour downstairs, sat still on the grass with her back against the tree. Her eyes were partly open, and she saw me coming, and stood up.

"It is a hot day," she said and patted the dirt on her pants. "Do you feel cool in that light blue dress?"

"Not any better." I stopped by the fence and smiled at her. "Why are you sitting on the ground?"

"I need to acquire the breath of the earth once in a while." She turned her head and looked at the towering building behind her. "I am not used to the home above in the air. It is not healthy. I have often felt dizzy and breathless since I moved in."

As I chatted with the old lady, my eyes fell upon a man who was standing beneath a willow tree on the side walk.

He was a stout man in his sixties, with sun-tanned skin and grey hair. The corners of his lips were closed firmly, and his dreamy eyes seemed to be gazing in an unknown direction. Though he was dressed in ordinary grey pants and white shirt, the solemn expression on his face somehow caught my attention. He looked unhappy and... lonely.

He noticed me, too. The quick exchange between us was only a couple of seconds. But when his eyes behind the glasses encountered mine, I thrilled with a strange feeling.

How could this be? It hit me that I had perhaps seen him somewhere. But when, and where? I searched in my mind. Well, I really couldn't remember where I had seen this man. Maybe it was only an illusion.

I said "Bye" to the old woman and walked into the building. On the elevator, I felt a little bit uneasy. Why? Was it because of the hot weather?

I got into my home and closed the door. There was no one at home. Everyone else in the family had gone to work. I put down the groceries on the kitchen floor and picked up the watering can.

"The flowers on the balcony need to be watered," I told myself, and turned on the tap.

At this moment, I heard a knock on the door. I turned off the tap and went over. As I opened the door, my eyes also opened. There, standing in the doorway, was the man I had just seen by the willow tree on the sidewalk. Within a second, my instinct told me who he would be!

"...Who are you looking for?" My voice was still calm but my hand grasped the door knob nervously.

"You," replied the man, his sad eyes looking straight into mine.

My heartbeat suddenly quickened and I tried unwittingly to close the door. "But I don't know you at all..." My voice sounded weak.

"Didn't your mother ever tell you about me?" he asked slowly, each word making my blood freeze. "I have been looking for you for years... I knew I wasn't wrong when I saw you. You look like your mother a lot..."

I stood there numb, my hands cold. He entered the living room. He scanned the furnishings briefly and seated himself on the sofa in front of the window, gazing at me silently. I stood against the bookshelf, my eyes staying fixed on the white lace curtains hanging behind the man. The ticking of the clock on the desk sounded loud. The air in the room was pressing heavily against my chest and my heart had risen into my throat.

I warned myself to remain as serene as possible. A volcano boiling with long repressed emotions was soon going to erupt.

He reached out his arms towards me and spoke in a husky voice: "Come to Father now, my child!" Tears were running down his lined cheeks.

Father?! His voice was not loud, but I felt I had been struck by thunder. My legs were shaking, my head was splitting. I stared at the tearful face and the arms in the air.

The long faded memories emerged cruelly in my mind like icebergs in a silent sea... The day a young mother sobbed all the way as she sent her one-month-old baby back to her hometown; the night Laolao and her four-year-old granddaughter walked alone through endless rice fields; the years spent in secret sobbing and heartbreaking imaginings...

My mother had told me the truth about my birth when I was twenty-four, shortly after her Rightist status was removed and she was declared innocent. She took me with her on a three-day vacation to Cheng De, the former imperial summer palace a few hundred miles north of Beijing. On the second day after our arrival, my mother and I took a walk around the lake in the evening after we had our supper in the hotel. The few-hundred-acres-large palace was built in the mountains. It was cool and quiet in the summer time, far away from the noisy and crowded city of Beijing.

There were few tourists around and birds were singing happily over our heads in the trees. My mother was unusually silent. I was silent, too, feeling the tension inside her. We had walked this way for an hour and dusk was spreading through the air. We came to a big-roofed pavilion by a pond filled with blooming lotus flowers. My mother suggested that we have a rest. We sat side by side on a wooden bench facing the pond and watched the big pink flowers on the water's surface. I had no courage to look at my mother. I feared to listen to what she was going to tell me soon. Yes, she had planned this trip deliberately, I now realized, to reveal the secret buried deeply in her heart.

In a calm voice, my mother started to talk. She told me briefly about her first marriage with Evergreen, my birth, and his sudden imprisonment. "I concealed this from you for so many years, to prevent you from being regarded as the daughter of two problem parents. Now that I have been declared innocent, I feel I am strong enough to protect you and it is high time I let you know who is your father by birth..." As she finished her words, I buried my face in my hands and burst out in loud cries.

"I knew, I knew this when I was thirteen years old..." I said as I wept.

My mother felt stunned. "How did you know? Who told you about it? Why didn't you ask me anything?" She stared at me, her voice revealing her alarm at my unexpected response.

I cried for a long time. My mother didn't comfort me. She just watched me. At last, I felt I had released all the sorrow accumulated over the years and I gradually calmed down.

"Where is he now? Is he still alive?" I asked my mother.

"I don't know... He might have died a long time ago..." My mother gazed at the starry night sky and shivered with cold.

Over fifteen years I had often chosen to remain alone to imagine his look, his character, his possible life experience, his love and sorrow, and his possible death... When I had serious conflicts with my mother and felt terribly lonely in this cruel world, I would cry miserably under my blanket for hours and call "Father" silently in my heart again and again, dreaming the man in my fantasy would come out to give me care and love, if he was still alive...

He had come, finally... Should I throw myself into his arms to satisfy his, as well as my own, long cherished wish? I hesitated...

No, no... At this moment I found my mind becoming surprisingly cool. It was clear what a hell of emotions would follow if I did not control myself. I and my mother had both had enough tears and sorrows in the past twenty-eight years. I did not want to break the hard-won peace and tranquillity I and the whole family had just acquired...

Besides, the uneven life I had gone through since my childhood had provided me with little chance to be held or kissed by someone. I would feel uneasy and awkward to be in the arms of a man. A man? I knew he was the man who had created my life, and the man who had been the mysterious shadow in my dreams for all these years. Yet, when he really appeared in front of my eyes and claimed to be my father, I found it very hard to connect him with the word 'Father'. Ever since I could remember things, I had thought Tian-zhi was my father, and he deserved the title 'Father'! And how could I ever forget the days with him in Xi An, and his diary! Yes, it was unfortunate, but true, I could only feel that Evergreen was a man, like any male stranger I met in the street.

Look at him now! He was expecting me to call him 'Father' and cry loudly in his arms. But it was too late. I was already twenty-eight years old when I finally saw the man whom I should have called 'Father'. Times had changed and I had changed. I might have been able to do it more easily when I was a weak, vulnerable little girl, but through the years I had become hardened, and I had learned well to cover my sorrow and my sense of inferiority with fake laughter and over-emphasized arrogance. Yes, it was too late...

I watched him silently. It was difficult to open my mouth. I would like to call him something else instead of the burning word 'Father', which, I felt, belonged to Tian-zhi.

"I... I am not used to this. It is true... Forgive me..." I muttered some meaningless sounds with difficulty, while he was still gazing at me in warm expectation. A few more seconds passed in silence. He heaved a deep sigh and withdrew his arms.

There were still tears in his eyes, the eyes of an old man. I went into the washroom and brought a cold towel for him. He took off his glasses and buried his face in the towel.

The clock on the desk struck ten. He raised up his head. I felt we were both breathing normally now. I smiled at him and showed him the family picture under the glass on the desk.

"This is my brother, an engineer, my sister, a doctor, and my..." I glanced at him secretly and found his eyes stayed fixed on my mother. I stopped talking.

✳   ✳   ✳

WHEN THE SUN WAS IN THE MIDDLE OF THE SKY, Evergreen and I were sitting in an old pavilion with an octagon-shaped roof in the imperial garden beside the Forbidden City. The pavilion was built halfway up a small man-made hill shaded with pines and cypresses. The palace roofs were visible with their splendid golden and green tints. Centuries of wind and rain had peeled off the crimson paint on the pillars and railings of the pavilion and the naked wood looked old and dull.

This was a safe place. No one would bump into us up here. I stared at Evergreen bravely, trying to find out if he bore any resemblance to me. His sun-tanned face looked as coarse as the bark of the pine trees on the hill. He was an ordinary looking man. There was no trace of a handsome and passionate poet and writer, the picture I had created in my imagination.

"Here is the only photo I have preserved. You can see what your mother and I looked like when we were young." He took out a black and white picture with worn edges, two inches square.

The young couple in the picture were dressed in army uniforms. They stood side by side against the railings on the bank of the Forbidden Lake, not far from where we were sitting. They were both smiling, the man confidently, and the woman, shyly and happily. I was thrilled when I noticed the similarity between the young man and me!

"The short time I shared with your mother was the happiest time in my life." His voice was gentle and moving. "Everything is still fresh in my mind even today. I remember the time when your mother came to attend my class. She was so pretty, graceful, innocent, intelligent, well educated... I was deeply attracted. We became friends. We cooperated to get many of our articles and books published...

"I still remember the evening after I attended the state banquet held for heroes. I joined your young mother at the corner of the Tian-an-Men Square. We talked and laughed heartily... We were so young then and so confident in our futures. We felt that even the lotus-shaped street lamps were lit up for us, and the red flags on the Tian-an-Men tower were waving to us...

"Did you ever see a silk quilt cover at home? It was pink, with small silver stars embroidered on it." He was soaking in happy memories, and his wrinkled eyes sparkled with a youthful light. "That was a gift sent by your grandma from Han Zhong, when we got married..."

The silk quilt cover? My heart shrank. I knew it was still kept at home. The small silver stars had worn off over the years and left only little round holes on the faded pink cover. Somehow, my mother would not throw it away.

"After we got married, every night under the soft light coming through the lamp shade, your mother would read novels in bed for us. She read with emotion, as if she were performing on stage. I would lie beside her, watching her silently... the graceful movements of her lips and brows... I felt I was the happiest man in the world...

"We had never expected that an abrupt snowstorm would destroy our small, warm nest which had been set up for only a few months! I was jailed. I knew I had been wronged and I denied all charges, but no one believed my innocence, including your mother...

"When I was cutting woods in the snow-covered wildness in the border area, I kept on studying and writing every night in the icy-cold shack. There was no desk or chair in it. I made a 'table' with a piece of board and set up a piece of log as a stool. Under the dim light of an oil lamp, I forgot the whole world outside and was intoxicated in the world I created...

"In the second winter there, a heavy snow storm one night crushed the little shack and I was buried underneath it as I slept. I thought about death, at that moment. I thought I'd rather be buried in the snow forever and never wake up...

"I wasn't sure how much time had passed as I lay in the snow, numb. My body was frozen and my mind was in a trance. The whole universe seemed dead and empty.... Faintly, I saw your mother staring at me, her face pale and tears welling up in her large eyes. Her lips moved, but I couldn't hear what she was saying. I wanted to reach out for her, but my hands couldn't move. All of a sudden, my mind became clear! Your mother disappeared. The snowstorm was over and there were shining stars over my head in the cold dark sky... I struggled to get out of the crashed shack and told myself again and again, 'Evergreen, Evergreen, you must never lie down! There will be one day when your innocence can be proved. When that day comes, you will stand in front of your wife and your child as brilliant as before, and not a devastated man at all!...'

"It was in late 1966 when I received a letter from your mother. She said she had lost hope of living in this world and had sent you away to Yi Chun. She hoped I would be able to find you and take care of you, if I became free one day... I was totally in despair after reading her letter. I didn't know what had happened to her. But I knew the Cultural Revolution was turning everyone crazy. How I wanted to find her and change her silly idea! How I wanted to tell her that there was still hope as long as you lived in the world. But I was not allowed to send any letters to anyone...

"A few years ago, the Party's organization finally re-investigated my case. I was proved to be innocent. When I regained my freedom, the first thing I did was to look for you. I thought you must have finished your secondary school in Yi Chun and become a new peasant in the border area. My footprints covered almost all the villages and state farms in that area but I could find you nowhere. When I became disappointed again and again, I shouted to the heaven: 'Tell me where is my poor daughter?'"

He stopped and looked at me pensively. My handkerchief was all wet. He reached out his hand and wiped the tears on my cheeks. His hand was firm and rough as an old tree's bark.

"Over the past few years, I have asked numerous people and gone to different cities to look for you and your mother. Last week when I was attending an authors' meeting in the south, I met an old friend from the nineteen fifties. He told me that Qin now works in the institute in Beijing. I was so excited, I flew to Beijing the next day.

"I went directly to the institute and asked to see your mother. While waiting in the reception office, I was extremely nervous. Actually, I wasn't even sure what I was going to tell her. My friend told me Qin had married again, divorced again, and been reunited again. I wasn't sure of the state of her relationship with her present husband. All I knew was that I had a very strong impulse to ask her to come back to me!

"I waited and waited. Time seemed to pass slowly in my state of anxiety. But your mother didn't show up. An institute leader came out and told me: 'Qin refuses to see you.'

"The next day, I phoned her office. She didn't know it was me and picked up the phone.

" 'Who is calling?' The familiar voice on the phone made me shiver.

" 'Qin!...' I was choked and couldn't continue.

"A long silence. She must have recognized my voice.

" 'Congratulations! We are both still alive!' I contained the sorrowful torrent rushing against my bosom and spoke calmly.

"She was still silent.

" 'Can we see each other? I have waited for twenty-eight years just for this day!'

" '...I...' She finally talked. Her voice had lost the quality of a silver bell I used to be so familiar with. 'We'd better not see each other. It is better that way for everyone.'

" 'But...' I stopped. Though disappointed, I knew she would not change her mind. 'Can I see our daughter?'

" 'No!' she replied quickly. 'She has gone through enough since she was born. She has become a very nervous and sentimental girl. And seeing you will upset her once again!'

" '...What does she look like?'

" '...Like you. Her skin is dark, and her nose flat, too.'

" 'Qin, I beg you, come to see me with our daughter.' I couldn't control myself any more and cried out.

" '...No, it is not good for anyone. Please, forget me, and forget us.' She hung up the phone.

"I don't understand why she refused to see me... I am not a shame to her any more..." Evergreen looked at me, as if I could answer his question.

I looked away to avoid his eyes. There were little kids running up and down at the foot of the hill, making happy noises. An old couple, perhaps the grandparents, were sitting on a long green chair looking at the kids with contentment.

Evergreen's story answered many of the questions which had accumulated in my mind. Now I understood why my mother looked heavy-hearted and often stared blankly in the air these days. Several times I found her looking at me inconspicuously, with a perturbed facial expression.

I felt surprised that everyone in my family, including Mother, Father, and Evergreen, had become victims in all the political campaigns launched by the government in the past few decades.

The question also puzzled me: why did Mother refuse to see Evergreen?

Perhaps she still hated him, as she used to tell me, for destroying her life from the very beginning of her career. But I didn't want to tell Evergreen about that. I knew it was not correct to blame him. Who had destroyed his life and career, after all?

Actually, until this moment, I had still been puzzling over my mother's real feelings. She might not hate Evergreen at all. But for the sake of my father, for the sake of the family of five as a whole, and perhaps for the tranquillity of her mind, she might think it a better policy to lock up her own emotions and never try to stir up the dead water in the pool.

On the other hand, she might really hate Evergreen. When he was accused as a counter-revolutionary twenty-eight years before, she let herself hate him, for she trusted the Party's judgement. Gradually, she might have found it easier to hate him, when she was under repeated attack and could not get out from under the spell-like web covering her up. Hating him provided a way to release her agony, her resentment, and the frustration she had built up over the years.

But finally, when she found Evergreen coming back to her as an innocent man, she was confused. Life had played such a cruel joke on her! Now, whom should she blame for causing her unfortunate fate? The Party, which had made a series of mistakes during its rule of China? No! She would never be bold enough to think that way! Then, should she herself be blamed after all? But that would mean she was wrong from the very beginning, and had kept being wrong again and again in the following years. That would be terrible! To acknowledge this would mean to negate her lifelong effort in pursuit of... What? Truth? Perhaps she might have found it was simpler just to close her eyes and insist on her original hatred, to keep the balance in her heart.

One thing was clear, the shadow of the Red Terror she had gone through over the years still lingered in her mind and might never be got rid of. Until recently, she still screamed aloud or wept miserably sometimes during her dreams, deep in the night.

We stood up and walked around in the imperial garden. We passed the Platform of the God of Earth, where five colours of soil were laid in a square. We watched the white marble pagoda built on a island on the lake. We stepped on top of the bridge on the imperial river.

Evergreen pointed out in detail the exact places he and my mother had visited decades ago. He was inundated with happiness for a while and then felt at a loss the next moment. He talked all the time as if he wanted to tell me everything saved up in his mind over the long years.

After he had been declared innocent a few year ago, the Party and the government appointed him to the position of president in a teachers' college, as a compensation for the unjust treatment to him over the years.

"What's the use of the position to me, anyway?! I lost my wife and child, I lost my youth in the wilderness. All the things I have ever valued are gone! They treat human life as a piece of straw. It is easy for them to say sorry for their wrong policy, but my life will not return, and nothing can compensate for that, nothing..." He shook his head in agony.

I found his attitude was sharply different from that of my mother when she was proclaimed innocent, years before.

The day passed quickly. I suddenly noticed the sun was setting behind the golden roofs of the palaces. Mother and Father might be on their way home from work now, and it was time for me to end everything before it was too late.

"Well," I said to him, carefully avoiding the embarrassment of calling him anything, "before I leave you, I'd like to present two of my sincere wishes to you. I hope you will promise to accept."

"Tell me whatever you want and I will certainly satisfy you, my child." He was eager to know my wish.

"First, I hope you will start by applying to be a Party member as soon as possible..."

"No, never!" he cut off my words excitedly. "The Party has destroyed all the hopes in my life and taken all the valuable things away from me. If it were not that I hoped to see you and your mother one day, I would not have survived till today... No, no, I hate it, I will never join it!"

"But you must know," I said, "it is only by joining the Party and being a member that you might be able to protect yourself better in the future. The Party is strong and mighty. You cannot break a stone with an egg. And this is not only my wish. I guess... No, I am sure... This is my mother's wish as well." I glanced at him quickly, catching an expression in his eyes.

I paused for a while and went on. "She will be very happy to know that you have become a Party member and have a better future. It is only when you can live happily that she will feel consoled and live in peace."

"My second wish is, I hope you will control yourself and never try to see us again: Ever since she left you, my mother and I have tasted life's bitter fruits. It is only during the last couple of years that we have started to enjoy peace of mind. My mother is anxious to forget all her sorrow in the past and I, to tell you the truth, I love my father very much and I am already used to thinking that he is my father... Your coming would certainly disturb the still water and break the hard-won peace in the family... And your effort to mend the broken dream would produce no sweet fruits. Please, forget the past and try to start a new life! I beg you..."

He gazed up in the air silently. A long time passed. Maybe it was only a few minutes, but I felt it was unbearably long. He finally gave out a heavy, heavy sigh and nodded his head.

We had to part at the bus stop in the corner of Tian-an-Men Square. He looked at me miserably. I avoided his eyes and tried to squeeze out a smile. I was fully aware that he had been expecting to see love and closeness from me, like that between a daughter and a father. But my good sense told me to be detached, that he might forget me sooner if I looked indifferent, and that, once healed, his wounds would not bleed again, leaving the poor man in the constant recollection of his lost youth.

A bus stopped beside me. I glanced at Evergreen, murmured a "Bye" and quickly stepped onto the bus. The bus moved. I moved to the back and watched from the rear window.

He was still there, standing frozen against the blazing setting sun. Once again, I tried to give him a peaceful smile, but this time I was not successful. Tears filled up my eyes immediately and his face became blurred. I suddenly realized that this was the first time, but might also be the last time for us to see each other in our lives. The man had waited for twenty-eight years to see his daughter, yet I had not satisfied him even by calling him 'Father'! I might have been too cruel to him, and too cruel to myself!

"Oh, I am sorry! Forgive me, please! Forgive me, Father... There is really no better choice..." A painful cry was trying to get out of my throat. I bit my lips tightly and restrained my intention to cry out. I wiped off the tears with my hand and looked hard through the bus window, only to find the motionless figure of Evergreen buried in the sea of on-coming bicycles...

end

Farewell, My Old Land

"WHAT ARE WE GOING TO DO FOR CHRISTMAS, MRS. Thompson?" I asked.

"I have no idea." She shrugged her shoulders. "Perhaps we can have dinner in a restaurant."

"I went shopping in town this morning. I saw that people have decorated their houses with colourful lights. Shall we decorate our house a little bit as well?"

She thought for a while and said, "Maybe we can cut a tree from the garden and put some lights on. I remember the lights are kept in the basement."

"OK! Let's go out and look for a nice tree!" I suggested in high spirits.

I put on my overcoat. Mrs. Thompson put on her hip-long dark blue wool coat and her crimson scarf. Max jumped for joy.

On the floor of the cottage I found the big hatchet. I had seen George cutting logs into fine fuel with it.

Mrs. Thompson led me to the farther edge of the orchard. A few rows of fir trees stood there, their tips reaching the sky.

I raised up my face and looked at them. "Is this the tree we are going to cut?" I asked in suspicion.

"No, of course not." Mrs. Thompson smiled.

We went further on a small path lined with shrubs on both sides. At the turn of the path, we came to an open space. It was a large swampy area. In summer, I had seen geese and ducks honking around the water beneath the dark woods. I had also suspected that this untouched land, covered with wild trees and plants, dead and alive, might contain the hidden homes of the various animals appearing frequently in the garden. But the swamp looked quiet in winter. There was no trace of the animals.

Mrs. Thompson scanned the trees standing or lying in disorder in front of her. She pointed her hand forward and said, "What do you think about this one?"

I followed her pointing finger and noticed a small tree standing a few yards away on a piece of dry land. It was about five feet tall, its trunk as thick as a baby's arm. There were no leaves on the bare branches and I could not tell what kind of tree it was.

"Don't you think this tree looks too naked, without any leaves?" I asked, afraid she might be wrong. I had seen Christmas trees on the TV, in advertising flyers and in other Canadian homes. They had all been green.

"I think it looks beautiful," she said firmly.

"...OK! We'll have this one." I didn't want to argue with her and started to cut it.

After lunch, I erected the small tree in a pot and put it on top of the white iron table in the middle of the back porch. Mrs. Thompson found the tiny red lights linked on a wire. I put the wire around the branches of the tree and plugged it in.

"It looks beautiful!" I watched the red lights and praised the appearance of the tree. "Your aesthetic judgement is certainly excellent."

She smiled proudly. I knew she was happy to hear my praise.

On Christmas Eve, Mrs. Thompson took me to dinner at a local steak house. It was hard to book seats during this season and we were given only two hours.

All the seats in the restaurant were full. The ceilings and the walls were dazzling with colourful decorations, proclaiming a festival atmosphere. We sat by a window quietly. The loud laughter from the neighbouring tables served as a foil to our desolation.

The smiling waitress brought us the steak, deep fried scallops, Caesar salads, and liquor.

"I'd exchange all my property for a big son, just a big son!" Mrs. Thompson gloomed, her eyes gazing at the dancing snowflakes through the window glass.

"It's too late, I know." She squeezed out a smile, lighting up another cigarette with her trembling fingers.

"Well, you do not need a son." I smiled to cheer her up. "You are rich and healthy. There is no doubt that you will live well past your ninetieth birthday..."

"Humph! If I lived to ninety, somebody would want to kill me!" she said coldly. The forced smile had gone to nowhere.

A blue car and a red dress swept through my mind.

It was in the afternoon. I had been to the Chinese grocery store and bought some tofu. I had convinced Mrs. Thompson to accept this healthy bean product and now she was trying to replace meat with tofu once a week.

On my way back, at the entrance of the property, I saw a blue car coming out of the driveway. I slowed down my speed and let the car pass by. In the driver's seat was a grey-haired woman dressed in red. She didn't even look at me.

Entering the house, I saw Mrs. Thompson sitting by the big dining room table, looking pensive. There were some documents on the table. I didn't want to disturb her, so I went into the kitchen. We never had meals in the spacious dining room. That place, decorated with exquisite antiques, was used only when her lawyer and financial advisor came.

A moment later, Mrs. Thompson entered the kitchen, looking upset. "Lilac..." she said. "I am not feeling well."

"Is there something wrong?" I was very concerned.

"...My step-daughter has just been here."

The grey-haired woman in the blue car jumped into my mind. "But... why?"

"Well..." She stared blankly at the cherry tree outside of the kitchen window. She was hesitating about what to tell me, I could see. "Well, I am not happy, of course." She seemed to have decided and quickly went on. "She and her family are going to have a two week vacation. But I am staying here."

This didn't sound logical to me. She may be lying, I thought. She had travelled in almost every corner of the world and she should not feel jealous about someone else's two week vacation. The worried clouds in her eyes were still thick. My thoughts fell upon the documents on the dining room table.

I had anticipated that the grey-haired woman would show up again during Christmas season. But nobody came. The door had been knocked on once. I quickly went downstairs to answer it. Outside was the son of Mrs. Thompson's housekeeper of twenty years ago. The man was delivering a gift box from his aged mother now lying in hospital.

The two hours in the restaurant passed slowly amidst our silence. I tried to make her happy, telling her some Chinese jokes. She smiled politely, but I knew her heart was not smiling.

Back at our quiet house, we both felt tired. I said "Goodnight" to her and returned to my own room on the other side of the second floor.

"Lilac!" Mrs. Thompson stretched her head out of her door.

"Yes?" I stopped and looked back.

"No coffee for me tomorrow morning."

I nodded. George had dropped into the house this morning, carrying a big cardboard box upstairs. There might be six bottles inside the box, at least.

*　　*　　*

LATE IN THE MORNING OF NEW YEAR'S DAY, I SAT BY THE kitchen table and watched the cloudy sky outside of the window. It was going to snow soon. Mrs. Thompson had told me a few days before that we were going to a concert downtown tonight, but it would be hard to drive the Cadillac in the snow.

I stood up and opened the fridge. What should I cook for lunch? Mrs. Thompson would not want any lunch when intoxicated, and I lacked the motivation to cook only for myself. I took out a tomato and washed it under the running water. I should not worry about the weather, perhaps. She might have forgotten the concert totally, as she often did.

"Bang!" A loud noise came from the front hall. I turned off the water and listened attentively. There was no more sound. I dropped the tomato and rushed to the hall.

Oh, my God! Lying at the foot of the staircase was Mrs. Thompson, barefooted and in her pink flowered pyjamas. On the floor, tiled with large square stones, was a tray and pieces of the exquisitely-carved long glass. A strong smell of vodka was suffusing the air.

Oh, dear! I was horrified to notice a stream of blood coming from Mrs. Thompson's head.

I bent over and looked at her face worriedly. She seemed to be sleeping. Her sparse curly white hair was tangled up in a mess. The floor around her was covered with a sort of strange liquid. It looked like something from her stomach.

"Mrs. Thompson! Mrs. Thompson! Are you OK?" I shook her arm and called her anxiously.

She opened her eyes and gave me a dreamy smile: "Oh, Lilac, I am OK..." Her voice sounded happy and relaxed. She was not like a person who had been hurt, but a singing dreamer.

I tried hard to lift up her body and move her onto the Persian carpet a yard away, but her hundred-and-eighty-pound body felt incredibly heavy at this moment. No matter how hard I tried, I simply could not move her a single inch.

"Her back might be hurt as well," I thought, and gave up my effort. Blood was still dripping down from her scalp. I did not have the courage to touch her hair and have a careful look, but I was frightened by the small pool of red blood on the smooth stone surface.

"The wound must be serious and I should call an ambulance." I told myself.

I rushed into the small sitting room and picked up the phone on the side table. I dialled 911. My hands were shaking vehemently.

"...There is an accident in my home... An old lady was hurt and... she is bleeding... My address?... It's... It's..." Oh, God! I just couldn't remember where I had been living! I stammered and hung up the phone.

I looked around and found George's telephone number beside the radio. Thank God I had always kept it there in case I needed help. I dialed his number. The ring rang for a long time and I waited impatiently... Oh! It suddenly hit me that George had already gone to England!

It was about a month before that that George had received a telephone call from England. He trembled when he heard the voice of his old flame of fifty years before. As a young Canadian soldier, George served in England during the War and it was there that he fell deeply in love with a girl.

"We cuddled and kissed each other warmly on the sofa in her home that night, after we had spent some happy hours in the only bar in the small town..." George told me in a nostalgic tone. "But that was all we did. I was married to my wife then..."

Fifty years had gone by without any communication between them. The girl — no, an old lady today — started to look for George after her husband passed away, in the hope that George might have become a widower. It was a miracle that the federal government's agency in Ottawa had helped her find George so quickly.

George suddenly felt the big-boned woman who had been living in his stone house for two months intolerable. She moved out the following week.

"Lilac!" George told me happily. "I am going to spend my New Year's Day in England!"

I looked at his old face shining with a brilliant youthful light and felt deeply touched. "Isn't it a nice thing to be able to love and be loved till an old age!" I sighed silently.

I felt calm now. All of a sudden, a number came into my mind. I picked up the phone and dialed again. "I am calling from 1841 Vanity Fair Drive..."

I returned to the hall, feeling somewhat relieved. She was still lying motionless on the stone floor, her eyes open.

"What has happened, Lilac?" she asked weakly, still smiling.

"You have fallen down the staircase and hurt yourself," I said, deliberately concealing the facts of her wound and the blood. She might be scared if she knew.

It was cold on the stone floor. I should find a blanket to cover her, I thought.

When I rose up, I was horrified to see Max licking greedily at the pool of blood on the tiles.

"Oh, no! Go away!" I shouted out, feeling disgusted at the sight of this. I waved to the dog, trying to drive him away.

"What is it?" Mrs. Thompson asked, trying to turn her face that way.

"Well... Nothing." I didn't want to tell her. I found a mop and cleaned up the blood and the liquid, while Max fought silently with the mop for the stuff underneath.

Thump! Thump! Someone knocked loudly on the front door. The ambulance must have come.

Three policemen rushed in and quickly checked the old woman's wound. One of them sniffed the air and asked me, "Is she drunk?"

"Probably. She has been drinking since Christmas Eve," I told them honestly.

When they brought in a stretcher and moved her to it, Mrs. Thompson said in a weak voice, still with that intoxicated smile on her face, "I don't want an ambulance... I don't want to spend the taxpayers' money..."

"I am sure you have paid enough taxes," one of the police officers said, glancing at the expensive furniture and decorations in the house. I saw the men were trying hard to force back their impulse to laugh out.

"No, I won't go... I don't need an ambulance."

"But your head is broken and you need stitches," the officer explained.

"What? My head?" Mrs. Thompson seemed to have woken up from her dream.

The officer carried the stretcher into the ambulance in the driveway. I hurried upstairs, took up her purse, and rushed down to the side-door closet to get her dark blue wool coat. Then I stepped into the ambulance.

"No! Lilac!" Mrs. Thompson waved her hand at me from the stretcher. "Don't come with me. Somebody has to stay and watch the house." She seemed to have regained consciousness.

"But who is going to take care of you in the hospital?" I hesitated.

"Don't worry. We will." One officer took the purse and coat from my hands.

The ambulance drove away and I returned to the house and cleaned up the mess in the hall.

Max walked in. He came close to me and reached out his mouth to touch my hand. I withdrew my hand.

"Get out of here!" I shouted at him. The memory of a bloodthirsty beast was still fresh in my mind. I found my feelings towards the black Doberman totally changed. He made me sick.

At six o'clock, the sky was dark. I locked up all six doors of the house.

There were too many windows and the curtains were never drawn, so I turned off all the lights. No one could see me from outside now.

I sat on the sofa in the TV room for a few minutes, and then went into the kitchen and sat on the chair beside the round table. I felt nervous there, too. I started to walk around the downstairs rooms silently.

The house seemed particularly quiet. In the big library, I felt the wigged man in the portrait watching me with an enigmatic smile. Was he the ancestor of the house? What had the house been like when this man was alive? Would he care what had happened today in his home? What would happen to this home when Mrs. Thompson was gone?

I came to the hall and stood in front of the door to the back porch. The lawn was covered with thick snow. The starless sky looked heavy and solid. My eyes fell upon the small Christmas tree standing in the centre of the porch. I plugged it in from inside the door. The tiny red lights on the bare branches of the tree lit up at once. The lights looked vulnerable, and the tree desolate against the dark curtain of the huge universe.

When Mrs. Thompson was in the house, though she stayed in her upstairs living quarters most of the time, I never felt as lonely and restless as I did now. I was surprised that I had become so attached to her.

Almost a year had gone by since I moved into the big house. What had I done for so long? I had been cooking, washing, cleaning, shopping, and... pleasing the old lady when she was not drunk. What else had I done? Nothing! I felt a sudden flutter in my heart.

I had become a genuine housekeeper, I realized. Over the year, I had gradually convinced myself to accept this sluggish, unchallenging life in this big house with this old lady. I had seldom questioned myself about whether there was anything wrong and there was certainly something wrong, I now felt. I had been killing my precious time, and I had totally forgotten my original intention for coming abroad. I had actually become the vassal of this old lady, and lost myself!

The wind became stronger outside and swept through the wildness, the valley, and the pine woods, in waves of sharp whistles. The wailing and the scene reminded me of the cold and lonely winter in Yi Chun when I was cutting firewood in the snowy forest as a twelve-year-old girl.

I got a letter from my mother before Christmas. Uncle Golden-birth and Uncle Honesty had both passed away as the winter started. They were in their sixties, much younger than Mrs. Thompson, but hardship over the years had seriously damaged their health. "If your life in Canada is not happy, you should come back as soon as possible," my mother wrote. "Many of our relatives are becoming aged. They miss you very much and want to see you when they are still in this world."

The bare branches of the Christmas tree were shaking in the wind. One of the tiny red lights went out. Then, another. I shuddered and turned around. Life in this big house was empty, depressing, and meaningless. Everything under the old roof now smelled mouldy and dying...

A taxi brought Mrs. Thompson back shortly before midnight. She was still in her pyjamas. There was a bandage on her head. I felt relieved.

"It's a small cut. The doctor said no stitches were necessary." She smiled at me, holding my arm to walk upstairs.

The next morning, she was up earlier than usual. After breakfast, she came to the TV room and sat on the sofa. Max jumped onto the sofa and rested his head on her lap.

She lit up a cigarette, inhaled deeply, and asked me, "What happened yesterday, Lilac? I cannot remember anything."

There was no smile on her face and her voice was serious. She was completely sober now, I knew.

I told her in detail about the events of the day before. She listened attentively and asked questions. She was most concerned about how many people had seen her situation and who they were.

In the end, she looked at me straight in the eye and said firmly: "Lilac, you are not telling the truth. I was not drunk. I simply fell off the staircase. That's all."

I gazed at her silently. I understood there was no need to explain anything any more.

"Mrs. Thompson," I said calmly, "I have decided to stop my work here. I will be moving out soon. You have two weeks to look for someone else."

"What?! What are you saying?!" She was clearly shocked at my announcement, as I had anticipated. She stopped smoking and stared at me, horrified.

I repeated my words.

"But why? Why do you want to leave? You never told me!"

"I have just made up my mind to leave..." I searched my mind to find a painless reason. "I like you and your home very much. But... I have been here for too long... and I need to change my environment."

"If you like me, why can't you stay? Oh, Lilac, I beg you to stay..." There were tears in her eyes. "I can't let you go! I need you! No. You are abandoning me!" She buried her face in her hands and started to cry. Max was scared. He jumped off the sofa and bumped her knees with his mouth.

I felt sad to see an old woman in tears. I came over and patted her shoulder with a confused feeling. I gazed at her shaking white hair and a feeling of guilt arose inside me. She was in her seventies, an age at which she would be well taken care of by her children, if she had been in China. But she had no children, and had to depend on other people's mercy, acquired by paying for it. My decision to leave her was certainly a heavy blow.

I waited patiently for her to stop crying. "You will find someone better than me. Perhaps a Canadian woman. She will be able to cook Canadian food for you," I comforted her.

"...People will eventually leave me, anyway." She sobbed. "Max is the only one staying with me."

She held Max's neck closely and rubbed her cheek against his. "He is my fourth dog... and the last dog I am going to keep. It is heartbreaking to watch my dogs die in front of me one by one... You know Max has heart disease. The doctor in Toronto told me that he could only live till February. I don't know what I will do if he dies..." She burst out crying again.

"Well, don't believe that doctor's words," I comforted her. "The first time we went to the animal hospital, he told you that Max could only live till Thanksgiving. The second time he told you that Max could only live till Christmas. But Max is still healthy today, isn't he?"

"No, you don't know." She raised up her face and shook her head. "My last dog died of the same disease. She was all right in the morning. But George found her body lying among the fallen leaves near the greenhouse at five o'clock in the afternoon. Her body was cold. No one knew how long before she had passed away..."

I knew the story. She had told me before. I wanted to lift her out of that sorrowful mood so I tried to smile: "But, she lived for nine years. Max is only seven. He may live even longer than she."

"Max is seven-and-a-half now." She stopped for a while before she continued slowly, her eyes staring at the window behind me. "I am going to keep his urn beside my bed, and, bury him in the same tomb with me..."

A current of sorrow swept through my heart. I suddenly remembered a heavy black coffin in a big, empty house.

✻   ✻   ✻

IT WAS A SUMMER NIGHT IN 1987 WHEN I SAT IN THE COURT-yard of the old house in Han Zhong, as Laolao was trying to piece together the broken threads in her memory in a slow and old voice.

Over the years, everything in the small ancient city had always existed in my memory like pieces of a beautiful dream. The quiet pool with ducks swimming in it, the old well with rusty windlass, moss-covered around its rocky edge, the prolonged voice of the vegetable pedlars and the squeaks of their wheel carts passing through the street, and the singing of magpies at dawn around the old roof against the colourful eastern sky.

Whenever my thoughts fell upon my picturesque home town, I would be overwhelmed by a nostalgic feeling. It was the place where Laolao had been staying. It was the place where my mother had grown up. And it was also the place I started my life, as a month-old baby. Though the time I had spent in this small city was much shorter than the time I spent in Beijing and all other places in China, I always felt there was an intimate blood relationship between me and Han Zhong.

Twenty-six years had elapsed since I last saw it at the age of six. As I walked on the familiar narrow streets laid with worn out flagstones, I almost wondered if time had stopped in this secluded small city!

Still squeezed one beside the other along the streets were the old fashioned business stores built a couple of hundred years ago. There were no windows at the front of the stores, but cumbersome planks painted dark red or black.

Among them I found the family cake store. From the dark, oil-smoked greasy doors came the same dull rhyme of rat-tat, rat-tat which I heard twenty-six years ago. I stepped inside, and was surprised to find that the layout of the furnishings was exactly the same as it was in my memory! A few men and women were still standing around the long board in the centre of the store and beating hard on the rice dough with the clubs in their hands. But by the stove with a big pot of boiling oil on it, there was no little girl pulling the hand bellows by the fire! In her place was a grey-haired old man with a bent back.

I found something new in the street a few yards away from Laolao's home. At the former location of the public well, a running-water tap had replaced the hand-turned windlass. But people still carried water home with two pails connected by a shoulder-pole.

In Laolao's home, the large back garden and the cloud-floating pond had disappeared. Three rows of brick flats were built on the site, with five families sharing each flat.

The back wall of Laolao's old house was a little out-of-the-perpendicular and was supported by a few big logs from outside. The exquisite wooden carvings on the eight-piece door of the main room were broken and worn. The legendary stories the carvings used to illustrate could no longer be deciphered. The floor of the main room sloped awfully towards the back wall. Anyone entering the room for a few seconds would want to escape the house at once for the natural fear of being buried under its collapsed roof the next moment.

Standing in the middle of the large empty room, I could hear the noise of mice chewing old papers on the second floor. The carved beams and painted rafters had lost their original rich colours completely and the naked wood looked dark and dismal.

The oleander tree in front of the broad porch had grown much bigger, its dense branches blooming with thick pink flowers providing shade overhead.

At supper time, I used fuel wood to light up the fire under the three-foot-wide iron pot over the brick stove, and worked the hand bellows clumsily. In the past week, I had learned to cook food this way, under the instruction of Mrs. Wang, Laolao's next door neighbour.

Mrs. Wang was over sixty now, and still looked as healthy and strong as thirty years before. Her seven kids had all grown up and left home. Her husband, Old Wang, the alcoholic, had withered to the size of a teenage boy, his small skinny face dry like a walnut. He had not thrown away his bottle yet. During the day, he always sat under the shadow of the oleander tree to play chess with another old man living in the front house. His right hand would move the chessman, and his left hand always held a narrow-necked white china bottle.

After I spent an hour in a muddle, the turtle soup was finally ready. I had been to the market in the morning and bought two soft-shelled turtles, the size of tea saucers, which were hardly seen in Beijing. Mrs. Wang told me how to cook them with a few pieces of ginger and green onion, and black pepper. I tasted the soup. Ah, it was the most delicious thing I had ever tasted! No wonder they were sold so expensively at the market — four dollars each. I shared the soup into two bowls and took one to Laolao.

In the shade of the front porch, Laolao was sitting motionlessly with her back straight in a bamboo chair. She was in an old fashioned white linen jacket, buttoned on the right, and a pair of loose grey pants. The silver hairs left on her scalp were countable.

I put the bowl and a pair of chopsticks on the small table in front of her and said happily: "Laolao, the turtle soup is ready. Try and see whether you like my cooking or not!"

Laolao turned her face in the direction where my voice came from. She had been blind for ten years.

"I am not hungry yet," she said slowly, while trying to open her eyes. "I'll wait for Mrs. Wang's supper. I have been used to eating the food she cooks..."

"But the turtle soup is something special. You should at least taste it."

"Oh, Peace! I have lived long enough in the world, and nothing is special to me any more. I am not as curious as you are about the soup. Eat it all! I'll feel happy to know that you have had something nice in grandma's home..."

"But, you know," I insisted, "I am leaving tomorrow morning. I hope you can have the soup with me today."

"You..." Laolao seemed to be touched by my words. She thought for a few seconds and nodded. I quickly passed the chopsticks into her hands.

When members of the five other families in the courtyard finished their supper, they all came out of their house. Old Wang brought out a twelve-inch black and white TV from his home, and put it on a small table in the middle of the porch. All the adults and kids sat on small stools in the yard, watching TV programs and chatting, to pass the hot evening.

I helped Laolao move slowly to the farther end of the yard, and sat by a stone table. We talked in low voices, paying no attention to the loud drum and gongs and the shrill singing of the local opera on the TV, and the noisy laughing and chatting of the people in the yard.

Around ten o'clock, the night air became cooler. People returned to their homes one by one and the yard quieted down.

The chirps of insects from the damp corners underneath the stone table sounded unusually loud in the quiet night. The jasmine tea on the table was already cold.

Laolao's talking was now and then interrupted by her failing memory and for a while she would move the palm-leaf fan in her hand slowly in silence, as if she was trying to find back the beads dropping off from a broken thread into the grass.

"...As I brought you to the labour farm, your mother was shocked to see us coming." Her voice was peaceful. "That night, she told me that she had no courage to present you to Tian-zhi and wanted to give you out for adoption... I blamed her. 'How does it come that you have become so weak?'

"Later, I found Tian-zhi in his home," she went on, sitting quite still. "I asked him to accept you and take care of you. 'Whatever you think about Qin, a four-year-old child is innocent, anyway.' I said to him..."

I closed my eyes. I saw the shadows of an old woman with a four-year-old girl walking haltingly among the endless rice fields under the starry sky...

A gentle night breeze brought a sweet scent from the blooming pink oleander flowers in front of the porch. I breathed the air heavily and felt a strong aroma of soil and rice shoots. It was a familiar smell coming out deep from my memory...

Tears ran down my cheeks silently and wet the front of my pale grey dress. I opened my mouth and breathed carefully to avoid making any sound. It was fortunate that Laolao was not able to look at me any more.

"You know what Tian-zhi replied to me? He said, 'The girl is innocent. I promise I will take care of her. But, as for Qin, she must work hard on the farm to remould her bourgeois mind before I can accept her again.' Well, I never told your mother about his remark. It might hurt her too much. You should not tell your mother, either..."

"I won't." I assured Laolao. But I knew my mother would not be upset any more even if I told her about this. The relationship between my parents had gone through much worse points over the years than Laolao actually knew.

My mother had already walked out of darkness. Shortly after her Rightist status was corrected, she took action to reverse the verdict about her 'adultery', the humiliating title over her head for fifteen years which deprived her of the dignity and decency an ordinary woman should enjoy. But this was not an easy case, not as easy as the correction of her Rightist status, where half a million people together could become normal citizens with the issuing of a government document.

The lengthy investigations, surveys and ratifications at various levels of government organizations took her years of effort, anxiety and exhaustion. A negative side effect of the procedure was that many of my mother's younger colleagues, who didn't work in the institute before the Cultural Revolution, now learned about the scandal and gossiped behind her back. She was fully aware of the new troubles caused by her struggle, but that only made her even more dogged about reversing the verdict!

After the humiliating record was finally erased from my mother's file, she was admitted as a Party member and her thirty-five-year-long dream came true. Her request to be transferred to another research institute was also granted. "I don't have to see the disgusting shadow of Sunshine any longer!" she exclaimed happily.

After she was appointed as the Vice-Director a year later, she was very happy and worked harder than before. "I'll make all effort to turn the institute into a first class one!" she once said with a confident smile, after my father gently persuaded her not to work too hard. There was a subtle change in my father's attitude now. When talking with my mother, I noticed he often looked at her with an appreciative smile.

One day I had lost my key, and I went to my mother's office. My mother's assistant, a very attractive young woman, met me in the office and we chatted briefly. Before I left, she asked my mother in a careless way: "Qin, I guess your daughter is prettier than you when you were young, right?"

Perhaps I was over-sensitive, but somehow I could read the words she didn't speak out. "How could this old woman with grey hair, deep wrinkles, loose teeth, presbyopic glasses and a shapeless body ever have had any 'affairs'!" she must be thinking.

My mother's eyes remained on the papers on her desk. She didn't even raise her head. "None of us has ever been pretty!" she said with a faint smile.

My mother's response was a typical Chinese attitude to other people's praises. You were always supposed to show your modesty by denying praises. An American professor from Stanford University actually stunned all his Chinese hosts during his visit to Beijing when he nodded agreement with other people's compliments to his virtually plain-looking wife.

From behind her back, I looked at my mother's right hand holding a pen. The light of the fluorescent lamp revealed the age spots on the back of her hand. I remembered the emotional tone in her voice as she talked to me one day. "I stood on the bus for a whole hour today," she told me as she got home. "It was so crowded and I never got a chance to sit down. Everybody standing was holding the bar overhead. I suddenly found that my hand looked so old and ugly, with withered skin and age spots, among so many smooth young hands..."

Her sorrow for her lost youth was deepened after she went to a beach resort for a meeting held for all educational research institutes in China. In 1986, it gradually became popular to hold official meetings at tourist cities so the participants could enjoy luxuries at the expense of the state, something strictly banned in Mao's time. Back home, my mother sighed about the loss of the industrious and thrifty manner popular in the past, and talked about her uneasiness at the four-day meeting.

"Everyone attending the meeting was a vice-director. I was the only female, and, the oldest one," my mother told me. A dry smile lingered at the corner of her lips. "We had ten-course lunches and dinners and sight-seeing programs everyday. As I was helped and taken care of by these men in their thirtieth or fortieth years, I didn't feel grateful, but instead, rather distressed. They were treating me like an old mother. I knew they meant to be kind to me, but they made me feel that I am indeed getting old..."

I understood the helpless sorrow deep inside her. She had struggled hard to recover the time, honour, recognition, everything lost in her youth, and to be useful and contribute to the society again. Unfortunately, she felt her incompetence in her position. Over the years, she had become used to physical labour in the fields, and she had become familiar with writing self-criticism reports. Now she found her mind was too blank and dull for a vice-director in a research institute. She envied the talents of many young people working under her and she urged herself to study and read more to update her knowledge as quickly as possible. However, it was at this time that she felt the weight of seniority unavoidably impending. The state restored the retirement ages, men at sixty, and women at fifty-five, to make space for the employment of young people. Qin was already fifty-eight. There was no excuse for her to stay in her position any longer.

* * *

"WHEN YOUR MOTHER CAME BACK LAST TIME, SHE TRIED to convince me to live with her in Beijing," Laolao's words broke up my memory. "But I refused. I cannot see. I cannot do anything for her. I don't want to become a burden to her in Beijing. She is eager to excel in everything and she needs time for herself, you know."

Last fall, my mother had returned to her hometown forty years after she left it. She planned to spend her one-month holiday with Laolao — a chance to do a little bit of her duty as a daughter. She came back with pride, no longer as a shameful Rightist but as a Communist Party member in a decent position. She visited her childhood friends, classmates, relatives and neighbours. However, she didn't find the admiration and jealousy she had secretly expected from the people around.

Some other visitors who had also returned to their hometown after forty years were hot conversational topics. They were people who escaped China at the eve of the communist takeover. With the government's open door policy, these people were now coming back for a visit from Hong Kong, Taiwan, North America and Europe. Their fashionable dresses and luxurious jewellery were dazzling in the ancient city's narrow streets. Wherever they went, they were escorted by city officials wearing ingratiating smiles.

Among the visitors, Qin found a high school classmate, a girl who quit school to marry a nationalist officer and fled from China before the communists came. This girl — no, a round woman now, though her hair remained jet black — returned from Vancouver, Canada, and attracted much more attention than she had forty years before. Qin felt sour when she watched the round woman being flatteringly called an 'expert' during her visit to a local high school, while the city officials fawned on her, anxious to hear her opinions.

"How could she become an 'expert'? She is just a high school dropout and all she has been for so many years is a Canadian housewife! What constructive opinions could she have? I am the Vice-Director of an educational research institute and I have plenty of good ideas to give, but they simply don't come to me!" Qin felt the insult of being neglected by the people in her beloved hometown.

She looked at and listened to everything going on in her small home-town city. An icy chill froze her heart. "A whole bunch of snobs!" she con-cluded indignantly. How could those old 'enemies' now be welcomed as 'distinguished guests' and be regarded as more worthy and respectable than those of us who stayed to work for the Communist Government all these years! Was it simply because those overseas visitors were rich? But where had the communist ideology gone, if money had become the criterion for everything today! She remembered her envy of her distant cousin forty years before when the female communist came back to her hometown in a jeep with several bodyguards. But she felt no envy for today's new visitors. Life was simply unpredictable!

The more she thought about it, the more confused she became. Finally, she found it was actually hard to tell who was wrong. "Perhaps those who escaped China forty years ago should not have been regarded as enemies at all in the first case. If I had chosen the same way, escaping China, would my life history have been written another way?" She felt dismayed. Life, or one's fate, was totally elusive, all manoeuvred by an unseen hand.

Each day in the small city became increasingly difficult for her to toler-ate. On the morning of the twenty-first day after her arrival, she left Han Zhong and returned to Beijing.

Would my mother come back again to the place where her youthful dream was bred? I wondered. During the day, as I passed through the Ancient Han King Palace on my way to the market and heard the tiny bronze bells hanging on the tower eaves tinkling in gentle breeze, I stopped by its ivy-ridden stone wall which was built on a high terrace. In front of me were the long stone steps leading towards the heavy wooden gates. A pair of stone lions stood on both sides at the feet of the dark-coloured old gates. The lions looked smooth from being touched number-less times over the centuries. I stared at them and asked them silently: "Did you ever see a teenage girl, with a pair of almond-shaped eyes suf-fused with perturbed feelings, standing by the gates and waiting for a young teacher who could sing beautiful songs in English? Did you ever see the ominous shadow of the Divinity of Fate hovering over the girl's head?..."

One day in 1983, my mother was helping my sister Little-red to choose a medical university for her graduate studies. Her eyes suddenly caught a familiar name among the faculty members of a university. My mother was sure it was the name of her young teacher's sister. He used to talk so much about his family at the coastal city that she remembered everyone's name.

My mother promptly wrote a letter to the professor, inquiring if her elder brother was called so and so, and if he had ever been to Han Zhong during World War II. The professor replied quickly, confirming everything. Her brother had finished his studies in England in the early 1950s and planned to come back to China. But he changed his mind when he learned that the Communist Government had started to drive away Christian missionaries, and he went to the United States instead. He had stayed there ever since and never came back, she wrote.

My mother remained silent for a whole week after reading the letter. She never mentioned her young teacher again after that.

∗   ∗   ∗

"...HAVE YOU GOT ENOUGH MONEY FOR YOUR TRAVELS abroad?" Laolao's voice brought me back to the present.

"Yes, I have scholarships from Canada."

"Canada is a faraway country, I know that." Something else seemed to float into Laolao's mind from the remote past. "When I was a young girl, I met some foreigners in big cities. There were both men and women. They looked strange with yellow hair and green eyes. But they were very nice to people. They could even speak the Chinese language... I heard they were from America and Canada, faraway countries on the other side of the ocean. They advised people to believe in their God... I forget the God's name... They set up a school and admitted young girls as students. I was really jealous of these girls at that time..."

I knew Laolao was talking about the Christian missionaries. They entered China in the early nineteenth century, with their numbers reaching a peak in the early twentieth century; they had left their traces in many cities and towns in China. But all the missionaries were driven out of the country in the early nineteen fifties.

"When and where did you meet these foreigners?" I asked curiously, remembering the rumours about Laolao's youth.

"Well, that was a long, long time ago. I was much younger than you are now... I cannot remember it so clearly now." Laolao seemed unwilling to continue this topic. She fumbled her hand as she reached for the tea cup on the stone table. I passed it to her. She sipped the cold tea slowly and became silent.

Everything in the small city looked old and sluggish. Time might have slowed down its pulse here.

Life in Beijing was changing rapidly, with exciting news almost every day. Freedom and democracy had become a hot topic since 1979 and student demonstrations had been escalating with each year's passing.

The government was making drastic efforts to boost the nation's economy, giving a green light to both private and official speculators, while watching the soaring inflation rate helplessly. On the other hand, any voice for political reform was strictly restrained and news blackouts, a popular practice used in Mao's era to fool the people, continued to facilitate the Party's rule.

The struggle at the Party's power centre was fierce, too. Earlier in 1987, the Party's General Secretary, Hu Yao-bang, a liberal-minded man, had been forced to resign, and a few well known outspoken journalists were expelled from the Party as a punishment for their appealing for freedom and democracy.

Many well educated young people, disappointed at the situation, had gone or were preparing to go to the West, in the hope of finding truth, for the nation and for themselves...

I joined this trend, and I was ready to bid farewell to this old land soon.

Life had taught me to become a little wiser. I had learned to act as a revolutionary-minded person during my three years in the journalism school. I won a good reputation and the trust of the Party's organization. I was made the President of the Graduate Students Association and, upon my graduation, was given the offer to become a Party member.

To be frank, I had hesitated for quite a while before I decided to turn it down. The honourable title was something I had dreamed about when I was younger, and it would at least please my mother, even if it was no longer attractive to me. But... but... I had the admission letter from a Canadian university in my hand.

Finally, I told the Party's Branch Secretary in a tactful way: "I am still too far away from the standard set for a Party member. I wish the Party's organization to put me on trial for a longer period before you finally grant me this honour."

He stared at me with his mouth wide open for quite a few seconds. My refusal must have been a first-time-in-his-life experience, I was sure. I was fully aware that I was risking my future. My refusal to become a Party member would undoubtedly deprive me of a brilliant life in China, while life in the maple leaf country was unknown and full of mysteries.

Over the past few years, I had become disgusted with the hypocrisy, bureaucracy, lying and cheating, deeply rooted in the Chinese media. I felt the thirst to breathe fresh air and I chose to face the unknown myth of the challenge overseas.

My mother's reaction when I told her that I had turned down the offer to become a Party member was complicated.

"Do you think your decision is too careless?" She looked at me with a troubled eye, and her voice sounded uncertain. "You have just started your career as a journalist in this prestigious news agency. To be a Party member is crucial to your future..."

"But I want to try my future abroad, not in China any more. And no one will care if you are a Party member or not once you are in the West," I replied without hesitation.

"Well, I don't know what to advise you." She paused for a while, her eyes searching the air as if she was looking for a ready answer. "Anyway, after all these years, I now feel that everything is empty, and life is just... meaningless, without any purpose..."

I felt uncomfortable when I saw the lost expression on her face. She had just come back from a trip to the Mongolian prairie. The one-week trip was organized for senior officials who would retire soon. She told me about her encounter with a fortune-teller on her last day there.

That evening, a banquet was held in a hot tourist spot, known for a group of ancient temples built a thousand years ago. My mother and the other guests were seated in a circle inside a large yurt decorated with colourful carpets and silk draperies. The hosts, young Mongolian men and women dressed in their traditional red, pink, purple and green long robes and head kerchiefs, served them with whole roasted lambs and hard liquor, while musicians played the rising and falling tunes with a bowed stringed instrument decorated with a scroll carved like a horse's head. The Mongolians were persistent in their unique way of entertaining the guests. They would kneel with one leg in front of the guest, hold high in their hands a tray with cups of hard liquor, and sing repeatedly their conventional 'Toast Songs' until the guests accepted the cups.

My mother would not take any liquor at first. However, she felt uneasy when she saw the girl continue to kneel and sing in front of her for so long and she finally forced herself to accept the Mongolian people's hospitality.

She felt a burning sensation and then dizziness after the drink. Afraid of being urged to drink again, she left the table, pretending to go to the washroom. Outside of the yurt, she found there were five other yurts, decorated the same way, entertaining tourists at the same time. She walked a few yards away from the noisy yurt hotel and breathed the cool fresh night air. A full moon was rising above the endless grassland. About fifty yards away was the entrance of a lama temple. She had seen the numerous golden statues and praying lamas swarming inside it during the day. It was dark and quiet now, but outside of the temple's rocky wall were a few pedlars still waiting patiently for possible late deals with the drunken tourists.

She paced over to the pedlars and scanned their tables under the soft moonlight. Some were selling traditional handcrafts such as bone-carved beads, earrings, bracelets and beaded knives. Some were selling grey-coloured, homemade dairy products which were unfortunately irritating the nostrils of the city dwellers. She was not interested in any of these. As she was about to turn around, her eyes fell upon an old man sitting on a small stool by the end of the pedlar line. There was no table in front of him, but a piece of white cloth with the big characters "Fortune-Telling" on the ground. The bald-headed man with a beard half-a-foot long smiled at my mother and said in a gentle voice: "Would you like to have your fortune told? I am accurate, or it's free."

My mother nodded and handed him a dollar note. She had never done this before, having restrained herself from all activities forbidden under communist ideology. "But what difference does it make now! I am going to retire soon and my whole career will be finished!" she said to herself.

After a careful examination of her palm, the old man asked about her birth date, including the exact hour at which she had been born. He then lowered his head and became silent.

My mother felt curious at his odd expression and said smilingly: "Please let me know what you have seen in my life. I won't be upset, whatever you say!"

The old man raised up his head and said slowly: "You have suffered many a setback in the past and your whole life has been wasted in useless struggles..."

My mother gave him an uneasy smile: "How did you know?"

"The reason is simple. You were destined to have a man's fate, but by an error, were born with a woman's body!"

My mother fixed her eyes on the old man's long dirty garb. She found it was hard to tell its colour under the dim moonlight. She stood motionless for a while and squeezed out a faint smile. Then she shook her head and walked away slowly. The moon overhead was hiding in the clouds and the night became deeper. There was the noise of music and song coming out of the yurt entrances left ajar.

* * *

MY FATHER'S REACTION TO MY DECISION WAS DIFFERENT from my mother's. "Nowadays, young people of your generation tend to seek truth in foreign countries and believe this is the only way to save China. But people of my generation think differently. We all know that the Communist Government has made a lot of mistakes in the past few decades and brought tragedy to many people and families. We feel, however, that no system is perfect in this world, and foreign systems may not be suitable for the Chinese environment. China has to rely on itself to work out a way, Communism plus something else, perhaps!"

* * *

THE NIGHT WAS GETTING DEEPER. THE LIGHT BULBS IN THE neighbours' homes were all turned off and the whole yard became dark. I helped Laolao stand up and move inch by inch in the darkness.

Entering her room on one side of the house, I turned on the lamp and started to catch the mosquitoes buzzing around. I had been doing this every night in the past week. I caught at least ten within ten minutes. I wondered how could there be so many in Laolao's room. The small insects were shrewd enough to see that the old blind woman had no power to resist their attacks.

"Peace, you might as well stop doing that," Laolao said to me. "I have been used to their attacks. And, you know, if you treat me this nice, I will be missing you too much and feeling sad after you leave..."

I kept on with my work. I worried, too, about who was going to deal with the mosquitoes tomorrow night...

One mosquito came out from underneath the table. I chased it around the room. Slam! My hand hit it against a hard surface in a corner of the room. Oh! I almost cried out. It was the black coffin! I withdrew my hand subconsciously and looked at the huge thing made with heavy wood.

During the day, I had always avoided looking at it. The ominous thing was a sign of the inevitable. Was this the place where Laolao would eventually sleep forever? How did she feel about preparing her own coffin and keeping it in her room?

Laolao sat quietly on the edge of her bed. She noticed my silence and seemed to understand what was in my mind.

"I have thought it over many times." She seemed to be talking to herself. "Death is something we cannot prevent anyway. I am no longer afraid of it. I have chosen a place for myself in the green hills alongside the Han River. I've always liked the dense bamboo bushes there," she said in a tranquil tone.

Laolao stood up and moved towards an old cabinet standing beneath the back window. Her hands fumbled in a drawer and brought out something. She passed the things into my hands and said: "This pair of ivory chopsticks is the only thing of some worth left from this family. Laolao has nothing to send to you when you are going far away, to the other side of the ocean... I used this for many years when I was young, and you may keep them as a souvenir..."

I held the pair of chopsticks in my hands carefully. They looked old and had a yellowish tint under the light bulb.

I was not sure how long I would stay outside of China, but Laolao was certainly too old to wait till the day I came back. The chopsticks would become a live memory, the last live memory of Laolao and my old mother-land.

I helped Laolao to lie down and sat beside her. I watched her silently. She tried to open her eyes wide and look at me. But I saw nothing inside her eyes except a dark shadow.

"It is late. You may go to sleep now," Laolao said, but her hand was still holding mine. I knew she actually hated to part with me, especially tonight.

The pressure of time and life could be felt in the quiet, large room. With a heavy heart, I stood up and walked towards the door.

At the door, I turned around and gave a final look at Laolao: "Good night, Laolao. May I turn off the light for you now?"

The light was off, and the room was dark. I realized it was all the same for Laolao, whether there was light or not. She had been living in a world of darkness every day and every night.

I closed the door and the darkness behind me.